CONNIE'S COURAGE

When Connie Pride finds herself alone and pregnant in the rough courts of Liverpool, she despairs. Deserted by her lover and too proud to ask her estranged family for help, there seems no hope, until she is offered the chance to train as a nurse. Finally Connie has a purpose in life, especially when the wounded of World War I start to arrive in droves, but when a face from the past turns up to disrupt Connie's new life, all she has built up is threatened. She will need every ounce of courage – and help from old friends and new.

CONNIE'S COURAGE

Connie's Courage

by

Annie Groves

Magna Large Print Books
Long Preston, North Yorkshire,
BD23 4ND, England.

British Library Cataloguing in Publication Data.

Groves, Annie
    Connie's courage.

    A catalogue record of this book is
    available from the British Library

    ISBN   0-7505-2320-4

First published in Great Britain in 2004 by HarperCollins Publishers

Magna Large Print is an imprint of Library Magna Books Ltd.

Printed and bound in Great Britain by
T.J. (International) Ltd., Cornwall, PL28 8RW

This novel is entirely a work of fiction.
The names, characters and incidents portrayed
in it are the work of the author's imagination.
Any resemblance to actual persons,
living or dead, events or localities
is entirely coincidental.

I would like to thank the following for their invaluable help:

Lynne Drew, who makes time for all her authors. Maxine Hitchcock, my editor, for her unfailing patience and support and encouragement during a very difficult year for me.
Jo Craig, for her marvellous editing and polishing.

My co-members of our Cheshire Chapter of the RNA, for their support and encouragement during what has been a difficult year.

Tony, who researched the music hall acts for me as well as driving me to and from my research trips.

And finally, I would just like to say how much it has meant to me to receive so many kind letters from the readers of *Ellie Pride* telling me how much they enjoyed her story. I hope they will get as much enjoyment from *Connie*, and take her to their hearts as I have taken her to mine.

I would like to dedicate this book to my mother who paid me the best compliment I have ever had in being so impatient to read Connie's story. Here she is, Mum – I hope you like her!

PART ONE

ONE

1912

Connie admired her reflection in the old spotted mirror she had propped up on the small chest by the window to get the best light. Not that very much light did come in through the small, filthy window of the room she and Kieron were renting in one of Liverpool's poorest areas – a huddle of terraced houses in an airless court down a narrow back alley – but Connie preferred not to think about their surroundings.

She had begged the landlord of the pub where she worked as a barmaid to let her take the mirror when his wife decided to throw it out. It was her sister Ellie who had always been considered the pretty one, and not her. She rubbed anxiously at her lips with a cloth, to try to give them a bit of colour, before applying a thin smear of Vaseline to them. She and Kieron might not have any money, but that did not mean she had to let herself go completely.

They might be living in straitened circumstances now, but things would be different once they got to America, she assured herself, picking up her skirts and whirling round, the reality of her situation forgotten, as her natural optimism brought an excited glow to her face. America! Oh, but she just couldn't wait to get there!

'We're going to America. We're going to America!' she sang at the top of her voice, dizzy with anticipation and happiness.

But her happiness turned to a sharp stab of discomfort, as the light from the window glinted on the cheap wedding ring she was wearing. A wedding ring she had no legal right to, because she and Kieron were not married.

In reality, she was not Mrs Kieron Connolly, but still Miss Constance Pride, daughter of Robert Pride of Preston. Not that her father cared anything for her now. No, he had a second wife to replace Connie's dead mother, and a new family to displace both Connie and her siblings from his affections.

Connie still hated to think about the unhappiness she had experienced after her mother's death. The four Pride children had been split up amongst their mother's sisters, without being allowed any say in their own futures. The Barclay sisters had been renowned for their beauty and grace when they had been young, and Connie knew that her aunts had never approved of her mother Lydia's marriage to a mere butcher.

When Lydia had died following the birth of her fourth child, Ellie, Connie's elder sister, had been sent to live at Hoylake with their Aunt and Uncle Parkes.

Mr Parkes was an extremely wealthy man – a lawyer – with a very grand house in the prestigious area of Hoylake where all the rich shipowners lived. Mr and Mrs Parkes had given a ball whilst Ellie had been living with them, and Connie had been invited to attend.

16

She had tried not to show how overawed she felt by the unfamiliar elegance of her aunt and uncle's home, or how upset and frightened she had been by the realisation that she and her sister Ellie were living such different lives. Her elder sister had seemed like a stranger to her, and she had felt so envious of her, and the wonderful life she was living.

It had seemed unfair that Ellie should be living a life of luxury with the Parkes, whilst Connie was stuck in a horrid, cold rectory with their parsimonious Aunt and Uncle Simpkins.

John, their brother, and the new baby, Philip, had been sent to live at Hutton with another aunt, and Connie hadn't had any contact with her family since she ran away with Kieron.

When Ellie found out that Connie had run away from their Aunt and Uncle Simpkins to be with Kieron, she had tried to persuade her sister to return to them, claiming that Connie would be socially ruined if what she had done should become public knowledge. But Connie suspected that Ellie was thinking more about her own social position, rather than Connie's!

Ellie had gone up in the world through her two marriages: her first into a ship-owning family, and then, when her first husband died, Ellie had married her childhood sweetheart, Gideon Walker. Gideon was a craftsman who had inherited a considerable amount of money, and a house in Winckley Square, the smartest part of Preston. This was much to the resentment of their Aunt Gibson, who also lived in the same square with her doctor husband.

Since their Aunt Gibson was used to considering herself of a much higher social status than Ellie and Connie's late mother, she no doubt thoroughly disliked having Ellie as her well-to-do neighbour. Not that Connie had any sympathy for their Aunt Gibson. She was the one who had insisted on splitting them all up following their mother's death, after all, even if she had claimed she was acting on their mother's wishes. But Ellie had been the one who had let her!

Connie had hated her life with her Aunt Jane so much. The Simpkins' household had been so different from the jolly comfort of the home she had known. She had missed its warmth, and her mother and father's love. Her Aunt and Uncle Simpkins had certainly not loved her. They had forever been finding fault with her. When she had met Kieron, she had been so thrilled and relieved to meet someone who seemed to love her. Kieron had certainly told her that he loved her. In fact, his boldness had overwhelmed her a little, and, if she was honest, made it impossible for her to think straight.

Deep down inside, Connie knew that their mother would never have approved of someone like Kieron as a husband for her. For one thing, they were of different religions, but, even more important in her mother's eyes, would have been the fact that Kieron had such a different background to her own. Connie's father was a respectable, hard-working butcher with his own business. A man who could hold his head up in any company. Connie's mother came from even more respectable stock. Kieron's family...

18

Connie had been shocked the first time she had visited his home, initially at the poverty of the small house itself, but later by the way she had witnessed Kieron's father treating his wife. Never would her own father have spoken to her mother in such a demeaning and unpleasant manner. Kieron's father had totally ignored Connie, and later Kieron had admitted that his family, especially his father and uncle, did not want him to continue seeing her.

'Seems like me uncle has a wife in mind for us – a good Catholic she is, with her family having a bit o' business wi' me uncle.'

Connie had been outraged by his disclosure and told him so, but to her shock Kieron had refused to condemn his family.

She bit her lip unhappily. Running away with Kieron had seemed such a romantic and exciting thing to do at first. And she had assumed that she and Kieron would be married virtually straight-away, but he kept putting it off, saying that he wanted to get them a decent place to live before he married her.

'But we are already living together, Kieron,' she had protested anxiously. 'And you promised me that we should be married...'

'Aye, and so we will,' he had agreed, taking hold of her and kissing her.

She began to pluck anxiously at the fabric of her dress. Kieron did want to marry her, she knew that. And he was going to marry her. He had said so!

But Connie knew that in the eyes of her family, especially her mother's family, she was now a fallen woman, someone they would refuse even to acknowledge if they should see her in the street. And it was not just so in the eyes of her family, but in the eyes of the world as well.

A sharp thrill of fear jolted through her. What had started out as an exciting adventure, had become something that, deep down inside her, Connie felt ashamed of, even though she stubbornly refused to admit it.

She twisted the cheap ring on her finger. Why should she care what anyone else thought? Especially her family! They had never cared about her, had they?

Anger and confusion darkened Connie's green eyes. She hated the starkness of the painful emotions that filled her whenever she thought about the life she had sunk to, and her family... Which was why she chose not to think about them at all, unless she had to.

Connie loved laughter and fun and excitement; she was in her element in the heady, giddy atmosphere of a music hall, or indeed anywhere where people gathered to have a good time.

Would there be music halls in America, she wondered naively. She was sure that there would. It was such a big exciting place, especially New York where she and Kieron would soon be going.

For the whole of the last month she had been bubbling over inside with excitement. She and Kieron were going to leave Liverpool and this horrid, dirty room they were forced to live in, and make a new life for themselves in America. And it had all been her idea! One of the best ideas she had ever had, she congratulated herself.

It had come to her when she had happened to pick up a copy of the *Liverpool Echo,* while clearing the tables in the pub. It had been left open on a page describing the wonders of the new liner, the *Titanic,* due to make its maiden voyage to New York, and Connie felt her heart skip with excitement as she read that the liner was going to be carrying steerage passengers at a very modest rate; ordinary people who would be able to travel to America to make a wonderful new life there for themselves.

In that moment, Connie's dream had been born. A dream of going to America with Kieron where they could live as man and wife, without the disapproval or interference of their families. At first, Kieron had rejected her suggestion, but Connie had gradually worn down his objections with her enthusiasm and her optimism.

Humming happily to herself, Connie deliberately refused to look at the grim poverty of her surroundings. She had always been an optimist, and never more so than now.

Where was Kieron? She wished he'd hurry up and return! He had gone out earlier to collect and pay for their tickets for the *Titanic.*

Connie had been avidly reading everything she could about the liner – the papers had been full of its magnificence and elegance. Of course, she and Kieron could only afford the cheapest of the steerage tickets, but that didn't mean that they couldn't go and sneak a look at the glamorous first-class salons, she assured herself, before going to have another anxious look at her reflection in the mirror.

She wanted to look her best when Kieron came in. Not that it was easy to look pretty when the only clothes she had were little better than rags! She had seen the way the landlady at the pub had looked at them – and at her! Her face burned with angry resentment. She had had pretty clothes, but Kieron had taken them from her and sold them. She had begged him not to, but he had torn them out of her arms, despite her pleas. He had insisted that they needed the money to pay their rent.

For all that she loved him, sometimes Kieron could be very unkind to her. And, as she had discovered, he had a quick temper – and he liked a drink! And, when he had had a drink, sometimes he flew into a terrible rage when he hurled angry and hurtful insults at her. Once or twice he had even raised his fist as though he was going to hit her. Not that he ever actually had! Connie gave a small shiver. On those occasions, if she were honest, she had felt slightly afraid of him. But she wasn't going to dwell on them. Everything would be all right once they were in New York.

The light coming in through the small window burnished her russet hair. Connie peered closer into the mirror. It was so unfair that Ellie should have been the prettier of them, she fretted, un-aware of the attractiveness of her own looks; her pretty oval-shaped face; her green eyes with their thick, dark, curling eyelashes, her neat straight nose.

Not that she did not have her admirers! She giggled, remembering how, not so very long ago, a cheeky baker's boy had stopped his bicycle to tell her that she had an extremely kissable mouth.

Connie loved flattery and compliments, almost as much as she loved pretty clothes and fun and laughter.

Why was Kieron taking so long? He should have been back by now!

Impatiently she started to pace the floor. In New York they wouldn't have to share a privy with all the other lodgers in the house, they would have one all to themselves, maybe even two! They would have a huge house, and she would have her own maid to help her change her clothes, just like Ellie had had when she had lived at Hoylake with Aunt and Uncle Parkes.

Kieron would become a very important man, and on her birthday he would present her with a beautiful diamond necklace. All the admiring new friends she would make in New York would be envious of her, especially when she told them the romantic tale of how Kieron had seen her and fallen in love with her, and how they had been married on the *Titanic*.

As she slid into the pleasure of her favourite daydream, Connie was able to forget her surroundings and her anxiety over Kieron's absence.

'Connie let me in!'

Connie woke with a start. She had dozed off and her body felt cramped. Quickly she got off the bed and hurried over to the door, unlocking it and throwing her arms round Kieron as soon as he stepped into the room. Her face was alight with excitement, questions tumbling from her lips.

'Where have you been? I fell asleep waiting for you! Where are the tickets, Kieron? Show them to me! I want to see them. Oh, Kieron, I can't wait for us to leave here and get to America.'

The smell of dirt, human excrement, vomit and alcohol that pervaded the whole of the boarding house where they were renting a room, was even stronger with the door open and Connie hurried to close it.

Of all the lodgings she and Kieron had occupied since they had run away together, this house in Back Court, one of Liverpool's most run-down housing areas, was easily the worst. Connie hadn't wanted to come to Liverpool, but Kieron had refused to listen.

His Uncle Bill had some work he wanted Kieron to do for him in Liverpool, he had told Connie. But when she had asked him what it was, and why, if he was working for his uncle, they did not have more money, Kieron had flown into one of his tempers and told her she asked too many questions.

If she wanted more money, he had told her, then she had better write to her sister and ask her for some! Connie had told him that she would do no such thing, and that she would rather starve than go begging to her sister.

They had quarrelled badly about it, and Kieron had become so angry that Connie trembled inwardly now, remembering how shocked and frightened she had felt.

But nothing would make her write to Ellie. She had begged her elder sister once for her help and been refused it, and now Connie was stubbornly determined not to do so ever again.

It was all right for Ellie, happily married to

Gideon, with everything she could possibly want, even if her first husband had committed suicide, leaving Ellie pregnant and alone and with his lover and her child on her hands.

Connie gave a small sniff. Now there was a scandal! Ellie's first husband, Henry, had taken a lover while working in Japan for his father's shipping line. The Japanese woman had given birth to Henry's child, and travelled to England, with her baby daughter, to find him.

But trust Ellie to come out of it all whiter than white, with everyone singing her praises, and a second husband in Gideon Walker who had loved her right from the start! As Kieron loved her, Connie tried to reassure herself. Even if he hadn't been showing it very much lately.

Uncomfortably, Connie admitted that she and Kieron seemed to spend all their time quarrelling these days. Since their arrival in Liverpool, he had taken to disappearing for hours at a time, returning the worse for drink and refusing to tell her where he had been, other than that it was on his Uncle Bill's 'business'.

He certainly always seemed to be able to find the money for drink, even when they had none for decent food or accommodation. Connie had seen the pitying looks the other women living in the court gave her, but she had refused to acknowledge them, hugging to herself instead, the knowledge that soon she and Kieron would be starting their new life together.

Titanic sailed in less than three days' time, and Connie had parted with the single reminder she had left of her past life and her beloved mother –

she had given Kieron the piece of jewellery her mother had left her, so that he could sell it to raise the money for their fares.

It had all been so different when she had been growing up in the comfortable, happy household her mother had run in Friargate above their father's butcher's shop. Theirs had been a home filled with love and laughter, and secretly she still missed those days dreadfully. She had certainly never envisaged that she might one day be in her present situation.

'Kieron, the tickets!' she begged again.

'Shut that bloody noise, will you!' he answered her aggressively.

Connie looked at him anxiously. 'Kieron, you did get the tickets, didn't you?' A pleading note had crept into her voice, and she was beginning to panic. 'We'll be sailing in three days, and you said that you would get them today!' she reminded him, unable to keep the anxiety and distress out of her voice.

'Aw, will yer stop nagging me, Connie. There'll be plenty of time to get the bloody tickets tomorrow.'

'But you said you would get them today. Why didn't you? Where have you been?'

'What I do wi' me time is no bloody business of yours. You don't have no rights over me!' he told her in an ugly voice.

Connie bit her lip, her face flushing at his deliberately hurtful reference to the fact that they weren't married.

At times like this, it was as though he had become a stranger. She could feel the mortified prick of tears at the back of her eyes, but she willed herself not to let them fall. No, she might not be Connie Connolly, but she was Connie Pride, and pride was what she had!

With that pride she turned back to look at him, and saw something in his eyes that made her heart start to beat with anxious, apprehensive strokes. 'What is it? What's wrong?' she demanded immediately.

'Nothing's wrong, exceptin' that I'm sick and tired of your nagging,' Kieron told her, pushing her away so roughly that she fell against the table.

'I'm beginnin' to think I should tek me Uncle Bill's advice and have nowt more to do wi' you,' he added bitterly.

Connie flinched at the sound of Kieron's uncle's name. There was something about him that was dark and frightening, and Connie was secretly glad that, in America, they would have the safety of the Atlantic Ocean between themselves and Bill Connolly.

'Kieron, you don't mean that!' she protested. 'You love me!'

'Get out of me way, I'm going out,' Kieron answered her angrily.

'Kieron!' Connie begged him, but he ignored both her protest and her shocked tears, pushing her out of his way as he headed for the door.

Things would be different once they were on board the *Titanic*, Connie comforted herself after he had left. She was unhappy and hungry, but there was no money for her to run down to the pie shop and get herself something hot to eat.

She blinked fiercely, determined not to let herself cry, and remembered her father's butcher's shop, and the happy home life she had known before the death of her mother.

Kieron glared furiously across the smoke-filled, filthy room at the man sitting opposite him. On the table between them was the money they had both staked – and the winning hand the other man had just gloatingly revealed.

Kieron could never resist a gamble. It lured and possessed him, like drink or women lured and possessed other men. It was a need and a lust that overwhelmed everything else in his life. His decision to run away with Connie had been made on the toss of a coin – heads, he took her; tails, he didn't.

'Bad loser as well as a bad player, are you, Connolly?' his opponent sneered as he made to pick up his winnings, including the money Kieron had gambled and lost. The money he had been supposed to use to buy his and Connie's tickets for the *Titanic*. The laughter of the men watching died abruptly, as Kieron swore and jumped up, reaching for one of the empty bottles standing on the table. Smashing it downwards to break it against the table, he lunged toward his opponent stabbing the jagged glass into his throat before anyone could intervene and stop him.

The bright red blood spattering everything matched the dark red murderous mist rising up inside him.

A barmaid coming in to collect the glasses screamed, and the man standing closest to

Kieron grabbed hold of him, gesturing to two of his companions to help him.

'Leave 'im, mate. We've got us own skins to think about,' one of them started to refuse.

'He's Bill Connolly's nephew,' the other man reminded him sharply.

Bill Connolly was well-known in the area, and not someone it was wise to cross. There would be some very unpleasant repercussions for anyone known to be here this evening, especially if Kieron Connolly was taken by the police.

As they dragged him toward a side door, Kieron made a savage grab for the money, crushing the bloodstained notes in his hand.

When midnight came and went and Kieron had still not returned, Connie finally left the chair where she had been sitting waiting for him, and crawled into bed.

It was almost lunchtime the next day when he returned, and Connie flung herself at him, sobbing in relief, and demanding, 'Where have you been? I was so worried... I hate this place, Kieron. I can't wait for us to leave. How could you leave me here on my own all night...'

'I didn't,' Kieron stopped her.

'What?' Connie's forehead creased in confusion.

'If anyone should come round here asking any questions, Connie. I was here all night. Never left the house all evening, I didn't,' he told her. 'And you better not be forgetting that if'n anyone should ask. Otherwise you'll have me Uncle Bill to answer to,' he said threateningly. 'If'n anyone was to come round here asking after me and where I was last night, you're to tell 'em that I was home with you, and that we was tucked up all nice and so cosy in bed together for ten o'clock... Understand? 'Cos you'd better had!'

Connie's mouth had gone dry, and her heart was hammering against her ribs.

'Kieron. What... What's happened? You aren't in some kind of trouble, are you?'

'You're asking too many questions, Connie. And me Uncle Bill wouldn't like that! It's him as says you're to say what I just told yer, if anyone comes asking,' he warned her.

Connie gave a small shiver. What was Kieron trying to say? What had he been doing? She was no fool and she knew he must be in some kind of trouble if he wanted her to provide an alibi for him.

'Oh, and I've got the tickets for the *Titanic*,' he added, almost as though it was an afterthought. 'So you can stop pestering me about it. Went out special like I did, this mornin', whilst you was still in kip.'

Connie hesitated. Kieron was concealing something from her, she knew that, but she was afraid to push him too hard, and at least he had got the tickets!

Kieron shifted uncomfortably from one foot to the other. He had used the money he had snatched back from the man he had murdered to buy their steerage tickets, more out of fear for his own safety than any desire to fulfil his promise to Connie. But of course he wasn't going to tell her that.

In fact, he was beginning to think that his father and his Uncle Bill had it right when they warned him that he would regret getting involved with Connie. She was a girl from a very different background to his own who did not understand their ways as one of their own would have done. Connie came from a respectable, hard-working family; Kieron's family inhabited a much darker world of thievery and violence, even though Connie herself had not realised it as yet.

Thrilled by Kieron's announcement, Connie dismissed her anxiety and flung her arms around his neck. This time Kieron didn't reject her.

The minute she opened her eyes, Connie was wide awake. It was only just dawn but she was too excited to go back to sleep. Today was the day they left for Southampton and the *Titanic!* They would reach Southampton by evening, and planned to go straight from the station to the port, ready to board the *Titanic* ahead of her departure at noon the next day. Connie's small case was already packed!

Eagerly she pushed back the thin, greying bedcovers, and got out of bed, singing happily under her breath.

'Mother Mary! Will you stop that caterwauling!'

Kieron had been out the previous night drinking, saying his farewells to his friends and his Uncle Bill, Connie guessed. It had been gone midnight when he had banged on their door, demanding that she let him in.

Now, in the pale morning light, he looked a very different man from the handsome young man she had fallen in love with. Drinking had bloated out his face, its flesh a pasty greyish colour, except for where his unshaven jaw bristled darkly.

'Kieron, get up. We've got to hurry. We mustn't miss the train,' Connie chivvied him. 'And I want...'

'You want. Who the hell cares what you want!' Kieron told her, staggering to his feet. 'You're a bloody rope around me neck, that's what you are. A bloody Protestant who 'ud open her legs for any un who'd have her! No decent Catholic girl would do what you've done. Me mam 'ud sooner see me sisters dead! Me Uncle Bill's in the right o' it. It's time I was rid of yer. An rid of yer is exactly what I aim to be!'

As always when he was angry, his accent broadened and Connie flinched at the venom she could hear in his voice.

'But you love me!' she protested. 'You–'

'There's only one of us will be sailing on the *Titanic*, and it won't be you.'

The cup she was holding slipped from her fingers to smash on the bare floorboards.

'No. No! Kieron, you don't mean that. You can't mean that,' Connie protested frantically, as she ran toward him and took hold of his arm, clinging to it in desperation.

'Who says I can't? Not you! You brung me down, that's all you done t' me. Persuaded me to run off with you like that and against what me family wanted. Me Uncle Bill says as how I'm to mek a fresh start for mesel' wi'out you!'

Connie couldn't believe what she was hearing. 'We're going to America to start a new life

32

together,' she persisted.

'You're goin' nowhere!' he told her. 'I'm t' one what's going t'ave a new life.'

Bill Connolly had instructed Kieron to leave Connie behind, and there was no way he would dare to cross his uncle. Not that he needed much persuading.

'But you've got us both tickets. I gave you the money, and the jewellery that my mother left me. You can't leave me here, I won't let you!'

As she flung herself against him in desperation, Kieron gave her a savage push that sent her careering into the bed. Connie cried out as her temple struck the sharp wood of the frame. Pain exploded inside her head, and she felt herself slide down into heavy, thick darkness, as she lost consciousness.

When she came round Connie was on her own. Frantically she tried to stand up, and then had to sit down again as nausea overwhelmed her. She was cold and shivering, and it was a long way down the stairs to the filthy outside privy they shared with everyone else in the house. Somehow she managed to will herself to get to her feet.

She had to get to the *Titanic*. Kieron could not have meant what he had said. She knew him. She knew his temper. He would be regretting what he had said to her now, she reassured herself pathetically, and besides he had their tickets. She had to get to Southampton and find Kieron. They would make up their quarrel like they always did; and everything would be all right.

Feverishly, Connie gathered her things together.

At the station, the guards shook their heads and averted their eyes from Connie's obvious distress. It was too late. There was no train that could get her to Southampton before the liner sailed, and anyway she had no ticket, nor any money to buy one.

She spent the rest of the day wandering round Liverpool in a daze, unable to accept what had happened – that Kieron had deserted her, cheated her not just of her money and her mother's jewellery, but also of her future.

It was dark when she finally let herself into the empty, cold room. Not bothering to undress, she crawled into the bed and wept until there were no tears left. It wasn't fair. It had been her idea that they should go, and now she was left behind whilst Kieron went without her.

On board the liner, Kieron joined in the excited celebrations. A pretty, blonde girl, overcome with excitement, threw herself into his arms and kissed him. He kissed her back enthusiastically, before releasing her to go and stand at the rail to watch Southampton and England disappearing. He had sold Connie's ticket to someone on the dock who had been desperate for one, aye, and got double what he had paid for it!

Around his waist he could feel the pleasing heaviness of the money belt secured there – filled with the money his Uncle Bill had given him in exchange for his promise that he would not take Connie to America with him.

'America she wants t'go, does she?' he had commented when Kieron told him of Connie's plans, and showed him the tickets he had bought with the money he had taken from the gambler, in an attempt to forestall his uncle's anger at the murder he had committed. Bill Connolly did not like anyone doing anything that might draw the attention of the law back to him.

'Aye, well, it 'ud be the best place for you right now, lad, there's no denying that,' he had acknowledged grimly. 'Arthur Johnson's dead. You were a bloody fool to go at him like that, and in public. Have you learned nothing, you bloody hot head! A quiet word to me and I could have had it sorted, no one the wiser and no danger of you being blamed for it either. Lucky for you that someone had their wits about them and got you away and cleaned up.

'You'd better make sure that Protestant whore of yours keeps her gob shut as well. America is it,' he had continued musingly. 'Aye, well, there's no denying that a fresh start is what you need now, lad. I've got a couple o'contacts there – men who ull be pleased to have someone who knows Bill Connolly working for them, but mind what I'm saying, lad, yer'll be a lot harder to trace without that Connie with yer. You don't want to be dragged back here and hanged for murder. So if yer've any sense, and yer tek my advice, yer'll leave her behind. In fact, yer can tek it that that's an order! And mind that yer obeys it, and does what I'm telling yer!'

Kieron knew better than to risk crossing his uncle. If he did, even in New York, he knew he wouldn't be safe from his vengeance. And besides, the truth was that he would be glad to be rid of Connie. She had been a novelty to him; a challenge, but now he was ready for fresh novelties and new challenges. 'So give us yer word, lad!'

Eagerly Kieron had done so. And had been rewarded by his uncle's approving, 'Yer da and mam will be right pleased t'ear you've come t'yer senses,' as he counted out a sum of money that made Kieron's eyes widen in greedy pleasure.

He felt neither guilt nor compassion for Connie or the man he had killed.

The blonde girl was giving him a poutingly inviting look. Whistling cheerfully, Kieron pushed his way through the crowd toward her.

Reluctantly Connie opened her eyes. It was still dark, but she was too cold to go back to sleep. It had been four days since Kieron had left, but, as she had now discovered, he had not left her without something to remember him by.

She moved underneath the thin, poor blanket that was all she had to wrap around her cold body, and immediately the small action made her stomach heave.

As she retched into the basin she had placed on the floor the previous night, Connie wept dry tears. She had missed her monthlies twice now, and had thought nothing of it at first, beyond being relieved to be spared its inconvenience, but now with this sickness, she was shockingly aware that the unthinkable had happened, and that she was carrying Kieron's child.

Running away with the man she loved had seemed a thrillingly romantic adventure, but the knowledge that she would bear an illegitimate child was neither thrilling nor romantic; it was a horrifyingly shameful prospect. She would be ostracised by everyone, not just her own family, and no decent people would want anything to do with her. There was no greater shame or disgrace for a woman than to have a child outside marriage.

Alone, and without anyone to turn to, she might as well be dead, Connie recognised bleakly. And, in fact, those closest to her would probably prefer her death to a disgrace that would contaminate them as well as her.

She retched again, as sick terror filled her. The room was cold with a dampness that was worse somehow than any sharp frost. Connie made no move to get up. What was the point? She wanted to hide herself and her shame from everyone.

She had no food, other than a stale half loaf, and no money to buy any, not even a couple of tatties from Ma Grimes' shop in the next street, never mind a juicy hot pie from the pie shop; but even if she had had the money she knew she would not have wanted to go out, fearful lest someone might guess her condition.

She had heard tales from her mother's servants, when she had sat listening in the kitchen to their gossip, of women being driven from their lodgings by their neighbours – sometimes physically – because of their sin in conceiving a child outside wedlock.

No one had any sympathy for a woman in such

a situation. Connie shuddered, terrified of the fate that lay ahead of her. Perhaps if she didn't eat she would somehow starve what was growing inside her of life, she thought desperately. Or even better, perhaps if she just went to sleep, when she woke up everything would be all right: she would be back at home in Friargate with her parents and Ellie and John. Oh, how she longed for that! To be a little girl again safe with her family; with her mother still alive to look after her and love her.

Shivering, she pulled the blanket round her body. Tears of despair and fear filled her eyes. The rent was only paid until the end of the week, after that... Even if he agreed to give her back her old job, the landlord at the pub wouldn't keep her on once her belly started to swell... Miserably she huddled into her blanket, unable to imagine what the future held for her.

TWO

Ellie Walker stood tensely in the elegant drawing room of her Winckley Square house and looked anxiously at her husband, Gideon.

The trauma she and all the other Pride children had suffered with the death of their mother might have ended for her with her marriage to her childhood sweetheart, but Ellie wanted it ended for all her siblings: Connie, who had so recklessly run away with Kieron Connolly; John, their brother, who had endured so much misery before he had become apprenticed to the Preston photographer for whom he now worked, and young Philip, who was in danger of growing up not knowing that he had a brother and two sisters. Ellie longed to have Philip safely here under Gideon's roof, and in the nursery with their two young sons, Richard and Joshua. But right now, it was Connie who concerned her the most.

Ellie knew that Connie had disgraced herself beyond redemption in the eyes of the world by what she had done, but she couldn't help but love her.

'Is there any news of Connie yet, Gideon?' she demanded, clasping her hands together. Gideon Walker frowned as he looked at his distressed wife. 'Come and sit down,' he urged her.

Waiting until she had done as he asked, he began gently, 'You know that through the agent my late mother used to find me, we've discovered that Connie and Kieron Connolly have stayed at a variety of addresses.' Gideon hesitated, not wanting to distress Ellie further by telling her that these addresses had, more often than not, been in areas no respectable person would ever want to admit living in.

'But where is she now, Gideon?' Ellie pressed him worriedly. 'Have you found her?'

'In a manner of speaking,' Gideon responded heavily. The last thing he wanted to do was to upset Ellie, but he knew that she had to be told the truth.

'Kieron Connolly bought tickets for them to sail on the *Titanic*. According to the passenger manifest he bought one in his own name and one in Connie's,' he told her quietly.

'What?' Ellie stood up, her hand to her mouth. 'But that means... You mean she's left England. She's going to America? Has he married her, Gideon?'

'Not as far as we can tell. Her ticket was in her own name, Connie Pride.' Gideon answered her, adding firmly, 'Under the circumstances, perhaps it will all be for the best.'

Gideon knew how much his wife's tender heart ached for her disgraced sister, but privately he acknowledged that Connie's departure for America was probably in all their best interests, including Connie's own.

Her reputation had been destroyed, and no one on her mother's side of the family was prepared to so much as speak her name any more, never mind find it in their hearts to forgive her and welcome her back into the fold, as his soft-hearted Ellie wanted to do.

Tears welled in Ellie's eyes, as she struggled to accept what Gideon was saying, but she didn't argue with him.

It had been nearly a week now since Kieron left, and Connie had done little other than sleep, and stagger weakly downstairs and across the yard to use the privy. She refused to refer to it as the 'bog' as her neighbours so cheerfully did.

It was on one of these occasions that she saw a new family, all wearing mourning, moving in to one of the other houses, and she smiled bitterly to herself to see how the mother, a small, fragile, obviously middle-aged woman, whose facial features were obscured by her heavy widow's veiling, glanced around herself in numb despair.

The small group were huddled together, the mother trying to comfort the young girl who clung to her skirts, whilst a tall, too thin, young man hurried to open the door for them. A lock of soft, brown hair flopped over his forehead, and would have fallen into his eyes if it hadn't been for his spectacles. He looked pale, and moved slowly, as though he had been ill.

Well, his health certainly won't mend living here, Connie acknowledged cynically. That they were not used to the kind of surroundings they now found themselves in was obvious. Their clothes might not be fashionable but they were clean and pressed, the young girl's apron immaculately starched.

Did they believe they were the only people here to think themselves above such a place, Connie wondered angrily, as the mother lifted her skirt above the dirt of the yard.

'Oh, I am sure the house will be better inside, Harry,' the woman murmured bravely.

The young man was shaking his head and looking very unhappy. 'Mother you cannot live here. We must find somewhere better.'

Connie glared at them. Better was it! Well, good luck to them. Normally the only place a person moved to from one of these poverty-ridden slums was either a wooden box or the poorhouse. Which reminded Connie, her own landlord would be calling soon for his rent money, and she had no idea how she was going to pay him. She cast an

41

anxious look toward the entry to the back alley, half-afraid to see him suddenly appear.

One of her neighbours, making her way to her own house, gave her a curious look. Connie hadn't made any friends amongst the other women living in the court. She and Kieron hadn't been there long enough, and besides she knew that they would shun her if they knew that she and Kieron weren't married.

Listlessly Connie made her way back to her room. She felt weak and light-headed, and she couldn't remember the last time she had eaten, but she wasn't hungry anyway. Perhaps if she was lucky she might just go to sleep tonight and never wake up again.

Self-pityingly she thought about how her family would react to her plight. They would be happy to see her dead, she was sure! Her aunts would not have dreamed of hiring a servant who lived in the kind of conditions Connie now did. Her grimy, darned clothes were shabbier even than those worn by her aunt's scullery maid.

She touched her concave belly, and turned her face into the grimy pillow to weep.

Three doors away, Connie's new neighbours were exploring their new home.

'Mother, you can't stay here,' Harry Lawson protested, as he looked around the shabby parlour.

'Harry, we'll be fine,' Elsie Lawson tried to reassure her son, but in reality she was as appalled by her surroundings as he was. Her elder daughter was yet to join them, so Elsie told Harry brightly,

'When Mavis gets here we'll set to and clean it up.'

It was only just a month since she had lost her husband. Thieves had broken into his grocery shop and bludgeoned him to death.

Elsie was still in shock. The shop had been a rented property, as had the pretty house they had lived in, and her husband had only left her a small amount of money. Of her three children, only one was working, and Harry's job as a junior schoolteacher at Hutton Grammar School paid him only a pittance.

She had been told that property was much cheaper to rent down in this part of the city, and naively she had not fully understood why!

'You can't stay here, Mother,' Harry was repeating. 'I'll leave Hutton when my contract finishes at the end of next term, and I'll look for another teaching job.'

'You will do no such thing, Harry Lawson,' Elsie stopped him angrily. 'What do you think your poor father would say if he could hear you saying that? He was that proud of you, Harry. Getting a scholarship and all! And there's no better public school hereabouts than Hutton. You said when they took you on, that you were lucky and what an honour it was to be chosen to teach there. I know they don't pay you much now, but when one of the older teachers retires, they're bound to give you a promotion,' she finished proudly.

Harry shook his head. Everything she had said was true, but he couldn't leave his mother and sisters to live here.

'This place will be all right for now,' Elsie assured him again, with a cheerfulness she was far from feeling. 'Once I've given it a good clean and got some of our own things in, it will look a lot better – you wait and see.'

Harry smiled. He knew how proud both his parents were of him. But he had seen the pretty young girl crossing the yard earlier, her face pinched with cold and hunger, her dress shabby and faded. His heart had gone out to her. There was no way he wanted to see his own sisters ending up like that. He had been granted some special leave because of his father's death, and he decided he would spend that time making enquiries to see if he could get a teaching post with a less prestigious school. He needed to find somewhere where he could live out, and not in, as he had to at Hutton, and to try to get some extra part-time work to help with the family finances.

'*Titanic* Sinks – Hundreds Feared Dead!'

Gideon's stomach lurched with disbelief as he stared at the headlines in his morning paper.

He picked it up and scanned the front page article. It was true! The liner its owners had claimed was unsinkable, had sunk!

That news, in itself, would have been shocking enough, without the fact that Connie had been on board it.

Ellie was upstairs in the nursery, and he had a mad impulse to throw the papers on the fire before she could see them.

He heard her footsteps crossing the hall and she came into the room, her eyes bright with happiness and love; her mouth curved into a delighted smile.

44

'Gideon, you'll never guess what! Joshua has just smiled at me! Nurse says he is still too young, but I know that he did. Oh, I wish you could have seen–' Abruptly she stopped speaking as she saw the look on his face. 'What. What is it?'

He went to her and gently led her to a chair, holding both her hands as he told her quietly, 'There is bad news, Ellie. The *Titanic* has sunk with a terrible loss of life.' He kept hold of her hands, and watched her as she struggled to assimilate what he had said.

'The *Titanic*... But no! That can't be true! She's unsinkable! It was in the papers! She cannot have sunk... Connie is on board her!' Ellie protested pathetically, before catching her breath and denying frantically, 'No, Gideon! No! No!' Shocked tears streaming down her face, Ellie turned to him. 'There will be survivors though, surely?' she begged.

Gideon felt the pity grip his throat. Connie had been a steerage passenger, but he couldn't bring himself to remind Ellie of this, and take her hope away from her. But something in his expression must have betrayed him because suddenly she demanded, 'You think that she's dead, don't you? Oh, Gideon! This is all my fault! I should have done more for her, Gideon. If I had she would never...'

Gideon was not going to allow that!

'Ellie, you have nothing to blame yourself for,' he assured her immediately. 'Connie was always headstrong and wilful, and you did your best for her.'

'The family will have to be told,' Ellie

45

whispered, as though she hadn't heard him.

'I shall do everything that is necessary,' Gideon assured her.

'She might have survived. There will be survivors, won't there, Gideon?' Ellie repeated helplessly. 'Such a new modern liner, there would have been lifeboats and...'

Gideon said nothing. According to the papers there had not been enough lifeboats to hold all the passengers, and those travelling steerage, like Connie, would have had the least chance of surviving.

As tears filled Ellie's eyes, Gideon took her in his arms. 'I'll get young John round here, aye, and send a message to your father as well. And your ma's family – the posh lot – will have to be told, I suppose.'

Ellie couldn't speak. How could it be possible that Connie could be dead, drowned? Wilful, naughty, reckless Connie. Connie, her little sister.

'Well, what I want to know is, what on earth Connie was doing on the *Titanic* in the first place?' Amelia Gibson's voice was sour-apple sharp as she looked accusingly at Ellie. Gideon had informed Ellie's mother's family, the Barclay sisters, of the news via Ellie's aunt, Amelia Gibson, who was also their neighbour.

Ellie shook her head and looked at Gideon. Connie had not been on the list of survivors posted by the White Star Shipping Line and published in the national papers, and nor had Kieron Connolly.

'Well, if you want my opinion Ellie, it's

probably all for the best,' Amelia Gibson was continuing virtuously.

'All for the best!' Ellie's whole body trembled as she stopped her. 'Aunt, Connie is probably dead. How can that be for the best!' Tears welled in Ellie's eyes.

Immediately Amelia bristled and fixed Ellie with an angry glare.

'I shouldn't have thought it was necessary to explain my words to you. I refuse to sully my lips by discussing any of your sister's disgraceful behaviour. She has brought shame on herself and shame on our family as well. If my poor sister had lived to see–'

'If Mama had lived, then none of this would have happened,' Ellie couldn't stop herself from bursting out.

Ignoring her, Amelia continued grimly, 'When I think of what she made your poor Aunt Jane suffer with her wilful ways. She and your Uncle Simpkins did their best for her, taking her in and giving her a good home, just as your Aunt Parkes did for you, and we all know how Connie repaid their generosity.' Her thin lips folded in a forbidding line. 'She was a disgrace to our family. She could never have returned to live amongst decent respectable people!' Amelia went on. 'And, in my opinion, she is better off dead!'

'Aunt, I won't have you speak of her like that,' Ellie protested immediately. 'How can you say such things about her?'

'I say them because they are true, Ellie! When a woman behaves as Connie has done and loses her reputation, she loses everything, and there can be no purpose to her continuing to live. Had Connie ever dared come to my door, I would not have let her in, and neither would any of my sisters. Indeed, I would not have spoken to her if I had seen her in the street. She was already as good as dead so far as I was concerned. I cannot understand why you waste your tears on her, Ellie, for she certainly did not deserve them.'

After they had gone, Ellie wept in Gideon's arms.

'Oh poor Connie, Gideon... How could my aunt speak so, and be so cruel!'

Gideon held her tightly.

'I know that Connie did wrong, but...'

'You would forgive her and take her in, I know that, Ellie, but there would be many people like your aunt who would not forgive or forget what she did, and who would shun her for it.'

Ellie knew that what he was saying was true. But she knew she would have forgiven her sister had she done a hundred times worse, if only she could have her back alive and safe!

There was a sudden commotion in the hallway, and her younger brother John came bursting in.

The moment she saw John, Henrietta – Ellie's stepdaughter, the child of her late husband and his Japanese lover – ran eagerly toward him. After her first husband had committed suicide, Ellie had made herself responsible for the frail Japanese woman who had travelled all the way from Japan with her young daughter to find the man she loved. But Ellie's compassion and care had not been enough to heal Minaco's broken heart. After Minaco's death, and Ellie's own subsequent marriage to Gideon, Ellie had insisted that they adopt the orphaned little girl, knowing herself how hard it was to grow up without loving parents.

Henrietta was both pretty and sweet-natured, and Ellie and Gideon loved her as though she were their own child.

'And how's my beautiful girl, today?' John asked Henrietta mock-severely as he set her on his shoulders. 'Have you been good and learned your lessons?'

As Henrietta giggled at his teasing, Ellie said quietly, 'John, there is bad news about Connie.'

THREE

Someone was banging on her door. Reluctantly Connie opened her eyes and stared at it in confusion. Had Kieron forgotten his key again?

Pushing back the bedclothes, she scratched absently at the marks the bedbugs had left on her skin, slid her feet to the floor, and stood up. To her shock, her legs refused to support her and she had to cling on to the bed. Her head muzzy with confusion, she went to unlock the door.

'By Our Sainted Mary, so you are here after all then, are you!'

Connie staggered back as Kieron's uncle, Bill Connolly, thrust open the door and strode in. Connie had never liked him, and she knew that he returned her feelings.

As he loomed over her, she could smell the

drink on his breath and her stomach heaved.

'Murdering bitch,' Bill yelled at her. 'Murdering whore. Sendin' our Kieron to his death. It should have been youse who was drowned, not our Kieron.'

He had slammed the door closed and Connie started to shiver, as she tried to make some sense out of what he was saying to her.

'Drowned,' she repeated uncomprehendingly, whilst she tried to control her nausea.

'Aye, drowned, when he went down in the *Titanic!*'

The room spun round and Connie struggled to grasp what he was saying.

'Aye, and you were the one as sent 'im to his death. It was you as nagged 'im into leaving – he told me all about it, how you were goin' at 'im and how as he were right sick of youse, and were feared to come home in case you followed him there. He knew his ma would never tolerate having the likes of you 'angin' around. A God-fearing respectable Catholic woman she is.' Bill's face darkened as he mopped the tears filling his eyes.

'I didn't send Kieron to America,' Connie defended herself weakly. 'I was supposed to be going with him, but he left me behind because you told him to – just like you told him to tell me I had to lie, if anyone came round asking where he was the night he didn't come home,' she added bitterly, forgetting her fear of him in the heat of her emotion.

Instantly Bill Connolly stiffened. 'What was that you just said?' he demanded menacingly.

How much had Kieron told her? More than he damn well ought to have done, that was for sure. Kieron might be dead and therefore no longer accountable for the murder he had committed, but if the stupid bitch in front of him started tattling, there were plenty enough people who would leap at the excuse to start sticking their noses into Connolly affairs.

Kieron had broken one of the cardinal rules of the Connolly family, which was never to talk to a woman about business. Had he been here, nephew or not, drowned or not, Bill would cheerfully have broken his neck.

Connie refused to answer him. She could feel the fear and shock trickling through her veins like ice. *Titanic* had sunk, and Kieron was dead. How was that possible? She was shaking so much that she turned back to the bed to sit down on it. She had barely eaten for days, and she felt sick with weakness and shock.

'I give our Kieron a hundred guineas afore he left, and that's a debt you are going t'ave ter pay back,' she heard Bill Connolly telling her menacingly.

Connie stared at him. 'But how can I do that? I haven't got any money! I haven't got anything,' she told him bitterly. 'Kieron took everything.' Her face twisted with misery, but Bill had no sympathy for her.

'How? Same way as yer earned it from our Kieron,' he told her in an ugly voice. 'On yer back, just like any other whore. I'm tekin you back ter Preston wi' me. I've got a place down by the river where you'll feel right at 'ome. Plenty o'

51

sailors callin' so you won't feel lonely,' he told her leeringly.

Connie froze in horror, as the meaning of his threat sank slowly through the numbness of her misery. He was suggesting that she become a prostitute. That he. That she... He couldn't mean it!

She looked into his eyes and a cold thrill of fear seized her. He did mean it!

'No! I won't!' she told him defiantly, the same rebellious streak that had got her into so much trouble before, spurting to life inside her. 'And you can't make me!'

She knew immediately that she had said the wrong thing.

'Whose goin' ter stop me?' he demanded tauntingly. 'That posh sister o'yourn?' He laughed out loud.

'I won't,' Connie repeated desperately, her eyes widening in terror as Bill advanced toward her, his fist bunched.

Connie screamed the first time he hit her, the blow knocking her clean off her feet. But, by the time his fists had laid into her body half a dozen times, she was beyond screaming; beyond crying; beyond anything only praying for the pain to end.

Straightening up over Connie's motionless body, Bill wiped the blood off his fist.

'Aye, let that be a lesson to yer,' he grunted, as he stared down at her. 'I've got business to attend to right now,' he told her, spitting onto the floor, 'but when I come back you'd better be ready to see sense, otherwise yer'll get another dozen o' the same.'

Aiming a contemptuous kick at her, he went to

the door and removed the key, taking it with him and locking her in the room as he left.

Waves of pain were surging through Connie like the tide on the beach, each one carrying her further and further into its agony. All she wanted to do was to be taken to a place where she could no longer feel it. But it wouldn't let her go. It was savaging her with brutal teeth, gripping her, and biting into her belly.

Connie whimpered and then cried out as each fresh surge brought her further agony. Through blurred eyes she looked at the locked door.

Anger filled her, streaked with blood red fear. She hated Kieron for leaving her and she hated him even more for what was happening to her now. Bill Connolly meant what he had said. And if she stayed here...

Somehow she managed to get to her feet. Bill had taken the key from the door, but Connie had another one, the one Kieron had left behind when he had abandoned her. Dragging herself to the small box beneath the bed, which held her few remaining personal treasures, she opened it, and removed the key.

She could feel herself growing more sick and dizzy as she turned it in the lock, but the fear that she might faint and not be able to escape, made her grit her teeth and ignore it.

She was conscious of someone from one of the other rooms staring at her as she staggered to the top of the stairs. Down at the bottom of them, the door was open, and a thin patch of bright April sunshine warmed the grimy stone of the court outside.

Connie could feel the pain dragging at her as she started to walk down the stairs. By the time she was halfway down, she had dropped to all fours and was crawling. She tried not to scream out loud, when suddenly she started to fall...

Harry turned into the alley on his way back to his mother's lodgings. His chest was aching, as it did whenever he was anxious, a legacy from the weakness he had suffered in it as a child, and he had to pause to take a deep breath. As he did so, he saw Connie tumble through the doorway and into the yard. She was moaning in pain and immediately he hurried toward her, unable to prevent the shock registering in his eyes as he looked down at her.

Her face was badly bruised and her lip was bleeding. He realised immediately that she had been beaten up, and Harry felt a surge of anger at the thought that a member of his own sex had hurt her so badly.

Connie looked up at the young man bending over her, his expression concerned. She recognised him as the son of the widow who had recently moved into the court. Somewhere, a part of her registered a feeling of shame and anger that he should see her like this, but then that feeling was overwhelmed by her fear that, at any moment, Bill Connolly would reappear.

A fresh wave of pain seized her and she tried to clench her teeth against it, but it was tearing at her again, even fiercer than before. She started to whimper, clutching at her stomach as she did so, struggling to get to her feet.

A couple of women came hurrying out of one of the neighbouring houses and came over to see what was going on.

'By the Blessed Mother Mary, what's happened to youse, love?' one of them demanded as she looked at Connie. 'Yer man got a temper on him, did he, love? Aye, he's given youse a right nasty thump.'

Her voice wasn't unsympathetic.

Connie was desperate to escape from the court. Somehow she managed to get to her feet, and ignoring both Harry and the women, she started to walk toward the alley. She had only taken half a dozen steps when the pain gripped her again; stronger this time, stopping her in her tracks and making her scream aloud.

Immediately the other woman's expression changed. ''Ere Mary Ann,' she called over her shoulder to the woman standing behind her. 'Get your Jim to run round to Ma Deakin's, will yer, looks like she's miscarryin'. 'Ere come on, love!' she told Connie comfortingly, bustling up to her, 'Let's get yer back inside. Ma Deakin 'ull soon 'ave youse sorted out. How far gone was yer?'

The girl was pregnant. Harry was filled with pity and shock.

As the two women bustled round her, Connie lifted her head and looked at him. Their glances met. In Connie's eyes he could see a mixture of fear and pride, and shame.

Turning away, Harry hurried toward his mother's lodgings. The two women had taken charge of Connie, and were trying to get her back inside the building.

'No. No. Don't take me back in there. He's going to come back for me.' She scarcely knew what she was saying, she was so terrified and so maddened by pain.

'What the 'ell's goin' on 'ere?'

The two women fell back as the local midwife hurried to Connie's side.

'She's losing, Ma,' one of them explained unnecessarily. 'Got beat up bad by 'er old man, by the looks o' it.'

Connie gave a terrified scream. She felt as though her insides were being ripped out. Mary Deakin frowned, and took hold of her. 'Too late to get her inside now!'

Discreetly Harry let himself into his mother's lodgings.

Connie felt as though the pain would never end, wave after wave of it, but all the time there was something else worse than the pain tormenting her. She heard herself scream, and then she was falling into burning hot blackness.

Connie opened her eyes. Her mouth felt so dry. She moved, and then cried out as she felt pain sear through her.

'Ma, she's awake.'

A woman was bending over her. A stranger! Terrified, Connie looked around the room. Had Bill Connolly carried out his threat, was she already in the brothel?

'Well, youse back with us, are youse? Must say I thought we was gonna lose yer. Had a real bad time of it, you have. Bleeding like youse were never gonna stop, and then being that bad wi' t'fever that youse looked fit to die. But I've niver lost a lass yet, and I weren't gonna lose youse.'

Connie blinked as she looked up into the beaming face smiling down at her.

'I've ... I've ... been ill?' she questioned uncertainly.

The smile changed to a frown.

'Aye, that yer have, lass. Lost yer babby, you did, and nearly died yersel. Eeh, but that bugger who knocked youse about left you in a right bad way. Although I says it m'sel, wi'out me to tek care of youse, yer would have been dead, right enough. 'Ere, our Jenny, go and get some water for the lass,' she instructed the girl standing behind her.

'Lucky youse was, lass, that them women in the court had the sense to send for Ma Deakin. The best midwife around these parts, that's what I am,' she told Connie proudly. 'Shame about the babby, lass. But...'

The baby. Connie struggled to sit up.

'Tek it easy, love,' the midwife warned her. 'Youse'ull be all right, but 'e give yer a right thumping and youse got a couple o' cracked ribs. Bound 'em for yer I have, and them'll fix easy enough. He didn't ought ter have knocked yer about like that and youse carryin' an' all! I'll tell yer straight, it were touch and go for the first few days you were here. Lucky yer was, too, that our Lily is away visiting m'sister, otherwise there wouldn't 'ave bin a bed for yer. Eeh, lass, youse were in a bad way. 'T'in't none o' my business, lass, but if I was yer ma...'

Connie shivered, as the midwife's words

brought back for her the full horror of what had happened to her. Tears of fear and misery filled her eyes.

'I haven't got a mother. She's dead,' Connie told the midwife, shivering again as she added, 'I haven't got anyone.'

It was true, after all, Kieron had deserted her, and Ellie, the sister she had turned to rescue her from the misery of her life with their aunt and uncle, had been more interested in her own life and her own happiness, than she had been in Connie's misery.

And, if she had refused to help before, how much more likely was Ellie to refuse to do so now! Ellie would probably tell her that what had happened to her served her right, Connie decided self-pityingly. No, she had no family now. They didn't want her, and she didn't want them!

Mary Deakin eyed her sympathetically. She had a soft heart, and if it hadn't been for the fact that she had a houseful of her own, she would have willingly offered Connie a bed.

'Eeh, I'm that sorry for yer, lass.' She shook her head. 'Ter 'ave no ma, and no folks o'yer own. It dunna bear thinkin' about!'

It was obvious to her from both Connie's shabby appearance, and what, to Mary, was her posh voice, that Connie was someone who had fallen on hard times. And, in Mary's motherly opinion, fallen in with a right wrong 'un man-wise, which reminded her.

'Jenny Parker says as how she 'eard from some-one 'oo saw 'im leavin', that it were Bill Connolly who belted yer. By, but yer'v got yersel' into a

58

pickle o' bother, lassie.' She shook her head gravely. 'Gettin' yersel on the wrong side o' Bill Connolly.'

Connie felt terrified. 'He doesn't know where I am, does he?' she demanded frantically. 'He mustn't know.'

'There, lass, there's no need to tek on so,' Mary tried to comfort her. 'We 'aven't told 'im nothing. We looks after one another round 'ere, and he ain't one o' us.'

Too distraught to be comforted, Connie struggled again to sit up.

'He mustn't find me,' she told the midwife, her eyes brimming with frightened tears. 'If he does...' She started to shudder. 'He said...'

Her face went white; her voice dropping to a terrified whisper, as she wept and told the midwife what Bill Connolly had threatened her with.

'Eeh, the bugger! Hangin's too good for him, and so it is. Eeh, lass, you've had a right bad time. 'Appen it's just as well yer lost the babby.'

'I've got to get away from here. He mustn't find me.' Connie repeated. 'But I don't know where I can go...' Not back to Preston, she acknowledged miserably, she certainly wouldn't be welcome there!

''Ere, I've just remembered sommat,' the midwife exclaimed happily. 'I've got a niece up at 'ospital, and she were telling us that they're wanting to tek on girls ter train up as nurses. Yer lives in whilst yer training, and I could 'ave a word wi' her if yer wants me to... By, but if'n I had me time again I'd jump at it. Yer'll be safe enough up there, lass, the Matron don't allow no men into

59

the nurses' 'ome! 'Ave their balls off if'n they tried, she would.' She laughed.

A nurse! Connie frowned. Working as a nurse was not something she had ever considered doing. Why should she have done? There had been no reason to think of such things in the life she had been envisaging for herself, up until Kieron had deserted her so cruelly. She had, Connie admitted, seen her future in very different terms, imagining it being more like her own mother's marriage to a man who loved her.

The rosy glow of believing Kieron loved her had faded long before their last quarrel, she admitted, but the fear of what separating from him would mean for her own respectability, had kept her clinging to the fantasy that, in him, she had found her one true love.

And she had yearned so for that love, desperate for it to fill the hurting space left in her life by the break-up of her family.

No respectable man would ever love her now though! Or marry her! So what was to become of her?

'I don't know anything about nursing,' she began doubtfully. 'And...'

'Lord bless yer love, yer don't need ter. Tek yer on and train yer up they will!'

A nurse! Vague memories of being taught at school about Florence Nightingale, the woman who had lifted the work of nursing from something no respectable woman would ever consider, to an almost saintly vocation, floated through Connie's head.

'It u'll give you a new start, lass,' Mary urged

her kindly. 'No one up at 'ospital needs to know nowt about what's 'appened down 'ere, and if youse 'ull tek me advice, you'll say nowt about it yersel. Best put it all behind you, and make out like it never 'appened, like.'

The picture she was drawing was a very tempting one, Connie acknowledged. A new start... She could have a whole new life, become a whole new person; she would be safe from Bill Connolly, and free from the shame of having run away with Kieron.

Connie's spirits started to lift. She could picture herself nursing grateful patients whilst an admiring, handsome doctor looked on. Of course, her cousin Cecily's husband was a doctor, and both he and his father practised in Liverpool. No doubt they attended patients at the hospital, but that knowledge did not put Connie off, far from it. Gleefully she imagined how graciously she would receive her family's awed praise of her nobility at giving her life to help others.

'Yes, please, I would appreciate it if you would speak with your niece,' she told the midwife, and already, although she didn't know it herself, she was sounding more like Miss Connie Pride, and less like the disgraced young woman who had run away with Kieron Connolly.

FOUR

Connie sat nervously beside Ma Deakin as the bus jolted through the streets. Thanks to the good offices of the midwife's niece, she had been granted an appointment to be examined by the Matron to see if she was fit to train as a nurse.

'Where are we going?' she asked anxiously, as she looked out of the bus window. 'This isn't...'

'Mill Road, o'course, ninny,' Ma Deakin answered her affectionately, giving her a dig in the ribs with her elbow as she chuckled.

'Mill Road, but that's where the poorhouse hospital is!'

'Aye, that's right, where else would we be goin'? Come on, 'ere's our stop,' Ma Deakin instructed Connie, heaving her weight out of the seat.

The Infirmary, in other words, the Poor Hospital. All the bright dreams Connie had been weaving suddenly collapsed. To have to be taken into one of the Poor Hospitals carried as much stigma as being taken into the workhouse, and, for a minute, she was tempted to get off the bus and run away. But she had nowhere to run to, she reminded herself in despair, as she followed the midwife.

Even on this sunny day, the Infirmary cast a dark shadow which made Connie shiver. When Ma Deakin had spoken of her going into nursing, it had never occurred to her that she had meant her to go into the Poor Hospital. Why, it would be as bad as though she were in the poorhouse itself.

'I'd best not come any further with yer,' Ma Deakin was saying. 'T' matron here don't approve of the likes of me – yer have to have a proper training to call yersel' a midwife round 'ere. Now, you haven't forgotten what yer have to do, 'ave yer, luv?'

The motherly concern in her voice gave Connie a pang of guilt. Ma Deakin had been so kind to her, she couldn't offend her by telling her that she could not work in the poorhouse hospital.

'Yer to go in and ask for t' matron, and to give 'em our Sarah's name. Tell 'em she's arranged everything like!'

Numbly Connie nodded her head. Was it really to come to this wretched place that Ma Deakin had washed and mended Connie's shabby dress, shaking her head over Connie's best one, 'No, lass, that's too fancy.' She had pursed her lips and added, 'Yer don't want 'em thinkin' yer flighty, like!'

'Connolly will never come looking for yer in here.'

Connie looked at her saviour, her eyes suddenly brimming with emotional tears. Flinging her arms round the midwife, she gave her a fierce hug.

'Eeh, lass, don't be such a softie,' the midwife told her, giving her a push in the direction of the hospital. 'Off yer go now, and think on, lass. No more getting yersel' into trouble!'

The entrance to the Infirmary loomed in front of her, and Connie knew that if Ma Deakin hadn't been standing watching her, she would have been tempted to turn and run away. The poorhouse hospital! The life she had known really was lost to her now, and as for her dreams about the fun she would have going to the music hall and the picture house... She gave a small shudder of fear. They locked you in your room at night at the poorhouse, didn't they? Everyone knew how cruelly its inmates were treated.

She checked, and turned to look over her shoulder. Ma Deakin was still watching her. With feet that felt like lead, Connie took a reluctant step into the new life she was now dreading.

Harry Lawson grimaced to himself in disgust as the pungent smell of bad drains filled his nostrils. The sooner he could get his mother and sisters out of their current accommodation, and into something decent, the better.

He had to return to Hutton in the morning, but he was hoping he might have obtained some translation work from the P&O shipping line. It would mean long nights spent working over complicated documents translating them from Spanish in the main, and sometimes French into English. The pay wasn't very good, but, so far as Harry was concerned, every penny helped.

As he passed the spot where Connie had gone into labour, he averted his gaze. The plight of the young woman had concerned him, for her own sake, and for his sisters' as well. He couldn't bear the thought of them being pulled down to such a level, but poverty dragged clanging chains of other ills with it, as Harry knew.

His mother was waiting for him when he opened the door to their shabby accommodation.

'Harry, the best of news!' she exclaimed happily. 'I took the ferry across to New Brighton to see your father's Aunt Martha. She has agreed that we may move in with her, Harry, on condition that I look after her. Oh, Harry, I am so pleased. The house is big enough for any family, and there is a garden for Sophie. The air is so much healthier there as well, and you are to have a room of your own for when you come home from Hutton! Harry, it is such a relief! I do not think I could have tolerated another night in this dreadful place.'

Harry looked ruefully at his mother. 'Great Aunt Martha is an old, cantankerous bully who will treat you like a servant, Mother. You know how Father always said how mean she was. I might have secured some extra work...'

'I shall not mind looking after her, and anyway it will give me something to do. I don't want you to put your career at risk by taking on so much extra work that you neglect your teaching duties, Harry,' she told him gently.

Harry sighed, but he knew better than to argue with her.

'There is more good news,' she continued merrily. 'We have heard today that they are taking on probationer nurses at the Infirmary. You know how much Mavis has always wanted to be a nurse!'

'The Infirmary!' Harry stopped her sharply. 'But mother that is the poorhouse hospital.'

'Well, we are poor, aren't we?' Harry heard his

sister Mavis challenge him, as she came into the room.

'I shall have my board and a wage, and I shall be training to do what I have always wanted to do,' she told Harry proudly.

Harry's heart sank. It hurt him inside that they had come to this, and that there was nothing he could do about it.

'It is what I want, Harry. To be a nurse!' Mavis told him fiercely.

'A nurse, yes,' Harry stopped her. 'But an Infirmary nurse is not...'

'Not what?' she demanded. 'Not as good as other nurses? Well, let me tell you something, Harry Lawson. I am going to be the best nurse there is! If the Infirmary will take me on, then that's where I shall go! And if you're ashamed of...'

'I shall never be ashamed of my family,' Harry stopped her fiercely, adding in a quieter voice, 'But I am ashamed of myself, for not being able to do better by you all.'

The Matron of the Infirmary was not a person to be trifled with, and she was no fool either. When she glided, like a ship under full sail, into the carbolic-smelling, scrubbed room in which the batch of would-be new nurses were waiting for her, it was with the express purpose of ensuring that they recognise her authority and quailed under it.

Her experienced glance took in the gaggle of young women in front of her, but it was the sudden giggle of one of them that caused her to turn her head and focus on her.

A potential troublemaker. Matron knew exactly how to deal with those and if she hadn't just had an interview with Mr Harris P Cleaver, Clerk to the Board of Governors of the Hospital, during which he had appealed to her not to turn down any of the new recruits so that they could meet the Government's demands, Connie would have been shown the door without any further ado.

However, the ears of the British Government had already caught the first threatening rumble of war, lying menacingly in the distance like thunder, and had started to prepare for it. More soldiers would be needed and more nurses to mend their wounds. Decisions were made and orders given.

Matron's bosom had heaved, as she had drawn herself up to her full height, and reminded him, 'Sir, this hospital has always put the thorough and excellent training of its nurses above their number. Quality before quantity has been our motto, which is why we have never, as some other Poor Hospitals have done, taken onto our wards untrained girls from the poorhouse itself.'

'Matron, it is because of your excellent reputation for training young women to become first-rate nurses, that we have been given this task of recruiting and training more.' Mr Cleaver had informed her. 'It is because our Government wants the very best of nurses to care for our wounded soldiers – should there be a war, our wounded heroes,' he had emphasised, 'that we are required to train more.'

There had been several more very flattering

remarks of this nature made to her by Mr Cleaver, and, eventually Matron had acknowledged that if the Government were in need of more nurses, then no hospital in the entire length and breadth of the country, was more equipped to train them to the highest of standards than the West Derby Union Infirmary.

And possibly no Matron! Because the Infirmary was no ordinary poorhouse hospital! Thanks to the foresight of one of its Guardians, its nursing practices and training methods had been recommended by no less personage than Florence Nightingale herself.

Matron was justly proud of that reputation, and she looked upon it as almost her sacred duty to maintain it. Her experienced gaze assessed and judged the freshly scrubbed faces in front of her.

Connie looked right back at her defiantly, ignoring the sharp tug the girl standing next to her gave her gown.

They had been waiting for nearly half an hour for the Matron to see them to assess their suitability, and Connie had learned that the calm steady-eyed, brown-haired young woman tugging her gown was Mavis, and that she had wanted to be a nurse all her life; and the anxious-looking redhead with the freckled nose and gangly body was Josie, whose stepmother had no longer wanted her at home. The blonde girl with her cheeky grin and upturned nose was Vera Harper, and Connie had already recognised that she and Vera were kindred spirits. In no time at all, they had been chattering happily together.

'So you all wish to train as nurses! Well, make

no mistake it is very demanding work and not for the work-shy or feckless.'

She paused and gave Connie a very long, cold look.

'No matter how humble your position, and how elevated my own, no error on your part will escape my notice.'

Josie made a small anxious sound, and Connie gave her a withering look.

'Do you have a problem with your eyesight, Miss?' the Matron asked Connie coldly. 'When I am speaking to you, your gaze, in fact the whole of your attention, should be on me and not wandering around the room.'

Connie fought back the blush she could feel wanting to burn her face. The teachers at the Park School in Preston had sometimes been strict, but nothing like this, and she wasn't a schoolgirl any more, she was... Connie tensed, as she remembered just what she was, and why she was here.

'You will be working a probationary period, after which your suitability to continue your training will be assessed.'

Matron had two strict rules, neither of which she ever allowed to be broken! The first was that her wards were, at all times, kept in a state of total cleanliness and the second, that her nurses were, at all times, kept in a state of total obedience. Occasionally, as now, there were situations when the two rules married admirably together.

'One of my nurses will come and escort you to a bathroom where you will wash and then present yourselves for inspection.'

Not even her imposing presence could check

the murmur of apprehension that ran round the room. One girl put up her hand 'Please, ma'am, does that mean we will have to take off our clothes?'

Matron pursed her lips. Of course, it was a good sign that a young woman should be modest, but as Matron had good cause to know, some of the girls who came to her for training were from the poorest families. Their clothes were removed from them and washed in the hospital laundry; every inch of their skin was scrubbed clean, and every hair on their head checked to make sure they were not bringing any kind of infestation into the hospital with them. Matron was as relentless, as she was tireless, in her war against dirt and its potential to carry disease.

Sternly she looked at the girl. 'Of course it does. How else would you take a bath? This is a hospital,' she reminded them, 'and within it you will see certain sights that would not normally be witnessed by an unmarried woman. But you will not be women – you will be nurses!'

'I won't do it. I'm not letting anyone see me without my clothes,' one of the girls announced, pink-cheeked.

Matron had left in a crackle of starched dress and apron, and Connie listened, waiting to voice her own refusal, when Mavis said quietly, 'It is simply a necessary precaution, and nothing to be feared.'

Feared? Who was afraid! Certainly not her, Connie decided!

And it seemed later, when they all huddled

together after undergoing their examination at the hands of a stern-faced Sister, that none of the others had been either.

'I felt a right Charlie,' one of the girls announced. 'A proper telling off I got for droppin' me drawers straight off, instead of waiting behind the screen for Sister to call for me!' 'Urgh, she had such cold hands,' one of the other girls laughed, and within seconds they were all chattering and giggling, trying to outdo one another as they described their embarrassment.

'So why did you decide to become a nurse, Connie?' Vera asked her.

For a moment Connie froze, feeling trapped. How could she tell them the truth? They would shut her out if she did. This was meant to be a fresh start for her.

She took a deep breath. She didn't want to lie to them but she knew that she had no alternative.

'Oh, it was a bit the same for me as it was for Josie,' she announced, as carelessly as she could. 'I was living in Preston with my father and my stepmother, but my stepmother didn't want me around. She'd got a couple of little ones of her own, and I heard they were wanting to train up nurses here.'

As she spoke, instead of feeling guilty, Connie felt as though a weight had fallen off her shoulders; as though suddenly she was the young woman she was describing; and as though Kieron, and all the horror she now associated with him, had never been. Her active imagination was already making her the girl she was claiming to be: Connie Pride, whose unkind stepmother had forced her to leave her home and fend for herself. And, after all, it wasn't completely untrue!

Connie felt her spirits lift, laughing and giggling along with the others.

'What is going on? Stop this noise this instant!'

The stern voice of the woman approaching them, shocked them all into silence.

'I am Sister Jenkins,' she told them. 'Come with me, please.'

She led them down into a tunnel, which connected the hospital to the nurses' home on the other side of the road. Once there, they were all handed a bundle which included their uniform, the cost of which, they learned, would be deducted from their wages. Clutching these bundles, they were then taken to the dormitory-like rooms where they would be sleeping.

'I am in charge of the nurses' home,' Sister Jenkins told them, 'and if I have any complaints about you, they will be referred to Matron. Let me warn you now, that Matron does not like receiving complaints about the probationers.'

The small dormitories contained eight beds each, and Connie was delighted to discover that she and Vera were sharing, but not quite so pleased to learn that Mavis was also in their dormitory. There was something about Mavis that reminded her, unwontedly, of her sister Ellie.

When Vera whispered conspiratorially to her, 'Pity we've got Miss Goody Two Shoes in here with us.' Connie couldn't help giggling in response.

Josie was also in the same dormitory, and Mavis, for all her apparent primness, turned out to have a good sense of humour so that, by the end of the day, Connie felt as at home with her new friends as though she had known them all her life.

It took less than a month for Connie to realise that her rosy dreams of being Florence Nightingale, were just that. The reality was that the probationers' duties were onerous and exhausting.

'Connie, you've forgotten your cap,' Josie announced, as the four of them got up from the dinner table.

'Oh grief, throw it over will you, Josie,' Connie begged her.

Obligingly Josie did so, but before Connie could catch it, Vera made a grab for it, and threw it to Mavis, calling out, 'Catch it, Mavis.'

Within seconds, the fun of the jape Vera had started had the four of them giggling as they threw Connie's cap to one another like a ball.

'Ouch!' As the cap sailed over her head and she made a leap to catch it, Connie bumped into something or rather, someone.

'What on earth is going on in here?' Sister Jenkins' ice-cold glance took in Connie's dishevelled curls and missing cap, and then travelled to where the cap was now lying on the floor. 'This is disgraceful behaviour,' she told Connie coldly. 'You are a probationer nurse, not a schoolgirl, and this hospital has certain standards of behaviour that it expects from its nurses.'

'But it wasn't just Connie...' Josie began, only to go bright red as the Sister turned a gimlet glare on her.

'I am well aware that all four of you have behaved disgracefully but...' she continued, turning to confront Connie, 'your behaviour is by far the worst. Laughing out loud, your hair half coming down, your cap...' Her mouth folded in a forbidding line. 'If you do not wish to train to be a nurse, then I can assure you that there are a hundred girls or more, who would be only too happy to take your place!'

As she listened to the lecture she was being given, Connie suddenly realised to her own shock that, despite the hardship their training involved, she did not want to be dismissed.

'Any more of this kind of behaviour and I shall report you to Matron.' Sister Jenkins warned Connie curtly.

FIVE

''Ere, Josie, that's my bed you're sitting on,' Vera protested without heat, as she came bustling into their dormitory room. 'I can't wait until we all get rooms of our own,' she added, as Josie reluctantly got up from her comfortable seat.

'I heard one of the Sisters saying that, with all the new nurses who have been taken on in case there's a war, some of the junior nurses may have to double up and share a room.' Mavis warned her, adding, 'Anyway, I like sharing. It reminds me of being at home and sharing with my little sister.'

'Oh, you would, Goody Two Shoes,' Connie

teased her. 'Personally, I can't wait for my own room – perhaps then my bed won't be covered in other people's things!' she announced, giving Josie a meaningful look.

'Well, it isn't my fault I've had to put my clean uniform on your bed,' Josie defended herself indignantly, recognising immediately that Connie's dig was intended for her, 'Vera has put all her things on my bed.'

By the time the good-natured squabble had been resolved, it was time for them to go down to the dining hall for their evening meal.

When the hospital had been rebuilt, thanks to the influence of Miss Florence Nightingale and her converts, a great deal of thought had been given to the needs of the nursing staff. Thus, the hospital was linked to the nurses' home by a tunnel, which saved the nurses having to go out in inclement weather. As well as their rooms, the nurses had been provided with a proper dining room, plus a recreation room, which they could use in their off-duty hours.

'At least they feed us properly here,' Josie commented, as they filed out into the corridor.

'Properly! Is that what you call it? I'm sick to me stomach of stew and steamed pudding!' Vera announced in disgust. 'I'd give half a week's wages for a decent pork pie and a glass of porter.'

'Well, we've all got an evening off on Saturday,' Mavis reminded them, adding with a sigh, 'I was hoping we might get the whole afternoon, then I could have taken the tram down to the pier, and got baggage ferry across to New Brighton, to see my mother and my sister.'

'Ooh, New Brighton!' Josie exclaimed excitedly. 'They've got ever such a good pier there. Me auntie took us once.'

'Well, since we're all off together, why don't the four of us tek ourselves out for a bit of jollity,' Vera announced.

'We could go to a music hall!' Connie joined in excitedly.

She had never forgotten the magical occasion on which Kieron had taken her to a music hall in the early days of their romance. She had been entranced by everything about the evening; the singing; the comedian, but most of all the excitement and fun of being amongst people who were determined to have a good time.

'Oh, yes,' Josie agreed eagerly. 'We could go to the Majestic, Marie Lloyd might be there.'

The mention of the famous singer made them all sigh a little enviously.

'We always go to the Christmas panto at the Royal Court, but I've never been to a music hall,' Mavis joined in wistfully.

'You'll love it,' Connie assured her.

'I can't wait,' Josie wriggled with anticipation. 'Which one do you think will be best, Vera, the Majestic or the Empire?'

'The Majestic!' Vera pronounced firmly. 'That's where me mam and dad allus go. They took me with them a few months back, and there was this singer. He was that handsome he made me come over all of a quiver!'

The saucy smile Vera gave as she extolled the virtues of the male singer made the other three laugh, and, within minutes, they were excitedly making plans for their evening out.

Looking forward to the fun which lay ahead of them helped to ease the hard work of scrubbing ward floors, cleaning the sinks and washrooms, and all the other drudgery that seemed to constitute their daily lives.

Not that they didn't have some contact with the patients. When she heard Josie complaining about the women on her ward, Connie felt pleased that she was working on one of the male wards.

'Not that some of them aren't hard work, if you know what I mean,' she confided darkly to the three, over breakfast one morning. 'I overheard Sister telling one of them off for trying to show her his you know what!'

Mavis went slightly pink, but a certain earthy heartiness was part and parcel of what they were learning, and even she laughed and admitted that she had heard that some of the male patients liked upsetting the probationers by behaving in an ungentlemanly fashion.

The Saturday of their outing to the music hall, Connie arrived back in their room a few minutes after the others, complaining, 'I've spent all afternoon winding bandages. My fingers feel as though they've gone numb!'

'You'd better get a move on, else we're going to be late,' Josie warned her. 'We're all ready!'

Grumbling, Connie hurried through her own toilette, trying not to feel too envious of the smart new dress that Vera was wearing.

'Can I have a spray of your gardenia scent, Vera?' she begged. 'Otherwise I'll be going out stinking of carbolic.'

'You can have some of my lavender water, Connie,' Josie offered, and Connie had to accept it with good grace, whilst wishing that she could go out scented with the more exotic gardenia fragrance.

The four of them were in high spirits as they left the nurses' home and set off for the bus stop, linking up together at Connie's instigation, and laughing in the summer sunshine.

The conductor on the bus gave them a wink and said, 'Off to have some fun, is you, girls! By, I wish I was coming with youse!' as he took their fares.

'I'm hungry,' Josie complained. 'I was that excited I never ate me dinner.'

'Well they won't let us in with food any more,' Vera complained. 'So we'll get a glass of porter and summat to eat before we go in.'

The bus took them right up to the music hall. Vera had suggested that they got off a few stops short of it and had a look at the shops, 'whilst we've got the chance', but Mavis and Josie had both vetoed this suggestion.

'Ooh, look, they've got George Robey as the comedian,' Josie gasped in thrilled excitement, as they got off the bus and hurried over to look at the programmes posted outside the building.

Clinging together to avoid being jostled by the growing crowd, the four of them peered excitedly at the billboard.

'Look there, right at the top, there's Marie Lloyd, and he's there, too!' Vera burst out excitedly. 'It's him as I was telling you all about,

George Lashwood. He's that handsome...' She gave a deep sigh.

'It says here that there's an Ella Shields on as a male impersonator,' Josie began, and then stopped to demand, 'does that means she's a woman pretending to be a man?'

''Ere come on you girls, let someone else get a look at the billing.'

The jocular request, made by a young man with a ready smile and twinkling blue eyes, had them falling back, blushing.

'Going in, are yer?' he asked. 'Only I'm with a few of me pals and we could sit together, if you fancied it.'

Immediately Connie tensed. Kieron's desertion of her and its frightening aftermath had left her feeling very wary of the male sex. And aware, too, of her own shameful secret. She felt a fierce need to protect herself, not just from having her past discovered, but also from giving any other man the idea that he could treat her as Kieron had. This might go against the grain of her normally fun-loving, light-hearted personality, but men, in Connie's eyes, had become a species who were not to be trusted – and certainly not allowed to take any kind of liberties!

'What, let you sit with us? Not likely!' she answered him sharply, exclaiming to the others, as he stuck his hands in his pockets and laughed before walking off, 'Cheek!'

'You're turning into a right spoilsport, Connie!' Vera complained. 'It would have been a bit of fun sitting with 'em!'

The crowd outside the building was growing by

79

the minute, and when Mavis suggested that they get themselves something to eat and then go inside, the other three willingly agreed. By the time the curtain went up on the first act, they were sitting cosily in their seats, waiting expectantly.

The loud roar of approval with which the crowd greeted the first act set the tone for the whole night, and, well before the curtain had been rung down on the first half of the evening, all four girls had thrown themselves into the spirit of things.

'I'm hoarse already from singing,' Mavis complained, as the curtain swung down.

'Ooh, that comedian had me laughing that much me ribs ache,' Josie marvelled. 'No wonder they calls him the Prime Minister of Mirth.'

The interval gave everyone the opportunity to get up from their seats and stretch their legs, and when the four girls were entertained by an enterprising young man who came and stood in front of them, and provided an impromptu show of his own devising – complete with a song extolling their beauty – everyone around them started to clap and cheer.

The good-natured atmosphere couldn't help but lift your spirits, Josie announced.

'It's a pity it's so full, otherwise we could have done a bit of dancing ourselves, up at the back,' Vera complained.

All four of them exchanged slightly wistful looks, but their disappointment at not being able to dance was soon forgotten, when the curtain went up on the second half of the show.

Ella Shields came on first, dressed in her male clothes, and sang, 'Burlington Bertie from Bow', to catcalls and yells of encouragement and approval from the audience.

When everyone else got to their feet to join in the final chorus, so did the four girls, singing the familiar words at the top of their voices.

Red in the face and happy, they waited expectantly for Vera's handsome singer to appear.

When he did, his appearance was enough to cause an impressed silence to fall over the theatre, followed by a soft, muted sound, which was a sigh of pleasure from the whole of the female audience.

'Oh, isn't he handsome,' Mavis whispered in awe.

'Told you so,' Vera announced smugly.

In mutual silence, the girls focused on the stage, watching the man standing there as he took the part of a swell out on London town for the night. When his act had finished, the applause was so loud it hurt the ears.

'Oh, I did enjoy this evening,' Mavis exclaimed happily when the four of them got off the bus outside the Infirmary, and linked arms.

Mischievously Connie started to sing a few words from one of the numbers, whereupon Vera started to mimic the dance steps performed by the chorus girls.

Within a few seconds, the four of them had given in to their high spirits and were singing and dancing their way down the street, and enjoying the spontaneous applause of a couple of young men who stopped to watch them.

'Do you think he wouldn't have died if they hadn't cut off his leg?'

'Josie, will you please give it a rest. I'm sick of hearing about it.'

Even Connie felt that Vera was being unsympathetic when she saw the tears filming Josie's eyes.

'It wasn't like someone dying on the ward, Vera,' she felt obliged to point out. 'Josie and I were there in the operating theatre when Mr Clegg amputated the man's leg.'

'Connie, please don't!' Josie begged.

There was a greenish tinge under her pale skin and Mavis, too, was looking slightly pale. Connie, on the other hand, had found that her fascination with the operating procedure had overcome any squeamishness she might have felt. And Sister had certainly moved smartly when she realised that Josie was going to faint, Connie reflected mentally.

They were sitting in the large room which was referred to as the recreation room, and as Josie started to talk again about the awfulness of the patient's death on the operating table, Connie glanced absently round the room. There was a piano in one corner, but, as yet, Connie had never seen anyone playing it.

'This will cheer you up, Josie,' she announced, as she got up and walked over to it, sitting down on the stool and folding back the top. On top of the keys was a notice saying, 'This piano is not to be played without permission!'

'What are you doing?' Josie demanded.

For a moment Connie hesitated, and then she pushed the notice behind a sheet of music and announced, 'I'm going to play some cheerful music to drown out the sound of you going on about the amputation.'

'You can play?'

Suddenly, not just her three friends, but also several other girls who were also in the room clustered around her, their admiring attention making Connie feel very pleased with herself.

'Yes,' she confirmed. 'My mother sent Ell ... me for lessons,' she amended quickly, breaking into the opening chords of a rousing tune, uncomfortably aware of how easily she had nearly said her sister's name.

The song was a popular one and, before Connie had finished playing it, virtually everyone was singing.

'Play us something else,' one of the other nurses encouraged Connie.

'Yes, do,' another begged, and Connie acceded willingly to their pleas.

They were all of them enjoying themselves so much, an increasingly bawdy element creeping into their choice of songs, that none of them noticed at first that Sister Jenkins, who was in charge of the nurses' home, was standing by the open door.

Gradually the singing died out as the singers became aware of Sister's presence but Connie, with her back to the door, had no notion of the disaster about to befall her until she turned round to find out why the singing had suddenly stopped.

'It is strictly forbidden for any nurse to touch the piano without permission, as the notice on top of the piano keys would have told you.' Sister informed Connie coldly, adding, 'You will present yourself in my room at seven tomorrow morning.'

'You'll really be in for it now,' Vera told Connie warningly after Sister had gone.

'If Connie is to be punished, then we should all be punished,' Mavis chipped in. 'After all, we were singing.'

'There's no rule against singing,' Vera pointed out smugly. 'And anyway, none of us asked Connie to play. It isn't our fault if she wanted to show off.'

'Vera, that isn't fair,' Mavis protested.

Numbly Connie listened to what they were saying. They had all been singing, but she was the one, as Vera had just pointed out, who had been playing the piano!

Hesitantly Connie knocked on Sister Jenkins' door, trying to swallow back her nauseous fear as she heard her call out sharply. 'Come!'

'So, Nurse Pride!' The cold, pale blue eyes surveyed Connie dispassionately. 'This is not the first time you have brought yourself to our attention with your bad behaviour.'

Connie felt her heart jolt against her ribs. Ma Deakin had been right when she had told her that the hospital would be a safe haven for her, and Connie had no wish to leave it.

Sharing a room with the others gave her the same feeling she used to have when she was with Ellie and their cousins: a feeling of warmth and happiness, and of somehow belonging. The thought that this feeling might now be taken away from her was making Connie sick with fear and panic. But being Connie, she was far too stubborn to show it.

'So! Have you anything to say for yourself?' Sister asked grimly, folding her hands together on the desk.

Connie could only shake her head.

Sister sighed. 'Nurse Pride, the piano was a gift to this nurses' home, from a very religious gentleman. And, as such, it is only used on very special occasions, and with permission! When did you learn to play?'

It was very unusual for the class of girls who trained at the Infirmary to have such an accomplishment.

The question caught Connie off guard, and automatically she responded truthfully, 'My mother insisted on us having lessons.'

'Indeed. Well, in future, I trust that her indulgence and my own forbearance will result in your humility and regret,' Sister announced sternly.

Connie held her breath. Was that it? Was she not after all going to be dismissed and sent packing?

Sister, who had a fair idea of what Connie was thinking, reflected that if she had not already made up her mind that Connie was showing all the signs of turning out to be a first-rate nurse – and a first-rate theatre nurse, at that – then she would, indeed, have been told to go.

The ominous rumblings of war were growing ever louder. It was unthinkable, of course, that they should go to war with Germany. But the

Government had insisted that every hospital in the country had to prepare itself for that eventuality, which meant that they could not afford to turn away a probationer with any kind of promise.

For war meant injured men. Injured men needed skilled and dedicated nursing. And more than that, many of the poor souls would need operations. Mr Clegg had made it clear that he wanted Matron to give priority to providing him with skilled operating theatre nurses. In Sister's opinion, Probationer Pride did not realise how very fortunate she was!

All this talk of war was extremely disturbing, and Sister Jenkins, for one, hoped that good sense would prevail and that the Germans would recognise their folly and cease their sabre-rattling forthwith!

The other three were waiting anxiously for Connie when she got back to their room.

'What happened?'

'What did she say?'

'Are you to leave?'

'I can't answer you all at once,' Connie complained, trying not to feel hurt that Vera should be the one to ask if she was to leave, and, moreover, that she should show so little concern at the prospect.

'I am to stay,' she told them firmly, only just beginning to believe and accept her reprieve herself.

'Oh, Connie!'

'Connie!'

'Lucky you!'

As all three of them hugged her, Connie felt

tears prick her eyes. For all that Vera complained constantly about the long hours, and the hard work, and everything else, Connie knew that, compared to the way she and Kieron had lived, her current life was a huge improvement. She got regular meals, she had equality with her peers, and she was even paid – albeit a very modest sum. But best of all was the fact that the hospital was clean; their room was clean; her clothes and her own self were clean! In fact, even the privies were spotlessly clean.

You had to have lived somewhere like Back Court to truly value something as simple as cleanliness, Connie acknowledged.

'No more getting in trouble,' Mavis told her mock-sternly.

'No more getting in trouble,' Connie agreed, and meant it.

She wondered if Mavis was as aware as she was herself of the fact that both of them spoke rather better than their fellow probationers? Vera teased her sometimes about what she called Connie's 'posh' accent, but Connie had noticed that it wasn't just her own mother's insistence that all her children spoke the King's English properly, that set her just a little bit apart from Vera and Josie. And, it was obvious that, like Connie herself, Mavis had received a far better education than the others, and had better table manners.

Connie could still remember how shocked she had been the first time she had seen Kieron eat a meal. Kieron! What was she doing thinking about him! He and the life she had lived with him were things she wanted to forget and pretend had never existed. Just thinking about Kieron was enough to bring back all her dread and fear of Bill Connolly.

Never did she want to return to that life, and she had been more mortally afraid than she wanted to admit to herself, never mind her friends, that, that was exactly what might happen to her.

Only now with her future here at the Infirmary safe, could she allow herself to recognise how terrified she had been of being sent away.

SIX

'I'm sure Sister makes us do all this scrubbing just to punish us,' Connie complained wearily to Vera, as she dropped her scrubbing brush into the bucket beside her, and wrinkled her nose at the strong smell of carbolic. 'We're supposed to be learning to be nurses, not scrubbing ward floors,' she grumbled.

'Cleanliness is the first law of good nursing,' Vera mimicked, repeating Sister Jenkins' favourite mantra.

'Don't you go making me laugh,' Connie protested. 'My ribs still ache from everyone practising their bandaging on me yesterday.'

It was several months since they had first arrived at the Infirmary, and during that time the four girls had become close friends, often spending their rare time off together.

'Look out, Sister's watching us,' Vera muttered warningly out of the corner of her mouth.

Diligently Connie bent over her task, grimacing as the hot, soapy water stung her raw hands.

'We might as well be skivvies in service,' she complained to Mavis and Josie, later that evening. 'I spent hours polishing the brass this morning, and then Sister came and told me to do it all again.'

'You'll never guess what!' Vera interrupted her excitedly, as she burst into their room. 'Remember that singer we saw at the music hall, George Lashwood, well, he's going to be singing at the Palais dance hall, a week Saturday just for the one night!'

'Saturday! My next day off isn't until a week Wednesday,' Connie told her in disappointment. 'And neither is yours.'

'Who needs a day? We all finish our shifts at three that day, I've checked, and we aren't on again until six the next morning, so that means we could easily go into town without being missed!'

'You mean the four of us should sneak out without telling anyone?' Connie questioned frowningly.

Mavis was already shaking her head, looking shocked, 'Oh, Vera, how can you even suggest such a thing! We aren't allowed to leave the hospital unless we have been given permission, you know that!'

'So, who's to know!' Vera demanded, shrugging impatiently. 'And anyway, what's the harm? After skivvying away here like they make us do, I reckon we deserve a bit o' fun? Connie'll come, won't you, Connie?'

'Connie, don't listen to her,' Mavis begged. 'You've already been in trouble twice – and if you were to get caught...'

'Come on, Connie. I dare you!' Vera challenged her.

Connie's heart sank. Vera was putting her in a very difficult position. Part of her wanted to refuse, but the stubborn, rebellious streak which had caused her so much trouble in the past, was whispering in her ear, and goading her not to lose face by refusing Vera's dare!

'Stop nagging me, Mavis, I'm going!'

As soon as the words were out of her mouth, Connie regretted them, but it was too late to call them back. Vera was looking triumphant whilst Mavis looked worried and upset.

'Oh, Connie!' she protested unhappily. 'You really shouldn't, you know!'

Mavis had that look on her face again that reminded Connie far too much of the kind of look Ellie used to give her. In fact, she decided crossly, Mavis was getting altogether far too like Ellie. Telling her what to do! Claiming to know what was best for her! Always being the 'good' one who never did anything wrong! She had even developed the same irritating inclination to act as Connie's conscience!

Although she loved and missed her sister, deep down inside Connie still felt the pain of Ellie's refusal to make it possible for them all to go home and live with their father, instead of being farmed out with their aunts and uncles. Of course, it had suited Ellie not to do anything because she had been quite happy living with their rich Aunt and Uncle Parkes who had spoiled her. It was Connie's resentment about Ellie's behaviour that sparked dangerously inside her now, making her reject Mavis's well-intentioned warning.

'Vera's right,' she claimed stubbornly. 'It's time we had some fun!'

The anxiety in Mavis's eyes deepened, but Connie was in the grip of a mood of defiance and recklessness.

'So I take it you two aren't coming with us then?' Vera challenged Josie and Mavis.

'I daren't.' Josie shook her head. 'Me auntie would never forgive me if I was to get thrown out of here, and me stepma would never let us go back.'

'And of course there's no need to ask whether you're coming, Miss Goody Two Shoes,' Vera taunted Mavis.

'It's against the rules,' Mavis answered her firmly.

'Well, it's you who will miss a good night out,' Vera told her, giving an exaggerated shrug of her shoulders.

'You'll be in very serious trouble if you get found out,' Mavis warned, as Vera got up from the table and Connie followed her.

'No one's going to find out!' Vera told her dismissively. 'And even if they do, we don't care, do we, Connie. Sick of this place I am.' As they left the room, she added to Connie, 'It isn't as though Sister guards the door or anything. And they can't lock it, can they, because of the night staff?'

Giggling together they hurried down the corridor, whilst Connie ignored the small inner voice trying to warn her that she was asking for trouble.

'I'm on one of the Nightingale Wards this afternoon, what about you?' Josie asked, as she and Mavis caught up with them, a few moments later.

'We're on the same,' Connie told her, trying not to laugh as Vera pulled a mocking face behind Mavis's back, when she answered that she was working in the operating theatre.

As they came up from the tunnel that connected the nurses' home to the hospital, Mavis almost bumped into a young policeman who was standing close to the tunnel entrance, holding his helmet beneath his arm.

'Steady, miss! I mean, Nurse,' he apologised, dipping his head politely, his face red with self-conscious embarrassment. His reaction caused first Vera, and then Connie, to burst out into fresh giggles.

'Ouch, Mavis, I think he took a bit of a shine to you,' Connie teased her good-naturedly.

'Yes, a big red shine by the looks of his face!' Vera added, as they both went into gales of laughter.

There was a faint tinge of colour on Mavis's own face, but she maintained her dignity, and kept her head held high as she stepped past the unfortunate young man, leaving Vera and Connie to giggle in her wake.

Cursing himself under his breath, Frank Lewis watched the girls walk away from him. He had only been working in the area for a few days, and his sergeant had told him that the hospital would be part of his regular beat.

He was waiting for his sergeant now, the older man having told him that he had a bit o' business to attend to. Frank suspected that the bit of business was probably a cup of tea and a gossip, but he knew better than to suggest as much.

If all the nurses were as pretty as the serious-eyed brunette he had just bumped into, his hospital beat was going to be a very pleasant one indeed!

'Oh, that Sister Miller, she knew my shift was finished, but she made me go and clean the sinks before she'd let me go,' Connie puffed, as she hurried into the bedroom and immediately began to pull off her cap and gown and start to tidy herself up.

'I told my ward sister that I'd got me monthlies,' Vera giggled. 'I told her I were too sick to finish me shift and that I might be sick. Mind you, I'd have loved to see the face of those miserable besoms I've had to run round after this week, if I had been!' Vera continued. 'Women's wards, I hate 'em. You don't know how lucky you are working on men's, Connie.'

'Vera, Connie, please don't do this,' Mavis begged them worriedly. 'If anyone should find out...'

'No one's going to find out!' Vera told her, confidently tossing her head. 'Connie's finished her shift, and I'm in me bed poorly.'

Behind Mavis's back, Vera pulled a face at Connie.

'Oh, I do hope you don't get into trouble,' Josie told them. 'Mavis told me this morning that she was really worried about what you're doing and that she thinks it is wrong!'

Connie could see a pink tinge of embarrassment on Mavis's face, and, for a moment, she hesitated. But Vera was tugging her arm, impatient for her to finish getting ready.

Quickly Connie put on the pretty summer dress she had saved up so hard to buy. She had fallen in love with the Herrick's cotton the minute she had seen it, and not just because the familiar name had reminded her of Preston where the company owned a large mill; the white background with its dainty sprigging of tiny pink flowers on green stems, suited her colouring perfectly, and she had enough of an eye for such things to have immediately changed the original pink ribbon trim for a much softer green – even if her sewing skills were such that she had stabbed her finger a dozen times, at least, whilst sewing on the new ribbon.

Vera, in contrast, was wearing a much fancier dress in blue silk ornamented with bunches of flowers.

'Blacking on your eyelashes!' Josie exclaimed. 'But what if it rains? You'll end up with awful smudges!'

'Do you think I need a bit more rouge on my cheeks, Connie?' Vera asked her self-critically, after giving Josie a withering look.

'Rouge! You're wearing make-up!' Josie exclaimed in shock. 'But, Vera, that's ever so fast.'

'No, it's not. All the nobs are doing it!' Vera told her. 'Do you want some, Connie?'

94

Cautiously Connie dipped her fingertip in the proffered cream powder and rubbed it carefully into her skin.

'Connie's looks better than yours,' Josie pronounced judiciously. 'She's not used as much as you, Vera.'

Finally they were ready to leave, but not before Vera had insisted on adding another smear of Vaseline to her carefully rouged lips, and demanding to know if her hair looked all right.

Ten minutes later, they were standing at the bus stop, arm in arm, Connie's eyes bright with excitement, as they waited for the bus that would take them to the city centre.

Since it was a warm, late summer evening, there was no need for them to wear heavy coats over their summer dresses.

'If you ask me, it's a good thing we're both fair,' Vera commented smugly as they climbed on the bus. 'I mean, that way we go together, don't we? I'd hate to have red hair like poor Josie's, or brown like plain Mavis.'

'She isn't really plain,' Connie objected. 'She's quite pretty.'

Vera gave her a sharp-eyed look but didn't say anything, turning her attention instead to trying to persuade the bus conductor to reduce their fare.

'We're poor probationer nurses,' she wheedled. 'You never know, one day you might have a horrible accident and we could be the ones to look after you.'

The conductor's heartfelt, 'I'd rather be dead,'

made them both giggle as they hurried to their seats.

They got off the bus in Bold Street, and Vera complained, 'Oh, my poor feet. These shoes are crippling me!'

'I told you they would be too tight,' Connie reminded her promptly. Unlike Vera, she had no special new shoes to wear, and had had to make do with her summer shoes from the previous year. Not that she minded too much. As she had already told Vera, being on their feet so much and for such long hours tended to make them swell, which in turn made new shoes uncomfortable.

'It's all right for you. You only take size two and a half. My feet have gone huge since I started at the Infirmary,' Vera retorted.

Connie gave her dainty feet a discreetly smug look. Her mother had always said that dainty feet were the hallmark of gentility, and that no lady ever admitted to requiring a shoe size above a three.

'I take after my mother,' Connie responded automatically. 'She had small feet.'

Her mother! Connie's eyes clouded.

'What's wrong?' Vera demanded sharply, watching her.

'I was just thinking about my mother,' Connie told her honestly.

Immediately Vera gave her a brief hug. 'Oh law', I forget sometimes about you and Josie losing your mas.' She wrinkled her pert nose. 'You must miss her, Connie.'

'I do,' Connie admitted truthfully, sadness clouding her expression. 'Nothing was the same after she died.'

Vera gave her a sympathetic look. 'My mam and dad might have their barneys, but me mam can wind me dad round her little finger. When I get married it's going to be to someone as does as I tell him!' Vera announced firmly. 'And he won't be some jumped-up Johnny either, nor one who tries to take too many favours, if you know what I mean. I know me worth and any lad who walks out with me is going to know it as well.'

Her words touched a place inside Connie that hurt, and made her feel not just afraid, but also as though she and Vera stood on different sides of a hidden divide.

Once she had been like Vera, happily confident about her own future and the man who would share it – a man who would love her as her father had loved her mother. The reality of her relationship with Kieron had been bitterly painful, but of course she could never admit to the knowledge she had gained or how she had gained it.

'Oh, look at that pretty crêpe-de-Chine blouse, Connie,' Vera demanded, losing interest in the subject of men. Dutifully Connie gave her attention to the window display Vera was admiring. 'It would go a treat with my new twill skirt. It's a bit pricey though.' Vera heaved a big sigh, 'I think I'll go in mind, and ask them to put the blouse to one side. I've got a birthday coming up and me mam and dad can get it for me.'

A little enviously, Connie followed her friend into the shop. A brand new crêpe-de-Chine blouse was a luxury she could not afford.

'There, I'll telephone me mam and tell her that

me birthday present is all sorted out for her,' Vera announced triumphantly as they left the shop, the blouse having been put to one side after the payment of a small holding deposit.

'We're going to be late for the dance,' Connie warned Vera.

'Oh, we'll get there in time if we hurry, and if we do miss anything it will only be the supper, that's all. I can't wait to see that George Lashwood again. I've never seen anyone so handsome or so smart. When he was singing, my heart fair turned over inside me chest,' Vera sighed.

Because of the popularity of the weekly dance, the entrance to the dance hall was thronged with people, and once they had bought their tickets, Vera and Connie had to squeeze past a group of young men in obvious high spirits, laughing and telling one another jokes.

'By, but me throat's dry. I wish we'd thought to get ourselves a glass of porter.' Vera told Connie, nudging her as one of the young men winked broadly at them, and swept them a bow.

'Looking for a seat, ladies?' he invited, indicating the seat from which he had just removed his own hat.

'We want a seat where we can see the dance floor,' Vera told him chirpily, whilst one of his companions gave them a bold stare and exclaimed, 'You two are a pretty pair, and no mistake.'

Vera stuck her nose up in the air and pretended to be offended, but Connie noticed that she didn't seem to be in any hurry to walk away.

'Not walking out with anyone then, or meeting

up with someone here?'

The question was directed at both of them, but it was Vera who answered it, tossing her head and saying, coquettishly, 'And what business of yours might that be then?'

'Just the business of a normal red-blooded man who's seen a real beauty of a girl,' he quipped back. 'Two right beauties they are, eh, Charlie?' he added, nudging his friend in the ribs and winking.

'Well, for your information, we've come here to listen to Mr George Lashwood singing, and not to listen to no impertinence from the likes of you!' Vera told him firmly.

But she was still lingering near to their table, and when one of them asked if she would like a glass of porter, she pretended to hesitate and then announced, 'Well, I'm not bothered for mesel', but Connie, me friend here, said just as we came in that she was sorry we hadn't got ourselves a glass and a bit o' sommat to eat.'

'Vera, I said no such thing.' Connie objected, adding determinedly, 'We'd better go and find somewhere to sit.' She turned and started to walk away leaving Vera with no option other than to follow her.

She didn't want to encourage the young men's overtures. In fact, she didn't want anything to do with them. After all, she had already learned the hard way what happened to girls who gave their love too easily. It would be a long time, if ever, before she ever trusted a man again.

As soon as she had caught up with Connie, Vera demanded crossly, 'Why did you have to go and do that? I was enjoying m'self.'

Connie made no response, knowing there was no way she could explain how she felt to Vera, or why!

'Connie, I thought we was coming out for a good time and now that's the third time you've refused to stand up with someone!' Vera objected, when Connie shook her head obstinately at the young man who had just asked her to dance.

'My feet are killing me,' Connie fibbed. 'But don't let me stop you, Vera.'

Vera pouted and protested, 'It's not the same if you're going to sit here being miserable all night.'

The truth was, Connie admitted inwardly, that she had agreed to come, more out of a stubborn determination not to let Mavis tell her what to do, than anything else.

'It's a good job that Josie and Miss Goody Two Shoes didn't come with us, mind. Josie would have gone as red as fire every time a lad came anywhere near us, and Mavis would have stuck her nose up in the air.'

'Mavis enjoyed the comedian the last time we went out,' Connie felt obliged to point out. 'It would have been more fun, too, if all of us were here!'

'It u'd be more fun if you'd give some of these lads a chance and have a dance wi' one or two of them,' Vera told her forthrightly.

'If you want to dance, then don't let me stop you.' Connie told her again, but she herself wasn't prepared to give in to the blandishments of the young men who tried to coax her onto the floor. Logically, she knew that all men weren't tarred with the same brush as Kieron, but somehow she just couldn't stop herself from being suspicious and wary. The miscarriage she had suffered might, in some ways, have been a blessing, but, in others, it had left her shocked and afraid, and she knew it would cast a shadow over her life that would last for ever. No woman could go through the pain and humiliation she had suffered and not be marked by it.

The evening was over and the dance hall was starting to empty. Tiredly, Connie linked up with Vera whilst they made their way outside, and then fought their way through the crush to their bus stop. Connie rubbed her stomach as it gave a hungry rumble.

'I'm starving,' she complained as they climbed on the waiting bus.

'Well, whose fault's that?' Vera challenged her. 'If we'd stayed with them lads as first showed an interest in us, like as not they would have treated us to a bit of sommat to eat.'

'Yes, and what would they have been expecting to get from us for it?' Connie demanded pithily.

'Well, expectin's one thing. Getting it's another,' Vera giggled.

The bus dropped them outside the Infirmary, and quickly they made their way inside.

There was a bit of a to-do in the reception area: an elderly man whose face was covered in blood, and an elderly woman with him who was obviously his wife. Connie noticed that one of the two burly policemen with them, was the same one who had taken such a shine to Mavis.

Skirting past the commotion they hurried into the tunnel.

'We're later than I thought we were going to be,' Connie commented a little bit apprehensively, as they came out of the tunnel. 'I... Oh!'

They both came to an abrupt halt as, suddenly, Sister Jenkins was standing in front of them.

'And where, may I ask, have you two been?' she demanded.

SEVEN

Connie could feel all the pleasure of the evening draining out of her body as though it had been her blood. In its place was a cold, icy feeling of deathly despair.

'We ... we've just been out for some air, Sister,' Vera fibbed.

'I see. I take it then, Nurse, that you are recovered from the indisposition which took you off Sister Hughes' ward this afternoon?'

Vera went red, and said nothing.

'And you, Nurse Pride?'

There was nothing that Connie could say. She suspected that Sister Jenkins knew exactly where they had been!

'This is not the first occasion on which I have had to speak to you on a matter of discipline, Pride.'

Connie quailed beneath her disapproving look, her apprehension growing.

102

'I have no option but to report your behaviour to Matron.'

Connie sucked in a shocked breath, her apprehension turning to a cold, hard ball of fear. Suddenly, and too late, Connie realised how much trouble she was in. It was obvious both from Sister's expression, and her reaction, that she was taking their breaking of the rules very seriously.

The warning she had received the last time she had been in trouble flashed through Connie's mind. She had been afraid, then, of what would happen to her if she was dismissed from the hospital but, foolishly, she had chosen not to think of that fear earlier. Now though, she was forcibly reminded of it by the cramping dread seizing her stomach.

Why on earth had she been so stupid? Unlike Vera, Connie loved working at the Infirmary. And besides, if she were to be sent away, where would she go?

'You will both go straight to your room, and you will remain there until Matron sends for you. The Guardians of this hospital expect its nurses to behave with obedience and decorum. You have been extremely fortunate to be taken on as probationers. And yet, you in particular, Nurse Pride, have repaid the generosity of the Guardians toward you with disobedience and the most shameful kind of behaviour,' Sister announced coldly, further reinforcing Connie's fearful awareness of how much trouble she was in.

Her stomach was a mass of nauseously churning nerves, whilst her head was a mass of equally churning fears. Now, when it was too late, she

103

bitterly regretted her own foolish stubbornness. She had put her precious hard-won security at risk, she realised. And for what? A dance?

'The nurses of this Infirmary have a reputation to maintain, and an example to set to those less fortunate than themselves. You will not go on duty in the morning, and you will not leave your room without permission. Is that understood?'

'Yes, Sister.' Connie said numbly, bowing her head in despair.

With a further quelling look, Sister Jenkins turned on her heel and sailed away, leaving Vera whispering wrathfully to Connie. 'Someone must have told her, and I can bet I know who it was!'

Connie said nothing. She was barely aware of what Vera was saying. She felt too sick with worry to listen to her. All she could think of was the morning and Matron. Matron would tell her to leave, she was sure of it. And all because she had given in to Vera. Tears burned the backs of her eyes. She could feel herself trembling inwardly with shock. It had never occurred to her that they might get caught. Oh, how she wished she had not been so foolish!

When they reached their room, Josie was waiting anxiously for them.

'Eeh, but you are late!' she told them. 'Sister has been round and your beds were empty!'

'And I suppose you told her where we were, did you, Goody Two Shoes,' Vera accused Mavis who was sitting up quietly in her bed. 'Well, we might have known that you would give us away!' Vera added nastily.

Josie's face had grown bright pink. 'Vera, that's

not fair!' she protested. 'Mavis told Sister that you were right bad with your monthlies and that Connie had gone down to the kitchen with you, to make you a hot water bottle and a cup of tea!'

When neither of them said anything, Mavis herself said quietly, 'I don't think you were the only nurses who went to the dance, not with George Lashwood being there!' She gave a small sigh. 'I would have liked to have heard him again myself. Connie, what is it? What's wrong?' she demanded with concern, getting up off her bed and coming over to Connie, as she saw the tears in her eyes.

'Sister caught us coming in,' Connie told her, too upset to hold back the truth. 'We... She's going to report us to Matron!'

'Oh Connie!' Mavis's hand went to her mouth, and her eyes reflected her shock.

'I'm starving! You'd have thought Sister would have let us have our breakfast,' Vera announced angrily.

'I couldn't eat anything,' Connie told her numbly. 'I feel that sick! I didn't sleep a wink last night. Oh, Vera, what will we do if Matron dismisses us?' she whispered, unable to keep her fear to herself any longer.

'As to that, I don't rightly care!' Vera retorted. 'I'd be glad if Matron did send us packing. I'm fair sick of this place, Connie. I thought nursing was going to be exciting, not spending all day scrubbing and polishing.' She gave a defiant toss of her head. 'I was thinking of leaving come Christmas anyway!'

As Connie digested her friend's comments, she

reflected bleakly that it was all very well for Vera to talk of leaving: she had a home to go to, and two parents who, by all accounts, doted on her, whilst Connie...

Connie stiffened as the door opened. Sister Jenkins was standing outside the room, a nurse on either side of her.

'Matron will see you first,' she told Vera, coldly.

After Vera had gone, marched away like a prisoner, Connie smoothed the fabric of her dress, and fidgeted nervously with her apron and her cap. Would this be the last time she would be wearing them? Although she had never said so, she had felt so proud and so smart in her uniform.

Whatever happened to her, she couldn't go back to somewhere like Back Court, she would rather die, Connie told herself fiercely. And she would certainly rather die than embrace the life Bill Connolly had planned for her. A sick shudder gripped her. Oh, why hadn't she thought properly about what she was risking, instead of being so stubborn!

She was on the verge of bursting into tears, but she knew she mustn't do so.

It seemed a lifetime to Connie before Sister Jenkins returned for her. It was certainly more than long enough for her to think about, and regret, her stubborn rebelliousness, over and over again. Just as she had regretted running away with Kieron, and wished she had listened to Ellie when she had begged Connie to leave him.

Even though she had been expecting it; waiting for it, in fact, the abrupt opening of the door made her start. There was no sign of Vera, and

Connie wondered frantically if she had just been told to leave without any more ado.

'I trust you have had time to repent of your shocking behaviour, Nurse Pride?' Sister Jenkins demanded, as she looked at Connie.

Too distraught to speak, Connie swallowed and nodded her head.

Matron studied the report she had in front of her. Normally with transgressions as serious as Connie's had been, especially after her two earlier warnings, she would have dismissed the girl immediately. But here in front of her were reports from the Sisters in charge of the wards on which Connie had worked. All of them, without exception, praised not just the high standard of her work, but each, in their own way, revealed that they considered that Nurse Pride – whilst as yet a very rough and uncut diamond – had, nevertheless, the potential to become not only an excellent nurse, but, in time, something much more. Good Sisters were born, not made, or so Matron considered, and good Theatre Sisters, even more so.

But no matter how promising a young nurse might be, discipline was, in Matron's opinion, the single most important thing she had to learn. It was impossible to be a good nurse without it! Straightening the reports on her desk, she rang the bell for Connie to enter.

Forbidden to leave their room, it was thanks to Josie and Mavis that there had been water for them to wash in this morning, and for Connie to smooth down her unruly curls before putting on her freshly starched cap, Connie acknowledged, as she advanced towards Matron's desk. There was a chair she could have sat in but Matron did not invite her to do so, and so Connie remained standing.

'You are, of course, aware of why you are here, Pride?' Matron began.

'Yes, ma'am,' Connie acknowledged, swallowing hard against the tension locking her throat muscles.

'You have already been warned, not just once, but twice, about certain unacceptable behaviour.'

Connie bowed her head in silent assent, fiercely blinking away her frightened tears.

'Your fellow probationer has informed me that it was at your suggestion that the two of you broke the rules by leaving the hospital without permission.'

Connie felt sick with disbelief. Vera had blamed her? When the whole idea had been Vera's own? She wanted to defend herself, but feared to do so in case she made her own situation even worse. How could Vera have done such a thing to her? She was supposed to be her friend! Connie knew that, had their positions been reversed, it was not something that she would have done.

Matron frowned a little as Connie remained silent. She had a pretty fair idea of just who the instigator of their transgression had been, and whilst she had accepted Vera's version of events without any comment, she had expected that Connie would refute it. Matron's opinion of Connie began to improve. Loyalty was an excellent virtue in a nurse, and so was the ability to hold one's tongue, especially under pressure.

'You realise, of course, the serious nature of your behaviour, and the consequences of it?'

Connie went white. She knew what was coming, and she bowed her head.

Matron stood up and came round from behind her desk. Connie could feel herself starting to shake. Was Matron going to remove her cap and her apron and send her thus from her office so that everyone could witness her disgrace?

Matron was tall and rather rotund, and her steely inspection made Connie clench all her muscles. She must not. She would not break down in tears and plea to be spared.

'When this hospital was rebuilt on the lines laid down with the assistance of Florence Nightingale, it was part of her recommendation that nurses be trained here in such a way that their training, and their demeanour, would reflect well on both the Infirmary and those who ran it.

'I look upon the task of maintaining the standards set down by Miss Nightingale as a sacred trust, Pride. I will not have that trust, or the exemplary record of my nurses, damaged or sullied in any way. One bad apple can contaminate the whole barrel, as we all know. My first instinct, so far as you are concerned, is to dismiss you from this Infirmary forthwith, and in disgrace.'

Connie dared not raise her own gaze to meet Matron's. A horrid feeling of light-headedness and nausea was beginning to spread unpleasantly through her.

Matron cleared her throat. 'However, it seems there are mitigating circumstances in your defence.'

Connie's eyes widened. Unable to stop herself, she looked at Matron.

'I have received some degree of praise for your work from those in charge of monitoring it, Pride. It seems that they consider you show a glimmer of promise of eventually becoming a good nurse. And for that reason, I am disposed to give you another chance.'

Another chance? Connie was terrified that she might faint with shock, and relief! She, who hadn't come anywhere near to fainting in the operating theatre!

'Good nursing though, Pride, is not just about practical diligence. It is about duty, responsibility, obedience: these are the virtues I wish to see growing in you, Pride. The virtues I intend to see growing in you,' Matron concluded ominously. 'Virtues which, I fear, are currently lacking in you.

'The only reason you are not now facing dismissal and disgrace is because of those members of my staff who have expressed their faith in you. I trust you will not let them down!'

'Connie, are you all right?'

'What did she say?'

Connie looked from Mavis's concerned face to Josie's anxious one. There was no sign of Vera, and somehow Connie was not surprised. She could well understand that Vera would feel uncomfortable having to face her so soon after having laid the blame for what had happened entirely on her shoulders.

'She said I am to have another chance,' Connie

110

told them shakily.

'Oh Connie!'

As they both hugged her tightly, Connie could feel the tears rolling down her face. 'Oh, I was so frightened I would be sent away,' she admitted.

'Vera's been let off as well,' Josie informed her. 'Haven't you, Vera?' she added, as the other girl came into the room.

Although Connie looked immediately toward her, Vera refused to meet her gaze, her face turning a guilty red, before she turned it away and tossed her head defensively, sniffing unconvincingly, 'Pooh, I don't know what all the fuss was about!'

'Vera, there's something I wanted to ask you about...' Connie began quietly.

But before she could finish what she had been about to say, Vera broke in quickly, 'I can't stay, I've got to get back on me ward.'

Silently Connie watched her leave. One of the links in their friendship had been broken by the lie Vera had told to protect herself, and Connie knew that things would never be quite the same between them.

And Connie was right. Whilst on the surface the four of them remained firm friends, a subtle shift in their loyalties began to develop over the months that followed. Connie emerged as the leader of what, essentially, was a trio of herself, Mavis and Josie, whilst Vera began to distance herself from them.

They still went out together on their rare evenings off, the music hall remaining a favourite venue, especially when George Lashwood was appearing. But whilst she retained her mischievous sense of fun, Connie was becoming increasingly involved in her work.

And then, out of the blue, Vera, announced that she was walking out with a young man she had met at the music hall.

'If I'm going to be skivvying, then I might as well be doing it in me own home and not this bloody Infirmary,' she told them sharply. 'Bert's dad has a little bit of a business that Bert is going to take over from him, and I reckon, if I play me cards right, I could be married to him within the year, and mistress of me own house.'

'But I thought you wanted to be a nurse,' Mavis protested.

They were in their room, drinking the sweet, hot cocoa Connie had made in the kitchen and brought up for them all.

'Maybe I did, but I've changed me mind,' Vera told her tossing her head. 'I'll give it 'til Christmas and then I'm off!'

None of them said anything but Connie was not surprised. She had suspected from certain comments that Vera had made to her that she would leave.

To her own relief she was not as upset by this as she had thought she would be. She and Vera had been close friends, and two of a kind, or so Connie had thought, but increasingly recently she had begun to grow impatient of Vera's constant complaints and time-wasting tricks.

Only this morning Sister had praised Connie's bandaging, and told her approvingly that she had done a very professional job. The glow of satisfaction that praise had given her, had felt much better than the pleasure Connie had once got from being rebellious.

It was Mavis with whom she felt she had the most in common now, as they discussed what they were learning, and how much they enjoyed their work. And although neither of them ever said, there was a shared awareness between them that they had both come from homes and backgrounds a little higher up the social scale than either Josie or Vera.

Where, originally, she had found Mavis's similarity to her sister Ellie got her back up, now Connie found it strengthened her affection for Mavis, and made her feel closer to her.

'I'm going Christmas shopping today, Mavis,' Connie announced, as she sat down with her breakfast opposite the other girl, she stifled a yawn. There had been an emergency on the ward the previous night, a patient suffering from delirium, and Connie had quick-wittedly noticed that something was wrong, and hurried to tell Sister.

'You and me have the same half-day, we could go together if you fancied it? Josie was saying that they've got all the Christmas decorations up now in the shops on Bold Street, and in George Henry Lee's.'

'Connie, what a good idea,' Mavis replied enthusiastically. 'I haven't done my Christmas shopping, yet. I want to get something special for everyone, my mother, my sister, and, of course, Harry, my brother.'

Connie had heard a great deal about Mavis's family since they had become more friendly, and, every now and again, when Mavis was talking about them, a sharp spear of pain pierced Connie's heart, and she felt very envious. Mavis's closeness to her family brought home her separation from hers. She missed them so much. Especially Ellie, even though once she had thought she would hate her elder sister for ever. She was an older and a wiser Connie now than that girlish Connie had been.

Unlike Connie, Mavis's brother was older than her, and her sister, younger, but when she talked about her family and the happiness of her life before the death of her father, Connie couldn't help recalling, again, how happy her own life had been before her mother had died.

'I do feel for you, dear Connie, in not having the comfort of a brother or sister!' Mavis said gently, now.

Connie bit her lip. 'I do have a sister, Mavis, and ... and two brothers, but after our mother died we were split up. Then my father remarried and...'

'Oh, Connie how dreadful for you!'

'Yes, it was,' Connie agreed bleakly, tears pricking her eyes. 'If you don't mind, Mavis. I prefer not to talk about it...'

'No, of course. I understand!' Mavis assured her sympathetically, squeezing her hand gently.

She couldn't say too much about her family, Connie acknowledged, because after all she could hardly tell Mavis the full truth. She could just imagine how Mavis would turn away from her in shock and disgust, if she knew what she had done.

And Connie knew how much she would hate that. There was a bond growing between her and Mavis which Connie deeply valued.

For once, there was no mischievousness or teasing in Connie's eyes as she looked at her friend, and said truthfully, 'You have become as dear to me as a sister, Mavis.'

'Oh, Connie!' Tears in her eyes, Mavis flung her arms around Connie and hugged her tightly. 'That is exactly how I feel about you!'

'Do Josie and Vera want to come shopping with us?' Mavis asked, when they had released one another with pleased and shamefaced, emotional smiles.

Connie shook her head. 'Josie is going to see her aunt, and Vera doesn't want to come.' Connie gave a small sigh. 'She's changed since she met Bert. You know she says that she isn't going to continue with her training.'

'Well, to be honest, I don't think she would have made a very good nurse. Not like you, Connie!' Mavis responded.

'Me?' Connie gave her an astonished look. 'You are the Miss Goody Two Shoes,' she reminded Mavis, teasingly. 'I'm always getting into trouble.'

'I don't suppose I should tell you this, but I heard Sister saying that you are a natural.'

Connie tried to look nonchalant, but her face went pink and inside she was secretly thrilled to have been picked out for praise.

Ellie was grateful for the warmth of the beautiful new furs Gideon had bought her, as she stepped out of Cecily's husband's motor car, to join her cousin on the pavement on Basnett Street. Cecily was one of Aunt Gibson's two daughters, and Ellie had always got along with her cousin very well. They were outside Liverpool's most exclusive store, Bon Marche, where they had come to do some Christmas shopping. This store, whilst owned by the Lee family, carried a far more exclusive stock than George Henry Lee's across the road from it. Bon Marche catered for the cream of Liverpool society, and it was here that women flocked to buy the latest Paris fashions.

Gideon had driven her over to Liverpool the previous evening, and he was picking her up this evening, and then driving her to Hoylake so that they could pay a visit to her Aunt and Uncle Parkes, before returning home to Preston.

'Oh, Ellie, this takes me back! You and I going shopping together.' Cecily smiled, as they stepped into the deliciously perfumed warmth of the store. 'Do you remember when we used to meet Iris at the Adelphi for afternoon tea? Not that we can do that today, of course, for they have pulled it down and are rebuilding it.'

Ellie nodded her head. She knew that Gideon had hoped that this visit to her cousin would lift her spirits, but Cecily's comment had simply reminded her of a time when her sister Connie had been alive.

'Connie always loved Christmas so much,' she said sadly. 'I think it was her favourite time of the year. We used to hurry home from school so that we could make our Christmas cards together. I miss her so much, Cecily.' Tears filled Ellie's eyes.

'Ellie, you really must try to put her loss behind

you,' Cecily told her firmly. 'I know it was very sad, but under the circumstances, bearing in mind the disgrace she had brought upon herself...'

'I know that what she did was wrong, Cecily, but...'

'Indeed it was. Very wrong! I suppose I should look for something for the maids,' Cecily fretted, deliberately changing the subject, 'although not in here, of course. It would be far too expensive. I thought perhaps a pretty handkerchief, Mama always gives her maids gloves which she buys from the Church bazaar. What are the children to have this year?'

Ellie smiled, roused from her sadness by the mention of her family.

'Gideon has insisted on buying a brand new train set for Richard, and we've ordered a new rocking horse for Joshua. Henrietta is to have a set of paints. She is very artistic, and Gideon thinks that we should get her some private tuition.'

Cecily started to frown. 'Well, I know how much you love her, Ellie, but I have to say that with her looks – and she is quite strikingly oriental-looking now, although very pretty – you may regret making her so much a part of your family. Mama says that it would have been far better if you had had her adopted, or sent her back to Japan.'

Ellie was shocked.

'Cecily, I look on Henrietta as my daughter, as much as though I had borne her myself,' she told her cousin in outrage. 'Gideon and I have adopted her legally and, to us, she is our eldest child.'

Really, Ellie thought crossly, sometimes Cecily

seemed to be growing unpleasantly like her mother!

'Brrr, it's cold!' Connie exclaimed, as she huddled into her thin coat.

'Oh, do let's look at Bon Marche's window,' Mavis begged her, catching hold of her arm.

Arm in arm, the two girls studied the elegant window displays, and the luxurious furs worn by the mannequin.

Still arm in arm, they crossed over the road to look into the windows of George Henry Lee's.

'Oh, Connie! Evening-in-Paris perfume. I can remember my father buying my mother some! And look at those gloves!'

They walked happily from the store to Bold Street, 'the Bond Street of Liverpool', lingering over each window display and teasing each other, their laughter ringing out in the cold air, as they drew level with Cripps shawl shop.

'Oh, do let's go in, Connie,' Mavis urged. 'I would love to buy my mother a really good warm shawl!'

The shop was busy with customers, and whilst they waited to be served, Mavis fingered some of the shawls.

'Oh, look at that one, Connie,' Mavis exclaimed, pointing to a particularly warm, soft, lavender blue shawl. 'It is so pretty.'

Connie looked at the shawl. It felt warm to the touch, and it was obviously expensive.

An hour later, after Mavis had finished her shopping, and Connie had mentally earmarked the small items she had decided to buy for her friends, Mavis said tiredly, 'I'm parched. Shall we go and have a cup of tea?'

'Yes, let's,' Connie agreed, and linking up together they started to walk down the road.

They had just reached the teashop, when Connie exclaimed, 'Oh, I've just remembered there's something I wanted to get. You order that tea, Mavis, and I'll just dash back for it!'

It didn't take her long to hurry back to Cripps, and, mercifully, this time there were no other customers. Connie pointed out the lavender blue shawl and opened her purse.

'It's one of my favourites,' the saleswoman said to her approvingly. 'Fair lifts the heart that colour does.'

Thanking her, Connie paid for her purchase and left. Connie hadn't forgotten the help Ma Deakin had given her, and when she had seen the shawl, she had thought immediately of the midwife.

The late autumn afternoon was already closing into dusk, as Ellie walked out of a shop ahead of Cecily. The street was busy with shoppers, but Ellie's attention was caught by one girl who was crossing the street, a few yards away from her.

Ellie froze, gripped by shock. The girl had her back to her, but something about her made Ellie's heart pound. Connie. It was Connie! The angle of her head, the way she walked. It was her sister! Frantically Ellie started to hurry after her, calling out her name, desperate to catch up with her, oblivious to the attention her urgency and strained expression were attracting.

She was walking so fast that she accidentally

turned her ankle, and would have fallen if a kindly fellow shopper hadn't reached out to hold her arm steady. Choking back a sob, Ellie thanked him before begging, 'Please, I must go. My sister ... I must find her...'

'But your ankle – you gave it a nasty twist...'

'Please...' Ellie pulled away. She had to catch up with Connie, before she was swallowed up in the busy crowd and lost to her.

'Ellie. What is going on? I saw you slip,' Cecily told her anxiously, catching up with her.

'Cecily, I just saw Connie...' Ellie burst out immediately. 'We must go after her. We must find her, Cecily...'

Tears were running down Ellie's face, as her frantic gaze searched the crowded street.

Cecily stared at Ellie in consternation. She knew how distressed Ellie had been by her younger sister's death, of course, but... 'Ellie, you can't have done ... you must have been mistaken,' she told her gently, taking hold of her arm.

'No, Cecily, it was Connie,' Ellie insisted again. 'We must go after her.'

'Oh, Ellie, my dear, be reasonable. How could it possibly be Connie?'

Ellie stared at her cousin, suddenly realising how she must appear to her.

And Cecily was right. How could it have been Connie? Connie was dead. Ellie had let her own pain overwhelm reality! Bleakly Ellie let Cecily lead her away.

'I'm sorry, Cecily,' she apologised shakily. 'It was that just for a minute...'

'Let's go and have our tea,' Cecily told her

firmly, tightening her grip on Ellie's arm.

'I've ordered us tea and some crumpets,' Mavis told Connie, as she hurried into the teashop. 'I'm really looking forward to Christmas at the Infirmary now. I wasn't at first, but Josie told me that Sister said that it is the most jolly time, with every ward having its own party and all manner of festivities taking place. There's a proper Christmas dinner and Matron herself hands out presents from a huge tree.'

'And, with a bit of luck, that handsome young policeman who's got an eye for you might be on duty?' Connie teased her mischievously, laughing when Mavis blushed.

'If you mean Frank, the only reason he stopped me to talk to me the other day was because he wanted to ask after old Mr Beddoes. He brought him in, you see, and he wondered how he was getting on!'

'Oh, I see, it was just to talk about the old man that he stopped you, was it?' Connie asked guilelessly. 'I'm only asking, seeing as how Mr Beddoes is on my ward.'

Seeing how self-conscious Mavis looked, Connie relented and stopped teasing her. 'Did Frank say if they've found out who it was who knocked him about so badly? Poor old thing's got a broken leg and Gawd alone knows what happened to his insides! Mr Clegg isn't saying anything, but somehow I don't think he's going to be going home,' she added darkly.

'Frank said that Mr Beddoes wouldn't tell them anything, but that Mrs Beddoes said something about them being pestered for money by some man. Frank says there's some sort of gang been set up that goes round demanding money from people. But they can't do anything, because everyone's too afraid to talk to the police.'

EIGHT

Connie shivered as she climbed reluctantly off the bus, and huddled deeper into her coat, wrapping her scarf more closely around her face against the taste of the freezing vapour shrouding the street.

It was the week before Christmas, Mavis had gone to New Brighton to see her family and to take her Christmas presents to them, as they were both working on Christmas Day. Vera had gone out with her young man and Josie was on duty, which had left Connie free to complete her self-imposed task.

Apprehensively, she turned to look over her shoulder, but to her relief the dingy street was empty. Even so, Connie was nervously aware of being in a part of the city which was neither safe nor desirable.

And yet, she had lived here with Kieron, she reminded herself, as she hurried down the street, hoping that she did not look as vulnerable and out of place as she felt.

It might be less than a year since she had left this area, but already the time she had spent here was a dim memory she wanted to forget rather than to remember.

The laughing, loving girl who had come here with Kieron had gone. She was a different person now, Connie recognised. A wiser, more cautious, person who bitterly regretted what she had done. She knew she would never forget what had happened to her here, neither Bill Connolly's harsh cruelty nor the wonderful kindness of Ma Deakin. But for her, Connie suspected that her miscarriage might well have taken her own life, as well as that of the child she had been carrying.

A small stab of guilty pain ached through her. She was glad, of course, that she had not had to endure the stigma of bearing an illegitimate child, but, even so, the thought of that small lost life saddened her.

The corner of a building loomed up marking the entrance to Back Court where she and Kieron had lived. As Connie hurried past it, she turned her face away from it, and fought her compulsion to turn back to look into the dank sour-smelling opening, in case Bill Connolly was waiting there to pounce on her, and drag her into the pit of sin he had planned for her.

It was only a few more steps to Ma Deakin's small house, and, as she stepped up to the door and knocked quickly on it, she looked anxiously up and down the street. It was unlikely that if anyone saw her, they would recognise her. But what if they did? What if they were to tell Bill Connolly?

Not for the first time, Connie questioned the wisdom of what she was doing. But something stronger than her fear had made her come here, and although Connie herself did not know it, it was the same something that her superiors at the Infirmary had recognised in her: a strength of character and a fortitude, which she had been born with, but which her circumstances had forged into true strength and inner courage.

The door opened, and a sullen-faced, unfamiliar young woman stared aggressively at Connie.

'If it's me mam youse is wantin' she's away at a laying-out,' she announced brusquely, and made to shut the door.

Quickly Connie put her hand against it, and produced the small package she had brought with her. Inside it was the lavender blue shawl she had bought for Ma Deakin, and which had cost her more than she could easily afford. Wrapped in bright-coloured Christmas paper, it looked almost obscenely out of place in such grey surroundings, and Connie could see the woman's eyes widening, as Connie thrust it toward her.

'You will give this to your mother, won't you!' Connie asked her anxiously.

''Course, I will,' the young woman replied fiercely. 'I ain't no thief, and even if I was I wouldn't take from me own mam. What do you take me for, and who are you anyway?' she demanded suspiciously.

Satisfied that she was speaking the truth, Connie guessed that the young woman must be Lily, whose bed she had taken whilst Ma Deakin was nursing her back to full health. Whoever she was, Connie was glad that she did not recognise her.

The moment the other girl had taken the

parcel, Connie turned and plunged back into the thickening, freezing mist, hurrying away from the shame of her past and toward the bus that would take her back to the safe security of her present and her future.

'Connie, I'm glad you're on your own.'

Connie smiled as Mavis sank down onto her bed.

'Were your mother and sister well, Mavis?' she asked.

'Oh, yes, they were fine, that's what I wanted to say to you. I...' She went slightly pink as she hesitated, and then burst out. 'Connie, my mother has asked if you would care to come and stay with us when we get our two days off in lieu of Christmas. I have told her so much about you, and that you have no family of your own.'

Connie had gone pink herself as she listened. Those nurses who were going to work over the Christmas period had been given two days off after it, and Connie had already wondered how on earth she would spend hers.

'Did your mother really mean it?' she asked Mavis excitedly.

'Connie, she said she would love to meet you, and so did my sister, and I would love you to meet them. I know that Josie is to go and stay with her aunt, and I expect that Vera will be seeing Bert and her parents.'

'Isn't it funny how things turn out?' Connie murmured thoughtfully. 'When we all met that first day, I thought that Vera and I were so alike, and we were, then, but now...' Connie paused and shook her head. 'I never imagined that learning to be a nurse would make me feel the way that it does.'

'I always knew I wanted to be a nurse,' Mavis said quietly.

Silently they looked at one another, both recognising in each other a kindred spirit, in a way that went far deeper than mere shared interests.

Putting her hand out, Connie touched Mavis's arm and said huskily, 'I am so glad that you have asked me to come home with you, Mavis.'

Unbidden, the thought came into Connie's head that both her mother and her sister would have liked Mavis, and approved of her as a friend. But neither of them would ever know her. Her mother was dead, and she, Connie, was as good as dead to Ellie.

'Connie, you look so sad, what is it?' Mavis asked her worriedly.

'It's nothing, really,' Connie fibbed, but inside she was acutely aware of how much she wished both her mother and her sister might be able to recognise how truly she repented of her stubbornness, and selfish foolishness. She longed to feel that both of them might be able to witness her remorse, and forgive her for her past sins. Especially Ellie. If Ellie could see her now, would she hold out her arms to her, and tell her that she still loved her? Did she ever think of her and wonder about her?

Suddenly Connie was filled with a longing to see Ellie again ... to talk with her. It was almost Christmas after all. A time when families came together.

'But Vera you can't do that! We all have to work over Christmas,' Connie protested.

'Well, I'm not going to. Bert wants me to spend Christmas day with his family, and that's what I'm going to do. You won't catch me missing out on a good opportunity like that! I'm lookin' to better meself!' Vera answered her, tossing her head belligerently.

'You'll be found out,' Connie warned her, 'and after what's already happened...'

'So what if I am found out,' Vera shrugged. 'I don't care. I'll be leaving here anyway just as soon as I've got Bert's engagement ring on me finger, and like as not he'll be putting it there Christmas day! Do you know something?' Vera continued sharply. 'The trouble with you, Connie Pride, is that you are getting more like Mavis every day!'

'I've got to go,' Connie told her, quickly finishing her meal and getting up from the table, 'I'm back on duty in a few minutes.'

Connie walked as quickly as she could through the tunnel, without breaking into a run, which was strictly forbidden by Matron, since the sight of a nurse running might panic the patients.

The operating theatre, and the wards for the surgical patients were on the top floor of the Infirmary, and Connie knew she would have to hurry to be back on duty in good time.

Mr Clegg the Infirmary's senior surgeon, a man who was admired both by his patients and those who worked under him, had the previous day had to perform an emergency amputation on a young

127

man who had slipped under the wheels of a brewery dray. Mr Clegg had had to remove both his legs, and Connie was thinking of the young man as she hurried onto the ward.

The sight of his empty bed, stripped of its bedding, and the set, stiff faces of her colleagues told its own story.

Connie felt tears burn the backs of her eyes, but she knew better than to let them fall. It was a strict rule that nurses were not supposed to become emotionally involved with their patients.

'What happened?' Connie asked one of the other nurses in a hushed whisper.

''E started bleeding about six o'clock this morning. Nothing we could do could stop it and, in the end, Sister sent for Mr Clegg, but it was too late. Poor lad had died 'afore he got there.'

The young man's death had cast a pall of sadness over the normally cheerful ward, and Connie could see the fear in the eyes of the other patients.

Even after her shift had finished, Connie discovered that she could not forget about the young man and his sad death, and she said as much to Mavis, when Mavis joined her in their room after her own shift had finished.

'It is sad, Connie. I felt the same way when we lost Mr Beddoes, the old man who Frank brought in so badly beaten.' She gave a small sigh. 'It reminded me of how my own dear father lost his life.'

'What did happen to him, Mavis? I don't want to pry, of course, if it's too painful for you to talk about what happened.'

Mavis shook her head.

'It was dreadful, Connie. My father's shop was broken into and my father was attacked – murdered.' She gave a deep shudder. 'I must admit, I still can't bear to think about it. Not really. We were all so shocked, especially my mother. She and my father were devoted to one another. My father's death left us virtually penniless, and we had to move from our lovely house to this horrible, horrible place.

'Harry, my brother, said that he would take on some kind of clerking work, for a junior teacher does not get paid very well at all, but my mother begged him not to. You see, our father was so proud of Harry's cleverness and scholarship, and the fact that he was to be a teacher. He talked of nothing else, and swore that one day Harry would be a headmaster!

'And then father's aunt, who is not very well, said that she would take us in, provided that Mother would run the house for her and look after her. Mother said it was the answer to her prayers, but Harry was not so pleased. He feels that our great-aunt puts on Mother and does not treat her at all kindly. But Mother says that it is just her way, and that she does not mind, and that all that matters to her is that we are happy.

'I know that Harry does without himself so that he can send Mother money, even though he pretends that he does not. I try to save something from my wages to help out as well, although it is not easy when we are paid so little.

'But there I am, speaking as though we have nothing to be grateful for, or happy about, and are very sorry for ourselves. But that is most

129

certainly not true!'

'I could never think of you as someone who feels sorry for herself, Mavis,' Connie assured her truthfully.

Mavis smiled gratefully. 'I am so glad that you are to come home with me next time, Connie. I have told my mother and my sister, Sophie, so much about you.'

'I'm looking forward to meeting them!' Connie smiled, her mood lightening. It was true that she was looking forward to going home with Mavis and being part of a proper family again, if only as an outsider.

'And I've just learned that my brother will be home at the same time, so you will be able to meet him as well,' Mavis said to her happily. 'He is the dearest person, Connie.'

'Happy Christmas!' Connie called out to the others as she hurried to get dressed, her glance resting briefly on Vera's empty bed. 'I've got to be on the ward for six,' she added cheerfully. 'See you both later.'

A large party for all the nurses who were on duty, was being held in the evening, and there was a buoyant, happy atmosphere in the nurses' home.

Morning prayers were longer than usual, and whilst she listened dutifully to them, Connie said a mental prayer of her own for her family. At home on Christmas morning, she had always been the first to wake up, scrambling out of bed and going to wake Ellie. No matter how early it was, the house had always smelled deliciously of

130

the feast to come. And although she had grumbled, Ellie had always let Connie snuggle into bed with her whilst they delved into their stockings to see what Father Christmas had left them.

Connie could still remember the thrill of discovering little pink and white sugar mice, and Ellie's scream when Connie had pretended that they were real. Then there had been the fat, shiny nuts and a twirly stick of barley sugar; folded rolls of paper with jokes on them that John would collect later, and keep on repeating all day until they were heartily sick of him, and them.

One year Connie remembered, John had received a wooden parrot on a stick that squawked and flapped its wings when one moved the string, a gift from Gideon Walker the young apprentice who had been courting Ellie. Their mother had threatened to confiscate the toy and banish John himself to his room, because of the noise it made.

That had been the year she and Ellie had received the gift of beautiful silk-lined sewing baskets from their parents, Ellie's palest blue, and her own in pretty pink. Within a matter of weeks, hers had been a tangled mess of cottons, whilst Ellie's had remained pin neat. Of the two of them though, she had been the better watercolourist, or so Ellie had always said, although Ellie definitely had a better ear for music.

A tear splashed down onto Connie's hand, followed by another. Quickly she shook them away, and reminded herself how fortunate she was to be here in the Infirmary, and how foolish it was

131

of her to think of a past happiness that could never be re-created.

By the time prayers were finally over, and they were able to sit down for breakfast, her stomach was rumbling with hunger.

Every ward had put up Christmas decorations and a tree, and even the sickest of the patients seemed to have caught the mood of excitement and happiness.

It was a long day with those on duty having to take on extra work, and Connie's feet and back were aching by the time six o'clock came and she was able to leave the ward. In their room, the three of them tidied themselves up, and then hurried down to the dining room.

'Ooh, just look at the Christmas tree!' Josie exclaimed as they walked past the recreation room, and saw the huge present-laden tree in one corner.

All week long, the nurses had been helping to decorate the large tree in their spare time. Connie, Mavis and Josie had made decorations for it themselves, and Connie sniffed the pine-scented air appreciatively.

'One of the senior nurses told me that even Mr Raw, the Medical Superintendent, comes to the nurses' Christmas day party,' Josie exclaimed in an awed whisper.

Certainly there was a much more relaxed atmosphere in the large dining room than was normally allowed, with nurses laughing and chattering as they sat down. Matron herself was seated at one of the tables, with, as Josie had predicted, the Medical Superintendent on one side of her, and Mr Cleaver, Clerk to the Board of

Governors, on the other. The Sisters on duty were all seated lower down the table.

The rich smell of roasted turkey filled the air, and, to Connie's relief, Mr Cleaver kept his grace to a reasonably short fifteen minutes.

Hungrily, Connie tucked in to her dinner, inwardly reflecting that whilst the turkey was welcome, it was not as moist or as succulent as those cooked by her mother. But then her mother, a butcher's wife, had always had first pick of the very best of meat and fowl.

The thought of her parents brought a shadow to her eyes. Ellie, of course, would be celebrating Christmas in her fine mansion, and, no doubt, John would be with her. Wistfully Connie wondered what they would be doing right now. Would they think of her at all? Connie bit her lip and fought back the lump in her throat.

Dinner was over, and they were in the large recreation room where they had seen the Christmas tree. A huge log fire was burning in the grate, and Matron was seated in front of it flanked by Mr Raw and Mr Cleaver.

'Pride, Matron wishes to see you!'

Immediately Connie was filled with dread. Was Matron going to question her about Vera? Had she discovered that Vera had illicitly left the Infirmary? And, if so, did she think Connie had been involved in her leaving?

Her legs trembling, Connie walked apprehensively toward the fire.

Since Matron was in conversation with Mr Cleaver, Connie had to wait in silence for several minutes until her presence was acknowledged.

'Ah, Pride. Sister Jenkins has just reminded me that you can play the piano. Since Sister Biddy is not on duty this evening, you will have to stand in for her and play us some festive carols. Sister Jenkins will give you the music.'

Matron wanted her to play the piano! Connie went limp with relief, and then immediately became freshly anxious. She could play the piano it was true, but nothing like so well as Ellie ... and she had certainly never played in public in front of so many people! It was one thing to lark about for a bit of fun, but quite another to do what Matron had instructed her to do.

Connie could almost feel the silence as Sister Jenkins escorted her over to the piano and then gave her the music. Nervously Connie looked toward her friends. Josie was watching her round-eyed, and Mavis had her hand against her mouth in apprehension.

The notes of the music score in front of her danced up and down. Fiercely Connie blinked and made herself focus. These were, after all, carols that her own Mama had played for them every Christmas as far back as Connie could remember.

There was nothing to be afraid of, she told herself firmly, as she lifted the piano lid and flexed her fingers.

'Oh, Connie, what a wonderful evening!' Mavis exclaimed, as she smothered a tired yawn.

'You say that every time we do something,' Connie teased.

'But it was wonderful,' Josie insisted, adding happily, 'what with you playing, and all of us singing, and then when Matron handed out presents to all of us. Just wait until Vera finds out what she's missed!'

It had been a good evening, Connie acknowledged. Once she had overcome her nervousness, she had realised that the enthusiastic singing led by Mr Cleaver was bound to drown out any occasional wrong notes she might play.

The small gifts they had all been given had added to the pleasure of the evening. Josie had loved the gloves Connie had bought for her, and Mavis had chided her gently for her gift of silk stockings saying that Connie had been far too extravagant. But, as Connie had discovered when she opened her own presents, Mavis had been equally generous in her gift to her. Her eyes had sparkled with excited pleasure when she had seen the small bottle of scent she had so yearned for when they had been in George Henry Lee's. Josie's gift of matching soaps had made her guess that Mavis had had a hand in guiding Josie's choice.

And Connie knew that she would cherish Matron's few sparse words of praise for her piano-playing, more than she would cherish the cheap handkerchief that had been her gift, from the Infirmary.

As she undressed, she suppressed a deep yawn. She was back on duty at six, with another long day in front of her, but she didn't mind. Sister had as good as told her that she expected her to get high marks in her Final Examination, and Connie certainly hoped that that might be so.

She might work long hours, and she might receive poor pay in comparison to other hospital nurses, but as Connie slipped between the cold sheets of her narrow bed, she discovered that the feeling bubbling up inside her, despite her tiredness, was actually happiness. She was still smiling when she fell asleep.

There was a large queue already waiting for the New Brighton ferry when Connie and Mavis got off the tram. Hurrying over, they tagged on to the end of it, huddling together against the icy cold, their breath forming white vapour puffs.

The ferry to New Brighton was, in actual fact, more of a cattle boat, and used to ferry passengers' trunks to and from the Pierhead on carts pulled by dray horses.

In the crush of people on the boat, Connie and Mavis were squashed up against one of the drays, and Mavis gave a small nervous squeak when the huge, blinkered carthorse blew softly on her.

'It's all right, missie, Prince won't hurt ye,' the driver laughed, winking at them and spitting out a plug of tobacco. ''E's just got a bit of an eye for a pretty lass.'

'I wish we could stand somewhere else,' Mavis told Connie nervously. 'But there isn't anywhere. The boat is full.'

'Don't worry,' Connie told her, as the inquisitive animal started huffing down her own neck as well. 'At least he's keeping us warm!'

Once off the ferry, the two girls hailed a hansom cab to take them to Mavis's great-aunt's house.

'Harry won't be home until later this afternoon,'

Mavis informed Connie, as they paid off the cab driver. 'Otherwise, I know he would have come down to the terminal to meet us.'

Mavis's great-aunt's home was much more imposing than Connie had expected, much larger than her parents' home in Friargate, but, of course, nowhere near as big as Ellie's mansion in Winckley Square.

A pretty girl, who bore a close resemblance to Mavis, opened the door before they reached it, giving them both a beaming smile.

'Oh, Sophie!' Mavis exclaimed, hugging her and then saying, 'Connie, this is my sister.'

'You are very pretty!' Sophie told Connie forthrightly, 'Mavis said that you were.'

Mavis blushed slightly as Connie looked at her. 'Sophie begged me to tell her what you look like,' she explained.

'Girls, come inside and get warm.'

'Oh, Mama,' Mavis smiled, hurrying to embrace the small-boned woman urging them inside.

'And you must be Connie.' Mavis's mother smiled gently. 'Mavis has told us so much about you. I am so pleased that you were able to come home with her.'

Although Elsie Lawson didn't hug Connie as exuberantly as her younger daughter had done, Connie could sense that she was warmly disposed toward her, and that the welcome was genuine.

'You both look frozen, but, don't worry, I have some hot broth waiting on the stove for you. Mavis, why don't you take Connie up to your room, to freshen up. Then you can both come down and have something to eat, and tell me all about what you have been doing.'

'Where is your great-aunt?' Connie asked Mavis curiously, when Mavis took her up two flights of stairs to a large attic bedroom with two prettily-covered beds.

'Aunt Martha has her own part of the house,' Mavis explained. 'The best parlour; a bedroom, and a bathroom on the first floor.'

No further mention was made of Mavis's great-aunt, but Connie realised what the real situation was when, no sooner had they sat down to drink the soup Elsie Lawson had prepared for them, a bell clanged noisily.

Immediately Mavis's mother stood up, looking apprehensive. 'Oh dear, I wonder what's wrong. I'd better go and see.'

'Mother, finish your soup first,' Mavis urged, but Connie could see how uneasy the older woman was looking.

As soon as she had scurried out of the room, Sophie announced angrily, 'Poor Mother, Great Aunt Martha treats her like a servant! Just because she's rich and we're poor, that doesn't mean...'

'Shush, Sophie,' Mavis urged her sister worriedly. 'You know how upset mother would be if she were to hear you speaking like that!'

'That's only because she's afraid that Great Aunt Martha will tell us to leave. She only lets us live here because Mother looks after her, we all know that! She promised that she would pay my school fees, but it's Harry who has to pay them! I hate her. She's horrid!'

'I'm sorry about that,' Mavis apologised to

Connie later when they were upstairs unpacking. 'Sophie is still too young to understand that she should not be so outspoken.'

'It must be very worrying for all of you,' Connie tried to comfort her friend.

'It is Mother I worry about the most,' Mavis confessed. 'Since my father died, things have been so difficult for her. And Sophie is right, Great Aunt Martha does not value Mother, as she should. And certainly no servant would ever look after her as Mother does,' Mavis burst out angrily. 'But Mama says that she prefers to be here with a sound roof over her head, and Sophie attending a good school, rather than having to struggle to manage in rented accommodation and worry about bills.'

There was no sign of any unhappiness on Elsie Lawson's face, or in her manner, when later in the day, she did everything she could to make Connie feel welcome and a part of her family.

Connie soon felt completely at home, joining in a game of snakes and ladders with Sophie, and then giggling with her over the jokes she and Mavis had saved from their Christmas dinner crackers.

It had grown dark, and the heavy, velvet curtains had been drawn over the windows and the fire stoked up, before a tattoo of knocks on the door heralded the arrival of Mavis's brother.

'That's Harry's knock!' Sophie exclaimed excitedly, springing up from her chair and rushing to the door.

From the hallway, Connie could hear male laughter. The parlour door opened and Sophie danced in. Connie looked up, poised to smile politely, and then paled as shocked recognition ran through her body seizing her in its stranglehold. She could neither move nor speak, as she stared into the face of the young man she had last seen looking at her with such embarrassed pity in Back Court, the day Bill Connolly had attacked her and she had miscarried her child!

By what appalling and cruel mischance of fate could such a thing have happened?

Her head was swimming, her heart, thudding erratically inside her chest. If only she could close her eyes, and then discover when she opened them again she had been mistaken, and that Mavis's brother was not the same young man who had witnessed her shame.

'Oh, Harry, do come and meet my friend, Connie,' Mavis was demanding excitedly. 'I have already told her what a wonderful brother you are.'

Connie couldn't look at him. She could barely even speak, although she managed to stammer some kind of response, as he came over and shook her hand. His grip was cool, and firm, but Connie withdrew from it as though it was fire. His acknowledgement of their introduction, like her own was a jumble of words, which could not penetrate her shocked fear.

'Connie has been playing snakes and ladders with me,' Sophie was telling him importantly. 'And she's better than you, Harry.'

'Harry, my love, you must be cold and hungry! We have waited supper for you, though.'

'I was later leaving school than I had hoped.

The Headmaster called us all into a meeting to tell us that our Housemaster is to leave, and that his replacement will be starting when the new term begins.'

'Mr James, but surely he has only been there a little while, Harry?' Mrs Lawson queried.

'Yes, he has, but he has a connection with one of the Governors at Rugby, and he has been offered a post there which will pay more money.'

All the happiness Connie had felt at being here with Mavis and her family was draining out of her like blood from an open vein, she acknowledged sickly. How could it not be? Had Mavis's brother recognised her? Or could he not see any resemblance in the healthy, well-fed young woman she now was, to the dirty, half-starved, beaten creature she had been?

Did he perhaps not even remember the incident that was burned into her own memory; her own soul, to leave her branded, and desperate to put aside what she had once been?

Connie felt so on edge that she could barely touch the meal Elsie Lawson had prepared for them. She knew that her conversation was lacklustre, and she was aware of the concerned, anxious looks Mavis was giving her, although she pretended not to be.

'Connie, I have told Mother how well you play the piano,' Mavis announced, when they had finished eating. 'And I know she would love to hear you play. There is a piano in the front parlour,' she added.

Connie bit her lip. How could she refuse? She could not. And yet she was loath to do anything which might draw attention to her, and thus prompt Harry Lawson into recognising her. Her legs felt like lead as she got up and allowed Sophie to escort her into the parlour.

'Perhaps Great Aunt Martha would like to join us?' Harry suggested, but immediately his mother shook her head and looked uncomfortable.

'Great Aunt Martha is still treating Mama like a servant, Harry,' Connie heard Mavis whisper angrily to her brother.

Afterwards Connie had no notion of what she played, other than that her heart had jumped into her mouth when Harry Lawson had suddenly appeared at her side, to sing in warm tenor voice, whilst turning the pages of the music for her.

'You play well, Miss Pride,' he commented.

Elsie Lawson sighed, 'I do wish you and Sophie might have learned, Mavis. It is such a genteel accomplishment.'

Connie winced, her face burning, half-expecting to hear Harry Lawson immediately denounce her, as she stammered, 'My mother wanted me to learn.'

'You have a large family, Miss Pride?'

Connie tensed, as Harry addressed her, but she did not look at him as she answered in a low voice. 'My mother is dead, and my father has remarried. I ... I have a sister and ... and two brothers...'

The visit she had anticipated with so much pleasure, Connie acknowledged miserably, had turned into the darkest kind of nightmare.

NINE

1913

'Lord, but you'd think no one had ever been engaged before to listen to the way Vera is carrying on,' Josie commented crossly to Connie, as they hurried to reach the dining room, their shift over. 'And fancy coming back, bold as brass, and showing it off to everyone after what she's gone and done. Leaving without so much as a by-your-leave, and not saying anything to us as was supposed to be her friends.'

A small frown pleated Connie's forehead, as she listened to Josie's indignant tirade. The Vera who had come proudly into the nurses' home flaunting the engagement ring, which had been Bert's Christmas gift to her, wasn't the Vera who had shared their lives for so long.

The fun-loving girl who Connie had initially liked so much, was now showing a boastful, and sometimes even slightly spiteful, side to her nature, which was far less attractive.

'Well, I don't envy her her Bert, no, nor her engagement ring either!' Connie told Josie forthrightly.

Josie giggled. 'No, me neither. That Bert, he's got a right pudding face on him, hasn't he, and after how Vera was allus going on about how she wanted to marry someone 'andsome like that

143

George Lashwood!'

'Connie, Josie. Guess what?' Mavis demanded excitedly, hurrying up to them. 'Harry, my brother, has obtained tickets for the panto at the Royal Court, and you are both to come with us.'

'Ooh, Mavis. He hasn't, has he? Oh, I'm that made up! The panto, I have never bin to a panto before.'

Connie could feel Mavis looking at her waiting for her response.

She had tried to distance herself from her friend following their return to the Infirmary. Not because she no longer wanted Mavis, she did! But she was terrified that, even if Harry Lawson had, by some miraculous chance not recognised her the last time they had met, as time went on, and he saw more of her through her friendship with Mavis, he might at some stage do so.

The alternative, that he had recognised her but had, as yet, for reasons she could not fathom not chosen to say so, was an even more frightening prospect. She realised now that the heavily-veiled woman she had seen in Back Court must have been Elsie Lawson – and that Back Court itself was the horrible place Mavis had described to her with such distress. Mavis would surely want nothing more to do with Connie if she were to find out the truth about her.

'Connie, what's wrong? You do want to come to the panto, don't you?' Mavis asked her later, catching her on her own, and tugging worriedly on her arm as Connie tried to turn away from her.

'I don't know as I want to be beholden to your

brother,' Connie answered her stiffly, not knowing what else she could say.

'But Harry wants you and Josie to come with us,' Mavis told her, looking bewildered. 'Connie, what's the matter?' Mavis demanded. 'You've been offhand with me ever since we came back from New Brighton. If I've said or done something to offend or upset you...'

Mavis's concern broke through the barriers Connie was trying to put up against her. Mavis was the first proper friend she had ever had, and secretly Connie knew that their friendship had gone some way to filling the cold, empty space in her heart and her life, left by her rift with Ellie.

'Oh, Mavis, no! You mustn't think that!' she protested unhappily. 'As if you could, or would, upset anyone. It's just.'

'Just what?' Mavis demanded.

'Well, I ... your brother ... I don't think he cares for me a great deal – perhaps he thinks that I'm not a suitable friend for you?' Connie suggested warily.

'Connie! How could you think such a thing?' Mavis objected. 'Harry is not the sort to say very much about a person, but I know that he likes you, I can tell. And Mama and Sophie have both told me how much they enjoyed your visit.'

Connie could feel the air leaking from her lungs, as her tension eased. Perhaps she had been worrying unnecessarily, after all. Mavis's brother had certainly not given her any indication that he had recognised her, Connie reassured herself, her natural ebullience reasserting itself.

Squeezing Mavis's hand, she told her, 'Of

course, I would love to go to the panto.'

Bill Connolly looked savagely at the man standing in front of him.

'What do you mean he won't pay? Did you tell him what's going ter happen to his shop and to him, and to his family, if he doesn't?'

'Aye, us 'ave told him how 'e needs to be protected in case anyone should brek into his shop, and that us'ull mek sure that no one does, but 'e says he can't pay.'

'Well then, you'd better get some of the lads and go back and show him what happens to folk when they can't pay their insurance, 'adn't you,' Bill told his henchman grimly.

'Harry isn't going to be able to come to see "The House that Jack Built" with us, after all,' Mavis informed Connie and Josie over breakfast on the day of their planned trip. 'The new Head of Harry's House has called a meeting of all the Masters, and Harry is obliged to go.'

Although she sympathised as vocally as Josie, inwardly Connie was relieved that Harry was not to accompany them to the pantomime. She willingly offered to go down to the Pierhead with Mavis to meet her mother and sister off the ferry, so that they could all go to the Royal Court together.

Although Connie had intended to affect a sophisticated disdain of the pantomime which could not possibly compare with the delights of the music hall, within minutes of the curtain going up she

146

was as transfixed by the performance as young Sophie.

When the dame yelled out, 'Oh, no, he isn't!' Connie was yelling back with gusto, 'Oh, yes, he is!' and screaming, 'look behind you', laughing until tears ran from her eyes.

Harry frowned as he checked his watch. His class had just finished, and it was another five minutes yet before he had to present himself at Mr Cartwright's door.

Unlike the junior schoolmasters, the Head of House, lived in great comfort in a house of his own with its own private garden. Harry had seen Miss Rosa Cartwright, the Head of House's daughter, walking there with her little dog.

Mr Cartwright did not have a wife, being a widower. From the window of his cramped attic room, Harry could look down on the quadrangle where some of the pupils were huddling out of the way of the chill winter wind.

Harry could not concentrate on the impending meeting, though. And for the very simple reason that his thoughts were already consumed by something else, or rather someone else; Miss Connie Pride! In fact, from the moment he had set eyes on her in his great-aunt's house, Harry had scarcely stopped thinking about her.

When Mavis had begged him to include her two friends in the treat he had to battle with his conscience. He had been shocked to recognise in Mavis's friend the young woman he had seen in such an appalling and unhappy state in Back Court. Initially he had supposed that the two of them must have met when his mother and sisters were living in Back Court. Even so, he knew that Mavis could not possibly have the knowledge about Connie's true situation whilst living there, that he had. But very quickly, it had become plain to him that this was not the case, and Mavis knew nothing of Connie's past.

Harry knew perfectly well that, even if he could not bring himself to denounce Connie, he should, at least, put an end to her friendship with his sister. But she must have suffered so dreadfully, and she had obviously been very brave.

She spoke well; she played the piano; she even revealed, without knowing she was doing so, an awareness of current affairs and general knowledge that could only have come from receiving a good education. Those were not things she had gained in Back Court.

How had she come to such a pass in the first place? Through naiveté and foolishness and the betrayal of a man, he suspected. Because, for all that he knew about her, there was a sweet innocence about her that touched his heart and made him loath to do anything that might hurt her. Such tender emotions? And for a young woman who was virtually a stranger to him? Anyone would think that he was in danger of losing his heart to her! He was certainly spending far too much time thinking about her.

Mavis had described her friend as pretty, but Connie was more than merely pretty, Harry decided. She had a fierce pride and spirit that shone out of her and made her truly beautiful. She aroused feelings of tenderness and protectiveness inside him stronger than any others he had known.

It was time for him to go.

The icy wind nipped at his ears and hands as he braved its coldness to cross the quadrangle and head for the house. Harry's salary did not allow for the indulgence of a thick, warm winter coat, although he had the new muffler which Sophie had knitted him and given him for Christmas, and he was still eating the hamper of food his mother had put up for him, after complaining that he was too thin.

A stern-looking maid admitted him to the house, 'I'll tell the Master that you're here,' she informed him, before disappearing.

The hallway was cold, and Harry wondered where the other teachers were. A door opened and Mr Cartwright strode toward him, saying bluffly, 'Ah, Lawson, excellent timing, do come in. Rosa was just about to ring for tea.'

Removing his muffler, Harry followed the Head of House into a comfortably appointed parlour, feeling slightly awkward as he realised that he was the first to arrive.

'Rosa, my dear, come and meet one of my teachers, Harry Lawson. Lawson, this is my daughter Rosa.'

As they shook hands, and Rosa gave him a demure look from beneath lowered eyelids, Harry noticed how soft and boneless her hand was.

'I've instructed Cook to send plenty of crumpets, Mr Lawson. All young men like crumpets, don't they?'

For some reason he couldn't explain, Harry found the soft voice grated on him.

'Papa has been telling me how clever you are, and that it is expected that you will become Assistant Master when Mr Thomas retires.'

'It is by no means decided,' Harry felt bound to answer her.

'But of course it is, my boy,' Mr Cartwright boomed out firmly. 'You have an excellent record, and as I was saying to the Head only the other week, it would be an excellent thing for the school to have a young man such as yourself as my second in command.'

Harry didn't know what to say... He knew that he should feel complimented, but what he actually felt was discomfort, and almost disquiet.

'My daughter wants to see us having a bit more jollity here, Harry, and she has commanded me to instruct you that you must put yourself at her disposal to that end. It will be good training for you in your eventual duties as my assistant to involve yourself in the social side of our calling. I have noticed that we do not have as many pupils applying to our House as the others. That needs to be addressed, and I intend to invite the parents of our boys here to take tea with us.'

'And in the summer we can have a garden party, Papa,' Rosa broke in excitedly, turning an animated face toward Harry. 'Do you not think that is a good idea, Mr Lawson? I do so love a garden party. And we can have punts on the river. Just like at Oxford... Oh, Papa, I do miss Oxford so...'

'My daughter is missing her friends, and who can blame her,' the Head of House told Harry. 'But, between us, I am sure that we can build a small Oxford for her here that will satisfy all her needs, don't you think?'

'I have so many plans, Mr Lawson. But I shall need your help with them,' Rosa told him.

She certainly did have plans, she reflected bitterly. Plans that would show her cousin Gerald that, whilst he thought he could toy with her and make her fall in love with him, and then cast her aside so that he could pursue some ugly heiress, two could play at that game.

A dull and poor junior schoolmaster like Harry could not possibly really compare with her handsome, dashing cousin, with his dangerous, flirtatious smiles and wicked whispered promises, but Rosa was determined that she would be wearing an engagement ring on her finger before her cousin placed one on the hand of his ugly heiress.

Gerald had laughed openly at her when she had foolishly let him see how much she wanted to marry him – but why else, after all, would she have allowed him the liberties she had, if she had not believed that he loved her, as passionately as she did him.

'Rosa, you are a sweet puss, and if things were different... But I am a lazy, expensive fellow and I need a rich wife.'

'I have money.'

Gerald had laughed and shaken his head.

'No, Rosa, you merely have a modest bequest from your mother. My heiress is rich, very rich...'

'But you do not love her. You love me! You said so yourself!' she had objected passionately.

'Ah, my sweet Rose. In your arms, tasting the nectar of your lips, I would say anything...'

'You cannot mean to marry someone else. You must not,' she had sobbed. 'I love you.'

But despite her tears and pleas, Gerald had refused to be moved.

So she had vowed that if she could not have his love, then she would have her own revenge. And that revenge would be her marriage to someone else. Harry would suit her purposes perfectly!

'I am only a poor, weak female and we are nothing without the support of a strong man.'

Harry said nothing, applying himself hungrily to the rapidly cooling crumpets.

'It is too cold for us to walk in the gardens to discuss our plans now, Mr Lawson, but Papa has given his permission for you to call on us whenever I need to speak with you,' Rosa told him, clapping her hands together in an affected manner. 'Oh, I am so pleased to have your help with this task. I don't want to disappoint Papa, when I know how important it is to him that the parents have the most favourable impression possible of our House.'

She had, Rosa decided smugly, been very clever playing on her father's vulnerability and pride in such a way, but then she had always been able to twist him around her little finger!

Later, as he made his way back to his own cold quarters, Harry wondered why he was actually enjoying the freshness of the icy air, and why he was not rejoicing at the opportunity which had befallen him to improve his prospects of advancement.

Connie shivered in the cold March wind as she hurried into the Infirmary. Officially it was her afternoon off, but Mavis had come to her, hesitantly and self-consciously, earlier in the week to ask her if she would mind changing half days with her.

'Of course not,' Connie had replied promptly.

'Oh, Connie, thank you. Frank has asked me to go out with him, and Thursday is his only half day free.'

'I told you he had a twinkle in his eyes for you,' Connie had teased her, but inwardly she believed that the young policeman would be a good match for her friend.

There was a sudden commotion in the corridor as Mr Clegg, the surgeon, hurried out of one of the wards, pulling on his coat, and carrying his medical bag.

'Ah Nurse!' he called out as he saw Connie. 'Come with me, and hurry.'

Connie hesitated uncertainly, but Sister had hurried out into the corridor behind the surgeon, and she told Connie immediately, 'Yes, Nurse Pride, go with Mr Clegg.'

The Surgeon was walking so fast that Connie could barely keep up with him as he raced through the Infirmary and across the forecourt.

'Someone has just brought word that one of my patients has gone into early labour and there may be complications. Fortunately, she does not live too far away, but we must make haste.'

It was said in the Infirmary that Mr Clegg was a man who never turned down work, and Connie reflected ruefully that that certainly seemed to be true. This patient must be one of the Infirmary's few paying patients, she decided, if Mr Clegg was prepared to attend her lying-in.

When they reached the house where the woman was giving birth, the midwife was waiting for them.

'Breach it is, Mr Clegg, and I cannot, try as I might, turn the little bugger,' she told them above the woman's screams.

Just for a second, Connie froze.

The woman's danger reminded her forcibly of the way her own mother had died, and quickly following on the heels of that still painful memory, came an unwanted acknowledgement that she, too, had come close to having her life bleed away from her with the child she had miscarried.

Pity for the woman on the bed filled her, and she made a small, silent prayer that she would deliver safely.

'Nurse. Quickly. There is no time to lose!'

In the bedroom, the air was foetid and sour, the woman's screams more like the sound of an animal than a human being. Connie had to steel herself not to think of her mother going through this same agony, only to die at the end of it.

The midwife had already instructed the husband to boil some water, and Connie used it to sterilise Mr Clegg's instruments as he commanded her to do.

'Tsk,' he exclaimed when he had finished examining his patient. 'The child will have to be turned, and quickly. Otherwise...'

Connie swallowed hard. If he could not turn the baby then Mr Clegg would have to ask the father who he wanted to live, his wife or his child, because saving the one, would necessitate the death of the other.

Silently she prayed that the baby could be turned and that both mother and child would survive, and she was sure that her own relief was almost as great as the poor mother's when Mr Clegg announced that he had successfully turned the child.

'Quickly now, Nurse,' he commanded. 'We do not want it turning again. I shall have to use forceps.' He looked at the woman on the bed. 'And perhaps a little chloroform.'

Connie nodded her head, holding the chloroform-soaked pad to the woman's nose as Mr Clegg went to work with his forceps.

Half an hour later, the mother was cradling her new son, who had suffered little more than some bruising as Mr Clegg had brought him into the world.

It was dark when they left the house and started to walk back to the Infirmary. The Street was eerily, and somehow Connie felt, almost menacingly silent.

'It's March now, spring will soon be here, Nurse,' Mr Clegg pronounced cheerfully.

'It cannot come soon enough for me,' Connie admitted. 'This cold weather...'

'Ah, thank you, Nurse, you have reminded me that I must speak with the Infirmary Guardians and warn them that we shall need to order more coals. The Government has given out instructions that we must have our hospitals and infirmaries in a state of readiness for war, and that means being fully stocked and equipped with everything that we might need.'

'Do you think that there will be a war, Sir?' Connie asked him.

'My heart wants to believe that there will not, but I am afraid that my head is not persuaded to agree with its optimism. What I do know though is that, if it does come to war, there will be dark days ahead of us. Very dark days, but we shall be ready, and... Goodness, what is this?' he broke off to demand, as suddenly out of the shadows two men, caps pulled down and mufflers pulled up high to obscure their faces, started to move threateningly toward them.

'Quick, Nurse. Get behind me,' Mr Clegg instructed Connie, but she refused to do so, standing firmly at his side, determined not to betray her fear.

'Give us yer bag,' one of them demanded, 'and empty yer pockets.' Connie gave a small gasp of shocked pain as the other man stepped forward and grabbed hold of her wrist, dragging her toward him and forcing her arm up her back.

'Let go of that young woman at once, you rogue,' Mr Clegg demanded, but the two men both laughed.

'You hold on to 'er and I'll do the searching,' one of them commented lewdly, 'and then you 'ave your turn after...'

Sickness and terror filled Connie, and suddenly she was back in Back Court with Connolly standing over her.

'Don't you dare...' Mr Clegg began, but it was

too late, the man had already reached out a dirty hand and placed it on her breast. A sensation of being dragged back into the past seized her; fear and loathing exploded inside her, and Connie lashed out with terror-driven strength, screaming at him and kicking his shin with all her might.

The man let go of her with a howl of rage, at the same time as a policeman walked round the corner, and seeing what was happening started to run toward them. The villains fled.

Mr Clegg was explaining what had happened, and Connie could feel the waves of fear-induced dizziness and nausea rising from the pit of her stomach. But she was a nurse and she was not allowed to faint, so she had to grit her teeth and assure the anxious policeman that she was perfectly all right, as he insisted on walking them back to the safety of the Infirmary.

Once there, Mr Clegg announced that Connie was a very brave, young woman, and Sister, who had bustled up to see what was happening, relaxed her normal starchiness enough to say, almost kindly, that Connie could go and get herself a nice cup of tea.

Conscious of the honour being bestowed on her, Connie managed a weak smile, but in reality all she wanted to do was to go to bed, and pull the covers up over her head, so that she could have a good cry.

She had been so afraid! The touch of the man's hand on her body, the look in his eyes, the sound of his voice, had reminded her terrifyingly of Bill Connolly. Never would she allow herself to be dragged back into that kind of life again!

'How the months are flying by, Harry. It doesn't seem two minutes since we were all altogether after Christmas,' Mavis told her brother fondly, as they sat together in the parlour of the New Brighton house.

'Mother tells me that you are walking out with someone, Mavis,' Harry answered, looking and sounding very like the older brother he was.

Mavis laughed and blushed. 'Yes. His name's Frank. You will like him, Harry. Mother says I may bring him home for tea the next time I have a full day off.'

'And your friend, Connie. Is she walking out with anyone?' Harry heard himself asking.

Mavis shook her head, a small frown pleating her forehead. 'No, she isn't. Poor Connie, the most dreadful thing happened to her, Harry.'

Harry felt his stomach lurch and his muscles clench.

'What do you mean?' he demanded.

Casting her brother a brief glance, for it wasn't like him to sound so grim, or be so peremptory, Mavis explained about the attack Connie had suffered.

'Mr Clegg, our surgeon, told Matron that Connie was very brave. And she was, Harry,' Mavis added earnestly. 'I should have been so afraid. Frank has told me that there is a very dangerous gang at work in Liverpool, preying on people and robbing them.' She gave a small shiver.

'I am sorry to hear that Miss Pride has suffered such an attack,' Harry told Mavis in a low voice, whilst inwardly he battled with his surge of very male, and very betraying, feelings. He wanted to hunt down whoever it was who had hurt Connie and teach them a lesson they would never forget. He also wanted to hold Connie in his arms and tell her that no one would ever hurt her again!

'Please do give Connie my best wishes, Mavis.' He paused to clear his throat, as his heart reacted to his intimate use of Connie's name. 'And ... and tell her that ... that I have asked after her.'

Mavis gave her brother a startled look. Harry's good-looking face was slightly flushed, and he was refusing to meet her eyes.

'Harry Lawson, I do believe that you are sweet on Connie!' she laughed.

Harry's face went even redder. 'Don't be silly.' He told her gruffly. 'I hardly know her.'

'What does that say to anything?' Mavis challenged him mischievously, 'Frank says that he knew I was the one for him the moment he set eyes on me!'

'I think I shall have to have a word with Mother about this young man,' Harry warned her mock-seriously.

'Well, if you would like to meet him...' Mavis began, going a little pink herself now. 'Since you have the whole week off, Harry, you could come to the Infirmary, and I could introduce you to him there. I am off duty the day after tomorrow at six, and so is Frank. He was going to wait for me and take me out for a bit of supper.'

Harry frowned. It certainly sounded as though the relationship between his sister and her young man was becoming serious and, if that was the case, then surely it was his duty and his responsibility to see Frank for himself?

Because of the shifts they were on, Mavis didn't get the opportunity to tell Connie about Harry's planned visit to the Infirmary, and so Connie walked totally unprepared into the large room where the nurses gathered in their off-duty hours, and came to a shocked halt as she saw Harry standing next to her friend.

'Connie!' Mavis exclaimed in delight. 'I was hoping I would catch you. Harry has come over so that he can inspect Frank!' she added drolly, pulling a face.

'You were the one who suggested that I meet him,' Harry pointed out calmly, but inwardly he was feeling anything but calm. Grimly he wrestled with those feelings he knew it was unwise for him to have.

'Connie, would you please look after Harry for me whilst I go across to the Infirmary and bring Frank back with me?' Mavis begged, unaware of the bombshell she was dropping.

Connie closed her eyes in despair, and then opened them again. She felt as though her tongue had stuck to the roof of her mouth and that she was indeed tongue-tied just like some of their afflicted patients. She certainly couldn't utter the refusal she needed to give, and Mavis was already darting away, her face alight with the expectation of seeing Frank.

He could have offered to go with his sister, Harry acknowledged belatedly, as she sped away.

He could almost feel the weight of Connie's silence, and he had seen the constrained, apprehensive look she had given him, before immediately looking away again. For a moment, they regarded one another in mutual silence, Connie's wary and watchful, and Harry thought he could guess what she must be thinking and fearing.

He had no taste for being in such an awkward situation, and couldn't help wishing that he had only met Connie for the first time when Mavis had brought her home. He had met her before though and, in all conscience, he knew he had a responsibility to his family to assure himself that Connie was a suitable person to be his sister's friend.

Taking a deep breath he plunged in, reluctantly, 'Miss Pride, Connie. There is something ... a matter, both delicate and ... er, in short a matter to which we were both privy and which I feel... When I arrived at my great-aunt's house and saw you there, I realised immediately that, that is to say, I recognised you immediately.'

Connie bit her lip, unable to say anything, her face burning with shame and misery.

Harry could see how white her face had gone, and how her eyes had become burning pools of fear and pain.

'Connie,' Harry urged her gently. He didn't want to frighten or hurt her, but he had a moral duty to put his sisters first.

'You intend to ... to denounce me, is that what you are saying?' Connie demanded tonelessly, her despair only too evident.

Watching her, Harry felt a fresh pang of pity for her, coupled with a desire to reassure her. He drew a deep sigh. 'Denounce you! No, Connie.

Please don't look so afraid! I have to think of my sisters,' he told her gently. 'You must see that, with our father's death, I must take the role of a father. Mavis has a very high regard for you.'

'Far higher than I deserve, you mean?' Connie challenged him bitterly.

He paused and took a deep breath. 'It is not for me to sit in judgement on you, Connie.'

'You say that, but others will do so if you tell them...' Her mouth had started to tremble so badly she had to break off, and force back her shaming tears. She would not further humiliate herself by pleading with him to spare her.

Even so, she couldn't stop herself from bursting out frantically, 'Don't you think I have regretted, over and over again, my own stubborn foolishness? I refused to listen when I was warned of the disgrace that would fall upon me for allowing my heart to rule my head. Such things are permissible for a man, of course! He may walk away from a situation such as mine with his character unstained! But a woman, no matter how respectably born, must lose everything!'

Harry frowned, stirred reluctantly to the admission that it was brave of her to speak so to him, and he could not help but admire her for her courage.

'The man...'

'He is dead,' Connie told him flatly. 'He was on *Titanic*. We both should have been, but he left without me.' Suddenly it was as though an old wound had opened up inside her, flooding her with sharp pain. 'He promised that he would marry me on board before we started our new lives together in America, but he deserted me, and then his uncle...'

Connie had no idea why she was telling Harry so much, or why she was exposing her own pain and shame. Abruptly, she swallowed. 'Denounce me if you must,' she began. 'But...'

Harry shook his head. 'I shall not do that. I have no wish to cause you any more pain. What purpose would it serve? My concern is for my sisters.'

'Lest I corrupt them?' Connie challenged him bitterly.

'I did not say that,' Harry told her quietly. 'But, naturally, I do not wish either of them...'

'To be tainted by my disgrace?'

'I think we should consider the matter closed, and say no more about it,' Harry told her gently.

Later, when she was on her own, Connie knew that she should be feeling much happier than she was. After all, Harry had as good as said that he wasn't going to tell anyone. But his comment about the matter being closed had left a thorn of pain inside her that pricked sharply at her. For her, it could never be closed, she recognised miserably. For her, it would always be there. A stain on her character for ever!

Spring came and went, and they were into summer. Connie was spending more and more time working in the operating theatre and on the acute wards. Connie found it rewarding work, although she knew that some of the nurses found the operations too harrowing and preferred to do other work.

163

They scarcely saw anything of Vera any more, but, unexpectedly, she turned up at the Infirmary announcing that she had brought them invitations to her wedding.

'Ooh, Vera, just look at that blouse you're wearing,' Josie squeaked round-eyed.

'It's the latest fashion,' Vera told her, preening herself as she sketched the neckline of her blouse with her fingers.

'Pneumonia blouses they're calling them in the papers,' Connie put in.

'Pooh the papers, who wants to read those!' Vera sniffed disparagingly. 'Bert says he'd 'ave 'em banned, if he were Lord Mayor.'

Connie and Mavis exchanged rueful looks.

'It's to be a full, posh, wedding breakfast and then there's to be dancing afterwards,' Vera told them, reverting to the subject which was of much more interest to her, before adding, 'It's a pity you and Josie aren't walking out with anyone yet, Connie. There'll only be a few spare lads, and me cousins will be wantin' to dance with them. And what about you, Mavis?' Vera probed archly. 'I know you're walking out with that Frank, but has he declared himself yet and shown his intentions?'

'Frank and I are perfectly happy as we are, thank you, Vera,' Mavis replied sedately, but as she told Connie later, she had felt more than a little put out by Vera's manner.

'It's all very well for her to boast of her plans, Connie, her wedding, and the rooms Bert's parents have let them have over one of the shops, but things are different for me and Frank.' Mavis gave a small sigh. 'Frank has his mother to think of. She is not in the best of health, and widowed, and she is used to having Frank to herself.'

Connie gave her a sympathetic look. Although Mavis was not the sort of girl who would say so, Connie had guessed from what she had not said, that Frank's mother was not the easiest person to get along with.

'Vera is having a September wedding and, personally, I think June would be much nicer,' Connie announced, trying to cheer Mavis up a little. 'What we need, Mavis, is a jolly night out.' Connie went on.

'I've got to go back on duty. I promised one of the patients, a soldier who fought in the Boer War, that I'd read the *Echo* to him this afternoon, if I've got time. He can't see very well, and he wants to know what the Government have to say about the Germans.'

Connie's forehead creased, 'Do you think there really will be a war, Mavis?'

Mavis looked worried. 'Oh, Connie, I do hope not. Harry and Frank were talking about it only the other day. Harry wants to join up if there is, but with his weak chest, I don't think he would be accepted.'

'Harry has a weak chest?' Connie demanded, unable to conceal her shock.

Mavis nodded her head and looked uncomfortable. 'I shouldn't have said anything. Harry hates it being mentioned, but sometimes, when he is overtired, he struggles so hard to breathe that it can be frightening. He was dreadfully poorly when he was little. I do hope there won't be any fighting, Connie. There are soldiers from the Boer

War on the non-acute wards.'

Both girls fell silent. The Infirmary being a poorhouse hospital was obliged to provide beds for non-acute patients, and many of them were occupied by the long-term sick of the parish, some of whom were old soldiers, whose injuries had left them bedridden and in pain.

'Harry, my daughter has been asking me why you have not been round to have tea with us of late?'

Harry's heart sank, as he avoided meeting Mr Cartwright's eyes.

The plain truth was that Rosa set his teeth on edge, and, even worse, bored him silly, but he could hardly say so to her doting father, especially since that father was his superior. And more than that, there was a boldness about Rosa's behaviour toward him at times, which made Harry feel acutely uncomfortable.

'You must come round today. I insist on it.'

Summoning a smile, Harry thanked him.

Officially the school term had ended, but Harry, in common with some of the other junior masters, had had to remain on the premises to take charge of those pupils who did not return to their homes during the holiday period – boarders who, in the main, were orphans or whose parents were abroad.

His job involved long hours as it was, but Harry wouldn't have dreamed of complaining. He felt he had been fortunate to secure a post at such a prestigious school, and, after all, he had his mother and sisters to think of. And not just because his mother depended on him to pay Sophie's school fees. He knew how proud they all were of him, and what hopes they had for him. In many ways, those hopes rested on him winning the support and approval of his superiors, especially Mr Cartwright, who was his direct superior – and Rosa's father!

His thoughts began to stray, as they did rather too frequently for his own comfort, from Rosa to Connie. He must not think of Connie, he told himself fiercely. But he could not help himself.

'And who are you then?'

Connie, her cheeks flushed from dancing, looked toward the young man who was addressing her.

'Family of the bride, are yer?' he persisted, whilst his gaze roved boldly over Connie's face and bosom.

'A friend actually,' she answered him. 'You're one of the groom's lot, are you?'

'Aye, he's me cousin. Fancy a dance wi'us?'

Connie gave him a haughty look. 'We haven't been introduced,' she pointed out firmly, slipping easily back into her long-ago role of Miss Connie Pride, one of the Prides of Preston, and happy to be so!

Her companion burst out laughing. 'Well, I'm Jack Baker...'

And a real flirt by the looks and manner of him, Connie reflected inwardly, as she gave him her own name.

Vera's wedding was everything she had expected it to be. Vera's dress was too fussy, and trimmed with far too much cheap lace, and too many flow-

167

ers and ribbons, even if Vera herself thought she looked the bee's knees in it. Connie knew that her own mother would have immediately declared the whole affair common and vulgar, but, despite that, Connie was enjoying herself.

She had been danced off her feet by a score of different partners, who, for all that Vera had said, had been far keener to dance with Connie and Josie than they had with the bride's cousins.

'My, but it's hot,' she complained, fanning herself with her hand.

'It'll be cooler outside,' her companion suggested, nodding in the direction of the French windows that opened out into the small private back garden belonging to the hotel where the wedding breakfast had been held.

It was a light, late summer evening and Connie saw nothing wrong in stepping outside with Bert's cousin for a breath of fresh air, but no sooner had they stepped away from the French windows, than Jack grabbed hold of her and pressed his hot, wet mouth over her own as he tried to steal a kiss.

Angrily Connie tried to free herself, stamping down hard on his foot with the heel of her shoe when he refused to let her go. ''Ere what d'you do that for?' he complained as he released her, but Connie refused to answer him, heading back to the hotel instead, her eyes burning with angry tears.

How could she have not realised what he had been intending? Just because they were at a respectable event like a wedding, that was no reason for her to think she could relax her normal guard! All men were the same, she decided darkly. All out for one thing! Well, they weren't going to get it from her! She could just imagine what Harry Lawson would have thought if he had seen...

TEN

'I can't believe it's nearly Christmas!'

Connie gave Mavis a weary smile as they met up in the dining room.

'It has been a busy year, what with Vera's wedding, an' all. I don't know where the time goes,' Mavis added.

'I can tell you where it goes,' Connie answered her, feelingly. 'Most of it goes with us up and down these wards!'

Mavis laughed. 'That's true,' she agreed. 'Which reminds me. How is that young patient you were telling me about, Connie?'

Mr Clegg had performed a major operation on a young man who had fallen off the roof he had been re-tiling, earlier in the week, and it was touch and go whether or not he would survive.

'The one as fell off the roof?'

Mavis nodded.

'He is in dreadful pain, but very brave,' Connie told her soberly, before adding ruefully, 'have you noticed, Mavis, how often, and how seriously, we talk about our work these days. It is almost as though we have become proper nurses.'

169

Both of them burst out laughing.

'My mother is hoping that you will spend Christmas with us, Connie. You know how fond of you she has become.'

Connie smiled. It was true that Elsie Lawson treated her almost as though she were another daughter, clucking round her when she visited in her fluffy mother-hen fashion, which secretly Connie adored, worrying about whether Connie was eating enough or working too hard.

'I'm not sure what time Harry will have off,' Mavis sighed. 'The Head of his House seems to be asking Harry to take on more and more responsibility. There will soon be a vacancy for the position of Assistant Housemaster, and Mr Cartwright has hinted to Harry that he is considering recommending him for it. If only he might, Connie. For not only would Harry get a rise in salary, he would also have more authority! It would be such a feather in his cap, and, of course, we all understand that he must work as hard as he can to prove to Mr Cartwright that he is worthy of his support.'

Connie kept her head bent, not wanting Mavis to know how relieved she was to hear that, if she went to New Brighton she would not see Harry. Relieved, and yet at the same time there was that unwanted, and very dangerous, little pang of something that was most definitely not relief!

'Vera came in today,' Mavis continued. 'I didn't see her, but Josie did.'

'I saw her as well,' Connie stopped her. 'She was wanting to know if she could come out with us.'

Mavis looked shocked. 'But she's married now.'

'That's exactly what I said to her,' Connie agreed briskly. 'But you know Vera.' Connie started to frown.

'Oh dear, I do hope that she isn't regretting marrying Bert,' Mavis replied.

The two young women exchanged looks.

'It seems such a long time ago now, since we all first came here and became friends,' Mavis sighed.

Christmas came and went, with Connie spending Christmas Day working, and having to forego the trip to New Brighton because of a sudden rush of emergencies.

Naturally she was disappointed, but a part of her was also relieved. She knew that there would have been a great deal of talk of Harry around the family dinner table, even though he himself would not have been there, and, just recently, Connie had had to catch herself up for the eagerness with which she was beginning to look forward to hearing Mavis talk about her brother. She could not afford that kind of silliness.

In truth, she was glad when Christmas was behind them, with its painful memories of her mother and the family life she had once enjoyed. It had been impossible for her not to think, too, of Ellie and the others, and to wonder sadly, as she had the previous year, if they were thinking of her.

January gave way to February, and then, in March, tragedy struck.

'Connie, I have had such bad news.'

Connie put down the apron she was folding, as

171

Mavis hurried into her room, her face pale and her voice shaking. There was a stark look of despair in her eyes.

For no reason she could account for, Connie's first thought was that something must have happened to Harry, but when she inadvertently put her hand to her mouth, and protested, 'Oh, Mavis, is it Harry?' Mavis shook her head immediately.

'No, it's not Harry! Connie, Mother has telephoned to say that Sophie has scarlet fever!'

'Oh, Mavis, no!'

Now Connie could fully understand the wretched note in Mavis's voice, and the look of sick worry in her eyes. Mavis started to cry, unable to contain her dread, and Connie instinctively put her arms around her.

She knew how close the whole Lawson family were, and she herself could hardly bear to think of Sophie suffering from such an awful disease.

'There are two others girls from her school who have it as well, and the doctor has given Mother instructions as to what she must do. She has already disinfected sheets and hung them at the window of her room, and over the door. I want so much to be there with them, Connie, but I can't! I used the last of my free days over Christmas and I cannot claim any more!'

'I am sure that your mother and the doctor will be doing everything that needs to be done, Mavis,' Connie tried to reassure her.

'Oh, yes. I know that, and I told Mother about bathing her and...' Mavis's voice was suspended, as her whole body shook with anguished sobs.

'I'm on duty in half an hour. I must go and tidy myself up. But, Connie, I am so afraid for Sophie. It is such a dreadful disease. So many of those who get it do not survive.'

'You must not think like that, Mavis,' Connie urged her, even though she knew what she was saying was true. 'You must be strong for Sophie's sake.'

But after Mavis had gone, a thoughtful look darkened Connie's eyes.

'You want to take all your remaining leave, now? But that is five days, Pride...'

'Yes, Sister,' Connie agreed.

'Is there any particular reason for this?' Sister was frowning, and Connie hesitated. Scarlet fever was a contagious disease and Connie felt sure that if Sister knew she was planning to go and nurse a victim of it, she would put her foot down and refuse to grant Connie her leave.

There had been an outbreak of it in Preston when Connie had been at school, and she could well remember her mother's fear when she had learned that the girl sharing a desk with Connie had been struck down with it. She had forced salt gargles, and worse, on Connie for days on end until she was sure the danger had passed.

'It is for family reasons, Sister,' Connie answered quietly. And, after all, that was the truth, even if the family was not her own, but Mavis's.

'Very well, then, Pride.'

There were other things Connie had to do, including making a visit to the Infirmary's dispensary.

The young man on duty grumbled as Connie told him what she wanted. 'It's for a friend,' she told him, when he had finished and handed her the bottles. 'So, shall I have to pay you?'

'So you shall, indeed,' he scowled disobligingly, 'wasting my time having me mixing private medications.'

Connie, already dressed in her coat and hat and with her bag packed, was waiting for Mavis when she came off her shift.

'Connie, where are you going?' Mavis demanded.

'To New Brighton,' Connie answered her calmly. 'You may not have any leave days left, Mavis, but I have five.'

'You are going to nurse Sophie!' Tears welled up in Mavis's eyes. 'Oh, Connie, I could not expect you to do that.'

'It isn't a matter of you expecting,' Connie told her firmly. 'It is a matter of me wanting to, Mavis. Sophie may be your sister, but she has become as dear to me as if she were mine.'

'Oh, Connie, if I cannot nurse Sophie myself, then to know that you will be with her is almost the same.'

'The same?' Connie teased her, deliberately trying to lighten the emotional mood. 'I'll have you know that Mr Clegg considers me to be one of his best nurses!'

When Connie arrived at the New Brighton house, she found Elsie Lawson almost on the point of collapse, through fear for her daughter, and the physical effort of looking after her, whilst trying to answer Great Aunt Martha's every querulous need.

'I daren't tell her about Sophie, Connie, in case she refuses to let us remain under her roof.'

'I am sure she would do no such thing!' Connie answered her stoutly. 'After all, if she did, she would be cutting her own nose off to spite her own face, for no one could make her more comfortable than you do. You must not be cross with her for doing so, but Mavis has told me herself how her great-aunt had used to employ a fresh person every six months because they were always giving her notice.'

'Oh, Connie, I cannot tell you how glad I am to have you here. When Mavis telephoned to say that you were coming, I knew that my prayers had been answered. Do you want to see Sophie now?'

'Not yet, I will change first if you don't mind,' Connie told her briskly, automatically assuming her nurse's manner, as she suggested that Elsie Lawson might instruct Cook to make them a pot of tea.

In reality, Connie wanted some time to herself to mix a disinfectant wash in which to soak some clean linen and some masks. If they were to care for Sophie in the best way they could, then it was imperative that they took every precaution with their own health.

Back downstairs, she explained this to Elsie Lawson, who immediately seized gratefully on her advice and told her, 'Oh, yes, Doctor Miles has said much the same thing.'

'And I have brought with me from the

Infirmary dispensary everything that I think we shall need. I do not wish to sound too officious, dear ma'am, but if I may suggest it, once you have taken me in to see Sophie, and she has accustomed herself to my being here, I think it would be a good idea if you were to go upstairs and rest for a while.'

'But what if Aunt Martha should ask for me?' Mavis's mother worried.

'If she does, then the maid will inform her that you have stepped out to go to the shops,' Connie told her calmly.

'Oh, Connie. You are such a tonic! Already I feel so much better!'

'Good. I am delighted to hear it.' Connie smiled. But whilst outwardly she might seem confident; inwardly, Connie recognised the moment she saw Sophie, how seriously ill she actually was. Not that she betrayed her feelings to Mavis's mother!

Sheets dipped in disinfectant had already been hung at the door, and as the doctor had instructed, everyone entering the patient's room had donned a cotton cloak which had also been soaked in the same preparation, in order to protect themselves from the disease.

But Connie decided to mix a stronger wash of her own, using the carbolic acid she had brought with her. At the same time, she mixed a little of the acid with water.

'What is that for?' Elsie Lawson demanded anxiously.

'I thought, ma'am, that we had agreed that you were going to rest.' Connie smiled at her.

'Connie, I cannot. Not whilst my poor child is suffering so dreadfully and in the gravest of danger. If she does not recover...'

'We must not think of that!' Connie insisted sternly. 'You have had much to bear, I know, but you must be strong for Sophie's sake. I have filled this jug with a mixture of carbolic acid and water, and it is for Sophie to gargle with. No one else must touch it, not even to wash it or refill it. I shall do that myself.'

'Dr Miles has left some Listerine spray for her throat,' Elsie broke in. 'But she hates it so, poor love, and protests that it makes her feel sick.'

Connie said nothing, knowing that the stronger medication she had mixed was even more likely to taste unpleasant.

'I shall take this up to her now, and I shall sit with her and see how she goes on. You must rest, dear ma'am,' she repeated firmly, smiling at Mavis's mother.

In the kitchen, Connie took one of the freshly soaked and wrung-out cotton sheets, cutting a hole in the middle of it and tugging it over her head. She then tied another piece of cotton around her head, and picked up a piece of disinfected cloth she had made into a protective mask for her nose and mouth. Then, she made her way upstairs.

As she had suspected, the sleep Sophie's poor mother had told her that their patient had slipped into, was more a state of feverish unconsciousness. After she placed a new sheet at the door, Connie took the old one back downstairs, and put it in a fresh tub of disinfectant solution.

She then made up a bowl of warm disinfectant water which she took back upstairs with her.

Mindful of Mr Clegg's insistence on absolute cleanliness whenever he performed any kind of operation, Connie washed her own hands again and then gently pulled back the bedcover from Sophie.

The flannelette nightdress Sophie's mother had told Connie the doctor had insisted she was to wear, was sticking to her skin, and Connie gently unfastened it and removed it. She carefully and thoroughly sponged Sophie's fevered body, with two different bowls of fresh water, before patting her dry and redressing her in a fresh nightgown.

Connie had given strict instructions that every piece of fabric which touched Sophie's skin was to be boiled and then soaked in disinfectant, and that everything worn by anyone who went into her room had to receive the same treatment, but separately from Sophie's own.

Sophie's long hair had become tangled and matted, and as she moved restlessly, Connie frowned. By rights her hair should be cut short, but Connie knew how she would feel were someone to do that to her. As a compromise, she dampened it with the disinfectant carbolic solution and plaited it, all the while talking soothingly to her patient.

Mr Clegg said that, although there was no medical proof of such a thing, he firmly believed that his patients could hear what he was saying, even under the direst of circumstances. He instructed all his nurses to talk only of hope for the patient's recovery and, automatically, Connie did the same thing now. Keeping up a gentle, low monologue whilst she busied herself making Sophie clean and comfortable. She had not, as yet, inspected her throat, which was where the real root of her illness lay – and the danger lay, as well.

Having removed the bowls of disinfectant and the dirty garments, Connie renewed her own protection and re-washed her hands before going back upstairs with her jug of carbolic acid and water, and a glass.

When she entered the room, Sophie's eyes were open but glazed and distant, and Connie knew that she did not recognise her.

Calmly, she approached the bed, and said gently, 'Sophie, it's me, Connie, and I am here to help nurse you.'

Sophie's tongue was pink and swollen, the infection giving off a noxious smell, the membranes of her throat swollen.

She was showing all the worst symptoms of the dreaded disease, Connie recognised. Her face was flushed, but she had the telltale pale area around her mouth that was one of the hallmarks of Scarlet Fever, along with a rash of spots. She looked, and was, very poorly, Connie acknowledged grimly. She could not, though, allow her personal anxiety for Sophie to affect her duties as a nurse!

At first Sophie refused to gargle, spitting the liquid out and shaking her head from side to side, but Connie persisted, and, in the end, her patience was rewarded. It would be hard for any mother, but especially one as loving and tender as Elsie Lawson, to have to perform such a task, Connie acknowledged, as she held Sophie whilst she vomited up the liquid she had swallowed.

'Oh, is it really you, Connie?' she demanded.

'Yes, it's me,' Connie assured her.

Later in the day, when the doctor called, he was openly relieved to find Connie in attendance on his patient.

'She should really have been admitted to an isolation ward, but the outbreak has been so severe that there are no spare beds. She hasn't reached the crisis point, as yet. You know what to look for, and what to do?' he demanded wearily.

Connie nodded her head.

'Perhaps she is better off being here than at the hospital. I have lost three young patients already this week,' he told Connie bleakly, as she followed him out of the room and they both removed their disinfected protective clothing. 'I shall leave you some peroxide of hydrogen which you can dilute to make a throat spray, if she gets worse.'

Connie said nothing. She knew that what he meant was 'when she gets worse'. She had seen in his eyes what he feared for Sophie, and with three children already dead, who could blame him.

'Connie, you need to rest as well. I can sit with Sophie during the day, surely?'

Connie put down the cup of tea she was drinking. It was three days since she had arrived, and she had been up each and every night, as well as most of the days caring for Sophie. But she knew that the crisis was approaching; and she knew she had to be there when it happened.

But rather than add to Elsie Lawson's anxiety, she simply said, 'I probably will have a nap later.'

'Mavis telephoned, and she said she had called Harry to tell him what has happened. I wish, really, she had not, because he will worry so – and there is nothing he can do.'

The Lawsons were fortunate in having a telephone, a luxury insisted upon by Great Aunt Martha who liked to be able to summon her own doctor whenever she chose.

'He would want to know, and feel hurt if you withheld the truth from him,' Connie told her gently.

'Can I go up and see Sophie?' Elsie asked her.

Connie hesitated. Perhaps it was better that Sophie's mother saw her now, rather than later, when the crisis would be at its peak.

'Dear ma'am, of course you may! You make me sound like a veritable dragon,' she teased her gently.

Sophie's glands were badly swollen and the thick, yellow membrane which had formed on her tonsils remained impervious to the spray Connie was using.

As the crisis approached, Sophie was growing weaker.

At least though, no one else in the household had succumbed to the illness, and Connie was tireless in her insistence on everyone maintaining the rigorous disinfecting procedures she had taught them.

'Connie, she looks so very much worse,' Elsie Lawson told her in an anguished whisper as she came out of the bedroom.

'Anyone would look unwell with this strong spring sunshine,' Connie answered her calmly.

Once inside the bedroom though, her own face registered her fear as she studied the sleeping girl.

The rash had gone now, but the danger was far from over. If the poison could not be cleared from her throat, Sophie would die. And, even if she survived, after having such a severe infection, there would be a risk of damage to her kidneys, and she could well be left with a weakness to her heart.

But although she was well aware of these risks, Connie refused to dwell on them, as she set about going through the same routine she had gone through since her arrival: bathing her patient, spraying her infected throat, sponging her down again, making sure she had something to drink.

The crisis came that night, with a sudden convulsion of the narrow, exhausted body, and a fit of vomiting followed by such a harsh rasping for breath that even Connie could barely endure to hear it.

'Mama,' Sophie croaked, and Connie immediately took her hand whilst ringing the small bell – a signal agreed between Connie and Mrs Lawson should either one of them need to summon the other.

Connie felt the fine draught of air as Elsie Lawson rushed into the room, but she did not relax her concentration on her patient.

'Oh no! My baby!' Mrs Lawson moaned, as she saw and heard what she had been dreading.

'Mama, I can see father,' Sophie whispered in a dry crackle of sound between laboured breaths.

'Oh, the poor child is delirious,' Elsie sobbed to Connie, but Connie didn't answer.

She couldn't because she was praying so hard that Sophie's words were not an indication that she was already slipping away from them. She had heard it from other nurses, and seen it for herself, that a patient in their last minutes would call out to a loved one gone before them.

'Your mama is here, Sophie,' Connie said firmly, stroking the thin hand, and all the time desperately aware of how shallow and frail the fluttering pulse was.

It would be so easy for it to stop altogether. Connie had seen it happen very many times. The one thing she must not do was to let Sophie slip into a deep sleep that could so easily become death.

'And so am I,' she told Sophie, determined to keep her awake. She tried frantically to think of some subject to talk about that would hold her interest. 'Do you remember how you said you wanted to go to the music hall? Well, when you are better, we shall take you.'

Sophie closed her eyes. 'I am so tired, Connie. I want to go to sleep.'

Connie could feel her hope draining away. Desperately, she refused to give in. There must be something she could say, some incentive she could offer, that would keep Sophie awake. And then she remembered. Sophie had begged and begged to have pierced ears, but, like Connie's own mother, Elsie Lawson had refused to give

183

her permission until Sophie was older. For some reason which Connie did not pretend to understand, it was not done for a young girl to have pierced ears unless she was from a Catholic family.

'Sophie,' she began urgently, 'do you remember how much you wanted to have your ears pierced? If you are very good and talk to me, then I promise you that you shall have them done just as soon as you are well enough!'

Anxiously Connie held her breath, but she might just as well not have spoken for all the response Sophie gave. She must stop Sophie from drifting into a coma. She must! Trying not to panic she began to talk again, 'Do you remember, too, last summer how we strolled down the pier and the wind buffeted our skirts and nearly stole my new hat? Soon it will be warm enough for us to do that again.'

The pulse was fading, and Connie felt despair fill her. She could not, she would not, give in and let her die.

She reached for the spray and opened Sophie's mouth, ignoring the moaned protest. In her attempt to stop her, Sophie's hand caught Connie's mask and it slipped from her face. But Connie refused to give in; her own nose and mouth exposed, she sprayed Sophie's throat thoroughly, not once, but twice.

Putting her lips to Sophie's ear, she whispered determinedly, 'Listen to me, Sophie. You will get better. You must get better. Your mama needs you. Your father wants you here with your mother, and Mavis will never be able to marry her Frank if you die, and Harry will...'

The thin pulse fluttered and died; the only sound in the room, the rattling of one long indrawn breath, and then silence.

From behind her, Connie heard Elsie Lawson cry out in anguished denial.

'No, Sophie! You are not to do this. You are not to die!' Connie insisted fiercely, 'You will not die, Sophie! Do you hear me?'

The seconds ticked by in the thick, smothering silence of the room, as death stole from the shadows.

'Sophie!' Connie leaned over her and gave the thin body a gentle shake. 'Sophie, listen to me.' Connie could taste her own defeat in the tears that ran down her face. 'Sophie, talk to me ... please...'

The sound of Elsie Lawson's grief filled the heavy silence.

Connie gripped the cold hand, and then froze in relieved disbelief as the still chest rose and fell, and a pulse jumped erratically beneath her thumb.

Two hours later, when Sophie was still breathing, and better than she had done in days, Elsie Lawson turned a pale, thin face toward Connie and announced emotionally, 'Connie, you are our saviour. But for you she would have died. You have saved her life, and with it mine...'

'All I've done is nurse her,' Connie protested, as they hugged one another and burst into relieved tears.

Although it was obvious that the crisis was

185

over, Connie insisted on remaining at her patient's bedside. It was there that Harry found her, grey-faced with exhaustion and looking far worse than Sophie, as he burst into his sister's bedroom, having feared the worst from the speechless tears with which his mother had greeted him.

'Harry.' Sophie's voice might be more of a croak than the sweet note of a songbird, but to Harry the sound of it was the best thing he had ever heard.

'Connie has saved my life,' Sophie whispered emotionally. 'I wanted to die but she wouldn't let me.'

Two pairs of brown eyes turned in Connie's direction: one brimming with tears, and warm with emotion; the other moist, but questioning.

'Sophie, you are exaggerating,' Connie responded briskly. 'All I have done is help to nurse you. And since you are now much better, I am going to leave you with your brother.'

But as Connie stood up, and moved away from the bed into the shadows of the hallway beyond, so too did Harry. He reached out to steady her as she swayed a little with her own exhaustion.

'I can never thank you enough for what you have done, Connie,' he told her emotionally. And then suddenly his own feelings overwhelmed him and he took hold of her.

Initially, all he had intended to do was just to hug her in fraternal gratitude, but he had misjudged both his self-control and the intensity of his longing for her.

She tilted her face up toward his in enquiry, lips

half-parted, and he was drawn helplessly toward her mouth. He was unable to stop himself from tasting its sweet softness, as he kissed her with a mixture of tender adoration, fierce longing, and gratitude.

The unexpectedness of his kiss caught Connie off guard, and to her own shock she could feel her mouth softening, clinging almost to Harry's, as though she were sweet on him and wanted him to know it!

Angry with both herself and with him, she pulled back from him hissing, 'Let go of me.'

'Connie, I'm sorry,' Harry apologised immediately, red-faced. 'I don't know what came over me.'

He was lying though, Harry acknowledged inwardly. He knew exactly what had come over him. And it was the same thing that came over him every damned time he saw her! But that was no excuse for him to have done what he had done.

'Well, you can't be as sorry as I am,' Connie retorted angrily. She could guess why he had done it and what he was thinking. After all, he knew the truth about her and her shameful secret past! And if he thought because of that, that he could treat her cheaply, and ... and force his attentions on her, then he was going to learn how wrong he was!

'And, if you think that because you saw ... that just because of what you know ... that, that gives you the right to...'

'Connie! No!' Harry stopped her in dismay. 'No. You don't understand ... I didn't mean. Connie, I know this isn't the time ... but ... I have to tell you that I hold you in the very highest regard, and that ... and that I have the tenderest of feelings for you, Connie. You are the sweetest and kindest of girls, and the prettiest. Every time I see you, I realise that the memories I have treasured of you do not do you justice.'

It was a relief to say what was in his heart, Harry acknowledged, and, for once, to ignore the stern voice in his head that told him that he must not think of Connie as anything other than his sister's friend. That voice told him, too, that he was simply not in a financial position to court a girl and marry her. Especially not a girl like Connie, when the nature of his chosen profession meant that he could not afford to have any kind of scandal attached to himself or his wife.

The emotions that had been building up inside him could not be repressed any longer. Secretly, he had been yearning for the longest time to tell Connie how he felt about her, and about the love he had kept in the most secret recesses of his heart.

A feeling that was both a pain, and a soaring wheeling arc of excited hope, was tightening Connie's chest and making it hard for her to breathe properly. Tears were stinging her eyes and she realised that she wanted, more than she had ever wanted anything, to allow herself to believe the sweetness of Harry's hesitant declaration. But how could she? She must not! She dare not! No man was ever going to take her in again with kisses and false words of love!

She must not listen to any more! Frantically she covered her ears with her hands and told him sharply, 'Stop, at once. You must not speak to me so! Do you think that I am really such a fool that I would believe such lies! Men are all the same! They think only of themselves and their ... their base needs and nothing of ... of the ... the hurt and ... shame they inflict on others through them!'

'Connie, I am not lying to you!' Harry protested. 'My feelings for you...' He hesitated, and then told her fiercely, 'My love for you is true and not false!'

'I do not believe you!'

Connie held her breath. Would he insist on repeating what he had said? Would he try to persuade her; convince her, that his declaration was serious? And if he did that, would she be able to find the strength to reject him a second time, or would those secret hidden feelings of her own – feelings she had not even allowed herself to acknowledge properly until now – have their way?

She was, Connie recognised, trembling on the brink of something so wonderful and precious, but at the same time so frightening that she hardly dared to breathe.

Harry went white. His words had been wrenched from his heart, and against the warnings of his head. They were the truth and not lies! It hurt his heart and his pride that Connie should refuse to believe him.

It was obvious that she did not feel the same way about him as he did her, he decided miserably.

'I apologise. I spoke out of turn. I had no right

189

... I shouldn't have said anything.'

The wooden voice; the way Harry was turning away from her without making any attempt to break down the barriers she had put up against him; without even trying to change her mind or convince her that he had truly meant what he had said, told their own story – at least so far as Connie was concerned. He did not love her at all, despite what he had claimed.

Bitterness and pain filled her, destroying the fragile bubble of joy that had shimmered inside her. If Harry had really loved her, he would have fought harder to convince her. The truth was that he had probably regretted his words as soon as he had uttered them, she told herself fiercely, and had been only too relieved to have her reject them.

Too upset to remain, she turned and hurried down the stairs.

Of course, word had got round the hospital about what Connie had done and she was summoned before Matron to explain herself.

'I understand that you wanted to help your friend, but did it occur to you to consider the risk you might be putting your colleagues and our patients under? And if you did not, why did you not? You realise that I shall have to insist on you being quarantined?'

Connie bit her lip. 'I observed all the safe practices, just as if I had been nursing a patient here in isolation,' she protested doggedly.

'I understand what you are saying, Pride, but you will present yourself in the isolation ward upon leaving here, and you will remain there until our Chief Medical Officer permits you to leave. You will, of course, not receive any pay during the time you are not working.'

Blindly Connie turned and walked through the door to where another nurse, heavily protected from any chance encounter with germs Connie might be carrying, was waiting to escort her to the isolation ward.

If she had been privy to Matron's thoughts though, she would not have been quite so down-hearted. Although Matron naturally had to think of the Infirmary first, inwardly she was aware that Connie had shown not just first-class nursing techniques, but also selfless dedication. She was, Matron decided, her bosom heaving with approval, an excellent example of the high standards and effectiveness of the Infirmary's teaching practices!

ELEVEN

'Harry, you aren't listening to me.'

Woodenly Harry tried to force himself to smile politely, as Rosa chided him and gave him a reproachful look.

The warm summer sunshine shone in through the windows of the stuffy parlour, and Harry suddenly longed sharply for the fresh salty air of New Brighton, and to be walking along the pier with his mother and his sisters. And Connie!

Connie! Just thinking about her brought a sharp ache of longing to his heart.

Her rejection of his foolish declaration of love still hurt him, but he acknowledged that he had, in part, only himself to blame. He should have courted her more gently, more slowly. Shown her that he respected as well as loved her.

Were the world privy to what he knew about her, it may well make a different judgement, and one that would reflect badly on him, as well as Connie herself. But he no longer cared. There were other schools where he could teach – not as highly acclaimed perhaps, but they would have one another and somehow they would manage.

Lost in his own dreams, Harry was barely aware of the angry grimness in Rosa's eyes as she watched him. He was not behaving as she had planned for him to do. And yesterday she had received a letter from her cousin Gerald's sister, Phyllis, confiding to her that she was sure that her brother was about to propose to the heiress he had been pursuing. Which meant that she had to move fast if she were to announce her own engagement first, as she was determined to do.

Phyllis had no idea of Rosa's feelings for her brother, or of her already considerably intimate involvement with him. Those secret meetings, and stolen kisses and caresses, were known only to the two of them for obvious reasons, and her frequent visits to see her 'dearest' cousin, had been little more than a device to enable her to be with Gerald.

She couldn't understand why on earth Harry was taking so long to propose to her. After all, she had given him enough hints and opportunities. She couldn't afford to waste any more time though. She would have to take matters into her own hands now.

Fixing a smile on her lips, she began sweetly, 'Papa has been asking me if you have yet made a formal declaration to me, Harry! He will be very angry with you if he thinks you are trifling with my affections, and indeed he has told me that he is disappointed that you are being such a laggard, and so am I.'

Whilst she was speaking she had placed her hand on his arm, and Harry had had to control an ungentlemanly desire to shake it off. Now he could feel the shock surging through his body like ice water freezing his veins. The tiny hairs at the back of his neck lifted, as he struggled to make sense of what Rosa was saying.

How on earth could half a dozen forced and uncomfortable meetings between them; meetings which had been forced upon him by Rosa's own father, possibly constitute any attempt to trifle with Rosa's affections? There was nothing about Rosa he had any desire whatsoever to trifle with, Harry acknowledged guiltily. In fact, if anything, what he felt toward her was something much closer to wary distaste than desire.

For all her outward docility and sweetness, Rosa had an implacably strong will, and could produce hysterical outbursts of shattering intensity whenever she was thwarted. To Harry, she was a duty her father had thrust on him, and one he felt increasingly burdened with. Rosa's announcement appalled him, and his first instinct was to roundly and soundly contradict her words. But Harry had a gentle soul and had been brought up to be good-mannered, and thoughtful of the feelings of others. Even so...

'Rosa, I have behaved toward you with propriety at all times,' he told her firmly. 'And I am sure that your father knows this. After all, it was at his suggestion that–'

'Harry, what are you saying?' she interrupted him immediately, her voice starting to rise as she added, 'you know how much I love you. And you have made me believe that you return my feelings!'

She had started to tremble and her eyes were filling with tears.

Why on earth was he being so difficult, Rosa wondered angrily. Surely he must know how very fortunate he would be to get someone like her for his wife. He was the poorest of all the teachers, with no income other than what he earned, whereas she – whilst according to Gerald, not a wealthy heiress – did have an allowance from her father and an income from the money left in trust for her by her mother.

Marriage to her would greatly enhance his financial position and his status within the school, and were it not for her all consuming desire to get back at Gerald, there was no way she would consider him as a husband.

That he should seem so unaware and appreciative of his good fortune was fostering resentment inside her that she was finding hard to contain. It was, she decided furiously, a great pity that she couldn't find a more suitable candidate for the role of her husband!

The plain truth was that Rosa was used to getting her own way. She had learned young that the merest hint of a temper tantrum from her was enough to have her father cravenly giving in to her. Gerald, of course, had been totally impervious to such manipulation, but Rosa had believed that Harry was made of much weaker, and far more gentlemanly, stuff than her cousin.

Gerald she knew, for instance, would have no qualms whatsoever about forcing his heiress into marriage by compromising her, if he had to; just as he had had no qualms about seducing Rosa, and then laughing at her when she had let him see that she had expected a proposal.

Harry could feel his discomfort growing, and to his shame, with it, his panic. He felt as though he was being sucked down into a frighteningly dangerous quicksand from which there was no escape. Behind the emotion in Rosa's eyes he could see a sharp gleam of hard calculation, which alarmed him even more.

'You must not tease me so, Harry,' she told him determinedly. 'How can you be so cruel? I know you love me. Do you think I would have allowed you the liberties I have, if you didn't?'

Harry stared at her. What on earth was she talking about? There had been no 'liberties' either taken or wanted, even if he had been forced into Rosa's company by her father's insistence that he helped Rosa with her plans to impress the parents of their pupils.

'Do you think my father would have allowed us to be alone together if he did not think of you as my fiancé?' she continued, pressing home her advantage. 'If you do not propose to me now, Harry, you will be totally disgraced. My father will see to that!'

Rosa cast him a reproachful look.

'You should have proposed to me at Christmas. I was expecting you to do so, and so was my father! Everyone was expecting you to do so, Harry,' she told him dramatically, and Harry felt untruthfully, 'and you have shamed me by not doing.'

Propose to Rosa? There was only one woman he wanted to make his wife! Harry tried to think of Connie behaving as Rosa was doing but it was impossible to imagine Connie playing out such a role. Connie. How his heart ached with love for her! As it would never ever ache with love for Rosa.

He took a deep breath. This whole ridiculous business had to stop right now. 'Rosa. Please listen to me. I beg you to...' He was trying to be gentle, but as he struggled for the right words she suddenly flew toward him and gripped hold of his gown. Her waiting ears had caught a sound that Harry's had not – her father was approaching.

'No, Harry. I beg *you*,' she interrupted him passionately. 'I beg you not to deny my love. You must not deny me. I shall not let you!'

As he opened his mouth to protest, to Harry's shock, Rosa suddenly pressed her own mouth hotly and intimately against his. Harry felt his whole body stiffen in rejection, but Rosa continued to press herself up against him.

'Dear me! I trust this tender scene I am inter-rupting means that I am about to receive a request from you for my daughter's hand, Harry.'

Harry went cold as, as though on cue, Rosa's father walked into the room.

He was a charitably minded young man but he could not help noticing the gleaming look of triumph Rosa cast him, as she stepped demurely away from him.

'Harry has just asked me to be his wife, Father, and was about to seek you out.'

'I should hope so, indeed,' Mr Cartwright agreed sternly, before adding, 'Harry, you may present yourself to me in my study before you leave.'

Harry listened in disbelief. This couldn't be happening!

But it was, and as he looked into the faces of the Head of House and his daughter, Harry was filled with the heart-sinking realisation that he was caught in a trap from which, as a gentleman, there was no possible escape.

A little enviously Connie paused as she crossed the busy entrance hall. Outside the sun was shining brightly, and she had just seen Mavis saying an obviously reluctant goodbye to Frank.

Sometimes just recently, it seemed to Connie that everyone she knew, apart from herself, was courting, and all the rumours that there could soon be a war had not helped. Young lovers were rushing to marry for fear of being parted.

Even Josie had confided blushingly to them the previous week that she had been asked out. ''E's nobbut a delivery lad, like. He delivers me aunt's bread.'

197

'Well if you like him, Josie, there's no reason why you should not go out with him,' Mavis had assured her in a kind motherly voice, before adding firmly, 'but you mustn't let him take any kind of liberties with you.'

'Oh no, Ted's not that sort,' Josie had assured her quickly. 'But if there is to be a war and he gets to be called up...'

'We don't know that there is to be a war yet, Josie,' Connie had told her sharply, 'and if there is to be one, somehow I don't think His Majesty will be needing the likes of a baker's lad, not when he's got so many fine soldiers to call on.'

Josie had bristled a little at Connie's dry comment, but, as Connie had confided to Mavis later, she didn't want Josie doing something she might regret, because she thought her admirer was going to be called for a soldier.

'Everyone says that if there is to be a war then it will be over within weeks,' Connie had reminded Mavis.

'Oh, Connie, I do hope it doesn't come to that,' Mavis had responded. 'When one sees some of the poor soldiers from the Crimea.'

They had both fallen silent, thinking about the limbless men who sold matches on street corners, in an effort to earn a few shillings. Sometimes little more than rags were wrapped around the stumps of their amputated arms or legs, and there was always somehow a look in their eyes that made one want to hurry away.

She wouldn't have anyone thinking that she was envious because her friends were walking out with someone, and she wasn't, Connie decided, tossing her head a little. Because she wasn't. Not for one single minute!

Mavis had seen her and was making her way over to her, beaming happily. 'Connie, it's the most beautiful day,' she announced dreamily.

'You'd think any day was beautiful if you were going out with your Frank. I reckon you think the sun shines out of his backside,' Connie teased Mavis earthily. 'Time was, when all we ever heard of you was, Harry this, and Harry that, and now that brother of yours might just as well not exist, because it's all Frank says, Frank thinks...'

No sooner was Harry's name out of her mouth than Connie wondered angrily what on earth had made her utter it. The last thing she wanted was to have Mavis thinking she was sweet on her brother! If she did, she was bound to say something to him, and then he might start thinking that she, Connie, was regretting the way she had turned him down. And then he might...

Well, whatever he might do, she wasn't interested! All men were the same so far as she was concerned. You couldn't trust a one of them, no matter how much they sweet-talked you, Kieron had proved that to her!

Unaware of Connie's unhappy thoughts, Mavis was both blushing and laughing at the same time, as she tried to look prim.

'For your information, the reason I haven't mentioned Harry recently is because he's been so busy that he's barely had time to telephone or write home, never mind visit. We all know that it's because his Housemaster thinks so highly of him that he gives Harry so much extra responsibility,

199

but I know, too, that although she doesn't say so, Mother misses seeing him. I shall ask Mama to tell Harry that you were asking after him though, Connie.'

'No ... no you mustn't do that.'

When Mavis stared at her, Connie amended hurriedly, 'What I mean is, that I wouldn't want your brother to think I was being critical of him for not coming home more frequently, Mavis. After all, it's nothing to me what he chooses to do!' she added sharply.

What on earth had made her say that? Connie was furious with herself. Why should she be interested in Harry? She wasn't. Not one little bit! Anyone would think she was regretting having turned him down, and she wasn't. After all, she had given him a chance to reassure her and he hadn't taken it, had he? And she knew why! It was because he had been lying about loving her in the first place! How could he really love her, knowing what he did about her? How could any decent young man?

She only had to think about what their own mother would have had to say if John, for instance, had brought home a girl with a past like Connie's. She wouldn't even have been allowed in over the doorstep!

And folks – families – did ask questions when one of their number made plans to wed. Vera had told them all, in an aggrieved voice, how many questions she had been asked by Bert's mother and grandmother. 'Nosy pair!' she had told them, tossing her head.

'We've both got time off at the end of August,

Connie, and I was hoping that you would come to New Brighton with me,' she heard Mavis saying placidly, as she finally managed to drag her thoughts away from her friend's brother. 'I know that Mother and Sophie are longing to see you, and Sophie hasn't forgotten that, thanks to you, Mother has agreed that she may have her ears pierced.'

Immediately Connie's expression softened. 'Sophie has written to me to tell me that she's grown nearly three inches, and that soon she will be nearly as tall as your mother.'

'Oh, Connie!' Emotional tears filled Mavis's eyes. 'None of us will ever forget that, but for you, she would not be here.'

'That's nonsense,' Connie told her bracingly. 'I nursed her, that's all. Anyone...'

'No,' Mavis stopped her fiercely. 'You saved her life, Connie. You will come to New Brighton with me, won't you?'

'Oh, go on then. I'll be needing a bit of bracing fresh air by then, especially seein' as Vera caught me at a weak moment, and I've promised to have tea with her on me next full day off.' She pulled a wry face. 'Like as not she'll be on at me to go out dancing with her – Josie said that she was trying to persuade her to go out with her last Saturday night,' Connie added.

'I know,' Mavis agreed. 'And I told Josie she should remind Vera that she's a married woman now, with a husband to take her out.'

'Yes, and that, unlike her, we are on our feet all day long, not sitting on our backsides. I thought they had us working hard in our first year, Mavis, but that was nothing to what we have to do now. Sister has me working flat out from the minute I get on the ward – and she's got me looking after the new First Years,' Connie complained.

'That's because she knows what a good nurse you are, Connie,' Mavis comforted her, loyally, knowing that it was the truth.

'If you say so, Mavis,' Connie teased her. 'But it doesn't stop my poor feet aching fit to burst out of my shoes!'

They talked for several minutes about their work, and then Connie exclaimed, 'It's coming up for your birthday in September. I expect that Frank will be popping the question then, and giving you a ring.'

Mavis blushed and laughed, and then shook her head, but before she could say anything, another nurse came over to join them, putting an end to their private conversation.

'Ah, there you are, Pride. We've had a new admission whilst you were off duty. A stab wound. He was lucky that Mr Clegg was here and was able to deal with it promptly, otherwise he would have more than likely bled to death. As it is, his breathing isn't very good, and he's going to need careful watching.'

'I'll keep my eye on him, Sister,' Connie responded dutifully and calmly, her hands folded neatly in front of her stiffly starched apron, as she stood waiting to receive the Ward Sister's instructions. The two new First Years were standing next to her, and Connie could feel their awe and their apprehension.

It seemed such a long time ago now since she herself had been in their shoes, and after Sister had dismissed them, Connie gave the bolder of the First Years a warning frown as one girl immediately started to hurry away.

'No running, Nurse,' she reminded her sharply, whilst secretly she couldn't help comparing them to how she herself had been. She smiled ruefully, remembering her impetuosity of those days, shaking her head a little over her youthful folly.

Tonight was her first night on night duty, after two weeks on days, and automatically Connie paused to check the corners of the beds to see that the sheets and blankets were straight and tight.

'You know that new patient who was stabbed,' the other First Year told Connie excitedly. 'He's a real bad lot, by all accounts, and should have bin left to die and not had his life saved. Leastways, that's what I heard Sister saying. Seems like he's been goin' around terrorising folk and threatening them, and now he's got his comeuppance. Sister said as how it was a crying shame that whoever stabbed him didn't do the job properly.

'Sister knows all about him, on account of her cousin, who runs a pub down on the dockside. He was beaten nearly senseless by the gang of thugs this chap runs because he wouldn't pay him protection money to leave his pub alone. Sister says it isn't right that someone like 'im should go around threatening decent law-abiding folk, and getting away wi' it like 'e's bin doing, and that if she 'ad her way...'

'You are here to work, Nurse. Not to gossip,'

Connie stopped her firmly, well aware that the two girls were pulling faces at her behind her back, in the belief that she didn't know. After all, hadn't she and Vera and Josie, and even Mavis, at times, done exactly the same thing!

The new patient might be a thoroughly bad lot but it was still her duty to nurse him, Connie reminded herself. She sent the two First Years about their business and made her way to the last bed, and pulled back the screen. She could hear the laboured sound of the man's breathing as it faltered unsteadily, warning Connie that Sister had been right when she had said that he would need careful watching. He might have survived his wound and his blood loss, but that rasping, tortured breathing said that he was by no means out of danger.

Connie stepped up to the bed and then froze, as recognition washed sickly over her.

Fear and loathing filled her. She wanted to turn and run like the girl she had been; would have done, but she was not that girl any more, she reminded herself fiercely. She forced herself to stay where she was and look down into the unconscious face of the man who still haunted her worst nightmares.

Bill Connolly moved restlessly and turned his head to one side, coughing up blood. His open mouth was pressed against the pillow, obstructing his breathing. Automatically Connie reached out, intending to remove the pillow and lift his head so that he could breathe properly. And then stopped.

Was it right that a wicked evil man like Bill Connolly should be helped to live to inflict misery and pain on others? He was already struggling to breathe, his efforts to drag air into his lungs simply pressing his mouth deeper into the pillow. It would ultimately smother him unless she removed it, and helped him.

Could fate have deliberately handed him over to her?

Slowly and purposefully, Connie reached out to the pillow. It was already covering his mouth. All she had to do was to move it higher to cover his nose. His own weakness would do the rest. She didn't even need to be here.

She could hear another patient further down the ward moaning and calling out for her. All it would take was one firm push and a handful of seconds. Then she could leave, and when she came back it would all be over. It couldn't be wrong, surely, to rid the world of a man like this one. Even Sister had said that Bill Connolly didn't deserve to live.

Connie closed her eyes, her hand resting motionless on the edge of the bed. How long was it since he had taken that last dragging breath? The cries of the other patient were becoming louder and more demanding. Bill Connolly had rolled over and his face was totally buried in the pillow. She didn't need to do anything other than just walk away.

Tears welled in her eyes and her hand started to tremble. Swiftly she reached for the pillow and wrenched it away, turning him back onto his back as she did so, one of her own tears splashing down on her hand.

She couldn't do it! She just could not do it.

Something in her was filled with revulsion at the mere thought of taking his life, never mind actually doing it. And it was not just that her training was overwhelming her own feelings, Connie admitted. She could not stand by and see a man die, not even when that man was *this* one – and she certainly could not take a life, no matter how much a part of her wished that she could.

She cleaned away the blood mechanically, and waited until his breathing had steadied.

Ten minutes later, as she attended to the other patient, her hands were still shaking.

'Oh, Connie, I am so looking forward to this weekend! It's the first Bank Holiday we've had off in ages. I hope we get good weather, we should do since it's the end of August. I've promised Sophie that we'll take her on the pier. Oh, and I almost forgot, Harry is coming home – not for the full weekend, just for the day.'

They were on the baggage ferry, hanging onto the side, the wind blowing their thin summer dresses against their bodies, and tousling their hair.

Connie raised her hand to her hair, as her heart jerked like a child's toy on a string at the mention of Harry's name.

'Frank is coming over as soon as he comes off duty and I thought the four of us, me and Frank, and you and Harry could p'raps go out for a bit of something to eat together.'

Connie said nothing but her smile curved her mouth, and her eyes were sparkling.

'Mavis! Connie! You're here at last.'

Sophie had been right about how much she had grown, Connie reflected, as she returned the younger girl's loving hug, and teased, 'Miss Impatience!'

Elsie Lawson looked tired and slightly strained though, and Connie could feel Mavis's anxiety as she, too, looked at her mother.

'Has Harry arrived yet?' Connie heard her demanding, as she finished hugging her mother.

'Yes! He got here about an hour ago.'

'What, and he didn't come down to walk us home?'

'He had... That is ... there was something he wanted to tell me...'

A curious sense of foreboding iced down Connie's spine.

'The very best of news, my dears. Harry has become engaged to the Housemaster's daughter, Miss Rosa...'

Harry was engaged. Shock, followed by anger, followed by a sharply unbearable pain caused Connie's heart to thump in huge hurting thuds. So she had been right all along! He had not meant a single word of what he had said to her! Either that, or he had very quickly switched his affections to someone else, Connie acknowledged cynically.

Well, she hoped he wasn't going to expect her to congratulate him! She certainly pitied the poor girl who had been so taken in by him, though. Had she been able to do so, she would have turned round and made her way straight back to

207

the hospital, but of course she couldn't, not without having Mavis, his mother and Sophie wondering what on earth was going on.

Perhaps she ought to tell them. That would show him up for what he really was! But of course they would never believe her. To them Harry was perfect, and no doubt to his new fiancée as well! Had he said the same words to her as he had to Connie? Had he told her that she was the sweetest, the kindest, and the prettiest girl he knew? Connie nearly cried out at the pain that gripped her heart.

No, she wasn't hurt! She didn't care like that; she wasn't really thinking that, if she hadn't rejected him, she could have been the one calling herself his fiancée!

She could hear Mavis and her mother talking about the engagement. Mavis's voice was full of sisterly curiosity and excitement.

'Harry's engaged! I can hardly believe it! He has never so much as mentioned anything, or given us any kind of hint! What a dark horse he is.'

'They are to be married before the new term starts,' Sophie broke in importantly. 'In the school chapel. We are to be bridesmaids, Mavis, and Miss Cartwright has sent with Harry some fabric patterns for us to see. She has chosen palest blue for our dresses.'

Connie had started to shiver. Her throat felt raw and her head was pounding. She must be coming down with a summer cold, she told herself numbly.

Harry was going to be married. Harry who had

kissed her... Harry who was now, quite obviously, saving all his kisses for someone else. Someone else who he was going to marry. Miss Rosa Cartwright! And Harry was going to marry her.

'I still cannot believe that this is happening,' Mavis announced sitting down, a little later. 'I have not even met Miss Cartwright, and yet she is to be my new sister...'

'She has written me the sweetest of letters,' Elsie continued, 'begging me not to be cross with her for taking Harry from us, and saying that she longs to meet us all. She wants me to be a mother to her, since she has lost her own mother. She says that she knows she will love all of us because Harry loves us; and she loves him so much that she could not endure to live without him. She says she loves him so much that she cannot bear to be apart from him, not even for the shortest time.

'And, of course, there is no reason why they should wait to marry. Everything has been arranged. After they are married, Harry will move in with Rosa and her father, so that Rosa can still run her father's household for him.'

For the first time since she had met Mavis's family, Connie felt like an outsider, excluded from their shared excitement and family intimacy.

'Oh, I can't wait to meet her. Did Harry bring a photograph with him?' Mavis asked her mother.

'I haven't had time to ask him yet, but Rosa had sent me one with her letter.'

'Oh, Mama, quickly let me see it please,' Mavis begged. Connie told herself that she wouldn't look, but somehow her gaze was drawn to the photograph Mavis was holding. The image looking back at her, showed a very pretty young girl, her curls threaded artlessly with pink ribbon, whilst her eyes held a look of vulnerability and innocence.

'How sweet she looks!' Mavis exclaimed.

'She is very pretty,' Sophie announced.

Connie couldn't say anything.

She was as much shocked by her own feelings as she was by the news of Harry's engagement. How could she have known she would feel like this? As though something had gone from her life that could never be replaced... As though she had suffered a dreadful loss.

Technically at least, she had been the one to reject Harry, and not the other way around, Connie reminded herself fiercely.

Upstairs in his attic bedroom, Harry could not find solace and comfort amongst the books and small personal treasures – mementoes of his father, in the main – which he kept there.

Normally, he spent the first private hour of his return to his family up here, enjoying his personal transformation from a poorly paid and junior schoolmaster of no account, to a son and brother who was very deeply loved.

Normally, too, he looked forward, and longed for, his rare visits home – but not this time. In fact he had dreaded the event, and finding that Connie was here had made it a hundred, no, Harry mentally corrected himself bitterly, more like a thousand times worse than his worst imaginings.

His mother had done her best, as he had known she would, but beneath her immediate warm acceptance of his engagement, he had seen quite clearly her hurt and confusion. She must be wondering why he had not mentioned Rosa in his letters; why he had not taken her home to introduce her to his family. But how could he tell his mother the truth, when he knew that knowing it would only hurt and distress her even more.

The now familiar feeling of black despair burned angrily inside him. His future, his life, was trapped in the sickly morass of dramatic emotion and outright lies Rosa had deliberately concocted, and there was no way out for him. Not now. Not ever.

On the third finger of her left hand Rosa was now wearing the diamond ring which had been her mother's engagement ring. It was a decision she had taken herself, without discussing it with him, announcing that people would expect her to be wearing a ring – and that she would have to wear her mother's, seeing as he had not bothered to buy her one.

As always when he had to talk to her now, Harry had been overwhelmed by a mixture of anger against her; compassion for her; and the shocking awareness that, intellectually, they were on two different planes, with a chasm between them so deep and wide it could never be bridged.

Rosa obviously thought nothing of wearing a ring it was clear he could never have afforded to buy her. Had he really loved her her decision would have been a bitter blow to his pride, but she seemed oblivious to that fact.

'Father is to see the Headmaster and request that you are appointed as his deputy, Harry. It is unthinkable that I should be expected to live on the miserly sum you earn – even with us living here with Father.' She had given a trill of laughter as she added, 'Goodness, my allowance is nearly twice as much as you earn!'

Rosa's father had already dropped several hints to Harry that his daughter had inherited, through her mother, a respectable sum of money which she would receive on her thirtieth birthday, and that, moreover, Mr Cartwright himself paid her an allowance, 'a trifling amount for her fripperies'.

In the eyes of the world he would be making an advantageous marriage, Harry recognised bitterly, but in his own eyes; in his own heart; there was no advantage at all in binding himself to a woman he did not love and could never love.

He was committed to Rosa now though. In her eyes, in the eyes of the world, and now in the eyes of his family, too.

'Connie, my umbrella!'

Although Connie made a valiant bid to grab hold of Sophie's umbrella, the wind caught it and turned it inside out, dragging it from her grasp. It was soon sailing over the pier and across the waves.

'I'm afraid you've lost it, Sophie,' Mavis sympathised, as she cuddled closer to Frank under the much stouter brolly he was holding.

'Urgh, some Bank Holiday this has been...' Sophie complained, as the four of them huddled together trying to seek shelter from the heavy rain.

It was 4th of August, the Tuesday following the Bank Holiday Monday – Mavis and Connie having arranged to extend their short holiday by an extra day.

'I'm wet and I'm cold,' Sophie grumbled.

'Come on, there's a café not far away. Let's go and get a pot of tea and some teacakes. My treat!' Frank suggested.

As Sophie slipped her cold hand into Connie's own, Connie tried to summon a cheerful smile for the younger girl's sake. But the truth was that it wasn't just the awful weather that had lowered her spirits.

The previous evening, after dinner, his mother and two sisters had plied Harry with questions about his wife-to-be, whilst Connie had sat silently, wishing herself a thousand miles away – just as she was sure Harry had been doing, to judge from the discomfort she had seen in his face. In the end, unable to bear it any longer, she had excused herself saying that she had a headache. But first she had made sure that she had openly, and publicly, congratulated Harry on his good fortune in securing Rosa's hand. Connie wasn't going to have him thinking she was having second thoughts.

They had just reached the end of the pier, when Sophie tugged excitedly on her arm and called out, 'Look, here comes Harry!'

Immediately Connie's heart turned over and for a moment she was tempted to do as Sophie was doing, and run toward him.

'He looks very serious. I expect it's because he's missing Rosa,' Mavis whispered to Connie.

'Then perhaps he should have brought her home with him to introduce her to your mother,' Connie couldn't resist replying tartly.

She had seen how, behind her loving smile, Elsie Lawson was secretly disappointed to have received the news of Harry's engagement without having met his wife-to-be. Privately Connie thought it thoughtless and selfish of the couple not to have considered, in the midst of their own excited happiness, Elsie Lawson's feelings. And now, no doubt, Harry would be wanting to talk about his wretched fiancée again!

'Harry, you are just in time to join us for tea,' Frank announced jovially.

Immediately Harry shook his head. 'No thanks. I am glad I have found you though. There is the gravest news.'

'Oh Harry, what is it?' Mavis demanded anxiously.

'Mr Asquith has just announced that there is to be War!'

PART TWO

TWELVE

Spring 1916

Bodies:

They were everywhere. All the time. Her hands, her skills, her time and those of her fellow nurses – no matter how fast and ceaselessly they worked – were just not enough to stem the unending tide of them. Some of them still alive; some of them not; but all of them hideously, horrifyingly damaged and wounded, so that the stench of gangrenous flesh and gas-damaged rotting lungs was one that filled Connie's days and nights.

The War, which so many had believed, as Mr Asquith had predicted, would only last a handful of weeks, was in its second year with no end in sight. Those who had stoutly believed and supported Lord Kitchener's harsh warning that it would be a long and bloody business, had been proved right.

The Infirmary had become a hospital for wounded soldiers from local regiments, its wards crammed and overflowing.

Connie was glad that she was working on Mr Clegg's ward – there at least, once they had passed through his caring and skilled hands, although they might be without a limb, the soldiers did stand a good chance of survival.

On the other wards lay men in the most pitiful condition, who no amount of skilled surgery or nursing could restore to health; some of these men had been exposed to gas attacks – and Connie's heart wept when she heard the tales of how, without gas masks to protect them, the first wave of men had faced attack with nothing more than handkerchiefs and cloths to cover their faces.

And then there were other men, separated when they could be from their fellows, and whom no one talked about: men with their minds destroyed by the War; and who ranted day and night, sobbing and sometimes screaming about the horrors of the trenches.

It took nerves of steel to nurse these poor creatures, but both Connie and Mavis had volunteered for extra duty in order to do so.

Regular shifts were something that had become almost forgotten, as every nurse who could went on duty so that she could be there to receive the wounded when they arrived off the trains.

Solemnly by night, the trains brought an unending line of grey-faced, exhausted, injured men – and, more often than not, the bodies of those who had been alive at the start of the journey, but who had not survived it.

Connie couldn't count the number of times she had heard a Tommy telling her brusquely, with tears running down his face, 'I knew he was a goner, Nurse, but I 'ad to bring him 'ome. It was what 'e would have wanted, aye, and me, too. I couldn't leave 'im there to die in the mud.'

And so the bodies were taken and cleaned and

laid out – all of which took up precious nursing time, but no nurse trained under Matron's regime would have thought of denying a dead soldier this last respect.

'Connie, over here,' she heard Mavis calling out wearily to her, as she held on to her supper tray and looked round to find somewhere to sit.

She and Mavis were lucky if they saw one another in passing these days, and she gave her friend a warm smile as she sat down beside her.

'Sorry if I don't stay long – we're expecting another trainload tonight. We've got the ward so full of truckle beds you can hardly move, and Mr Clegg is concerned that having so many wounded men in such close proximity might lead to the spread of infection – so we're double-scrubbing everything and everyone.'

'Sometimes, Connie, I think this War is not going to end until every single able-bodied man is either dead or wounded,' Mavis responded sadly. 'I swear I can smell putrid flesh in my sleep.'

'How is your great-aunt?' Connie asked her, deliberately changing the subject.

'Her heart is getting weaker, but Mother nurses her so devotedly her doctor says she will probably outlive us all.'

'Like Frank's mother?' Connie suggested drily, and then wished she had been more tactful as she saw Mavis's eyes fill with tears.

'Connie, she is so very angry with me. Now that the Government have brought in the conscription bill, she wants me and Frank to get married quickly, as married men are exempt for conscription. But neither Frank nor I feel that it would be morally right to do something like that. As a policeman, he isn't subject to conscription anyway – although at Christmas he confessed to me that he feels that he should join up,' she admitted heavily.

Connie gave her a sympathetic look. Mavis, like many other nurses, had chosen to put her marriage plans on one side so that she could continue nursing, and because she felt the help she could give others was more important than her own personal happiness.

'I know how torn he feels. His conscience is urging him to serve our country, but he also has his mother to think of.'

'And not just his mother, Mavis, he has you to consider, as well,' Connie reminded her fiercely.

'I would not hold him back, Connie. Even though what we see here in the wards makes me so very afraid for him.' Mavis gave a small shudder. 'One sees the merest boys – for they are no more, Connie, you know that – pitifully wounded and yet so grateful for what little we can do for them, and so proud to have given their best.'

Their best, and in so many cases their health and their lives, Connie acknowledged inwardly.

'I saw Josie the other day. She has gone so thin, Connie.'

'You cannot know how much I wish I had not made that cruel comment about Ted,' Connie admitted in a low voice.

Immediately Mavis covered Connie's hand with her own and the two friends exchanged understanding looks.

Ted, the delivery boy, had joined up in the first wave of enthusiastic volunteers. He had also been in the first wave of men to be gassed by the Germans.

He and Josie had been married within days of his return home, a sad, quiet, little wedding conducted more as though it was an occasion for mourning rather than one for celebration.

Josie had been devotedly nursing him ever since, lovingly tending the body that was now merely a rotting carcass, whilst Ted died slowly and painfully in the narrow bed they had never been able to share.

All over the country there were thousands of other Teds and thousands of other Josies too.

'Have you heard anything of Vera?' Connie asked.

'Josie said she was still working at the armaments factory, so far as she knew.'

'And your family? Everything's all right with them?' Connie asked, as casually as she could.

Try as she might, she couldn't say Harry's name. She hadn't attended his wedding, even though Mavis had pleaded with her to do so, insisting that she couldn't possibly ask for extra time off.

The wedding had taken place in the chapel at the school and had, according to Sophie, been the most wonderful affair.

'It is such a pity you could not be there,' she had told Connie. 'Rosa is the most lovely person. She told Mother that she had fallen in love with Harry the moment she first saw him, and it is as plain as plain that he feels the same way about her.'

Even now Connie could still feel the searing stab of pain she had felt listening to Sophie's excited revelations. How could she love Harry so deeply when loving any man was the last thing she wanted? When she knew that neither he, nor any other man, was worth loving? And knowing that, why couldn't she be strong enough to stop loving him? Why wasn't the fact that he had so easily overcome his supposed feelings for her, to turn to and marry someone else, making her feel glad that she had realised her own vulnerability and turned her back on him?

Connie had thought she had learned the folly of loving another human being. She had lost her mother; seen her family torn apart by her aunts; experienced the desolation of having her father turn his back on his children; felt the shock and despair of her elder sister's betrayal. And then, when she had believed she had found the love that would make her world right again, she had discovered that what she had so foolishly believed was love had been nothing of the sort. She had told herself that she was far better off without love – and she had believed it.

She still believed it, she told herself fiercely, but that belief could not stop the pain she was feeling. A pain so intense that she could scarcely endure so much as to hear the sound of Harry's name. Her only comfort was that no one else knew of her feelings, not even Mavis her closest friend, and certainly not Harry himself! After all, it was too late for her to long for things to be different now, Harry was married to someone else.

Yet it hurt so much having to listen to Sophie singing Harry's wife's praises, whilst she herself burned with misery and envy.

'Rosa told me that she has always wanted a sister, and that getting two is just like having the best Christmas and birthday presents she could have asked for, both at the same time,' Sophie had told Connie excitedly, her eyes sparkling with pleasure. 'She said that she would write to Mother and beg her to lend me to her for a visit!

'She has the most beautiful clothes, Connie, and although we are not supposed to talk about it, I overheard her telling Mother that she has no need to worry about them managing on Harry's wages, because she has her own allowance from some money left to her through her mother's family.

'And you should see the house she and Harry are going to be living in, Connie. It is so pretty, with the sweetest garden all surrounded by a wall. Rosa told me that when Harry was courting her, he came every day, no matter what the weather, to walk in the garden.'

Connie had felt her heart jerk against her ribs in angry protest, but fortunately Sophie had been too engrossed in what she was telling her, to be aware of Connie's tension.

'Rosa has had the whole house newly decorated in the latest style. And their bedroom! The bed is after the French style with blue drapes to match Rosa's eyes and an embroidered satin coverlet. There is a chaise longue to match, and Harry has his own dressing room, and Connie you'll never guess what ... Rosa and Harry have their own private bathroom!'

Even Mavis had not been able to resist praising her new sister-in-law, confiding happily to Connie, shortly after the wedding, 'Rosa is the most delightful girl, and she loves Harry so much it would be impossible not to love her just for that alone. She begged Mother so prettily to consider her to be a new daughter, and not merely a daughter-in-law, and she told us all that we are welcome to visit just any time we wish, and not to stand on ceremony at all.

'Of course, knowing that Harry loves her and that she loves him is the best thing of all. You can see in their wedding photograph how she gazes up adoringly into his eyes.'

'I am very happy for you all,' Connie had responded woodenly. But somewhere deep inside of her there was a pain that just would not go away. A pain that became so much more intense whenever she thought of Harry so blissfully happy in his marriage, and so tenderly in love with his wife. And it was obvious to Connie, from what Sophie had innocently said, that Harry's marriage to Rosa had been much more advantageous to him than marrying Connie would have been.

She had told herself fiercely that it was just as well she knew what men were all about, and that she had not taken Harry's declaration of love seriously. Even if he had genuinely believed that he loved her, he had proved how unreliable that love was, with the ease with which he had fallen out of love with her, and into love with someone else.

Not for the world, had Connie been prepared to admit right away to her other feelings: the ones she had buried deep down inside herself; the ones that mourned the death of the tender, burgeoning shoots of potential new happiness she had felt beginning to grow. Instead, she told herself that she did not care how happy Harry was, whilst inside she ached with misery.

But, as the weeks of Harry's marriage had slid into months, Connie had realised that the emptiness inside her was growing, and not fading, and that her thoughts were filled more and more with regrets and longings for what she could no longer have.

It shocked and frightened her that she should feel like that, her nights filled with longing for Harry and emptiness without him. How had it happened? How had the sharp thrill of awareness she had felt every time she saw him, or heard Mavis mention him, which she had thought of as so small a danger to her, turned into this? Connie didn't know, but she did know that she had to put Harry out of her thoughts and out of her heart.

Determinedly, she flung herself into her work with fierce dedication finding a temporary escape in its demands.

Bodies:

Harry's mind was filled with them day and night.

225

The bodies of fit, fighting men torn apart by the grim reality of war; the bodies of the not-yet-fully-grown boys he had taught, who had gone off to war with the same excitement with which they had anticipated a cricket match. But it wasn't their silent stillness that tormented him, so much as the look of bitter reproach and contempt in their eyes. The same contempt he felt for himself.

It didn't matter that he had been declared medically unfit to fight, not once, but twice. Harry still felt like a coward; like a man who did not have what it took to be a man and do his duty.

As he crossed the quadrangle, the wind tore at his gown and whistled through the quad's silent emptiness.

He was on his way home from what was now a regular weekly service to mourn the loss of those who were old boys of the school. Initially, it was just a spare trickle of names, the service conducted in a chapel containing just the members of the school, and the odd clutch of agonised relatives. Now, the trickle had become a deluge, so that there was standing room only in the chapel for the families of those killed.

None of the Houses now possessed a senior year, nor the year below it: those pupils, those boys, those *children*, had all gone to war, and many would never return.

Harry felt their loss very heavily, and so he felt, ultimately, must England itself. Many of the brightest and the best, and certainly the noblest, were already gone.

He stood still as the cold silence was suddenly

pierced by the sound of a woman's grief. Today they had mourned the loss of the third son in one family. He had been fifteen and had joined up during the Christmas holiday, lying about his age.

Her loss was more than his poor mother could bear. All her sons were gone, and her daughter's fiancé as well.

'I wonder who shall provide England with her future soldiers Mr Lawson?' The woman had asked him grimly. 'For mine shall be a generation of women without husbands. This War has robbed us not only of our husbands, but of our children as well.'

Deep down inside himself, Harry knew that intellectually he could see no virtue in such a terrible waste of lives; but another part of him longed fiercely and passionately to be able to do his bit, and to fight, not just for his country, but also alongside his fellow countrymen.

And if he did enlist who, after all, would miss him? Not Rosa his wife!

Harry knew how upset and shocked his mother and sisters would be if they knew the truth about his marriage. But he would never hurt or distress them by allowing them to know. In their eyes, he was an extremely fortunate young man, married to a charming young woman who loved and openly adored him. Only he had seen the other side to Rosa's nature – the private shocking darkness and hysteria, that was in such total contrast to the public sweet lovingness she exhibited to everyone else, as she clung to his arm and gazed soulfully into his eyes.

There seemed no logical explanation for the moods which suddenly possessed her, dark destructive moods which Harry had come to dread, during which she would scream and hurl all manner of verbal insults at him. Sometimes she would even attack him physically, and threaten to take her own life, before collapsing into overwrought exhaustion.

Harry had thought initially that they might be caused, in some part, by guilt because of the way she had trapped and blackmailed him into marriage; but then her father had taken him on one side, and told him that Rosa had inherited from her mother a delicacy of the nerves, which led to the outbursts.

Harry had listened to his father-in-law as stoically as he could, whilst inwardly he had been filled with despair. In spite of everything, he pitied Rosa more than he could hate her. No, he could not hate her. But neither could he love her.

In the place of the love and physical adoration he should have felt for her was only the pale shadow of his pity, and more shockingly the physical revulsion he tried so hard to hide. He reminded himself sternly that it was not Rosa's fault that she wasn't Connie, and he tried to hold in his heart the vows he had made toward her. But the truth was that their marriage was empty and barren, devoid of any real kind of love and shared intimacy, and empty, too, of respect and even affection. They had nothing in common, and Rosa claimed frequently, and he suspected truthfully, that she wished she had never married him.

If her uncontrollable rages were hard to bear though, they were not so hard as their aftermath: those times when, after sleeping all day, she would awake in tears and full of remorse, begging him to forgive her.

'Punish me as you wish, Harry,' she would plead emotionally. 'Do with me as you wish, beat me and chastise me, if that is your desire, for I have surely deserved your punishment.'

And then when he told her not to distress herself, she would cry out, 'Then if you will not punish me, I must punish myself.' And she would start to claw and tear at her own skin so that he was compelled to restrain her physically, to stop her from hurting herself.

There would be no calming her until he had told her that she had his forgiveness, but contrary to what she appeared to think, her sad debasement of herself filled Harry not with righteousness, but rather with repugnance.

He had reached the house, and he hesitated outside the door, and then took a deep breath. The rich smell of roasting fowl filled the hallway, but its aroma failed to arouse Harry's appetite. How could it when he had just come from a service mourning those who could never indulge such appetites again?

'Harry, you haven't kissed me!'

He looked blankly into Rosa's pouting face.

'You aren't a very romantic husband at all, Harry.'

His stomach muscles started to clench, as he recognised the sharp aggrieved note in her voice.

'All wives complain that their husbands are not

romantic, my love,' her father joked. 'It is a condition of being married, eh, Harry?'

'Is that true, Harry? Would you be so unromantic if you were married to someone else, do you think?'

His clenched muscles became a tight knot of mingled anger and despair. The very last thing he felt like doing now was humouring her.

'Rosa, I have just come from the memorial service for Jack Burton. His poor mother was–'

'Harry, who is Connie?'

The knot in his stomach became a clenching fist of ice and fire.

'If you mean Miss Pride, she is a friend of my sister's,' he answered her carefully, whilst his heart burned with contempt for his denial of his love.

'Is she so, indeed? A friend of your sister's, you say. You are lying to me, Harry. That is not the truth! How can it be when last night you called out her name in your sleep? Who is she? I must know. I will know.'

'Rosa, my dear,' her father started to protest, but Harry had seen the look in her eyes and knew that her father's warning would not be heeded.

'Who is she, Harry? I demand to know! I am your wife! What is she to you, some ... some harlot you have lain with, is that what she is? Is that why you cry out her name because you would rather be with her than with me? Did she crawl into your bed Harry, or did you take her there? Tell me, I demand to know! I have to know!'

Harry could feel himself recoiling from the

ugliness of the whole scene as he heard the venom in Rosa's shrill, accusing voice, and saw the look on her face.

Grimly he swallowed against the bile blocking his throat. For one mad moment, he had actually felt that he wanted to take hold of Rosa and demand that she stop sullying Connie's name.

'Answer me!'

A plate flew past his head and shattered against the wall.

Loathing and disgust burned and twisted inside him, withering the last shreds of the compassion he had fought so hard to hold on to. He could not, and would not, stand here like this and allow Rosa to insult Connie. But how could he protect and defend Connie without exposing her to even more of Rosa's malice?

A surge of mingled anger and helplessness rushed through him. Rosa's father had already left the room and Harry was afraid of what he might do himself if he stayed. Nausea and despair clawed at his stomach and his lungs cried out for the cleansing coolness of fresh air, in place of the putrid, fouled air of the dining room. Unable to trust himself to speak, he turned and walked toward the door.

'What are you doing? You cannot leave. You must not... Tell me who she is, Harry. I demand to know... Harry... Harry!'

As he walked out into the quadrangle, Harry could still hear Rosa's wild screams. His heart was racing and his lungs felt as though they might burst. There was a pain in his chest and an even sharper one in his heart.

He was, he recognised, afraid to go back. Because for the first time Rosa's hysteria had filled him, not with aching helpless pity, but with raging savage anger. Hearing her sully Connie's name had sent a red mist burning through him that had made him want to choke her into silence.

He started to shudder, his body hot, and then cold. There would be no peace for him now, not now that Rosa had Connie's name.

He started to walk through the school gates and into the main thoroughfare that lay behind it, and the busy jostle of other pedestrians and traffic, his mind in turmoil.

''Ere mate you goin' ter enlist too, are yer? Didn't think they 'ud 'ave the likes of me before, but now they need every man they can get, and I wants to do me bit. Ernie Henshaw's the name.'

'Harry Lawson,' Harry responded automatically, shaking the other's extended hand.

Ernie was a thin and undersized man with a pronounced limp who looked nothing like the popular image of a soldier. He also appeared malnourished and pale as though he had been ill, but Harry could see the fervour burning in his eyes, and suddenly he was filled with shame and guilt.

Today in the school chapel, he had been overwhelmed by a need to honour the youthful fallen of the school who had sacrificed themselves so bravely. What better way could there be for him to do that than to follow their example?

Surely only by winning this fearsome War could their deaths be vindicated, and he himself might find some kind of peace, even if it was only in death, he acknowledged bitterly. And if the Army would take this wretched-looking man then surely they would take him, weak chest and all?

That his marriage was an empty sham, he had already known and would have endured, but the knowledge of how easily he might have reached out and physically restrained Rosa, had shocked him. He felt as though he had turned a corner, and seen in a mirror an image of himself he could not recognise, and he had not liked what he had seen.

Was it true that violence begat violence? Surely man had control over his own reactions, if not his own destiny, and could choose how he might, or might not, react to whatever came his way? It withered something of himself deep inside to know that he could not trust himself always to deal gently with Rosa. An unfamiliar sense of reckless passion filled him.

Since he could not live the life he had wished to live, since he could not be with the one woman he loved and would always love, what point was his life to him in reality? Surely it was far better for him to use it in the service of his King and Country, than to waste it in an empty marriage and on an unrequited love?

A savage purposeful determination filled him, and he nodded his head brusquely in Ernie's direction, and fell into step with the other man.

THIRTEEN

'Sister Pride!'

Connie was still not quite used to her new title, and mindful of the danger of too much pride, she had warned herself to remember that her elevation to the rank of Sister probably owed more to the War than her own merit. Even so ... to be thus addressed gave her a warm glow of achievement, despite her constant exhaustion. She paused on her way through the tunnel that linked the main entrance of the hospital to the nurses' home, as she heard her name called out by a fellow Sister.

'If you are on your way for dinner, let me warn you that Cook is obviously not in the best of moods. It is cold mutton again and tapioca pudding!'

'Ah, but at least it will be served on Derby china,' Connie riposted, repeating a joke made by one of the soldiers about the fact that they were served their meals on china bearing the stamp of the Western Derby Union.

'Oh, these Tommies.' Her colleague grimaced. 'Have you heard the latest?'

Connie shifted her weight tiredly from one slender leg to another.

'Well, you know Sister Biddy. It seems like one of the patients was playing up like, and threatening to jump out of the window, you know how some of them get! No one could quiet him

234

down, not even Dr Stead, and then calm as you like, Sister Biddy told him to get on with it but to give her his dressing gown before he did, because she wasn't going to have a good dressing gown wasted! Calmed him down a treat it did.'

Connie was still listening to her when she saw Mavis hurrying past, her head down and in obvious distress. Quickly excusing herself, she hurried after her friend, touching her on her arm as she caught up with her, demanding, 'Mavis, what is it, what's wrong?'

'Nothing,' Mavis told her, and then shook her head. 'Oh, Connie I can't lie to you.' Pain darkened her eyes as she lifted a strained, white face toward Connie. 'I know it is wrong of me to feel like this,' she paused, and bit her lip, whilst Connie guessed what she was about to say.

'Frank has decided to enlist,' Connie guessed.

Mavis nodded her head. 'And it is not just Frank.' Tears filled her eyes. 'Harry has already enlisted,' Mavis continued shakily.

'No. That's not possible,' Connie denied flatly, whilst her heart raced in a frantic despairing anguish that told her far more about her true feelings than she felt she could bear to know. 'He's a married man and ... and there is his chest, his medical history.' Her voice tailed away as Mavis bit her lip and struggled with her tears.

'It is true, Connie. He has offered himself for enlistment and been accepted. He told Mother that he felt it was his duty. I know how very much upset he has been by the loss of so many of the school's former students.'

Connie couldn't say anything. Her throat felt

not just raw with pain but as though it was lined with broken glass, so that every breath she tried to take savaged her. How could Harry have stolen so quietly and unknowingly into her heart, and lodged himself there so deeply, without her realising it until it had been too late?

'Poor Rosa is distraught, according to my mother.'

A different, sharper pang of emotion bit into Connie's heart at the mention of Harry's wife. 'There will be a good many wives who will share that emotion if the Government has its way, and married men are called up for active duty,' she reminded Mavis.

'It is a little different for Rosa, Connie,' Mavis's voice was almost sharp now. 'Naturally she will have assumed that Harry would never be accepted for enlistment because of the weakness to his chest, and she will have had no time to prepare herself for such an eventuality. Besides, she is not like you. Rosa is so very sensitive, and ... and fragile. Harry is her whole world. He is everything to her and she is devoted to him, and dependent upon him...'

Not like her! Connie tried not to show how much Mavis's words had hurt her, and not to show either how very envious she felt of Rosa. Wasn't it enough that Rosa had Harry's love, without her having Mavis's support and protection as well? Mavis was supposed to be *her* friend, but of course, Rosa was now family, and as such she would be more important to Mavis than Connie ever could be!

Resentfully Connie started to turn away, but

then Mavis's voice altered and she added quietly, 'Frank wants us to be married as soon as it can be arranged.'

There was a note in her voice that broke through Connie's resentment and touched her heart on behalf of her friend, arousing both her understanding and her sympathy.

'So when is the wedding to be?' she asked, trying to make light of things.

Mavis shook her head, fresh tears welling in her eyes. 'It isn't as simple as that, Connie,' she protested in anguish. 'And you know it. There is nothing I want more than to marry Frank, especially now. But how can I when—'

'How can you *not!*' Connie stopped her firmly, taking hold of her arm and almost dragging her into the privacy of a nearby linen cupboard. She then closed and locked the door.

'Connie, you can't do this,' Mavis objected worriedly. 'We both have work to do and we shall be missed!'

Connie shook her head. 'This is more important than anything else, Mavis. Tell me why you can't marry Frank? Have you stopped loving him, is that it?' she demanded, even though she already knew the answer.

As Connie had known she would, Mavis protested immediately, 'No, of course not!'

'So you still love him, but you are afraid that he might come back from this War injured, and that you will have to spend the rest of your life taking care of him like Josie with her Ted?'

'Connie, how can you suggest such a thing? Of course, it isn't that.'

Connie looked at her. She had known that Mavis's insistence that she could not marry Frank was for neither of those reasons.

'So then, what is it?' Connie asked her gently.

Mavis was obviously trying hard not to break down completely.

'If we get married then I shall have to leave the hospital, you know that, Connie. And we both know how desperately short of trained nurses every hospital is, and how desperately our skills are needed. It is all very well for Frank to speak of his duty and to expect me to understand, but what about my duty? There is nothing I want more than to be his wife,' Mavis declared fervently, 'especially now, and knowing that...'

Unable to go on, she placed a hand to her mouth to steady her trembling lips.

'Is it selfish of me, Connie, I know, to feel that I would bear what has to be borne much more easily if I was playing my own part, here in the hospital instead of sitting at home fearing and waiting?'

'Of course, it isn't,' Connie assured her robustly, quickly adding, 'but there is no reason why you should not marry Frank and continue to nurse here, Mavis. In fact, I should say that it was your duty, twice over, to do so – firstly, it is your duty to give Frank the comfort of wifely love before he goes to war, and secondly, it is your duty to nurse those poor soldiers who come here to us for our care.'

'Connie, you know I cannot do that,' Mavis wept, shaking her head. 'The Infirmary has a rule that once a nurse marries she has to leave.'

'Maybe so, but rules are made to be bent occasionally,' Connie stopped her quietly. 'Oh, I know officially we cannot continue to nurse once we marry, but Mavis, believe me, you will not be the first, nor the only nurse here to do so.'

'Connie, if that's true...'

'It is,' Connie assured her firmly, and then crossed her fingers behind her back, as she added with more optimistic fiction than true fact, 'you may be sure that Matron is aware of what is happening and is turning a blind eye to it, just so long as the nurse concerned is discreet. Heavens, I could name you at least a dozen nurses I know of myself who are wearing their wedding rings on a chain around their neck, and pretending that they are no more than merely engaged! Mavis, you cannot let Frank go to war without giving him the blessing of your love.' Don't spend your life wishing for what you cannot have, Connie wanted to tell her, but instead she simply said starkly, 'Don't risk creating any unnecessary regrets for yourself, Mavis.'

'You are right,' Mavis agreed. A watery smile banished her tears. 'Connie, you are so good for me. And so close to me. It will have to be a quiet ceremony but I want you to be my bridesmaid, you will, won't you?'

'Of course,' Connie assured her emotionally.

'Everything is arranged for the wedding, Connie.' Mavis was speaking in a hushed whisper, as she and Connie snatched a few minutes together between shifts.

'Sophie, as you might guess, is madly excited.'

239

Mavis gave a small, painful sigh. 'She still sees war as something romantic and chivalrous and she does not realise just what its realities are... She is insisting on wearing the bridesmaid's dress she had for Harry's wedding, and Mother says she thinks she can alter my own to fit you, although of course she will have to take it in, since you are so much more slender than me.

'I am to wear Mother's own wedding dress, and Harry has been promised leave from his barracks so that he can give me away. He has written Mother to say that he does not expect to be sent to France until June, and that is weeks away yet.'

Connie stiffened in shock. Knowing that Harry had joined up, she had assumed that he would not be able to attend the wedding. Why on earth hadn't she anticipated this and guessed that Harry would apply for leave? And of course, she reflected bitterly, leave wouldn't just enable him to give Mavis away, it would enable him to see his wife!

Wretchedly Connie recognised that it was impossible for her to say that she had changed her mind and would not be Mavis's bridesmaid, without either hurting her friend or arousing her suspicions.

And not only would she have to see Harry, she would have to see his wife as well. Connie could feel the pain tightening its grip on her heart. She would have, in fact, to see them together and be forced to witness their happiness.

'It will not be a grand affair like Harry's marriage to Rosa – we do not have either the time, or the money for anything like that! I am so looking forward to you meeting Rosa, Connie. You will love her just as we do I know, for she is the sweetest girl.'

Fresh pain tore at Connie's heart. Quickly she dipped her head so that Mavis couldn't see her expression. She didn't know who she hated the more, Harry for stealing her heart, or herself for not being strong enough to stop him.

Despite all her attempts not to do, Connie had wasted more tears than she could count in the folly of wondering what would have happened if she had responded to Harry's declaration to her. No matter how hardily she had reminded herself that he would not have remained constant, a part of her still daydreamed foolishly of what might have been. It was so hard to make herself sound normal whenever Mavis spoke about him, and not to give away what she was truly thinking.

'I am so glad you made me see sense, Connie,' she could hear Mavis confessing. 'I could not have endured to let Frank go to war without... When we haven't...' Mavis broke off and blushed self-consciously, but Connie knew what Mavis was too uncomfortable to say. She didn't want Frank to go to war before they had been man and wife. Before they had known one another completely and truly as lovers.

Because of course Mavis, being the old-fashioned sort of girl she was, would not have allowed Frank to step over the mark with her. That was the kind of girl Harry's wife Rosa would have been, Connie reflected bitterly, as pain twisted her heart, and she admitted how much she wished she might too, have been that kind of girl – for Harry! How could he really have loved her knowing what he did about her? He couldn't and she was far better off remembering that Connie told herself grimly, than dreaming foolish hurting pointless empty dreams.

'Connie, I am so afraid for Frank and Harry!' Mavis suddenly burst out in anguish. 'I know that is cowardly and selfish of me, but seeing what we do here...' She shook her head in despair. 'Sophie, of course, is desperately proud to have a brother who is a volunteer, and talks of nothing else. She still doesn't realise...' Mavis looked at Connie, and said helplessly, 'I have not said too much at home about what we see for fear of alarming them. Mother has enough to bear as it is, and Sophie just wouldn't understand, for all that she says she wants to be a nurse.'

Silently they looked at one another. The full horrors of war and what it did to the men who engaged in it were no secret from them.

'They've given you a forty-eight hour-er? By, but you're a lucky sod, Harry,' Ernie commented without malice.

He had attached himself to Harry after their discovery that they were to be in the same regiment, not one of the new ones being formed, but instead a Lancashire regiment whose men had already seen service, and were held in high regard. An unlikely friendship had developed between the two of them.

'A damned lucky sod, that's what. And blow me if I don't think that's what we should call you from now on. Not 'Arry but Lucky!'

Harry smiled good-naturedly, and didn't argue. He suspected that his forty-eight hour leave had more to do with the fact that someone had got word that his sister was marrying an enlisting man, than anything else. And as for him being lucky in any other way! Unlike Ernie, and some of the others, Harry didn't discuss his personal life with his comrades, but he knew that if he did, lucky was the last thing they were likely to think him.

His decision to enlist had led to a bitter quarrel, followed by Rosa refusing to speak to him, for three days, and then announcing challengingly that she intended to go and stay with her cousin, Phyllis.

Harry hadn't felt able to prevent her, even though he considered that the other woman was not the best of companions for someone of Rosa's temperament. It was rare for him to dislike anybody, but he had disliked Phyllis, and he had disliked her brother Gerald even more.

'Well, I never thought I'd see Rosa married to a teacher, much less a chap with a weak chest!' Gerald had smirked as he had spoken to Harry, as though he felt that he had one up on him in some way. 'You'll have to be careful Rosa doesn't wear you out,' he had added, in what Harry had considered to be an overfamiliar manner. And then Rosa herself had come over, flinging herself into Gerald's arms and kissing him, enthusiastically.

'Cousin's privilege, old chap,' Gerald had told Harry, but Harry had seen the triumphant gleam in his eyes, and guessed that he had enjoyed

Rosa's attention, and the way she had flirted openly with him.

Rosa though would hear no word against her maternal cousins, championing them at every-turn, especially Gerald, who, as she frequently reminded Harry when she was in one of her rages, was everything that Harry himself was not.

Privately Harry thought that Gerald was the worst sort of fellow: the sort who boasted openly whilst in male company about his female con-quests, and who, so far as Harry could ascertain, lived the life of a well-to-do young swell without appearing to have any legitimate means of earning a decent living.

If there was a race on, a bet to be placed, a risk to be taken, then Gerald, as he liked to tell others, was their man. He had a habit of rubbing the side of his nose and winking, whenever anyone asked him how he always seemed to have money to burn, and Harry suspected that he did not always come by it entirely honestly.

Needless to say Gerald had not enlisted.

'Because he is a married man and, unlike you Harry, his first concern is for his wife,' Rosa had told him angrily.

Harry had had to bite on his tongue not to retort that, if that was the case, then how did she explain Gerald's numerous 'lady friends' and the exploits of which he freely boasted when amongst other men.

Gerald and his fiancée had married a few weeks after their own wedding. The bride was a thin, plain, awkward-looking young woman, and Harry had seen her blush a painful bright red when she had overheard Rosa criticising her to Phyllis.

'That was unkind of you, Rosa,' he had told her quietly later, but Rosa had simply shrugged mutinously, and answered that it was not her fault that Beth was so plain and had no taste.

'Gerald has only married her for her money. Everyone knows that!'

'If that is true, then you are certainly doing your cousin a disservice by saying so,' Harry had answered her sharply, with distaste. 'It would be kinder of you to show her some compassion, Rosa, for the poor girl certainly needs a friend.'

'Well, she need not look for one in me! She is dull and plain and I much prefer Gerald – who is my cousin after all!'

It was no secret in the barracks that they were being trained in preparation for some big offensive against the Germans, and that the Government wanted as many men to enlist as possible. Ypres had inflicted heavy and damaging losses on the British Army in terms of both manpower and pride, and the Government was determined to make the Germans pay for those losses!

No, Rosa had not reacted at all well to the news of his enlistment, throwing all manner of accusations and insults at him.

Harry had not trusted himself to make any response. At that stage, he had still not totally been able to take in himself what he had done, but he had been guiltily aware that his strongest emotion at the thought of parting from Rosa was one of relief.

And his guilt didn't just extend to Rosa either. Although she had not said so, Harry knew how his mother would worry.

Mavis though had been more outspoken, 'Harry, what can have possessed you?' she had demanded tearfully, when he had visited the New Brighton house on his last visit home before going into the Army. 'There was no reason for you to enlist, what with your chest and...'

'No reason maybe, Mavis,' he had stopped her quietly. 'But I did have a need!'

And, as he had spoken, suddenly Harry recognised, to his own relief, that what he was saying was the truth. Over and above his unhappiness in his marriage, there was a part of him that not only had felt compelled to volunteer, but that also felt proud of the fact that he had done so.

'I don't care what you say, Harry, I am not going to your sister's wedding and you can't make me!'

There was a triumphant glitter in Rosa's eyes, as she tossed her head and added, 'You can plead with me as much as you like, I won't change my mind! You didn't change yours about enlisting, did you, even though I begged and begged you to!'

The triumphant glitter had become a mutinous pout, and Harry's heart started to sink. With hindsight he knew that he should have anticipated something like this, but naively, perhaps, it had never occurred to him that Rosa would punish him for volunteering by refusing to attend Mavis's wedding.

It wasn't that he particularly wanted her company, he admitted guiltily. But for form's sake she should be there. His mother would certainly wonder why she wasn't.

'Phyllis said she'd never heard the like of it when I told her that you'd volunteered, and if she and Gerald hadn't been so good and kind to me and comforted me, I don't know what I would have done. Gerald said that you'd never catch *him* leaving a wife as pretty as me to go and join up.'

'I dare say he did,' Harry stopped her grimly.

'Beth is so lucky to have a husband like Gerald,' Rosa told him.

'I doubt that she thinks so,' Harry muttered under his breath.

'Oh, I might have guessed you would say something like that! You've never liked my cousin Gerald, and I think that's because secretly you are jealous of him.'

To his own shame, Harry was unable to stop himself from saying contemptuously, 'Well, you could not be more wrong. If you want my opinion, your precious cousin is a sight too slippery for his own good!'

'How dare you say that! Gerald is charming and dashing, and ... and more of a real man than you will ever be, Harry Lawson. Given the choice I'd far rather be married to someone like him than a dull, moralising stick of a husband like you! Gerald is a proper man; a proper husband!' Rosa flung at him, wildly. 'He has been far kinder to me than you ever have, and you are not to insult him!'

Harry had remained stiffly silent during her outburst, but his own strong moral beliefs would not allow him to let Rosa's remarks pass unchecked, even though he knew that to challenge them would result in a further furious tirade from her.

'Your cousin is a man who cares for no one apart from himself. He lives off his poor wife whilst openly scorning her. He has led more than one naive young man into a life of drink and debt, solely for his own gain. He boasts openly of his ability to avoid any kind of moral responsibility or duty, and before you start to defend him, Rosa, I am merely repeating what he has publicly declared about himself. If you really think I would want to emulate him...'

'If Gerald lives off Beth, then it is no more than you do yourself. For you most certainly live off me! And more than that! Do you really think that if you hadn't married me you would have been elevated to your present position?' she demanded scornfully. 'Father told me himself that he had to plead with the Headmaster to make you his assistant, and that the Headmaster thought you neither educated enough, nor strong enough, to fill such a post!

'I don't know why I should have concerned myself about you enlisting, for I am sure that I would be better off if the Germans put a bullet in you and made me a widow!' she continued bitterly. 'After all, it is not as though your death would deny me the comfort of a husband, is it, or that I would really be missing anything?' Harry could feel his shame burning him soul deep, but he still could not bring himself to use the same weapons as Rosa and remind her that their marriage had been forced on him by her.

It would be so easy for him to retaliate; to tell Rosa that the reason he preferred to sleep with

248

his back to her, and a cold space between them in their bed, was that he had never wanted her for his wife in the first place. But he could see no point in descending to such a bitter exchange of home truths.

Rosa though had no such qualms. 'I cannot believe what a cold man you are, Harry,' she taunted him. 'It isn't natural for a man to behave so. I had wondered if it was perhaps on account of you having a weak chest and that normal marital relations might be too much for you. I am sure that if they knew the truth, no one would blame me if I were to take comfort with someone else. Perhaps I should go to the wedding after all, and tell your sister how unhappy your coldness has made me.'

'No! You will do no such thing!'

Harry knew that she was deliberately goading him, trying to incite him into exactly the denial he had made, but he still could not stop himself from reacting.

Rosa stared angrily out of her bedroom window. She had been planning to go and visit her cousins, and now Harry had spoiled things by coming home on leave. It had taken Gerald to point out to her that having Harry enlist could be of benefit to them.

'For I don't mind admitting to you, puss,' he had told her flatteringly. 'I do miss you.'

'You should have married me then, and not Beth!' Rosa had answered him angrily, but he had soon sweet-talked her round, and besides, she had missed him as well.

'Being a married woman will give you the freedom to do as you please,' Gerald had told her, adding meaningfully, when she had frowned, 'for one thing you could come and visit Phyllis whenever you chose – and if I just happen to be visiting her at the same time, well who's to say anything? We are cousins, after all. And if, occasionally, I was to take you out for the day and we were to have to stay at a nice little hotel overnight on account of not being able to get back...'

And that was exactly what they had done. Several times!

And now Harry had gone and spoiled things for her by coming home the very weekend that she had planned to spend with her cousins. But thinking of the secret intimacies she had shared with Gerald brought something else to the forefront of Rosa's mind. Gerald was always very careful, of course. But it would be foolish not to take such an opportunity of providing herself with some extra protection. If there were to be a mishap and she got caught out, it would be essential that Harry accepted any child she might bear as his.

It was gone eleven o'clock. Carefully Harry put down the book he had been reading and stood up.

The house was silent, everyone else, including his father-in-law and Rosa, were in their beds. Rosa had refused to speak to him after their argument earlier, apart from insisting that she would not accompany him to Mavis's wedding, and had gone to bed shortly after dinner.

Reluctantly, he went upstairs.

'Harry, I am sorry that I was so cross with you.'

He tensed as Rosa reached for him, his emotions, like his body, shrivelled by her proximity.

'Kiss me and we can make up, and I shall be good and come to your sister's wretched wedding! It will be nothing like ours, of course. Why I believe she is to wear your mother's old gown! It must be awful to be so poor! Kiss me, Harry. I am your wife, remember, and you have been very cruel to me!'

In the darkness, Harry closed his eyes. All he had to do was think of Connie, his love, his beloved, for his body to swell with aching longing and tender yearning passion. He knew that; but he refused to soil his precious memories of her by using them to enable him to fulfil his marriage vows to Rosa.

Nevertheless, he had to perform his marital duty...

FOURTEEN

The May sunshine might be sharp and bright, but the wind was still cold, Connie decided, as she stood patiently trying not to shiver in the flimsy dress, which despite Mavis's mother's skill was still overgenerous on her.

But then, the knowledge that she would be seeing Harry had stolen her appetite, and with a full two weeks to worry about that meeting –

both during her working hours and those in which she should have been sleeping – Connie knew that she had gone from slender to almost pinch-faced and thin.

She had surreptitiously pulled the ribbons that tied the dress a little bit tighter to mask its looseness, reassuring herself that no one was likely to pay close attention to her since it was Mavis who was the bride.

There had been a rush of weddings on these last few weeks, the Vicar had informed them, and of course everyone knew why. Patriotic young men were determined to enlist and serve their country; and equally patriotic young women were determined to show their support for their sweethearts by pledging themselves to them.

After a simple wedding breakfast at the New Brighton house, Mavis and Frank were going to spend a few precious days together in the Lake District.

'I try not to let myself fear that they might be all that I have of him,' Mavis had confided emotionally to Connie last night.

But at least Mavis would have something of Frank. Something with him, whilst Connie would never... Could never, have anything of Harry.

It had hurt so much seeing him walk into the New Brighton house not ten minutes ago, so dearly familiar, and yet a heart-stoppingly handsome stranger in his khaki uniform.

He was holding himself differently, Connie had noticed immediately with a jealous lover's eyes; standing taller and prouder, and watching first Sophie and then Mavis run to him to be gathered up in his arms, she had ached so badly to do the same. Only the kiss she wanted to press against his newly-shaven skin was not the chaste one of a sister, but the fiercely passionate one of a woman who loved him.

'Where is Rosa?' Sophie demanded excitedly, whilst Connie tensed. This was the moment she had been dreading, when she must look into the face of Harry's wife and try to smile at her as though she felt no envy of her.

'Unfortunately, she was not able to be here. She sends her apologies and her regrets.'

'Oh, Harry, is she not well?' Mavis enquired with immediate concern.

'I had not realised it, but she was already promised to her cousin Phyllis, and felt she could not cancel her visit since Phyllis was so looking forward to it,' Harry answered her calmly.

Inside though he was feeling far from calm. Rosa had made it plain that she was not finished punishing him, and the look in her eyes had been spiteful as well as triumphant when she had told him that she intended to visit her cousin rather than accompany him to his sister's wedding. In truth, he was glad to be relieved of Rosa's presence for his own sake, as well as lest she mar the occasion for Mavis in some way.

As yet he had not allowed his hungry senses to feed on Connie's silent, almost wraith-like presence, but he was aware of her with every single fibre of his heart and body and soul.

'Oh how noble that is of her, isn't it, Connie?' Sophie breathed on a small sigh. 'I am sure I could not have endured to give up so much as an

253

hour of Harry's company, when this is the first time she has seen him since he enlisted.'

Connie froze as she was drawn into the conversation, acutely aware that not just Sophie, but Harry, too, was looking at her.

'We are at war, Sophie,' she managed to say. 'And we are all of us called upon to make sacrifices.'

How stuffy and stiff she sounded, more like Matron than herself, but how could she be herself in such close proximity to Harry.

'Connie, is quite right, Sophie.'

Even his voice had changed, become sterner, harder. Connie tensed as Harry took a step toward her, unable to help looking fully into his face. Her breath seemed to catch in her throat, and a bittersweet longing filled her. She stepped forward, and Harry held out his hand to her.

'You have lost weight, Connie. I hope you are not working too hard.'

'She is Sister Pride now, you know, Harry,' Mavis broke in.

Silently they looked at one another. There was such a look of helpless yearning in his gaze that it dizzied her, or was it her own emotion that was deluding her and making her imagine it?

She could barely bring herself to look at him in case she gave herself away, and several minutes later whilst he hungrily devoured the breakfast his mother had made for him, Connie was not so much as able to pour him a cup of tea for fear of her hands shaking too badly.

'Connie, I'm so nervous. Do I look all right...? Is

my veil straight ... Mother? Sophie?'

'Oh, my darling girl...'

Connie felt her own eyes mist with tears as Elsie Lawson hugged Mavis. 'You look so beautiful.'

And it was true, Mavis did look beautiful, Connie acknowledged, as she carefully gathered up the veil and instructed Sophie to open the bedroom door.

She had known that Harry would be waiting in the hallway for his sister, and she had sworn a vow that she would not so much as look at him. But when she looked down, the gloss of his shoes gleamed so much that Connie could see his reflection in them. Helplessly, she allowed her gaze to sweep upwards.

Connie was too thin; too strained; too fragile; and he wanted to pick her up and ask her what on earth she had done to herself, Harry recognised. But of course he had no right to do any such thing. He was a married man and anyway Connie had already told him she had no use, or desire, for his protection or his love. And yet as he looked at her, Harry could see such pain in her eyes that it was all he could do to stop himself demanding to know what had caused it, and swearing to her that he would banish it.

'If only your father might have lived to see you both.'

His mother's emotional words broke into his private thoughts and brought him sharply back to reality.

'I think that he probably can, Mama,' Sophie was whispering softly. 'When I was poorly I often felt him near to me...'

For a moment they all fell silent. Unable to stop himself, Harry looked at Connie, but she had turned her head away from him.

Sophie meant no harm, and had no awareness of how bitterly painful the memories her innocent remark had stirred were, at least for her, Connie acknowledged. She saw Harry turning toward her, and quickly looked away.

Was he looking at her because he wanted her to see in his eyes his relief that she had ignored his advances? Because he wanted her to be aware of the happiness he had found with another?

A loud knock on the door broke into the sharp silence of the moment, causing Mavis's mother to exclaim, and hurry downstairs to admit the neighbour who had offered to sit with Great Aunt Martha for the duration of the ceremony. The elderly lady was now in her eighty-seventh year and virtually bedridden, although still very much a demanding martinet with a sharp mind, and an even sharper tongue.

'I hate the way Great Aunt Martha is so mean to Mama,' Sophie had burst out only the previous evening. 'I heard her telling Mother last week that when she dies we shall have to move out since she has left this house and everything in it to a charity.'

'It is her right to do as she wishes with her money, Sophie,' Mavis had chided her sister gently, before adding warmly, 'Frank has already said that you and Mother will always be welcome under his roof.'

With nearly as many horses as men recruited

for the war effort, and transport difficult to come by – even those with motor cars had been urged to either donate them for use where needed, or to use them as little as possible – they had decided to walk the small distance to the church. A small crowd had gathered to wish Mavis good luck, the children throwing flowers in front of her as she clung to Harry's arm.

The elegant little square in front of the church had already lost the railings to its garden and house, Connie noticed, gone no doubt to be melted down to provide much-needed raw material for new munitions.

As they reached the church, Harry hoped that the message he had sent saying that he would pay for the organist, the choir, and for the bells to be rung after the ceremony, had reached the Vicar, since his mother had informed him sadly that these were luxuries Mavis had felt unable to afford.

If anyone deserved a decent wedding then it was his sister, Harry reflected. For no one gave more to others than Mavis – unless it was Connie who had risked her own life to nurse his sister Sophie.

Connie almost missed a step as the church doors were thrown open and the organist began to play. Mavis had warned her that there would be no music and, as Harry urged his sister forward Connie couldn't help looking toward his proudly straight back, guessing that he was the one who was responsible for the soaring resonance and dignity of the traditional music.

Frank's Best Man was a fellow police officer

and Connie could see the brass buttons on their uniforms glinting in the darkness of the church, as they turned to watch their progress up the aisle. It touched Connie's heart to see Frank surreptitiously wipe away a tear as he gazed at his wife-to-be.

She could feel Mavis's hand tremble as she stood in front of the Vicar, and turned to hand Connie the bouquet, that had been part of her own wedding gift to her friend.

The last wedding Connie had attended had been Josie's and before that the marriage of her sister Ellie to her first husband.

How very different that occasion had been. Their Aunt and Uncle Parkes had spared no expense to make the wedding the most lavish affair.

Ellie! A small shadow crossed Connie's face. Increasingly since the start of the War she thought of her sister and their shared childhood. Did Ellie ever think of her, or did she only want to forget about the shame Connie had brought on their family? So many brave young men were enlisting. Was her own brother John one of them? A longing to see her family pierced her.

'Speech speech!!'

Boldly risking Great Aunt Martha's wrath, Mavis's mother had set out the wedding breakfast in the dining room, and opened up the large double doors which led from it into the big front parlour. This meant that the euphoric married couple, and their family and supporters, could take their fill of the dainty sandwiches she and Connie had prepared, along with the cooked ham, and last year's elderberry wine.

And now the Best Man was getting up to make his speech.

He spoke simply and proudly of Frank, his strengths and his love for Mavis, and when he toasted their good health and a long life together, there was a small silence amongst those listening. Every last one inwardly praying that that might indeed be so, before lifting their glasses.

And then Frank nudged his friend and whispered something to him and the Best Man grinned, laughed, and announced, 'As if I'd forget that. Where are the bridesmaids?'

Someone urged Connie and Sophie forward, and they were each presented with a small box, in exchange for which they had to part with a kiss for the Best Man. This took place amidst much good-natured teasing and laughter from the watching guests, as he deliberately made a great play of relishing the small intimacy.

Sophie opened her gift first, her eyes glowing with delight as she lifted out one of the tiny pearl earrings for everyone to see.

Over her head, Mavis's tear-filled gaze met Connie's, and Connie knew she was thinking, as Connie was herself, of the special trip Sophie and Connie had made to New Brighton. To keep the promise Connie had made to Sophie when she was sick, Connie had taken the younger girl to have her ears pierced, at a local jewellers.

At the last minute Mavis had not been able to go in with her, and so it was Connie who had had to grit her teeth and fib robustly that, no it didn't hurt at all, or at least not very much, whilst knowing full well that it did.

But Sophie, bless her, hadn't done more than give a small, single squeak as she endured the pain of her small rite of passage into fashion.

Connie and Mavis had bought her her first pair of real earrings as a reward for being so brave, to wear once her poor sore ears had healed enough for the thin gold sleepers to be removed safely.

There were, of course, earrings for Connie herself, too, and Sophie was highly delighted that they would own a matching pair.

'You have such pretty ears, Connie, doesn't she, Harry?' she appealed innocently to her brother.

Acutely conscious of Harry's suddenly compressed jaw as he refused so much as to look, Connie burned with chagrin and pain, 'That is no question to ask a happily married man, Sophie,' she chided the younger girl, with more force than she intended. 'Naturally in your brother's eyes, no other woman's ears, or indeed any other aspect of her, could aim to match the perfection of his wife!'

Connie obviously realised that he still loved her, Harry decided miserably, and that was why she had chosen to remind him so sharply and pointedly of his duty to Rosa.

He had been achingly aware, throughout the whole of the wedding breakfast, of the way the Best Man's eyes had lit up the moment he had seen Connie. And Harry had seen too how the Best Man had drawn out that kiss he had insisted on being given before he had parted with her bridesmaid gift.

Pain and longing savaged him. Somehow he had thought that the pain of loving her would lessen with time, and not increase.

The guests drifted away until only the family was left. All too soon it was time for the bridal couple to leave, and Sophie, reluctant to release the happy excitement of the day, pleaded to be allowed to go with them as far as Liverpool station.

'Yes, why don't you all come, Mother?' Mavis begged. 'That way you can see Harry off as well, since he has to return to his barracks tonight.'

'An excellent idea,' the Best Man agreed. 'And you need not worry about getting back home, ma'am,' he assured Mavis's mother, 'for I shall undertake to bring you back here safe and sound.'

'Goodbye, dearest Connie. And thank you for everything!'

Silently Connie returned her friend's fierce hug and then stepped back only to have Frank give her a big bear hug himself, his honest face slightly red with embarrassment as he announced gruffly, 'Don't think that Mavis hasn't told me about the part you played in bringing this about Connie. As close as sisters, that's what Mavis says you are, and it's as much a sister you will be to me now as young Sophie is.'

'All of us consider Connie to be part of our family,' Mavis declared emotionally before adding, 'Harry, I pray that you will be kept safe and well. And Mother thank you for everything... Connie, I shall see you next week when I am back on duty, and Sophie, you help mother.'

Another round of fierce hugs and then the porter was blowing his whistle and Frank was urging Mavis toward the waiting train.

'I must take my own leave of you now, Mother,' Harry announced quietly.

He could see the anxiety in his mother's eyes.

'I pray that you will be safe, Harry.'

'Oh, since the other men have nicknamed me Lucky, I think you can be sure of it,' Harry joked, but Sophie's face was already crumpling and she flung herself into his arms.

'There, Sophie, no tears now,' he comforted her gently.

Connie had tried to distance herself from them, but as she stepped back from Harry, Sophie took hold of her hand and cried out, 'Harry, you have not said goodbye to Connie yet.'

Numbly Connie tried to force her lips into a smile, as her unwanted tears blurred her sight of Harry's face.

'Connie!'

Unable to stop himself Harry took told of her, holding her as tightly as he dared. *This* would be the memory he took with him into battle he admitted; the feel of Connie's warm flesh against his own, the scent of her, the soft brush of her hair against his chin. He felt her tremble, and instinctively he whispered her name.

Blindly Connie lifted her face to snatch one last look at him, one last memory to hold and treasure.

Her tears, the soft warmth of her breath against his skin, were more than Harry could bear. Bending his head he pressed a fiercely passionate kiss against her mouth.

Harry was kissing her, no doubt overwhelmed by the emotion of his departure, Connie acknowledged dizzily, as she clung to him and wished with all of her turbulent heart that he was hers, and that she had the right to share this sweetest and most tenderly intimate of embraces with him.

A shrill whistle pierced the air, bringing them back to reality. As Harry released her Connie whispered to him, 'Be safe, Harry.'

Connie watched as he plunged away from them and into the mêlée of men on the platform, reaching for Mavis's mother's hand as carriage doors slammed and the train disappeared into the smoky distance.

In the emotion of the moment, neither Mrs Lawson nor Sophie seemed to have noticed the kiss she had shared with Harry. But Connie knew she would never forget it.

FIFTEEN

'You'd have thought that Josie would have put on a better spread than this for her Ted's funeral. I mean it's not as though she mustn't have been expecting it like, him being so poorly an' all,' Vera complained, as she pulled a face over the sandwich she was eating.

Silently Connie and Mavis exchanged speaking looks. Unlike Vera, who had only arrived in time for the funeral tea, they had both not only attended the funeral itself but also done as much as they could to help Josie in other ways, too.

'I still can't believe he's gone,' Josie had sobbed piteously when Connie and Mavis had gone to help her lay out the body, a familiar task now so far as the two friends were concerned.

'And the Government can say what it likes, my Bert is not enlisting,' Vera continued defiantly, tossing her head. 'Why should he when it's against his principles?'

Connie and Mavis exchanged another look.

'And what principles would those be, Vera?' Connie couldn't resist challenging her sharply. 'The Bert put-yourself-first principles?'

'By, but you've got a cheek!' Vera retorted, her face going red. 'If you must know, Miss Clever Clogs, my Bert is a conscientious objector!'

Connie knew that if she hadn't felt so bitterly contemptuous she would have laughed.

'If your Bert possesses anything remotely resembling a conscience of any kind, I'd be very surprised to hear it,' she contented herself with saying cynically instead.

'Well that's all you know, Bert has been against this War right from the start. Said all along it shouldn't ha' been allowed, he did. Anyway, now that the papers are full of this big push that's going to knock the Germans for six, and put them in their place for once and for all, the whole thing is going to be over and done with. Bin working night and day down at the munitions factory, we have, for months now. That's why I couldn't get 'ere for the service. Not that it was much of one by all accounts, him being a Methodist. Can't beat a good Catholic funeral in my book. Know how to send 'em off proper-like the Catholics do...

'Pity your Frank and that brother o' yours rushed to join up, Mavis. Could have saved themselves the bother. If you'd have had any sense, you'd have married your Frank sooner and then he wouldn't 'ave needed to go, leastways not until they bring in this law for conscripting married men,' she added smugly.

'Frank and Harry both volunteered,' Mavis reminded Vera, white-faced. 'Unlike your Bert they put their duty to their country before their own safety!'

It was unlike Mavis to be so outspoken, and Vera looked resentfully taken aback. ''Ere keep your hair on, Mavis. Mind you, I must say I'm surprised that the Army 'ud take someone like that brother of yours, what with his weak chest and all. And fancy your Frank volunteering, as well, 'im being in the police, like.' She gave another defiant toss of her head. 'But then some folk don't 'ave the sense they was born with, do they, and all as they can think about is a row of medals and calling themselves a hero!'

'Vera, you've got no call to be speaking to Mavis like that,' Connie objected, immediately going to her friend's defence. 'And if you had a ha'pennyworth of sense, you'd know that for yourself, without having to be told it. If you want the truth, then your Bert is no better than a coward, and in your shoes I'd keep my opinions on others to myself. Mavis and me know better than most what happens to conscientious objectors once word gets out about them – and that's just before they end up in hospital. There's a Sister that I know of who mixes her own special enemas to give to men like your Bert,' Connie told Vera darkly.

An angry flush ran along Vera's face as she glowered mutinously at Connie, but she didn't try to retaliate.

'Vera really is the living end,' Mavis pronounced later, as she and Connie walked back to the hospital. 'I wouldn't mind so much, Connie, if I thought that her Bert really was a conscientious objector.'

'He and Vera have always been the kind to look out for themselves first,' Connie reminded her.

'I don't mind admitting that she fair got my back up,' Mavis admitted, before laughing, 'mind you, the look on her face when you said about that enema!'

Connie laughed. 'I couldn't help myself. Not that I don't feel a bit sorry for them.'

Mavis sighed. 'Me, too. We had one on our ward a while back. He'd been caught by a gang of women and forced to drink carbolic.' She gave Connie a speaking look. 'It was so pitiful to see him die, Connie, and his poor mother...'

'It isn't cowardice that makes them refuse to fight, no matter what some folks might say,' Connie agreed soberly. 'But it gets my goat to have Vera standing there and criticising your Frank and ... and your ... and Harry, when they're risking their lives for the sake of her and her bloody Bert!'

'Do you think Vera is right when she says it will all be over soon?' Mavis asked Connie shakily.

'I don't know, Mavis,' Connie answered her honestly.

She suspected that they were both remembering how, right at the start of the War, they had been promised that it would be over by Christmas – and that had been two years ago!

'It says in the papers that after the losses at Ypres the Government is determined to crush the Germans once and for all.'

Both girls looked at one another.

'I couldn't bear it if either Frank or Harry came back like those poor men who were gassed, Connie, or those others whose minds have been so badly affected.' Mavis stopped speaking and shuddered, whilst Connie gripped her bottom lip between her teeth and looked away from her. 'I'd rather they were killed outright than suffer that.'

There were soldiers in what had originally been the Infirmary's lunatic asylum ward, who raved and sobbed, or just sat silently never speaking. No one ever talked about them, not even their bewildered and shocked families.

'Have you had word from either of them?' Connie asked Mavis, as they neared the hospital.

'Yes, Mother has had a letter from Harry telling her that they were leaving for France, and Frank has written to me twice. Once saying that he hates Army food, and then a second time asking me what I would like him to bring me back from Paris!'

Dawn was already lighting the summer sky. Soon the order would be given for them to go over the top.

They had come up to the Front during the night, marching at a swinging pace. Ernie had got out his mouth organ, and started playing a well-known music hall tune. Someone had started to sing, and then the others had joined in, all of them aware of the bright spots of light stabbing the darkness as the British artillery pounded out its shells into the distant enemy lines. Every now and again a staff car had slid past them, raising a rousing cheer from the marching men.

As they had passed through one small French town, a French sentry had raised his arm in a salute and called out to them, *'Bonne chance, mes camarades.'*

'Wots he say 'Arry?' Ernie had demanded.

'He's wishing us good luck,' Harry had told him.

'Aye, well, for myself I'd rather have some bloody support from the French troops instead of his bloody *bon chance!'* Ernie had reported pithily, as a motorcycle despatch rider had raced past them furrowing up the road.

Around him everyone else was still asleep, and Harry reached into his jacket and removed the carefully-wrapped photograph he carried everywhere with him. Mavis had sent it him, and he smiled tenderly as he unwrapped it.

There was Mavis in her wedding dress with Frank standing proudly at her side. He himself was standing on her other side, next to his mother, whilst Sophie and Connie stood together next to Frank.

Connie! Harry closed his eyes and let his emotions roll over him. Maybe it was wrong to let himself think of her now, when rightfully his thoughts should be with his wife. But in his heart, Connie was the woman he cherished and worshipped above all others, and since God must surely see and know that, there was no point in trying to conceal his feelings from Him, Harry reflected. And He must know, too, that he had gone to sleep thinking of Connie last night, and that it would be her image he took with him today when he went into battle.

''Arry?'

As he heard Ernie's voice, he quickly rewrapped the photograph and put it away. The rations were coming round and the camp was coming to life. Automatically he reached out for his pack, even though he had already checked its contents a dozen or more times. The methodical, practical, physical action was somehow comforting.

'I can't do it. I can't … I'm too scared. We're all going to be killed, I know it. I'm getting out of here.' A pitifully young soldier, more of a boy than a man, had started to sob noisily in panic.

'Belt up, you young idiot,' Ernie, who was sitting next to him, protested sharply, swearing under his breath before warning him, 'if the Sergeant hears you carrying on like that he'll have you shot as a deserter and no messing. 'Ere 'Arry, give us a hand,' he urged, making a grab for the boy's arm.

'I don't care. I'd rather be shot now than left to die with me belly ripped open by some Hun.'

The other men were beginning to react to the boy's panic and Harry felt his heart ache with pity for the youngster, as he went to Ernie's aid.

The boy was their youngest recruit, and only just sixteen. He had admitted tearfully to Harry and Ernie that he had been bullied into enlisting by a group of female munitions workers who had virtually marched him down to the recruiting office, and stood over him whilst he signed his name.

All of them were on edge, knowing that as soon as dawn broke properly, they would be told to fall-in and wait for the order to go into action, storming across no man's land to drive back the enemy. The youngster's panic was doing neither himself, nor anyone else, any favours. But still Harry could not help sympathising with the boy, and feeling protective toward him, just as he would have done toward one of his pupils.

'Johnny, you can't turn back,' he told him gently. 'We can only go forward now.'

'No... No... I'm not going to do it, I can't, and you can't make me... I'm going home to me mam,' he sobbed wildly.

As he spoke the boy was standing up and trying to tear off his jacket, flaying against the hands reaching out to restrain him.

'For Christ's sake, if he starts spouting off like that to the Captain, he'll have him court-martialled,' someone muttered. 'And a right sod he is, an' all.'

'Aye, if he gets that far,' another soldier added, meaningfully.

Everyone knew that their Captain, who had a notoriously vicious streak, had given an order to shoot anyone trying to desert.

'Let go of me.' Johnny was pushing against their

restraining hands as he struggled to break free, sobbing noisily as he did so.

'For Gawd's sake, someone shut 'im up, before I do it me'self. 'E's making that much racket the Huns 'ull be able to hear 'im over on their lines.'

'Johnny, try not to be afraid,' Harry coaxed him gently, but the boy shook his head and stared white-faced, at him.

'It's all right for you, Harry. Everyone knows that you're lucky. They even call you that! Lucky Lawson.' His face puckered. 'But I'm not! I just know that some bloody Hun's bullet's got my name on it already. I might as well be shot down here as wait. I might as well get it over with now...'

He was starting to panic again and pull away, and Harry knew that he had to do something to stop him. 'Come on, Johnny, pull yourself together, and I'll tell you what. If you like you can wear my jacket and I'll wear yours. That way, you'll have my luck, and if there is a bullet with your name on it, it will find me instead of you!'

It was the kind of logic that made sense to men on the edge of war, and Harry held his breath as Johnny hesitated. The tear-filled eyes widened and a muscle twitched in the youthful jaw. 'You mean it, Harry?' he demanded.

'Of course,' Harry assured him, immediately starting to unfasten his jacket, shrugging it off, to stand in his vest as he held the jacket out to him.

Up the line they were already being given the signal to march out. Harry tensed as Johnny started nervously, and licked his lips. If he ran now he would be shot down without mercy, and whilst Johnny may not care, his family would, Harry reflected pityingly, as he watched the boy shudder and shiver, drenched in the sweat of his own terror.

'All right, men...'

'Give it to me then.' Snatching the jacket Johnny began to tear off his own.

'Hey, you up there. Why the hell aren't you dressed? Get a move on unless you want my bayonet up your bloody backside...'

'Come on, Harry, otherwise it will be you as gets shot,' Ernie muttered as he thrust Johnny's jacket at Harry and helped him pull it on.

The line was already moving out as Harry fastened the khaki. To his relief, Johnny had fallen into step ahead of him. Quickly Harry shouldered his pack. Each one weighed a good seventy pounds and contained entrenching tools, two gas helmets, wire cutters, two hundred-and-twenty rounds of ammunition, two sandbags, two Mills bombs, a groundsheet, a haversack, a water bottle and a field dressing.

The ceaseless pounding of the British artillery had been replaced by an eerie silence, as the barrage was lifted to allow the men to advance into no man's land.

Harry felt his stomach muscles clench, but he deliberately kept his gaze fixed forward on the back of the man in front of him, refusing to give in to the temptation to raise his eyes and look ahead.

'Right men, rifles at the ready. Fix bayonets.'

Harry felt the clamminess of his grip, as he responded automatically to the orders.

Every single man here was a volunteer. They had been trained for this very purpose, this very day, for this push that would bring them victory!

'Come on, you lot, orders is to push forward at a smart pace, not dawdle like you was taking your girl for a walk in the park. Pick up those feet. Keep up with the line in front of you... You there ... you're out of step.'

Somewhere ahead of them Harry could hear the sharp crackle of gunfire mingling with screams and groans. Smoke filled the air, sucking in the khaki-clad figures ahead. There was no jolly singing now, only a smothering silence broken by gunfire.

'Remember we've got forty thousand yards to cross before we reach the enemy, and it's going to be a piece of cake. Our lads have been out ahead of us doing the dirty work, cutting through the wire and clearing the way for us. All you namby pamby lot have got to do is put a bullet into the enemy,' the Sergeant roared. 'Keep moving.'

Out in front, Harry could see vague solitary figures in the mist and his stomach tensed and churned. Had they reached the German lines so soon?

A bullet whined past his ear, and behind him he heard a thin, high scream that lifted the hair on his scalp and made him shudder, but he knew he couldn't risk turning round.

They were surrounded by gunfire now, and suddenly a group of men came running toward them through the mist, calling out to them, 'Get back. Get back. You can't get through. We're being shot down like bloody sitting ducks.'

'Get back in line there.'

Harry heard a man scream as a bullet thudded into his back. All around them they could hear sounds of panic and death, but their Sergeant was urging them on, his face set and grim.

The sun which had shone so brightly earlier had gone, blotted out by smoke, its acrid smell scorching Harry's lungs as he struggled to walk and breathe. The ground had become bumpy and uneven, but it was only when his foot slipped on something wet that Harry looked down and realised that the obstacles he was trying to walk over were bodies.

For a moment he couldn't move, shock gripping him by the throat, a hand grabbed at his ankle and when he looked down again all he could see was a body ripped open to reveal spilling entrails, and a blood-pulped mess where the man's head should have been.

His stomach heaved, but before he could move the Sergeant thrust him out of the way and raised his gun. 'Better to put him out of his misery, poor sod,' he muttered, before demanding savagely, 'get a move on you lot. We've got work to do.'

For months, they had heard nothing but how noble their cause was, how honourable their calling, how assured their victory. But there was nothing noble or honourable about this: about your body jerking in agonising death throes, with your guts and your brains spilling into the dirt, to mix with the vomit of those who could see the horror of their own fate there in front of them.

The Sergeant was running at their side urging them forward, and abruptly through the gun smoke Harry could see the enemy lines.

'Get to it, me...'

Harry saw the look of surprise freeze on the Sergeant's face as the shell hit him. His arm, shorn off by the explosion, thudded into Harry's face, whilst the Sergeant himself lay face down amongst the other bodies.

Harry was vaguely aware that everything around him seemed to be happening in slow motion. A figure loomed up in front of him, and ran toward him, and he felt the heat of the bullet that whistled past his ear.

''Arry look out.'

He turned at the sound of Ernie's voice, just in time to miss the bayonet aimed for his gut. Harry retaliated immediately, not allowing himself to think that he was plunging his bayonet into human flesh; not allowing himself to hear the agonised scream of his victim.

Time and reality ceased to exist, here was only blood and death and the sound of bullets mingling with the screams of the wounded and fallen. The butt of Harry's rifle glistened red with blood. It had soaked his hands and run up his arms. He could taste it in his mouth and smell its hot, sweet death-scent.

Somewhere, somehow, they must have become detached from the rest of their unit, he recognised vaguely. Ernie was still beside him and he could see the Corporal several yards away, but there was no sign of any of the others.

Out of the corner of his eye, he saw the sudden lunge of an enemy figure and he cried out automatically to Ernie in warning. He lifted his rifle to fire at the German. Blood oozed from the hole in the uniformed chest.

'That one nearly had you, Ernie.' Harry grinned, and then froze as he saw his friend clutch at the bayonet piercing his stomach.

'Ernie...'

'I'm done for 'Arry...'

'No...' Frantically Harry dropped to his knees as Ernie sank to the ground, putting his arms around him.

'Bin the best pal I ever had you 'ave, 'Arry,' Ernie whispered to him. 'Do me a favour will yer mate ... mek sure you gets out of this. And when you do, mek sure you does enough living for both of us...'

'Ernie.'

Even as he sobbed his friend's name, and felt the hot flow of his anguished, denying tears sear their way down his face, Harry knew that it was too late.

Bullets hailed down around him like a metal snowstorm, but he ignored them as he tenderly wiped the blood from Ernie's mouth, and equally tenderly closed his eyes.

Bloody Huns! Bloody war! Bloody Ernie for going and getting himself killed! As he got up and staggered forward, slipping and sliding on the bodies of his dead comrades, Harry didn't even see the rifle being levelled at him, never mind hear the bullet's whine. All he knew was the pain tearing at his flesh, so agonising that he screamed and writhed, his body contorting, as he fell to the ground.

Semi-conscious, he lay amongst the fallen and

dying, unable to move. He could see the man lying near to him – no, not a man a boy – Harry corrected himself drowsily. A numb coldness seeped relentlessly through him.

The boy who looked as young, if not younger, than Johnny, had been shot through the neck, and blood bubbled from his wound with each breath he took. He was crying for his mother in German. A wave of helpless pity searing him, Harry inched over to him.

Miraculously, he still had his pack, and painstakingly he struggled to open it and find the wound dressing, his movements slow and painful. The boy was bleeding badly and Harry grunted in satisfaction as he finally managed to staunch the flow of blood.

Somewhere close at hand he heard someone scream and saw, out of the corner of his eye, the downward thrust of a bayonet. Instinctively he covered the boy's body with his own. The bayonet thrust toward his heart, but slid into Harry's arm instead, as its owner lost his balance.

Everything was pain. A thick red mist of it that clutched him in its sharp talons. Beneath him the boy's body, like his own, felt deathly cold. Harry could feel the will to live slipping away from him, along with the sounds of the battle.

Just before he lost consciousness, he whispered Connie's name, his lips curving into a smile as though they had somehow tasted hers.

SIXTEEN

News of the terrible disaster that was the Battle of the Somme cast a pall of shock over the country as thick and choking as the black pall of death that hung over the battlefield itself.

Horrific tales of the number of men lost had reached Connie and the rest of the hospital, long before the first of the injured men began to arrive. No one could remain untouched by it. Every woman had, or knew of, a man who had fought there.

Crowds of white-faced women waited to meet the hospital trains bringing back their wounded, some of them breaking into agonised sobs of deep despair.

At the Infirmary, like the other nurses, Connie worked grim-faced, hardly daring to whisper her own private prayers, and certainly not daring to ask any questions of her friend.

As the troop trains rolled in and the wards overflowed, she tried to comfort herself with the belief that the War Office was always mercifully quick to inform families of a death; and that every day, every hour, that slipped by, strengthened the possibility of both Frank and Harry having survived.

And then, three days after the battle, she saw Mavis standing in the door to her ward, and she knew immediately. Only her love for her friend enabled her to put Mavis first, and demand fiercely of her, 'Frank?'

Numbly Mavis shook her head. 'Not yet. But we have heard...' She stopped, her body visibly shaking, 'Rosa has received a telegram from the War Office. Harry was killed in action on the first of July.'

'No!'

At first Connie thought she had actually given the feral primitive scream that had torn at her heart and throat, but Mavis's stiff lack of reaction told her that, miraculously, she hadn't.

'My mother...' Mavis's mouth started to tremble and she fought to control her lips. 'I have to go to her, Connie, and I intend to stay with her for as long as she needs me...'

Sharply and painfully Connie suddenly felt excluded, aware that she had no right to grieve for Harry as anything more than a mere friend. 'I shall pray for Frank's safety,' she told Mavis quietly.

No matter how much she wanted to do so she couldn't leave her ward, and so she had to plunge on somehow doing what had to be done, whilst all the time her shocked grief savaged her.

How could Harry be dead? How could he no longer be here in this world? How could she continue to live in it without him inhabiting it? Only now did she realise what comfort she had taken just knowing he was there. She had thought she had known grief, that it had been her companion and her enemy, but now she knew she had not known it all. What she had thought of as grief had merely been a pale shadow of its reality.

She would rather bear a thousand times the pain of Harry loving someone else but living, than endure this unending agony.

Nothing could ever be the same. *She* could never be the same. The world could never be the same. Because the light in it that had been Harry's life had been extinguished, leaving it a dark and soulless place.

'I've seen Matron, she was very understanding.' Wearily Mavis sank down onto Connie's bed.

It was just over a month since they had heard the news of Harry's death, followed by the information that he had been buried with his fallen comrades.

Connie had known immediately what that had meant! She had had nightmares then – searing, shockingly explicit, and unbearable – about his poor mutilated body.

The family had had a simple service at the same church where Mavis and Frank had been married. Amongst the effects sent back to the family there had been, Mavis had told Connie between her sobs, the wedding photograph which she herself had sent to him.

Connie had forced herself to attend the service, steeling herself for her first meeting with Rosa, but Harry's widow had not been there. Mavis had told her that Rosa's grief was such that her cousin Phyllis had insisted on taking Rosa to live with her, so that she could recover in surroundings that would not constantly remind her of her lost husband.

'It's official now, Connie, I leave at the end of

the week.'

'Are you sure you're doing the right thing?'

Both of them, in common with virtually everyone else working at the hospital, were wearing the black armband that indicated a loved one lost to the War.

'Connie, I don't have any choice,' Mavis answered her almost sharply. 'My poor mother has been so greatly affected by losing Harry. There is that house to run and Great Aunt Martha to be taken care of. There is Sophie as well, and even though Frank has only lost a hand whilst others have been far more badly injured, he is no longer able to work as a police officer.

'The simplest answer to our problems is for me to give up nursing and for Frank and I to move into the New Brighton house. He can take over and easily manage all the outside work including the garden, whilst I shall be able to relieve Mother and take over nursing Great Aunt Martha.'

Connie looked away from her, unable to say what she was truly feeling, which was how alone, and despairing, and even abandoned, she herself felt at the thought of losing her friend.

The pain was, in its own way, as sharp as any she had known. Losing Mavis was like losing her anchor in life. And not just that. She was also Connie's closest link to Harry and her memories of him.

As the misery churned inside her, she felt a resurgence of the old Connie and had a childlike need to beg Mavis not to leave her.

'It won't change anything for us, Connie,' Mavis told her gently, as though she had guessed what she was thinking. 'We shall still remain friends.'

'But you will be in New Brighton, and busy with your new life, whilst I shall be here.'

'I don't have any choice. Surely you can see that? I have my mother to think of and Sophie and Frank.'

Connie could hear the impatience in Mavis's voice, and suddenly she badly wanted to cry. She had already lost so much, too much, and now she was losing Mavis as well. 'Couldn't Rosa help your mother, and then you and Frank could move in with his mother...'

Mavis exhaled tiredly, and shook her head. 'Rosa could not possibly cope, and anyway, as I have just told you, she is living with her cousin. And as for Frank's mother, she has decided to live with her widowed sister. We shall see one another, Connie. You can come to New Brighton on your days off and you know you will always be welcome.'

'Yes,' Connie agreed in a thin, empty voice. 'But it won't be the same.'

'Nothing can be the same for any of us any more, Connie,' Mavis replied bleakly. 'This War had changed so much. Taken so much!'

She felt as desolate as a deserted child, Connie recognised miserably. What was it about her that caused all those she loved to abandon her? Her mother; Ellie her sister; Kieron – even if she had loved him more out of foolish youthful folly than any real emotion or understanding of what love was; Harry. Her heart started to thud painfully, Harry, who she had lost not just once but twice over, and now Mavis.

A dull numbing bleakness filled her. Was she to spend the rest of her life never being truly loved? Truly wanted?

SEVENTEEN

'Aw for Gawd's sake, why doesn't someone shut him up? Yer mad Jinx, do you know that yer sitting there all bloody day rocking like that, and pretendin' to be a bloody machine gun!'

Connie paused halfway down her ward and frowned at the soldier who had just spoken.

Normally they tried to keep those soldiers who had been mentally affected by what they had experienced, separate from those who had suffered physical injuries. But when Jinx, as the poor man sitting cross-legged on the bed rocking to and fro, was known as, had been admitted, the only free bed they had, had been in her ward. Besides he had suffered a nasty bayonet wound in his back which had still not healed.

Although they were normally a good-natured bunch, it was obvious that some of the men were uncomfortable around Jinx, and none more so than the burly sergeant who was in the next bed.

On two occasions now, she had found Jinx lying on the floor beside his bed, confused and badly bruised, and on both occasions she had been told he had fallen there himself, but Connie had her suspicions as to how his injuries had been caused.

She felt sorry for Jinx who was a gentle soul, and who she sometimes heard reciting poetry in between bouts of imitating machine-gun fire and the screams of the injured and dying.

For his own sake, it would be better if he was moved to the old mental asylum ward, but as Connie knew it was already full with other men like Jinx – and worse – for whom the War was a torment that would never end.

'Bloody coward,' Connie heard the Sergeant muttering, as she walked past. 'He's orf his 'ead. Should have been shot for desertion, not given a bed amongst real soldiers.'

'He's an injured man, Sergeant Bailey, just like you and the other men on this ward,' Connie stopped him sharply.

'No 'e bloody ain't – anyone can see as how 'e's got it in his back – and we all know what that means, even if you don't, Sister,' the Sergeant answered her angrily.

Connie repressed a sigh. The Sergeant was a brave man, no one could doubt or question that. He had, after all, single-handedly dragged three of his injured comrades one by one through no man's land, rather than leave them there to be picked up by a stretcher party. The other men in the ward tended naturally to follow his lead, but the ward was not the Army, she was in charge here. And she already had more than enough work to do.

She went over to the Sergeant's bed and looked down at him. 'I shouldn't really be telling you this, Sergeant,' she said quietly. 'But I think for both your own, and Jinx's sake, I have to. He received his wound in his back when he threw himself on top of an injured comrade who had already fallen, so that he might protect him. The machine guns he imitates are our own British guns, which he lay listening to for three nights before a stretcher party found them. And the cries and the screams of the dying are those he had to listen to of the men around them, as they waited for help.'

A dull red tide of colour had crept under the Sergeant's skin. 'If that's the Gawd's 'onest truth, Sister.'

'It is,' Connie told him crisply, tensing as she saw the way the Sergeant had turned his head to look at her black armband.

'Ah, Sister!' she heard Mr Clegg, the senior consultant, addressing her, causing her to turn away from the Sergeant, and automatically hold herself straighter. She cast an admonishing look at the wan-faced junior whose scrubbing brush was not moving as rhythmically and efficiently as it might.

'We have a new patient.'

Connie frowned. They had new patients every day.

'One who Mr Raw has had sent especially to us for care.'

Immediately Connie's frown disappeared. Mr Nathan Raw, the Medical Superintendent, was now in charge of a mobile hospital unit at the Front which dealt with those cases deemed too serious to be moved. The whole hospital was intensely proud of the unit and their connection with it.

This would not be the first time that Mr Raw had sent one of his mobile hospital patients on to them and Connie, as befitted a surgical nurse, was immediately curious to know what manner of injuries this one might have sustained. Mere amputations were no longer considered serious enough to merit special treatment, and those suffering from gas poisoning were not sent to the surgical ward.

'The patient has lost one eye, and the wound has become badly infected,' Mr Clegg told her, as though he had read her mind. 'Captain Forbes's father is a close friend of one of our Governors, and for that reason he has requested that his son be nursed here. Oh, and the family have requested a private room.' There was a certain woodenness to Mr Clegg's expression.

Connie was frowning again, and forgot herself so far as to repeat questioningly, 'A private room?' before subsiding into pink-cheeked silence as Mr Clegg looked at her.

'I know that we don't normally give our patients private rooms, Sister, but I am instructed that we are to treat the Captain as a special case, in view of his family connection with the hospital. Matron has kindly agreed that the Captain might be placed in the small linen room off your ward. I think we might consider changing his bandages, and getting a closer look at his wound.'

'I'll scrub up immediately, sir,' Connie answered him briskly, even though she had just been on the point of leaving the ward for her already delayed evening meal.

The small linen room was used to store

bandages and was barely big enough to hold a bed, but somehow Connie managed to position one in it so that there was room for the Second Year to bring in a trolley, and for Connie to stand close enough to Mr Clegg to hand him whatever he might need.

They had seen all manner of wounds since the start of the War, and the Captain's looked by no means as severe as some had been.

He was an extremely good-looking young man, Connie had to admit, as he lay rigid on the bed, refusing to betray any sign of discomfort as she worked to remove the bandages, as quickly and as carefully as she could.

As she did so though, Connie had to clench her stomach muscles against the now familiar stench of rotting flesh. Behind her she heard the nauseous retch of the second-year nurse, who was supposed to be assisting her. The wound was certainly very badly infected.

Whoever had sewn up the Captain's wound was not very good with his needle. Her sister Ellie would have been shocked to see such uneven ugly stitches, Connie reflected, deliberately conjuring up the safety of such a mundane image as she worked on.

Ten minutes later when Mr Clegg had finished his examination, he motioned to Connie to follow him back onto the ward.

'The Captain has already lost an eye, Sister, and we shall have to work very hard if we are to ensure that he does not lose his life as well,' he pronounced seriously.

Connie folded her hands across her apron. They

287

were very proud of the fact that here in the hospital they lost so very few patients to septicaemia, unlike some hospitals, but that was when the patient had been operated on here and when they observed very strict cleanliness procedures, as laid down by Florence Nightingale. Those sorts of procedures were a luxury for those working in field hospitals. Connie did not need Mr Clegg to tell her that septicaemia was far easier to prevent than to cure.

'Have the Captain prepared for the operating theatre, please, Sister. I don't want to lose any time in cleaning out that eye socket. How soon can you have him ready?'

'As soon as you wish,' Connie answered him calmly.

So much for her supper, and her rest period.

Connie stood in the middle of the ward listening to the various sounds of breathing from her sleeping patients, interspersed here and there with the more raucous sound of someone snoring.

So far as Connie was concerned, a sleeping ward was a sign of a well-run, orderly ward, where patients had been tended to the best of a nurse's ability, and were not lying awake in their beds, in either pain or distress.

Slowly she walked down the ward. Even their newest patient, a boy of sixteen who had cried piteously for his mother after he had discovered they had had to amputate his feet, was peacefully asleep.

She had reached the end of the ward now, and she hesitated for a second before walking past the door to the Captain's room. It was just over a week since he had arrived, and Mr Clegg believed they had won the battle to stop the infection from his wound spreading.

He was certainly an extremely brave man – off the battle field as well as on it, Connie acknowledged, and a charming one according to everyone who had any dealings with him. Yet for all of that there was something about him that made her feel on edge and wary. Something about the way she had caught him looking at her when he had thought her unaware, a blatant, brutal kind of male scrutiny that raised memories and fears she had thought safely buried. And thanks to her own folly, the Captain knew of her fear.

She had just finished cleaning his wound this morning – a twice-daily ritual that Mr Clegg trusted only to her – when, before she could move away from his bed, he had reached out and taken hold of her wrist. His thumb caressed her bare flesh with bold intimacy, as he said softly, 'Your pulse is racing, Sister. Why? Surely you aren't afraid of me?'

And as her gaze had been jerked to meet his like that of a puppet on a string, she had known, oh, how she had known, that secretly he was exulting in the thought of her fear. His grip on her wrist had tightened past imprisonment to pain, and then he had slowly let his gaze move insolently over her body making her recoil from its lecherous intent.

It had been the sound of Jinx and his machine-gun fire outside in the ward that had broken his concentration, causing him to swear savagely, and allowing her to pull away.

Whilst the other men practically worshipped Captain Forbes, Jinx was petrified of him. Could only a poor deranged, damaged man, and a woman like her, sense that vile darkness about him; that dangerousness and evil intent?

Certainly the other nurses didn't share her feelings. They were always giggling about how handsome he was, and how gentlemanly his compliments.

Connie couldn't wait for the day when he would be well enough to leave. She had thought she had all but forgotten the horrors of her past; that they were buried deeply and safely out of reach, but now she had started having night terrors in which Bill Connolly and the Captain were trying to hunt her down.

Only today, listening whilst her junior nurses giggled over the Captain unaware of Connie's presence, their conversation as bold and flirtatious as her own had been as a girl, she had recognised abruptly how much she had changed, how alien that girl she had been now seemed to her.

Those dreams she had had then were so meaningless for her now; the carelessness with which she had flung herself heedlessly into her love for Kieron, the stubborn wilfulness, had all been tamed. She had learned too late what true love was, and she felt she had lost, too, the closeness of her friendship with Mavis, and that recent part of her life would soon be gone as well.

She had already decided that her future lay here in the hospital doing the work, which against all odds, she had come to love. As Sister Pride she was respected, and she respected herself and her own skills. She believed she had earned the right to cut herself off from the mistakes she had made and the shame she had brought on herself. But now suddenly, the Captain had created an unwanted bridge between the old Connie and the new, even if only inside herself. A wave of fear shuddered through her.

'Connie, I've just heard the best possible news.'

It was Mavis's last evening, and they were having supper together.

As she saw the happiness illuminating her friend's face Connie's heart bumped against her ribs. Putting down her cutlery she whispered, 'Harry...'

Mavis's smile trembled. 'No... No... Not that... How could it be? No, Connie, Rosa has written to Mother to tell us that she is to have Harry's child!'

The pain ripped and tore at Connie, unbearable and unending, her face drained of blood and a cold faintness spread out from the pit of her stomach. Harry's child! Rosa was to have Harry's child! The pledge and proof of his love!

'You can imagine how Mother feels, how all of us feel. Of course, nothing and no one could ever replace Harry, but to know that he is to have a son or daughter...'

She couldn't bear it. She could not bear it. Memories flooded through her. Kieron deserting her; the realisation that she was to have his child; the panic and fear she had felt; the knowledge of her shame – the shame that Harry had witnessed.

'We are going to do all we can to support Rosa, of course. We are her family after all, and the baby will be Mother's grandchild – Mother wants to have her to stay for a while...'

As she listened to Mavis, Connie tried to battle against the hurt and jealousy she was feeling. Years ago as a young girl, she had stood on the sidelines watching as a new closeness developed between Ellie and their cousin Cecily. She had felt shut out of what they were sharing, and not just shut out, but hurt and jealous. Ellie was *her* sister and not Cecily's she had reasoned childishly then, resenting having to share the sister she had thought of as exclusively hers, with someone else.

Now, although she was grown-up and Mavis was not her sister but her friend, what she was feeling – the sense of being excluded and the hurt that caused her – reminded Connie sharply of what she had felt then. She didn't want to lose her friend to someone else, but it hurt all the more knowing that the person she was losing her to, was Harry's wife.

Connie tried to be rational about it, and to tell herself that of course it was only natural that Mavis, as a young wife, should make friends with another young wife, especially when they were already related by marriage. And she tried to tell herself, too, that Mavis with her tender caring heart was bound to want to comfort and protect Rosa.

But a part of Connie didn't want to be rational and grown-up, and that part of her reacted to what Mavis was saying by deliberately withdrawing from her in hurt and anger, and to find excuses not to spend as much time with Mavis as she had.

It was, of course, Connie's way of protecting herself, but Mavis was not to know that!

'You've told them then?'

'That I'm to have Harry's child?' Rosa answered Gerald's wary question. 'Of course. They can't hear enough about it. They've even invited me to go and stay in that stuffy house in New Brighton – as if I'd want to go there!'

'You haven't told them that, have you?'

'Of course not. I've said as how I'm feeling too sickly to travel.'

'So what are they going to say when they find out you've travelled here to see me?' Gerald challenged her.

Rosa tossed her head. 'Who says they are going to find out? I told my father I was coming to stay with Phyllis. He doesn't know that she isn't here. What did you tell Beth?'

'The same. That I was coming to see Phyllis.'

'So does that mean we've got the whole day together, and maybe tonight as well?' Rosa asked him suggestively, drawing her fingertip along his arm.

'What about...?' Gerald gave a small nod in the direction of her stomach.

'Well you put it there and no one else,' Rosa pointed out coarsely. 'You should have married me you know, Gerald...'

'Don't you think I wish that I had,' he responded thickly, pulling her into his arms.

'We're a good match you and me, Rosa.'

'But you married Beth, and she's carrying your child as well.'

'More's the pity. All she ever does is complain. She's been driving me mad with her moaning about her bloomin' headaches.'

The Captain's parents had arrived to see him and the Captain's father had announced that he wanted to see Mr Clegg.

'Instantly and no messing! Tell him it's Councillor Forbes who is wanting him.'

Connie didn't care very much for the Captain's father, but for very different reasons than those that made her fear his son. Whilst the Captain spoke with the accent of a gentleman, his father was hewn from a much rougher stone. And obviously believed that his money could buy him whatever he wanted.

Had it bought him the thin, cold-looking woman who was his wife and the Captain's mother, Connie wondered?

They had brought the Captain's betrothed with them, Miss Burrell Howard, a haughty, proud-looking young woman, who had got the backs of all the nurses up good and proper.

'Fancy 'er being engaged to someone as good-looking as the Captain, and 'er that plain, an' all,' one of them had sniffed, after one of her earlier visits.

'Good-looking or not, she's welcome to him,' Connie had replied grimly.

'Ooh, 'ow can you say that – 'e's a fine well-set-up man the Captain is, and always got a cheery word and a bit of a twinkle in his eye, if you know what I mean.'

'Aye, well we all know what you are likely to get if you pay too much attention to it, and it won't be a wedding ring on your finger!' Connie had warned, not mincing her words.

The other nurse, a pretty, pert young woman who reminded Connie very much of the girl she herself had once been, had tossed her head and announced boldly, 'Well, you can't blame him for wanting sommat warm in his bed with a cold piece like 'er.'

Connie ignored her, but an older nurse who had happened to overhear the comment, came over to Connie once the girl had flounced off, and began disapprovingly, 'Little Madam, she wants to be tekken down to the women's ward to see what happens to girls who warm men's beds without a wedding ring. There's two of them on there now, two who got themselves into trouble and tried to get out of it!' she told Connie scornfully. 'Brung their disgrace on themselves they have. Shameful that's what they are, and shouldn't be allowed on the same ward as respectable women.

'Time was when the likes o' them would have been tied to the cart-tail and whipped through the streets. And if you want my opinions it's a pity that their sort isn't still made a public spectacle of. Any woman who bears a child outside of wedlock is a disgrace to her sex and should be punished accordingly, and I'm not the only one as thinks so.'

Connie knew that the other nurse was speaking the truth, but hearing it made her mouth go dry and her hands start to tremble slightly. She didn't want to be reminded of the fate that could have been her own, and she was relieved to see Mr Clegg walking toward her. Connie sensed, as she had done before, that Mr Clegg was no fonder of Captain Forbes than she herself was.

'There you are, Clegg. Took yer time, didn't yer. You know I'm a busy man...' The Captain's father puffed out his chest. 'I've got a munitions factory to run, I'll 'av you know.'

Discreetly Connie moved away from the door. She had other patients to attend to, and it didn't matter how much the Captain's father bullied and blustered, Mr Clegg would not allow the Captain to leave the hospital until he was well enough to do so.

Walking down the ward, she stopped by the Sergeant's bed. He was well enough to be discharged now.

'Mr Clegg tells me that we shall need to find a new patient for your bed, Sergeant.'

He beamed at her, whilst several other men on the ward started to cheer. As Connie knew, it always lifted the spirits of the whole ward when one of their number was declared fit enough to leave, just as the death of one of them plunged the whole ward into gloom.

'No doubt Mr Clegg will give you the news himself when he does his round.'

She was about to walk away when the Sergeant whispered urgently to her, ''Ere Sister, there's sommat I wanted ter tell yer!'

Frowning a little, Connie moved closer to his bed.

'It's about old Jinxy,' he told her in a confidential whisper, nodding his head in the direction of Jinx who, since Connie's quiet revelation to him, he had begun to treat far more kindly. 'I don't like to tell tales outta school like, especially not where there's an officer involved, but old Jinxy, well I feels I owes him one like, and knowing as how you 'ave a soft spot for him...' He paused and looked uncomfortable.

'It's the Captain you see, Sister... Yer gets men like 'im in the Army. All right if yer stands up ter 'em like, but they can be buggers – if you'll excuse me language – if yer lets 'em.'

Connie's whole body had gone bone cold. 'What is it you are trying to say, Sergeant?' she pressed him.

'Well, it's old Jinxy, Sister. Captain doesn't like 'im and he's stirred up one or two of the lads like, as well. Of course, whilst I've bin here I've kept me peepers on wot's goin' on like, and I've bin able to put 'em right about Jinx – tried ter tell the Captain as well but he weren't having it – and wi' me only being a Sergeant and 'im Captain... Aye, a real nasty piece o' work he is and no mistake! Jinxy is scared shi..., er, sick of him and, all and well, I just thought I'd give yer a warning like, Sister.'

'I'll remember what you've said, Sergeant,' Connie thanked him sombrely. It made her feel guilty that she hadn't realised for herself that the Captain might have had some part in Jinx's recent deterioration.

'Well, Sister, it's not my place to interfere, but he's not really a bad sort old Jinxy like – sorta got

297

a bit fond o' him mesel as it 'appens, although Gawd knows what's goin' to happen to him when he leaves here.'

'I don't know that either, Sergeant,' Connie answered truthfully, as she glanced toward the darkening sky outside the ward windows.

Mavis had written to invite her to join them for her Christmas off-duty days, adding excitedly that they were hoping that Rosa would return from her cousin's in time to spend Christmas with them, prior to her lying-in.

'For, after all, Connie, Harry's baby is far more closely related to our family than it is to Rosa's cousin's. We all grieve so for Harry, Connie, but Mother more so than any of us naturally.'

More so than her? In a different way, perhaps, but not more so, Connie thought painfully. She already knew that she would not accept Mavis's invitation and go to New Brighton. There would be too many painful memories there for her, and some even more painful reminders of Harry's love for someone else. And apart from that, she suspected that Mavis's invitation was borne more of duty than because she wanted to see her.

They had been exchanging letters it was true, but Mavis's had been full of the coming baby, and Connie had replied almost tersely to them, unable to express on paper how she was feeling, and how much she missed the closeness they had once shared. And she did miss it, and Mavis herself, most painfully.

In her most recent letter, Mavis had expressed her anxious concern for Rosa so strongly that Connie had felt a physical stab of misery. To make matters worse, Mavis had only made the most cursory enquiry into Connie's own happiness, leaving Connie feeling as though she didn't matter at all.

Stubbornly determined not to reveal how hurt she was, she had deliberately written back to Mavis describing her own life and work as though she was in the best of spirits, and even implying that she was too busy with her life without Mavis to have time to visit New Brighton over Christmas.

Mavis had taken longer than normal to write back to her, and she had not once pressed Connie to change her mind and visit over Christmas. Connie had shed more tears than she wanted to admit over that letter, before screwing it up and pushing it into the pocket of her cape.

Surely if Mavis had thought anything of her at all, she would have made some push to persuade her to go to New Brighton, Connie had thought forlornly, forgetting that the tone of her own correspondence might have hurt Mavis as much as Mavis's had hurt her.

At least she would be needed on her ward over Christmas, she tried to comfort herself. Her patients did not stop needing her just because it was Christmas.

She had come to accept that, from now on, the hospital must be her home and her security, and that her life would be spent here, and, as she already knew, her situation could have been much worse.

The Captain's visitors had gone. Reluctantly she made her way back to his room. The door was closed. How were her nurses supposed to keep a check on him on their way up and down the ward with a closed door? Frowning she opened it, and then froze. The Captain had one arm around the waist of the bold-eyed probationer who reminded Connie so much of her old self, whilst his free hand was cupping the girl's breast.

'Ooh, go on, you are a one you are, Captain, and no mistake. You're 'aving me on. That's no way to take a pulse...' Connie heard her giggling.

'Maybe not, but it is a sure fire way to get a good strong pulse going in any man who isn't a corpse,' Connie heard him replying thickly. 'Why don't you feel for yourself if you don't believe me.'

For a second Connie was tempted to slip back out of the room and to pretend she had neither seen nor heard what was going on – the probationer was plainly both encouraging and enjoying the Captain's attentions. And besides she herself... She herself was what? Afraid of interfering? Afraid of the Captain?

This was *her* ward, Connie reminded herself, and its standards and reputation, and those of the nurses who worked on it, were her responsibility. Would Matron – the yardstick by whom she now measured all her working actions – have walked away?

She took a deep breath and said coldly, 'Nurse, go back to your duties immediately.'

Hot-faced the probationer gave a shocked gasp and immediately started to pull away from the Captain.

'No stay Sukey!' he commanded the probationer, giving Connie a glittering look of malice, as he fastened his hand around the girl's wrist.

The probationer had stopped giggling, but the look she gave Connie was one of mingled excitement and rebellion.

'Still here Sister? Of course, if you want to join us...'

The probationer started giggling again. The small room suddenly felt icy cold to Connie and filled with danger. She wanted to turn and flee but she knew she had to re-assert her authority.

Thankfully the door was still open. Ignoring the Captain's comment, she turned her head and looked into the corridor.

'Mr Clegg is doing his round, Captain. I shall leave it to your own judgement as to whether or not you wish him to observe your behaviour. I understand your father is most anxious to know when your fiancée may commence preparations for your marriage.'

The probationer had stopped looking smug, and was now looking angrily sulky. Mutinously she pulled away from the Captain who released her without a word.

Connie felt sick as she saw the malevolence of the look he was giving her.

Ignoring it, she addressed the probationer telling her coldly, 'I shall wish to see you before you go off duty.'

EIGHTEEN

There was darkness, and movement and pain, so much pain, too much pain. It gripped and mauled him in fire-red, savagely sharp teeth. Sounds punctured the darkness, explosive and urgent, then voices uttering words that were unfamiliar to him, but which his brain and body registered with panic and fear.

He tried to move and could not do so, and the panic grew and changed and became a dread not of others, but of and for himself. He began to struggle but the pain seized him, dragging him bodily into the nothingness that was its hot, dark lair.

Sometimes the darkness was splintered by explosive noise he struggled to recognise, knowing only that it made him sweat with anxiety. Sometimes he could smell blood and fear and death.

There were the voices again speaking in an alien tongue. Harsh guttural words which he struggled to understand. And then there was movement; a cruelly rough jolting that made him cry out, but one split second before he did so, he suddenly recognised what he had not previously known. The voices he could hear were German voices, the hands he was in were German hands. He was a prisoner of war.

Now a different panic clawed at him, and the pain inside his head was the pain of sick fear.

There had been the most gruesome of stories told amongst his fellow soldiers. Stories of men done cruelly to death whilst they lay fallen and helpless, instead of being treated as a prisoner of war should be treated.

A sudden movement sent pain cascading through his whole body and swept him back into the darkness.

When he came round, he realised that he was strapped to a stretcher, lying on the floor of a train carriage surrounded by other injured men. A soldier in a German uniform walked up and down the narrow space between them, and Harry shrank back instinctively as the man's long shadow touched his own body. He was a prisoner of war being taken to wherever it was he was to be imprisoned!

He tried to turn his head, and had to bite back a scream as pain tore at his nerve endings.

The man on the next stretcher had a bandaged stump where his arm should have been, and Harry could see and smell the blood seeping steadily through the bandage. He looked in vain for a nurse, aware that the other man needed help but could see none.

The journey seemed to last for ever, through hot sweltering days and fever-soaked nights. The train stopped and stretchers were removed, but never his own. Only his pain and the sound of German voices, the German hands pulling at him – removing bandages, replacing them as pain exploded inside him and he escaped into unconsciousness – remained constants. He was too weak to do anything other than submit to whatever was inflicted on him, but whilst the pain was great there was no deliberate cruelty, he acknowledged.

Through that pain he thought longingly of home and his family, but most of all he thought of Connie. If he closed his eyes he could hear her quick, warm voice, and almost feel surely the calm coolness of her hands on his fevered skin. Surely it couldn't be a sin to think of her now, like this, when everything else was gone from him. Surely lying here alone in his pain-filled returns to consciousness, he had the right to let his thoughts embrace her. Connie. Connie. She would never know now just how much he had loved her!

The train stopped. He could feel his stretcher being lifted. So he had arrived at his prison! Pain skewered him and he sank back into the darkness.

A curiously bright light streamed in through the small window, and Harry immediately recognised its significance. Snow!

Snow. He could only remember heat. Too much heat. How could there now be snow? Panic flared inside him as his confused brain tried to make sense of vague, unconnected, and surely illogical, memories. He tried to lever himself up so that he could look out of the window and confirm his suspicions, but his body was too weak.

A tall man came into the room, not a soldier – he wasn't wearing a uniform – he was some kind of servant, Harry recognised.

'Who are you?' Harry demanded. 'Where am I? What...'

The man shook his head, his eyes widening as

he saw that Harry was struggling to sit up. Putting down the tray of food he had been carrying, he told Harry forcefully, 'Nein... Nein,' before hurrying back to the door.

As he heard the key turn in the lock behind him, Harry closed his eyes. He was a prisoner of war! He had to be. But where exactly, and why was he alone and not with other prisoners? The last thing he could remember properly was no man's land.

He could smell the coffee the man had brought and his stomach rumbled. The food on the tray looked simple but nourishing, a bowl of soup and some unfamiliar dark, flat-looking bread, along with several slices of sausage.

He knew he must have been wounded – he had sharp memories of pain, and a long train journey, and before that much hazier ones of low voices, of the sharp, harsh smell of carbolic and something else, sweeter and cloying ... chloroform? Did that mean he had had an operation? An amputation? Quickly he checked his body, trying not to groan as pain ripped at his side and spread through his chest, forcing him to sink back against the bed.

He still had his arms at any rate and his hands; although one of them was so heavily bandaged he could not move it properly. Why was he here alone? He could hear feet on the stairs, two sets of them and not just one. He tensed as he heard the grate of the key in the lock.

The tall man entered, followed by someone else, a smaller, darker, man – older – who looked as though nature had designed him to be plump but whose body and face had been stripped of that plumpness by some kind of anxiety.

'Ah, Herr Braun you are back with us. This time maybe for good, eh? That is good!'

Herr Braun? Why was he calling him that? There were more pressing questions he needed to have answered, Harry reminded himself as he tried again to sit up.

Immediately the older man was at his side, shaking his head, 'Ah, no, Herr Braun, please be so kind as not to move. Your wound is healing very well, but there were so many stitches, I had to dig deep to remove the bullet, and my sewing does not take too well to too much strain...'

Behind his steel-rimmed glasses, the man's dark eyes reflected more anxiety than humour at his own joke, causing Harry immediately to do as he had requested.

'Good. That is good. You have been a very good patient already but you still have a long way to go. You lose much blood and I was afraid...'

'You are a doctor,' Harry interrupted him, 'and you speak English.'

'A little English. I learned it whilst I was studying in Austria. But *nein*,' the man denied forcefully, '*nein*, I am not a doctor, Herr Braun. I am a professor. A surgeon, I am Professor Siegfried Freidmann Brante,' he told Harry fiercely.

'And you are German, Professor?' Harry demanded quietly. 'You are a German surgeon, and I am a prisoner of war? Where is this place ... this prison?'

The Professor's mouth compressed.

'I am Jewish, Herr Braun, and Austrian.' The

Professor hesitated and then continued in his careful English, 'As to the rest. Yes, you are indeed a prisoner of war, but, as to this being a prison... Indeed it is no such thing!'

At any other time, Harry suspected that the indignation in the man's voice would have made him smile. As it was, he felt far too anxious and apprehensive to do anything other than demand tersely, 'I do not understand what you are saying. I am a prisoner of war, but you say that this is not a prison. Is it then a hospital?' If so, where were the nurses, the other patients? Harry could feel his heart starting to hammer frantically, as confusion and dread gripped him.

'Please let me explain... After the Battle of the Somme we have news that the soldier son of my old friend has been badly injured. We go immediately to the field hospital, his father and I, and it is then that he tells us of the Englishman who has saved his life. He is badly injured but he tells us of how this Englishman comforted him, and how he placed a bandage around his wound.

'He points you out to us, for as luck would have it, there were so many wounded that you were only four beds away from him – the German soldiers and the prisoners of war had not yet been separated.

'My friend, his father, who has some influence in these matters, tells the authorities that he owes your family the same compassion you have shown his son, and that it is a matter of honour that he does not leave you to die alone and uncared for.

'My friend's son, Heinrich, is very weak and has lost much blood, but his wound is not so serious as your own. The army surgeon allows us to take you since he says it is obvious that you will die. That is what he says... I say that since you will die anyway, then there is no problem in us removing you and saving them a burial. The officer-in-charge commands us to take you, but first he removes your papers and we see that your name is Johnny Brown.

'We bring you here to the small village where both my friend and I grew up. It takes many days on the train and I fear that you will die. There is no hospital here, but I have my laboratory and, with the aid of the good nuns who nurse our sick, I am able to attend to the wounds of both my friend's son and your own.'

He was a prisoner of war, Harry recognised, and according to the Professor lucky to be alive. But he did not feel lucky. How could he? His family ... Connie ... did they know what had happened to him? His mother would worry so, and his sisters. But not Rosa, of course. She would not care if she never saw him again. And Connie, did she care? Did she think of him?... Connie ... his family. Would he ever see any of them again?

Filled with despair, Harry wrenched his pain-filled thoughts back to the Professor to hear him saying, 'Once I have cleaned the hole left by the bullet, Heinrich's wound will heal quickly, but your own is not so easy. The bullet had lodged deep in your chest and there was also a bayonet wound in your arm.

'I had not truly dared to hope that you would survive, I was able to experiment with a new procedure, a method that is all my own – I first

308

of all treat the gut I am to use for the stitches, and then... But my first attempt was not successful and your wound showed signs of infection. I had to remove the stitches, and clean the wound and then try again. It was very important that you did not move, and I had to sedate you in order to keep you still.

'It was Gunther's task to watch over you and make sure that you did not move too much, and that nor did your stillness give rise to bed sores.'

The tall, grey-haired man who had brought Harry his food, gave a small bow. 'Gunther is valet to my friend Baron von Hapsburg.'

'Baron?'

Harry struggled to make sense of what he was being told. He tried again to sit up but the sharp pain searing his arm stopped him.

'You have asked me if you are a prisoner of war. That is a matter for Friedrich to discuss with you himself. He is away from home at the moment, but when he returns you can ask him your questions.

'Now, Herr Braun, I should like to take a look at your wound. If there is too much pain for you then please to say so and I shall give you some chloroform.'

'I am not Herr Braun,' Harry started to say, but the pain was overwhelming him, and the smell of chloroform was dizzying him into unconsciousness.

Connie heard the scream as she entered the ward for night duty, an inhuman terrifying sound that lifted the hair at the back of her neck. It changed abruptly to the rattle of machine-gun fire, followed by sobs and a litany of muddled pleas...

She had been off duty for two days and immediately she started to walk as fast as she could, without breaking into a forbidden run, as she headed for Jinx's bed.

The bed itself was empty and Jinx was huddled on the floor beside it, his knees up under his chin and his arms wrapped tightly around them.

A white-faced, second-year nurse was standing frozen to the spot whilst a handful of the patients had got out of their beds and were standing in a small group in their dressing gowns.

''Ere stop that racket will yer!' someone shouted irritably from a nearby bed, whilst Connie swept aside the other patients and asked the nurse sharply, 'What is going on? Where are the other nurses?'

'I dunno Sister. I just come on meself.'

'It's all right Jinxy, everything's all right, you're safe here we don't need the machine guns,' Connie told him gently, crouching down on the floor beside him to speak to him, whilst he continued to rock himself to and fro.

As soon as he heard her voice, he turned his head toward her, and in the dim light Connie saw the glisten of his tears on his thin face – and she could see something else as well; something that made her recoil in disbelief, quickly followed by outrage and fury.

There was a wound on his face, the blood congealing on it from him pressing his face into his knee, so that it was plain to see what it was. Someone had carved a large letter C on the side

310

of his face.

Connie had no need to ask what it was supposed to stand for, nor she suspected whose hand lay behind it.

'Nurse, go into the next ward, and ask the Sister there if she will telephone Mr Clegg. I think he will want to see this,' Connie instructed the white-faced girl watching her bleakly.

'Well, it's no use anyone asking me anything, cos I weren't here.'

'And you, gentlemen?' Connie asked the silent soldiers. 'Am I to take it that none of you were here, either?'

She could hear them shuffling from one foot to the other as they felt the bite of her furious sarcasm.

She couldn't leave Jinx, who was still sobbing and moaning, whilst his body shuddered violently, her first duty was to him. But she could see that the door to the Captain's room was ajar, and instinctively she knew that he was the kind of man who would take pleasure in such a bestial action. Had he done it himself or had he somehow caused the other patients to do it? So far as Connie was concerned, it didn't make any difference. The guilt was his. The guilt and the cruelty.

One of the house surgeons had arrived, a thin, young, red-headed man whose Adam's apple bobbed nervously in his throat when he saw Jinx.

'What happened?' he asked Connie uncertainly.

'I don't know but he certainly didn't get a wound like that falling out of bed,' Connie told him tightly.

'Well, if you ask me it's all a fuss about noth-

311

ing,' one of the other nurses claimed, after Jinx had been stitched and sedated, and the ward had been restored to order. 'After all, that's what he is, isn't he? A coward... And what with 'is mind gorn, an' all, he should be in Bedlam, not a respectable hospital with decent soldiers and heroes.'

Connie had had enough. She marched across the ward and pushed open the Captain's door.

'I know that you're awake, Captain,' she told him fiercely. 'Mr Clegg is anxious to know what happened to Jinx.'

'Now how should I know that, Sister? I haven't left my room all day! And of course, if you wish to ask her, I am sure that Probationer Jennings will confirm that I was here in bed the whole time she was on duty.'

Connie could feel her face starting to burn. It had infuriated her to discover that the Captain's father had spoken to his friend the Governor about the wonderful nursing his son had received from Probationer Jennings. He had praised the hospital, and specifically Matron for the quality of her nursing staff. Now Sukey Jennings was treating Connie with a pert cheekiness that made Connie long to slap her face.

Connie couldn't say anything to Mr Clegg about her suspicions. It simply wasn't done, and besides, she reasoned, Mr Clegg was bound to take the word of a soldier and a gentleman, over her own.

Wherever he was, it was obviously high up in the mountains, Harry decided, as he stared out of

312

the narrow window of his small attic room at the snow-covered terrain beyond them.

As he already knew, there was no point in him opening the door of his attic prison, because the moment he did, Gunther would materialise silently from the corridor and bow impassively whilst blocking his exit.

As prisons go, his was far better than most, Harry acknowledged. Gunther brought a regular supply of fuel for the small stove in addition to his meals, and the Professor had even supplied him with several English books – a history of the Duke of Marlborough's campaigns, a history of Wellington's Peninsular Campaign, and a heavy volume of Shakespeare's tragedies.

But none of those things stopped him from desperately wondering how he might escape. So far though he had not been able to come up with any viable plan. He had several times asked for pen and paper and been refused, and he had also tried to make the Professor understand that he was not Johnny Brown, but to no avail.

All the other questions he had tried to ask, such as where he was, what had happened to the young man whose life he was supposed to have saved, and when the Baron was likely to return, had all met with no response.

He wanted desperately to be allowed to get in touch with his family... He heard the door open behind him and guessed that it would be Gunther bringing more logs for the stove. It had been snowing hard all day and soon it would be dusk.

Without taking his gaze from the darkening sky,

Harry demanded wearily, 'Gunther, when is the Baron to return?'

'I am sorry, Herr Braun, that I have been kept so long from my home and that I have not been able therefore to welcome you to it, and thank you for acting as a good Samaritan toward my son.'

Harry turned round immediately. The man standing in the doorway was as tall as he was himself, his face weathered, his eyes a brilliant blue. His aquiline profile, like his bearing, hinted at Prussian ancestry, but the heavy leather cloak that swung from his shoulders, and the knarled hand he was extending toward Harry, were those of a farmer rather than a member of the nobility.

'I wished I might have been able to be here sooner, but we had the sheep to move to their winter pastures. If we lose the flock then the village, my people – and I too – lose our livelihood. You look surprised, Herr Braun?'

Harry felt himself redden uncomfortably.

'No... That is... When the Professor referred to you as the Baron. I thought ... that is I imagined...'

The older man smiled. 'The title is an old one, and whatever lands and riches may once have gone with it were lost many generations ago. My inheritance was this ruined castle, an excellent library, the villagers who depend on me as though they are my children, and a flock of sheep.'

'You speak very good English.' Harry didn't know what else to say.

'My family connections are extremely extensive.

I have cousins of cousins who have cousins who are English, and in happier times I visited them. I had hoped that my own son might do so, too, but alas this War.' He started to frown. 'I owe you a great debt, Herr Braun.'

Harry started to shake his head in denial.

'But, yes,' the baron insisted. 'For there can be no gift a man values more than the life of his son. My son would have died but for you, Herr Braun.'

'I only did what any man would have done,' Harry felt bound to protest.

The Baron smiled thinly. 'You are a modest man, Herr Braun. My son, I am delighted to say, has fully recovered from his wound and has now returned to the Front.'

Harry's mouth tightened, as he reflected inwardly that that was exactly where he should be.

'Your expression gives you away,' the Baron told him quietly. 'But you cannot escape from here. And besides... The British cannot win this War, you know that, don't you. Sixty thousand British soldiers died in the Battle of the Somme – the cream of the British Army.'

'That is all the more reason for me to be there with them now!' Harry told him fiercely. 'Englishmen are renowned for their bulldog spirit. We will not give up.'

'I admire your valour but you will certainly not fight again in this War, Herr Braun,' the Baron told him sternly. 'You are a prisoner of war, and have been given into my care as such!'

Harry exhaled painfully. 'But this is not a

prison camp.'

'I am sure that the Professor has already told you that had we left you in the same field hospital where you had been taken with my son, you would not have lived.'

'He has said something of the sort, yes!' Harry acknowledged curtly, reluctant to acknowledge any debt of gratitude to an enemy.

'I can see that your honour is affronted by that, and that does you credit, but my honour demanded that I repay you for saving my son's life, which is why you are here and not in a prisoner-of-war camp.'

'I would rather be with my own people,' Harry told him stubbornly.

'I'm afraid that that is not possible, Johnny Brown.'

'I am not Johnny Brown!' Harry burst out.

'No?' The Baron started to frown.

'There has been some confusion,' Harry told him shortly.

'Confusion? What confusion?' the Baron demanded.

Harry took a deep breath.

'I am not Johnny Brown. My name is Harry Lawson.' Quickly he explained what had happened, whilst inwardly wondering if Johnny himself had survived. If so, he must surely have told the authorities about their exchange of jackets, but if he had not... As he had done before, Harry wondered if his family knew what had happened to him.

'The papers you were carrying said you were Johnny Brown. Think very carefully, please now,' the Baron warned him sternly. 'If you have falsely claimed another's identity then I must report that fact. Assuming the identity of another is a practice favoured by spies.'

'I am not a spy,' Harry protested. 'I am simply an ordinary soldier. But I would like my family to know that I am still alive.'

Inwardly he thought of his mother and his sisters, and what they must be feeling. He even thought of Rosa, and then, like a miser hoarding his gold, he thought of Connie, as he had thought of her every single day since he had regained his senses.

'I shall do my best to inform the authorities. We have no telephone up here this high in the mountains. Until spring, the only contact we have with the outside world is by skiing down the mountainside. Do you ski, Harry?'

Harry shook his head.

'So. But I shall still ask for your word as an honourable man, that you will acknowledge your position as a prisoner of war and not try to escape from the castle! In truth, I think you would do better to serve out your imprisonment here until the War is ended rather than in a military encampment.'

Worriedly Harry struggled with his conscience. If he were to give his word as the Baron was demanding, then he would have to keep it. But his duty as a soldier meant that he should do whatever he could to escape.

'You cannot escape from here,' the Baron told him calmly, as though he had guessed what he was thinking. 'And if you should try to do so, then I shall shoot you.' He added emphatically, 'And I am an excellent shot.'

Harry looked at him. 'But you have saved my life!'

'In repayment of my debt to you because you saved my son's – if you try to escape then that is a different matter, and I am honour bound to stop you, which is why I request your word as a soldier that you will not do so!'

What was he to do? He was still very weak, he had no gun, no money, no means whatsoever of making his way back to the Front.

'Very well,' he agreed reluctantly. 'You have my word!'

'Thank you! It would be impossible for you to escape from here anyway, I can assure you of that. Now, since the Professor has returned to his own home and his laboratory, you and I shall only have one another's company until the snows melt. So tell me, Harry, do you, by any chance, play chess?'

It was almost November, and the War was no nearer to an end. As she hurried on duty, Connie could hear someone whistling a love song and, just for a moment, emotional tears filled her eyes. There wasn't a single day when she didn't think of Harry. Not, if she were honest, a single hour. Quickly she blinked her threatening tears away.

It seemed impossible that he should be dead, not when he was still so very much alive in her thoughts and her heart, and she could still see him so clearly with her mind's eye. She could still taste, too, the warmth of his mouth on hers in that bittersweet kiss they had shared. But at least in her thoughts and her heart he was now hers – and she claimed that possession of him with hungry need. Her memories were her own to cherish. Her love her own to mourn.

The dark, pain-filled days of her grief clung one to the other, locking her into her own private sadness and pain.

But at least the Captain was being discharged today, and Connie couldn't wait to have him gone. They were even busier than usual on the ward, having had a new flood of casualties arrive earlier in the week, which reminded Connie that the cupboard in which the ward's supply of bandages and dressings were now kept needed restocking.

She would have to send a couple of the juniors down to the dispensary for some fresh supplies. They needed more dressing gowns as well, and that new patient with the head wound would need an extra special eye keeping on him. It would be such a relief to be rid of the Captain.

Jinx was still on the ward and Connie went over to talk to him for a few minutes. The attack which had marked his face had left him even more prey to his nervous attacks, and Connie knew that sadly he would never return to normality.

When he took hold of her hand and pressed his cheek against it, she didn't try to draw away. He was like a child now mentally, but possessed of a man's physical strength, and Connie felt some-how protective toward him. He, in turn, had become devoted to her.

Leaving Jinx she headed for the small Sister's

room off the ward, and told the senior ward nurse waiting for her there, 'The Captain will be leaving today.'

'Beggin' your pardon, Sister, but he's already gorn.'

'Gone?'

The nurse nodded her head vigorously. 'Yes. Left bright and early he did. Said as how Mr Clegg had given special permission like, and how he couldn't wait to get home and have a decent breakfast again.'

Connie nodded her head briskly, not wanting the other nurse to see how her relief was making her tremble slightly. Just recently she had felt as though he was watching her like a cat at a mouse hole, and although she had tried not to show it, she had felt vulnerable and afraid.

'Can I go and have me own breakfast now, Sister, seein' as how I should be off duty now anyway?'

'Yes, of course,' Connie agreed absently.

The door to the Captain's room stood open and Connie walked out of the ward and into the small room. The empty bed was still there, but in all other respects it was empty of any sign of the Captain's occupation other than the sharp smell of the cologne he had worn.

Connie sniffed and tensed, and then whirled round, alerted by some latent sixth sense, but it was already too late. The Captain was standing between her and the door.

Just outside it, Jinx, who must have followed her, was standing fearfully, watching. The moment the Captain saw him, he swore and grabbed him by the throat, banging his head brutally against the doorjamb.

As Jinx howled in pain, and then collapsed, Connie rushed automatically toward him demanding, 'Stop that at once!' But the Captain slammed the door closed and stood in front of it.

'You like giving orders, don't you, Sister, telling others what to do, and poking your nose in where it isn't wanted? Well I don't like others poking their noses into my affairs, and when they do, I make sure they feel the full weight of my displeasure. Like you are going to now!'

Connie could see the hot, feral glitter of enjoyment in the Captain's good eye as he witnessed her shocked reaction, and then suddenly the room was plunged into darkness as he extinguished the light.

Instinctively she tried to push past him to reach the door, crying out as she did so. Instantly, he covered her mouth with one hand, whilst the other turned the key in the door.

She could feel his breath against her ear, as he whispered savagely, 'Ah ha, got you now, Sister, and guess what I'm going to do with you. I'm going to make you pay me what you owe me, starting with this.'

As he wrenched open the front of her dress, Connie sank her teeth into his hand. She heard him curse as he lifted his free hand and hit her hard across her face, the impact of the blow jerking her head back painfully against the door.

'You had that coming. And you've got this coming, too, bitch...'

His voice was thick with lust and savagery.

Frantically Connie tried to claw at his hand as he grabbed hold of her breast and squeezed it painfully. In retaliation he placed his hand round her neck and banged her head against the door, before seizing hold of her hair and dragging her over to the bed.

Beyond the door she could hear Jinxy rattling off rounds of machine-gun fire mingled with dying screams.

Against her ear the Captain told her tauntingly, 'Listen to him, good, isn't it? No one is going to pay any attention no matter how much you scream – they'll just think it's that madman.'

His finger touched her face and Connie froze.

'C is for coward,' he whispered in her ear, 'and C is for Connie as well...'

She could hear him laughing as he pushed her down onto the bed, whilst she tried to break free, kicking out wildly at him.

'Bitch!' he told her roughly, hitting her again.

It was like being back in Back Court all over again, abandoned by Kieron and left at the mercy of his uncle, only this time it was worse. Much worse.

Bill Connolly had only threatened to let others rape her.

Connie tried to scream through the sickening dizziness of her pain, turning her head frantically from side to side, as the Captain forced open her mouth and thrust a wad of fabric into it. Terrified and hardly able to breathe, she felt him push up her skirts and then straddle her, pinning her beneath him with his weight.

She tried her best to resist him, pushing at him

with her hands, but he simply laughed at her resistance, hitting her so hard that her teeth rattled.

'See, this is what you are going to get,' he boasted to her.

Her eyes had adjusted to the faint light in the room now. Helplessly Connie closed her eyes against the sight of the dark red, pulsing male organ with its thick raised veins.

'I've been dreaming about this ... do you know that? Dreaming about punishing you for daring to interfere with my plans ... my pleasure...'

He was forcing open her legs. Connie kicked out at him and then almost fainted as he grabbed her ankle and twisted it until she thought it was going to break.

She heard him grunt in satisfaction as her body went limp and then he was thrusting into her; hurting her; forcing her; defiling her.

He was breathing heavily and hard, thrusting hard, grunting, lost in his own obscene pleasure, Connie recognised, as she lay sickly beneath him barely conscious.

'Whore. Whore ... whore...' He gave one final triumphant thrust, his weight pressing her into the mattress, as he relieved his lust, and then he was pulling away from her, and calmly dressing himself.

'I always get what I want, Sister – one way or another,' he told her tauntingly.

Connie heard the door open, and his voice sharp with loathing, as he demanded, 'Get out of my way, imbecile!' followed by Jinx's scream of pain, but it still took her several seconds to realise that he had actually gone.

She felt weak and sick, and her hands were shaking so much it took her what felt like a lifetime to remove the gag from her mouth and then straighten her clothes. Her face felt swollen and she could taste blood on her lip.

When she opened the door, to her relief the corridor outside was empty apart from Jinx, who was huddled on the floor, his face badly bruised.

Later Connie had no memory at all of how she got back to her own room or who might have seen her. A quick look in her mirror confirmed everything she had feared. Her face was swollen almost out of recognition and by tomorrow would be black and blue. No amount of bathing it with cold water or applying arnica to it was going to make any difference.

As for the rest. She simply wasn't going to allow herself to think about it. Far better to pretend it had never happened. Shudders were wracking her body but she ignored them. It had never happened. Nothing had happened. The Captain had gone and she was safe.

So why was she crying?

In the bathroom she scrubbed her skin as though she wanted to scrub it off, leaving it red raw.

She told everyone who asked that her bruised face and body were the result of a fall outside on the ice, and that was what she told herself she had to believe as well.

At Christmas, she thought she had succeeded.

By February, she knew she had not and never

324

could. She had missed her monthlies – twice – and not just that. She was wretchedly, heavingly sick on rising, and had come close to fainting in the operating theatre.

Thoughts of intense rage and bitterness filled her. She tried every old wives' remedy she knew to dislodge the hated life growing inside her, including drinking a bottle of gin before immersing herself in a bath of water so hot it scalded her skin – but to no avail.

There were other methods, crude and rarely successful, which were too horrific to try. She had seen young women on the wards who had attempted them dying in agony from septicaemia – even wealthy young women sometimes, who had thought themselves safe in the hands of the doctor who had operated illegally on them.

Instead she clung to the hope that she would miscarry naturally, and that life wouldn't be so cruel as to make her endure a fate she surely did not deserve.

But then they were in March, and she was over three months gone. Soon she would start to show. She would lose her job; she would lose everything and be right back where Kieron had left her. Her hope had gone, and in its place all she had was mindless dread and fearful panic.

She couldn't endure what lay ahead of her. It was too much for her to bear. Connie had never felt more wretched.

''Ere look there's a photo of the Captain and his new Missus in the paper.'

Connie fought back her nausea as the news-paper was passed up and down the ward whilst everyone looked at the photograph.

Would the Captain treat his new bride as he had done her? Bitterness filled her. What had she done to deserve such a fate? Surely she had already paid for her youthful mistake?

She had nothing left to live for now. Nothing! She had lost the man she loved, and now she was going to lose what had been left. Her respectability; her job; her home. She would be destitute and out on the street, pregnant with a child she already hated.

She had virtually stopped eating, unable to keep food down through a mixture of nausea and sick distress. As a result she was weak and constantly light-headed, gripped by spells of dizziness and stomach-churning despair, which she battled to hide from everybody else.

As soon as she was off duty, Connie left the ward and crossed the hospital's busy entrance hall, heading not for the exit to the nurses' home but instead for the main doors. Wild thoughts of taking her own life filled her head, even though she knew it would be a dreadful sin. The sour taste of her own nausea made her retch and grip her stomach, too caught up in her own despairing thoughts to be aware of anything or anyone else.

In such cold, icy conditions a person could surely slip easily and unnoticed into the cold waters of the Mersey. It would be over quickly if she didn't struggle, the water filling her lungs, and drowning out the unwanted life within her along with her own.

She would be safe then. Why she might even see Harry again! But of course Harry would go to heaven and she would not. People who broke God's law and took their own lives went straight to hell, everyone knew that! That's why they were not allowed to be buried in consecrated ground.

Numbly she started to cross the road, lost in her own dark painful thoughts. She was oblivious to everything bar her own despair, including the car bearing down on her. The driver tried to avoid her, but the road was icy.

Connie heard the screech of brakes and realised, too late, her danger. Her eyes widened as she saw the car coming toward her. She was going to be killed! In a split second she recognised that she did not, after all, want to die.

Panic filled her as she tried to turn and run, but it was too late.

A bystander witnessing the accident cried out in horrified shock. The car skidded to a stop whilst a crowd gathered anxiously round Connie's prone, still body.

A tall, striking-looking woman emerged from the back of the car and pushed her way through the crowd commanding sharply, 'Make way, please, I'm a doctor.'

'A doctor! And her a woman, too! Catch me letting her doctor me,' one of the onlookers commented in disapproval, as the tall woman knelt down in the road beside Connie. She frowned as she saw the blood trickling stickily from Connie's mouth. Then suddenly she tensed, as she looked closer and into Connie's face...

PART THREE

NINETEEN

As the car turned into the familiar square, Connie closed her eyes as tightly shut as she could. She had fought so hard against coming here, but in the end she had had to give in. Where else, after all, was there for her to go now that she was well enough to leave hospital?

Everyone kept telling her how lucky she had been to have suffered nothing more than a nasty bump on the head and a few sprains. And she supposed she ought to be grateful to Iris for her quick-wittedness in inventing Connie's fictional widowed status for her the moment it became obvious that she was pregnant.

And since she herself had still been unconscious at the time, Connie had not been in a position to reject the timely invention, learning of it only when one of her fellow nurses had come to see how she was, and told her breathlessly, 'My, but you are a dark horse, married and widowed, and in the family way and saying nothing of any of it to us!'

Now of course, it was impossible for her to remain at the Infirmary even if she had been well enough to do so.

But to have to come here!

She flinched as Iris drove past the house that belonged to her Aunt Amelia Gibson, refusing to glance toward it.

The house was ahead of them, elegant and immaculately kept. The gravelled carriageway crunched beneath the tyres of Iris's car, the same tyres beneath which Connie herself had so nearly met her death.

Despite her determination not to do so, Connie started to shake. Although she had not said so to anyone, she still experienced flashbacks to that moment when she had thought she must die. In those last, dark seconds before she had collapsed, she had thought instinctively of Harry, and even believed she had felt his presence.

But when she recovered consciousness she had been not in hell or heaven, but far more prosaically in a hospital bed, with Mr Clegg and Iris standing over her.

Iris, it appeared, had just been given the role of acting as a medical go-between by the Government, to direct injured soldiers to the hospitals in the area best able to deal with their injuries. Iris had been on her way to see Mr Clegg at the time of Connie's accident.

It had been a few days later that she had briskly explained to Mr Clegg, who had been examining Connie's injuries, that she suspected that it was Connie's grief at the loss of her husband that had caused her to lose concentration and step out into the road as she had.

The front door to the house was opening, Connie started to tremble again as she saw the familiar figure standing there.

'Let's get you out of the car, Connie, and then it's straight to bed with you,' Iris was telling her firmly, but Connie couldn't respond to her. All her attention was concentrated on the woman hurrying toward them.

The car door opened. Connie bit her lip as a soft hand touched her own, and an even softer voice said emotionally, 'Oh, Connie, Connie, it is you... Oh dearest, I hardly dared to let myself hope, even though Iris assured me that it was true and that it was you! Gideon, it is Connie. Come quickly and see. Oh, my dearest love... My dearest, dearest sister!'

Connie could feel Ellie's tears on her skin as her sister lovingly helped her from the car.

'I didn't want to come here,' she began, but immediately Ellie stopped her.

'Not come? But Connie, where else should you go? We are your family! This is your home!'

'No, it is your home, Ellie,' Connie started to say, but her emotions were clogging her throat and making it impossible for her to speak.

Iris had told her that Ellie was overjoyed to hear that she was still alive after believing her to have perished in the *Titanic*, but Connie had not truly dared to believe that her sister would welcome her.

'If only we'd known where you were, and that you were alive.' Ellie was weeping as Gideon took over from his wife, lifting Connie's frail form into his arms, to carry her inside.

'Please don't. I can walk,' Connie protested, but it was too late, Gideon was carrying her into the house and up the stairs. He took her through a doorway and into the prettiest bedroom Connie had ever seen.

Tears blurred her vision, but through them she

could still see her sister's anxious face and tear-wet eyes, as she instructed her husband to place Connie on the waiting chaise.

'See, Connie, from here you can look out into the square, and later on, when you are able, we can walk to the park together. Oh, Connie, why have you not written or telephoned?'

'Now Ellie, we agreed that there should be no questions,' Gideon broke in with quiet authority. 'At least until Connie is feeling stronger.'

Iris had come upstairs, and Connie heard her saying firmly that Connie would be better in bed so that she could recover from the journey. Within minutes of those firm words, Connie was tucked up in bed being given a drink of hot milk.

She was tired, more so than she herself had been prepared for, but her anguish at being forced on her sister's charity kept her awake. Once she was alone and there was no one to witness her misery and guilt, she plucked worriedly at the bedclothes.

Ellie couldn't possibly want her here, surely? Despite the warmth of the room she shivered. She had no right to be here. She didn't deserve to be here.

She closed her eyes trying to squeeze back her unwanted tears, as exhaustion, and then sleep, claimed her.

She was still asleep several hours later, when the door opened gently and Ellie tiptoed in. She stood by the bed and looked emotionally into her sister's sleeping face.

In her sleep Connie was aware of the gentle, loving hand touching her face. Without opening her eyes she whispered longingly, 'Mother.'

It was the hot splash of Ellie's tears on her hand that brought her to confused wakefulness.

'Oh, Connie...'

As Ellie took her in her arms and held her tightly, she could feel her sister's body shake with the pent-up force of her tears.

Suddenly she too was crying, clinging to Ellie as Ellie was clinging to her, their tears mingling, just as though they were still young girls.

'Connie, what on earth are you doing out of bed? You know Iris said you must rest, for your own sake, and for the baby's.'

'Ellie, I'm fine,' Connie assured her elder sister, as she stood in front of the window of the elegant guest room in Ellie and Gideon's Winckley Square home.

'Connie, you may think that you are, but dearest, you must try to remember that it is only just a month since Iris brought you here. And if I seem to fuss over you, it is just because I am so happy to have you restored to us! When Iris telephoned from our cousin Cecily's to tell us that you had not, as we had thought, been on *Titanic* and that you were alive, I could scarcely take it all in. For such a coincidence to happen! That Iris should have been on her way to the Infirmary for a meeting just as you stepped out into the road.'

'I didn't want Iris to involve Cecily in any of this! I know that Cecily's husband is her brother, but I can never forget that Cecily's mother is our aunt – and it certainly wasn't by my choice that

Iris wished me on you, Ellie!'

'Cecily means well and is very kind-hearted, Connie. And as for you being wished on me, no such thing! Where else should you go? My dearest wish has been that I might see you again.

'Iris says it is a wonder that her driver was able to stop! I can't bear to think about how easily I might have lost you! How easily you might have been killed.' Ellie gave a small shudder.

'You thought I was dead already,' Connie couldn't stop herself from pointing out prosaically.

'Which makes me all the more determined that you shall be properly looked after now that you have been restored to us,' Ellie returned promptly. 'Your return to us is like a miracle, Connie. I had grieved for you so much; wished so much that I might tell you how much I love you. Fate meant you to come back to us, Connie, otherwise why should it have been Iris who saw you and recognised you?'

Connie wondered what her sister would say if she told her that part of her still wished herself dead, despite the luxury and spoiling Ellie was surrounding her with.

'And it is not just a gift of your return I have been blessed with, Connie, but the hope of a new niece or nephew as well,' Ellie continued sentimentally.

Immediately Connie looked down at her left hand and the rings she was wearing on her wedding finger, a plain gold band and a small diamond engagement ring.

Ellie followed her gaze and blushed prettily.

'We thought it best that you had them. You

know how people talk, Connie, and with Aunt Gibson living so close. I know you were working as a nurse, but Iris says it is not uncommon for nurses to marry in secret before their sweethearts go off to war.'

Sweetheart! An icy coldness had started to invade Connie; nausea rushed into her as she compared the brutal reality of what she had endured with the idyllic image conjured up by her sister's words.

'You have not spoken of ... of anyone,' Ellie continued uncertainly, 'and ... and Iris said that you must be allowed to get your strength back before anyone bothered you with questions that might cause you pain. So many brave men have been lost in this War. I can only imagine how I would feel if I were to lose my darling Gideon!' Gideon's right hand had been crippled in a horrific accident before he and Ellie were married. To Ellie's relief, this meant he had been rejected for military service.

Ellie couldn't have made it plainer what she was wanting her to say, Connie recognised, and a part of her was tempted to lie and claim the respectability of marriage, and the widowhood to which she was not entitled.

But another part of her wanted her sister to know the truth; wanted her to know what had happened to her. Wanted what? To see Ellie recoil from her in shock and horror, because that was what she would do, Connie warned herself. The elegant, protected, respectable wife Ellie had now become, would never be able to understand the kind of situation she, Connie, had been in. Nor

337

the situation she now was in.

What was the matter with her? Connie asked herself in irritation. Why was she reverting to such childishness, especially when Ellie had been so kind and welcoming to her? Was it because her sister's use of the word 'sweetheart' had conjured up for Connie images of Harry?

'And that reminds me,' Ellie added. 'Iris will be here soon. She telephoned to say that she would be coming over, and that she would like to call and see you, to see how you are progressing.'

'There is no need for her to put herself out on my account,' Connie insisted ungraciously. 'I may not be a doctor, but I am a fully qualified nurse, Ellie, and I do not need Iris to tell me that a few bruises and scratches are healing.'

'A few bruises and scratches! How can you say that? The cut on your head alone!'

Connie could feel her impatience growing. What was the point in trying to explain to Ellie the difference between the few small wounds she had received, and the wounds she had seen soldiers bear?

She should be counting her blessings, and thanking God for His and Ellie's generosity, Connie admitted. But she could not relax when she knew that, sooner or later, she would be called upon to account for her past, if not by Ellie herself, then certainly by her husband Gideon, and even more certainly their Aunt Gibson.

The sudden sounds of an arrival downstairs in the hall had Ellie going to the door, exclaiming in relief, 'That is sure to be Iris. I must go down and welcome her.'

Once her sister had gone, Connie paced the room restlessly. To her despair, against all the odds and contrary to her secret hopes, she was still carrying the Captain's child.

There was a firm knock on the bedroom door and then, before she could call out in response, it opened and Iris came in.

'I was at the Infirmary yesterday, Connie. Both Matron and Mr Clegg asked after your health, and asked me to convey their good wishes to you.'

Connie almost flinched. 'Does Matron know?' Unable to go on, she turned away.

Behind her she heard Iris exhale.

'That you are to have a child? Yes.'

'I wish I might not be having it,' Connie burst out. 'I wish that...'

'No. You must not say that,' Iris stopped her firmly, coming over to her and grasping her shoulders. 'I do understand how difficult this is for you, Connie. And if, as I suspect, I am right in guessing...' Iris stopped and shook her head, whilst Connie tensed. 'Those of us who experience at first hand the frailty of life and its shortness, especially when that life is a soldier's life, can sometimes be forced to live by a different set of rules in wartime than those who do not have that experience. I can understand that there may not have been the time or the opportunity for you to marry the father of your child.'

'Is that why you told them at the Infirmary that I was a widow?' Connie asked her.

'I did what I thought was best,' Iris told her. 'My dear,' she added gently, 'you are far from being the only woman to find herself in such a situation, and I would be the last person to judge you harshly for it. Of course I may have guessed incorrectly, and if that is so then I apologise for any distress I might have caused you, Connie. However, if I am right, then please allow me to offer you some advice.'

Iris paused and gave Connie a very direct look.

'I shall not mince my words, for I believe that both of us are women who prefer plain-speaking. Whilst there are those who will understand your situation, there are many, many, more who will not, and who indeed will take great pleasure in not doing so. They will condemn both you and your child, and through you all those who are closely connected to you. Your sister, Ellie, for instance. Do you understand what I am trying to say?'

Of course she did, how could she not, Connie reflected bitterly, as she acknowledged Iris's statement with a brusque nod of her head.

'I know this cannot be easy for you,' Iris continued. 'But for their sakes, and for the sake of your child, I would urge you to think carefully, and to look ahead to the future when this war is over, and the urgency and immediacy that governs our actions now is forgotten...' Her glance fell to the rings Connie was wearing. 'Life, society will be much kinder to you as a widow, Connie, than as a young woman with a child who has no legitimate father, especially when...'

'Especially when that young woman is someone like me who has already brought disgrace on herself and her family?' Connie challenged Iris sharply. 'Is that what you were going to say?'

'No. It wasn't,' Iris answered her evenly. 'What I was going to say was, especially when that young woman is so highly thought of by her employers, and might one day want to return to her work, and to do so in the knowledge that she is respected.'

'Respected or respectable?' Connie challenged her.

'Both,' Iris told her coolly. Connie looked away from her. There was a certain truth, a good sense in what Iris was saying, she recognised.

'So far as your baby's father is concerned...' Iris continued, more gently.

'I do not wish to speak of him. I cannot bear to speak of him,' Connie stopped her, shuddering violently.

'So many brave young men have been lost to this War,' Iris told her quietly. 'So many children made fatherless, that as a widow you will be far from alone.'

It was obvious to her that Iris thought her pregnancy was the result of a reckless passion for a man who either could not, or would not, return to her.

Dry-eyed, Connie looked at her. The Captain might not be dead, but she certainly wished he was. And she wished the child she was carrying inside her might die also.

The child she was carrying inside her! A furious anger seized her. A child created out of lust and brutality; out of bestiality; forced upon her. Connie wanted to scream out the truth and with it her own pain and anger. But who here, knowing

341

her as she had been, would believe her? There was no point in telling Iris the truth. No point in telling anyone. She was condemned already by her own past.

She closed her eyes and protested passionately, 'I do not want this. I do not want any of it.' Her misery broke through her self-control and her voice trembled as she cried out, 'I cannot bear it.'

'You must bear it, Connie,' Iris chided her firmly. 'You must bear it as you will bear your child, with fortitude and strength. Believe me, there is no other way for you, and hard though it must seem now, one day your child will thank you for what you have done. For the respectability you have given it. The plain truth is that a bastard child must always carry a slur on its name, and so must its mother.'

Connie looked down at the rings she was wearing.

'You have already taken the decision out of my hands.'

'For your own good.'

Connie gave a small sigh. 'I understand that, of course Iris. I know it is better for everyone's sake including my own.' There was no point in her arguing the matter any further.

'I am trying to help you, Connie, although it may not seem so to you now,' Iris told her firmly, as though she had guessed what she was thinking.

'If you really want to help me, then will you please tell Ellie that I do not need to spend any more time in bed,' Connie asked her ruefully. 'I am used to working, Iris, not being mollycoddled, and besides...'

She stopped, reluctant to admit to Iris that without the busyness of her work to keep her occupied, the time seemed to drag, her days filled with too many hours in which to brood on her own misery. Too many hours in which to dwell helplessly and hopelessly, on impossible might-have-beens, and her even more impossible love for Harry.

'Of course, but you must not overtax yourself. Oh, and I nearly forgot, I have brought some letters and notes that have been left at the Infirmary for you.'

Connie took them eagerly, immediately looking for Mavis's familiar handwriting.

There were two letters from her friend; one which Mavis had obviously written in great anxiety having heard of Connie's accident, and then another written later which was far more formal and stilted. It offered her condolences on Connie's loss of her husband. Connie knew immediately on reading it, that Mavis was as shocked and hurt as she would have been herself, to receive such news of a close friend at second hand. And, of course, Connie could not write back and explain.

A tear squeezed its way into Connie's eye and rolled down her face to land on the letter. More than ever right now she longed for Mavis's friendship and understanding, but her condition meant that she had forfeited her right to them.

'I understand that you have left Liverpool and returned to your family in Preston, to await the birth of your child. Oh, Connie, how can it be that so much has happened to you, and I have not known? You were my dearest friend.'

Were... Connie closed her hand over the letter and gulped back a sob. There was no point in her writing back, other than to acknowledge Mavis's good wishes for her future. No point at all. If she were ever to see Mavis again, she would be afraid that she might blurt out the truth to her and she could not do that!

'There will be plenty of room in the nursery for the new little one, Connie,' Ellie gave a small sigh. 'I own that I had hoped that Gideon and I would have more children of our own, but it seems it is not to be. I can't wait for term to end and Philip to be home. He takes more after Mother than Father, Connie. We were so worried that Aunt Jepson would not allow him to come to live with us permanently, but Gideon was so wonderful, he finally managed to gain her consent.'

Connie frowned as she struggled with a sharp spear of jealousy. It hurt hearing Ellie talk of Philip, their youngest brother, who she herself had not seen since he had been a baby.

'Our aunts had no right to separate us all the way they did,' she told Ellie fiercely.

'It was mother's wish,' Ellie reminded her. 'But I have so much wished that I might have been older and braver so that we might have stayed together.' She gave a small sigh, which Connie deliberately ignored. 'You will be astonished when you see John. He is a man now, and our father all over again, only larger.'

'And what of Father? You have said very little of him,' Connie pointed out.

'He is not in the best of health, Connie, but I hesitate to interfere or say too much. He has married Maggie after all, and she and I do not see eye to eye. John sees more of him than I do. Our Aunt Gibson has been asking after you by the way.'

'And what exactly has she been asking, or can I guess?'

Ellie's face flushed slightly, and she looked up at Connie. They were in her pretty parlour where she had suggested that she and Connie might spend the blustery, wet, late April day stitching clothes for the coming baby.

Helpless and dependent though she sometimes felt living under Ellie's anxious care, Connie knew in reality how fortunate she was that Ellie had been so willing to take her in. Knowing that though, and being able to feel grateful for it, were two very different things!

'There are matters appertaining to your coming child that need to be discussed, Connie,' Ellie told her quietly, adding reassuringly, 'it is nothing very much, Connie, only what I know Iris has already discussed with you.' She broke off and looked at Connie before continuing gently, 'I don't want to distress you and I understand how painful... That is ... but dearest, I am concerned that people will gossip ... and ... well, I thought that it would be best if everything were to be made clear at the outset ... so that when you and the baby do go out amongst our family and friends, their ques-tions...'

345

Connie kept her head bent over her stitching, whilst guilt and humiliation flooded through her.

'Oh, Connie, I am distressing you and that is the last thing...' She heard Ellie sigh. 'What I am trying to say, is that for your own sake, Connie, it would be better if a little more is known about your past life and your husband.'

Connie shuddered wretchedly, her needle slipping and pricking into her finger leaving a small drop of blood on the tiny white garment.

Immediately Ellie put down her own sewing and went to her, sitting at her side and putting her arms around her.

'Oh, my poor sister, you must have loved him so! If you were married to him, my love...' Ellie paused hesitantly.

'And if I were not?' Connie asked her angrily.

She could hear Ellie making a small sound of protest.

What was happening to her? Connie wondered miserably. She was behaving, reacting, more like the Connie of old than the sensible woman she now prided herself on being.

'Connie, this is painful for both of us I know, but it has to be said. If you were not, then for your own sake you must at all times, in public at least, behave as though you were!'

'What you are saying, Ellie, is that I should claim the sanctity of widowhood, and a husband killed fighting for his country, whether or not I have a right to it.' Connie's mouth twisted painfully, as she thought to herself how she wished that that might be so: that the Captain might be killed, for that way she would know that she

346

would never have to bear the humiliation of seeing him again.

'Connie, please let us not quarrel over this,' Ellie pleaded anxiously. 'I know that Iris has already spoken of this matter with you, and with the Infirmary as well.'

Connie couldn't bear any more! The weight of her shame already weighed so heavily on her, and she didn't think she could endure having to live a lie for the rest of her life!

Ignoring Ellie's plea to her to stay, she ran to the door and pulled it open, heading for the sanctuary of her bedroom to throw herself on the bed and give way to her tears. She felt as though her shame and her grief were burned into her, and would brand her for ever.

She heard a soft knock on the bedroom door and just had time to dry her eyes and sit up before Ellie came in, her own eyes bright with tears. 'Connie, please don't be upset.'

'How can I not be? You all want the eyes of the world to see me as a respectable widow. But what if I am not, Ellie? What will you do then? Throw me out of doors ... leave me to the fate you must think I deserve?'

'Connie, you must not think such a thing!' Ellie protested in distress. 'No matter what, I shall never part with you. Never!' Emotionally Ellie reached for her hand. 'You are my sister, and I know you. I know your loving, impulsive heart, I know that, whilst you may sometimes act without thinking of all the consequences, you would never give any part of yourself where you did not love.'

A huge lump of unexpected emotion had

347

lodged in Connie's throat. She hadn't known that Ellie knew her so well, nor judged her so lovingly. For a heartbeat of time she longed, ached, to unburden herself to her sister and reveal her pain, but the caution life had taught her, stopped her.

'All I am trying to say to you is that if we were to offer a little information about your ... about your situation in an open and natural way – if we were to say, for instance, that you have been widowed by the War, perhaps that your husband was a soldier whom you nursed and whose family live in another part of the country, then you and your child will be treated as we would want you to be treated.

'You are to be a mother soon, Connie, and when you are, I promise you, you will want to do things for your child that you would not do for yourself. You will want to protect and guard it with a passion and a fierceness that will be greater than anything you have ever known. There will be no sacrifice you will not want to make.'

'No!' White-faced, Connie stopped her, her vehemence shocking Ellie into silence. 'No,' she repeated fiercely. 'I have made all the sacrifices – and more – that any woman could make for this ... this...

'Say whatever you want to about me, Ellie,' she told her sister wearily a moment later. 'Tell the world and our Aunt Gibson, that I am a poor widow whose husband died bravely on the field of battle, if that is what makes you happy, but make sure that you tell them as well not to pry into my pain, or my past!'

'So Connie, Ellie says that your late husband was a soldier. Presumably, he did not hold any rank, but what of his family? According to what I have heard, when Iris chanced to find you you were working as a nurse!'

Their Aunt Gibson could not have made either her distaste or her disbelief clearer, Connie reflected, as she sat in the stuffy parlour of her Winckley Square house, forced to endure Amelia Gibson's questions.

As Connie had quickly discovered, despite all Ellie's kindnesses to her, and her attempts to spoil her with small treats and draw her into her own busy social life, Connie desperately missed the hospital and her work.

It seemed impossible to her now that she had ever desperately craved and wanted the kind of life her elder sister and their cousins lived. Morning calls, afternoon calls, the ordering of what few servants the War had left them, and all the other activities that went to make that life, chafed now at Connie as though they were a hair shirt.

She had already extracted a promise from Iris that, on her next visit, she would take Connie with her to the Preston hospital where she did some of her work.

'But why would you want to do such a thing?' Ellie had asked perplexed and slightly horrified.

'Professional curiosity,' Connie had replied immediately.

Ellie had promptly taken hold of her hand as though she thought Connie in need of comfort and reassurance, telling her, 'But dearest, you have no need to concern yourself with any of that any more. Your home is here with us now.'

'Ellie, you don't understand,' Connie had had to protest. 'I miss my work ... and the Infirmary.'

A small frown had crinkled Ellie's smooth forehead, and she had looked upset and slightly disapproving. 'Connie, you are soon to be a mother!'

'Does that mean I can't be anything else? Thousands of mothers are working, Ellie.'

'Because they have to. You will not have to, and besides... Well, it wouldn't be fitting for you to return to nursing, Connie.'

'Why on earth not?'

Ellie had given her a reproachful look, 'Gideon is a wealthy man, and I ... both of us, want you to have every comfort you need.'

Bored with listening to their aunt's hectoring pronouncements, Connie looked across to where Ellie was in conversation with their cousin Cecily on the other side of the room.

Like her, Ellie was shrouded in head-to-toe black, as befitted the sister of a newly-widowed woman, Ellie having made it public, bearing in mind Connie's pregnancy, that her husband was only recently deceased.

Connie had protested at the number of new clothes Ellie had insisted on ordering for her, but Ellie had responded firmly, 'You will need them, dearest, for although as a widow and in your condition, it will not be possible for you to attend large public functions, you may be sure our Aunt Gibson will expect you to call. And then there is my sewing circle when we meet to do our bit for the War effort; and of course we must make sure that you take plenty of walks in the park – fresh air is an excellent thing for the constitution, and according to Iris an admirable pursuit for women awaiting childbirth.'

Connie could see a copy of the *Liverpool Echo* lying on the chair which had been vacated by Cecily's husband, Paul. He had sprung up in some relief as they were announced, saying teasingly that he wouldn't stay to inhibit their gossip.

Determined not to answer her aunt's probing questions, Connie looked idly at the headline, which ran 'Murder Most Foul'.

Absently she read on:

The Echo has to report the most shocking news of the vile and dastardly deed which last night resulted in the death of Captain Archibald Forbes, the son of Councillor Forbes, whose good work in providing our fighting men with munitions is well known in the city.

The Captain, who was clubbed to death by an unknown assailant or assailants, was to stand as a candidate for election to the Government, and was well known for his firm stance on the punishment of those cowardly men who refuse to do their patriotic duty by claiming to be conscientious objectors.

Only last week we reported in this paper, the Captain's rousing speech recommending the detention of those men returning from the Front who, being too cowardly to return, are spreading lies about the conditions there and the conduct of the war!

Somehow Connie managed to drag her gaze away from the newspaper. The room started to whirl around her and nausea clawed at her stomach.

'Connie ... Aunt ... Connie ... Aunt, I think Connie is about to faint!'

The acrid smell of burning feathers beneath her nose brought Connie back to her senses.

Ellie was seated beside her, watching her anxiously and holding one of her hands in her own, whilst their aunt looked on grimly.

'Aunt, I think I had better take Connie home.'

'Mama, perhaps you should not have mentioned Connie's husband,' Connie heard Cecily whispering reprovingly to her mother, as Ellie guided her toward the door.

TWENTY

'And take it from me, the side which controls this War in the air will be the side that will ultimately win this War...'

As unobtrusively as she could, Connie tried to ease the discomfort of the growing bulk of her body whilst at the same time listening attentively to her brother. Henrietta, the child of Ellie's first husband and his Japanese lover, sat transfixed, her openly adoring gaze never once leaving John's face.

Henrietta might still be very much a child, but one could already see the promise of the beauty she was going to be, Connie admitted.

Their Aunt Gibson frequently expressed her disapproval of the fact that Ellie treated Henrietta as though she were her and Gideon's own child.

'But Aunt, she is, since we have legally adopted her,' Connie had heard Ellie point out, with unusual steel in her voice.

'She is the child of a disgraceful and unlawful union,' their aunt had insisted sharply.

'No,' Ellie had corrected her, equally determinedly. 'She is the child of love!'

But Connie knew that, no matter what her sister might say, Henrietta would be punished by society both for her unorthodox parentage and her illegitimacy. Thanks to Gideon and Iris's determination and forethought, her own child would be spared that same slur, although Connie suspected that their Aunt Gibson was far from convinced as to the existence of her dead soldier husband.

'I am planning to call and see Father this afternoon, Ellie,' Connie heard John announcing.

Immediately she stopped him to say eagerly, 'I'll come with you, if I may, John, I would like to see Father, too.'

'Perhaps we should all three go,' Ellie agreed, although Connie could see that she looked worried and uncomfortable.

The subject of their father was not one that Ellie liked to discuss, although Connie had found out by accident, through an overheard conversation between Ellie and Gideon, that Gideon often had to provide his father-in-law with financial assistance.

'It is not Father,' Ellie had insisted, when Connie had demanded to know why Ellie seemed so reluctant to visit him or talk about him. 'It is Maggie, Connie. She has made it plain that she does not want Father to involve himself with us, and it is for his sake that I do not see very much of him.'

'He was our father before he was her husband,' Connie had pointed out quietly.

There had been a small telling pause whilst the two sisters looked at one another.

'I know what you are thinking, Connie,' Ellie had said in a low strained voice. 'You are remembering that time when you asked me to ask Father if we could all return home to Friargate.'

The time they had spent together since their reconciliation had brought a new closeness between them which was a mingling of the old relationship they had shared as girls, and a new appreciation of one another as young women. But there were still some barriers between them; some past hurts they had not discussed.

Connie had tensed a little, all too aware that none of those barriers had divided them more sharply or painfully than this one.

'You promised, Ellie!' had been all that Connie could say at first, as her own emotions threatened to overwhelm her composure. 'I missed you all so much and I was so unhappy. You don't know how much it meant to me when you said you would go and see Father and beg him to let us go home. I know things were different for you. And I can see now why you would have preferred to stay with our Aunt and Uncle Parkes, and why you broke the promise you had made to me,' she had managed to continue eventually.

'Do you still blame me for that, Connie? Can you not forgive me?' Ellie had wept.

'I wanted to go home so much,' Connie had answered her sadly, 'and perhaps, if we had, then Father would not have married Maggie.'

Ellie had looked at her as though she was about to say something, but they had been interrupted by one of the children, and Connie had not wanted to spoil the new closeness they were sharing by referring to the matter again.

At Connie's insistence they had decided to walk from Winckley Square to their father's shop and home in Friargate. And now as they crossed the market place, Ellie put a restraining hand on Connie's arm and warned gently, 'Things in Friargate are not as they were when we lived there, Connie.'

Connie made no response. Privately she suspected that Ellie's comments were coloured by the fact that she now lived so grandly in Winckley Square.

Just being in the familiar street tugged painfully on her heartstrings. She had grown up here after all, even if she felt as though there was a deep gulf now between the happiness she had known as a child, and the woman she had become.

A small group of children were playing in the street, and in the window of the baker's shop hung a sign reminding everyone of the King's exhortation to remember they were at war and to restrict their consumption of bread.

She could already see their father's shop and automatically she started to hurry toward it.

The sight of peeling paint and the unpolished doorstep brought her up sharply, but she didn't say anything as she saw the look John and Ellie exchanged.

It was John who led the way into the shop itself, surely smaller and shabbier than she had remembered. Like their father himself, Connie wondered, stifling a sense of shocked confusion as he looked up from the meat he was trimming, and she recognised how much older he looked. And how the set of his shoulders now had a defeated air about it where she had remembered it as jaunty.

The smile illuminating her father's face was the same though. Calling to his assistant to take over from him, he came toward them exclaiming in pleasure, 'By all things, this is a wonderful surprise. John and Ellie... And Connie! Come on into the house.'

Connie didn't need to ask why Ellie tensed a little before turning to follow him. The very air in the place had a musty, slightly sour taint to it that made her want to wrinkle her nose. Thanks to Matron's insistence on her nurses following the procedures set down by Florence Nightingale, the nurse in Connie abhorred dirt of any kind, for dirt was parent to disease. As she lifted her hand from the greasy banister rail and saw the unkempt, unbrushed state of the stairs leading up to the living quarters above the shop, she grimaced in disgust.

'Maggie,' she heard their father call out with

strained heartiness as he opened the door. 'Come and see who has come to visit us.'

Connie exhaled sharply as she looked round the once familiar parlour in disbelief. Whatever else she might be, their father's second wife was obviously no housewife. There were dirty plates on the table, a dead fire in the grate, dusty carpet on the floor; and two red-headed, snotty-nosed boys were fighting over some marbles, tussling and rolling together as they kicked and punched, with scant regard for either the furniture or adult limbs.

It was their father on whom Connie's attention most focused, though. With the light coming in through the parlour windows, she could see how thin and old he looked, his cheeks sunken in and his face a waxen yellow-tinged colour, that made her heart sink with foreboding.

Studying him, she felt as though a giant fist was clenching around her heart. The nurse in her had recognised the dread symptoms of the worst kind of incurable disease, as swiftly as the daughter in her wanted to reject it.

In peacetime, Mr Clegg had regularly operated to remove the tumours from patients afflicted with similar symptoms to her father, but no amount of cutting out the cancer that was clamped to their vital organs could ever prolong their lives for very long.

As though in confirmation of what she was thinking, their father started to cough, supporting himself against the wall as he did so, a sheen of sweat glistening on his forehead as he tried to massage his chest.

Immediately a furious, bitter anger filled Connie. Couldn't Ellie see how desperately ill he was? Couldn't she have done something?

'Give over you two.' Neither boy acknowledged the command, and it was left to John to pull them apart, saying briskly, 'All right, that's enough.'

'Where's your mother?' Their father asked breathlessly.

'In bed restin' and there's nowt for us supper. Ma said as 'ow you was to go out and get us some pies.'

Connie winced as she heard the rough accent, sharply aware of their own mother's fastidiousness in such matters.

''Ere let go o' me, you.' The taller boy wiped his runny nose on the back of his sleeve and aimed another kick at the smaller, who immediately howled and bit his arm.

'Jerry, Jack!'

Whatever Ellie might have been about to say to their half-brothers was lost as there was a thumping sound from overhead, followed by a screeched, 'Stop that racket, you bloody little varmints.'

Both boys exchanged wary looks whilst their father forced an embarrassed smile in his elder offspring's direction, and apologised, 'Maggie is a bit out o' sorts...'

'It's the stout. Allus gives her a bad head, it does,' the elder of the two boys explained knowingly, whilst a dark flush stained their father's thin face and a look of shame shadowed his eyes.

Connie's heart went out to him, and immediately she went over to him and kissed his withered cheek.

''Ere, 'oo the hell are you?'

The woman coming down the stairs was as fat as her husband was thin, panting and struggling for breath as she eased her bulk down their narrowness.

'Maggie, it's Connie come to visit with John and Ellie.'

Immediately the small eyes narrowed suspiciously. 'Oh, it's that fancy pants lot is it, and what might you be wantin'?'

'We've just come round to see Father, Maggie,' John answered her calmly. 'I've just got a couple of days' leave and...'

'Just to see him, eh?' she interrupted John sourly. 'Well that's a change... Putting on airs and graces you might be now, Missie, but I haven't forgotten how you come here beggin' and pleading.' This last remark was addressed to Ellie.

Astonished, Connie turned to look at her sister who had gone pale.

'That's enough, Maggie.'

Just for a minute it was the old Robert Pride speaking, the father and man Connie remembered.

'It's wonderful to see the three of you!' There were tears in his eyes as he turned toward them.

''Eard as how you was carryin' and widowed!' Maggie told Connie, ignoring her husband to come and stand between him and the three of them. 'Soldier, was he?' she demanded speculatively.

'Maggie, why don't you go and put the kettle on and then we can all sit down and have a chat over a cup of tea,' Robert Pride was suggesting eagerly, but Ellie shook her head and answered him hastily, 'There's no need for that, Dad. We can see that you're busy.'

'Bloody well should be. Bloody well oughta be in the shop and not up 'ere wastin' time!' Maggie announced aggressively. 'He's fathered four brats on me 'e has, and he's got no business wastin' time on you lot as is grown and gone, when 'e oughta be workin' to feed them.'

Connie's heart ached for her father, and she didn't argue when, after a few more minutes' conversation, Ellie suggested that they left.

It was their father who showed them downstairs, ignoring Connie's anxious protest that he stay where he was since they knew the way. Connie noticed how John slipped some guineas into their father's hand, and closed his fingers over them when their father would have protested.

Connie was reluctant to leave, but she had no option other than to follow her sister and brother.

'Ellie, how can you leave Father there like that, surely you can see how unwell he is,' she demanded accusingly.

'There's no call to speak to Ellie like that, Connie,' John objected. 'She's done her best, but Dad has his pride, and anyway, Maggie...'

'How could he take up with someone like that after Mother?' The shock of her father's decline had resurrected old pains and bitterness.

'He was lonely without us,' John replied quietly.

'Yes, and whose fault is that?' she broke in emotionally as her feelings overwhelmed her. 'I begged you to leave our Aunt and Uncle Parkes, Ellie, so that we could all go back home, but what was happening to Father and the rest of us didn't matter to you did it?'

'Connie, please,' Ellie begged her with tears in her eyes. 'You don't understand...'

'I understand that you broke your promise to me,' Connie told her sadly.

'Connie, that's enough!' Suddenly John, her younger brother, looked both older and sterner. 'You've no right to speak to Ellie like that, and anyway—'

'It's all right, John,' Ellie stopped him quietly. 'Naturally Connie's upset to see the deterioration in Father... Gideon and I do what we can, Connie, but Dad has his pride as John says.' She gave a rueful smile. 'Pride by name and Pride by nature, that's what he used to say to us when we were growing up, wasn't it? And besides, you can see how Maggie is for yourself. She persuaded Dad to mortgage the shop a couple of years ago, and if she thinks Dad has money...' Ellie stopped. 'Gideon is paying for both the older boys to get a decent education. I shouldn't say this but, according to Uncle Will, the younger two may not even be Father's...'

'Ellie, I'm not talking about giving Dad money! He's ill ... very ill.' Connie shook her head in frustration as she saw the look her brother and sister were exchanging. 'He needs to see a doctor. And, if I'm right about what I'm thinking...' Connie's eyes filled with tears which welled over and spilled onto her cheeks. 'It should never have been like this! You got what you wanted, Ellie, but the rest of us had to pay the price. Dad ... me ... Philip...'

They had reached Winckley Square and, too overwrought to say anything more, as soon as they were inside the house, Connie started to head straight to her room. But she turned on the stairs as she heard John's muttered, 'You've got to tell her, Ellie.'

'You've got to tell me what?' she challenged her sister.

TWENTY-ONE

The lower slopes of the mountains were clear of snow now, and Harry had journeyed with the Baron and those villagers deemed too old to fight to gather the flock from its winter pasture and drive it back to the mountains.

As a prisoner of war he was bound by his word and the fact that the Baron had stood as surety for it, not to try to escape. That was part of a code understood and adhered to by both of them, and one which Harry knew his own officers would respect.

He did still feel guilty though about the fact that he was living in what was, after all, relative comfort, whilst his fellow prisoners of war would be enduring far harsher conditions.

When he had said as much to the Baron, the older man had told him calmly, 'My kindness to you as you call it, Harry, is not the result of either luck or altruism but is in repayment of my great debt to you. Had you not had the compassion to reach out to a fellow wounded soldier – to protect and care for him – then that soldier, my son, would have died and you would not be here. You are, my friend, indeed the author of your own fate! You would be of no use to your Army anyway,' the Baron told him bluntly. 'There is little use left in your left arm even though the Professor managed to save it from amputation, and as for your chest ... here in the mountain air you can breathe easily, but not on a field of war!'

Harry knew there was a great deal of truth in what the Baron had said to him. He did have some very limited movement in the fingers of his left hand, although it could support no weight. One benefit, if it could be called that, of his imprisonment was that he could now speak German reasonably fluently, and ski rather badly, but he had vanquished both the Baron and the Professor at chess on several occasions.

Harry had written both to the British Authorities explaining his mistaken identity, and to his family, but as yet he had heard nothing back. Initially he suspected, because of the isolation of the village, but he was desperately anxious for news of them. And not just of them. It was impossible of course for him, a married man, to write personally to Connie, an unmarried young woman, but he had slipped a few lines into his letter to Mavis, enquiring after the health of her friends, 'especially Connie, Mavis, who must always hold such a special place in all our hearts for what she did for Sophie!'

That had been as far as he had dared let himself go in his letter to his sister. But in the privacy of his thoughts, Connie was the bright beacon from which he drew strength in his darkest moments. Those moments when he wondered if the War would ever end, and if he would ever see his home and his loved ones again. He liked the Baron and the Professor but these were neither his people, nor his land.

There were times when he bitterly regretted having given his word not to try to escape, and times too when he was angrily tempted to break it; but it constrained him far more strongly than any physical bonds could have done, and he suspected that it was because the Baron was aware of that fact, that he allowed Harry so much personal freedom.

For all the grandeur of the castle and his title, as Harry had quickly discovered, the Baron was not a wealthy man – far from it.

'We are poor relations who our family often prefer to forget,' he had told Harry drily, during one of their winter evening discussions.

A poor man maybe, but also an educated one, and Harry had enjoyed sharpening his wits against the Baron's erudition.

During the winter they had had scant news of the progress of the War, but spring's thaw had changed that, bringing them news not just of the War but of the situation in Russia as well where the Czar had handed over the reins of government.

In New Brighton, his mother's carefully tended garden would be coming alive with spring bulbs.

Valiantly Harry fought back his longing to hear news of his family and home.

'What is it Ellie has to tell me, John?' Connie demanded sharply.

It was the last day of her brother's leave, and since their return from their visit to Friargate, there had been growing tension between the two sisters. It was a tension which on Connie's part, sprang from the bitterness of remembered betrayal, and which, she judged, could only on Ellie's part, spring from her guilt.

Ellie herself had become uncharacteristically stubborn, refusing to discuss either their father or their past, so Connie had been left with no other course than to tackle John before he left.

'It is not really my place to say anything,' John protested, and then frowned as he added, 'but what I will say is that you are being very unfair to Ellie, Connie.'

'John, I love Ellie and I know what I owe her, but I still can't help how she promised me that she would go and see our father and beg him to let us come home, and then broke that promise!' Connie's mouth trembled.

'No, Connie, she didn't.'

Connie stared at him. 'She did!'

John was beginning to look angry. 'Connie,' he warned, and then broke off as the door to the parlour opened and Ellie herself came in.

'I was walking past the door and I heard the two of you arguing,' she told them quietly. 'John, leave us please. I want to talk to Connie on my own.'

'I don't care what you've said to John. He was too young at the time to be able to remember what I can remember, Ellie!'

'Connie, I understand how you feel,' Ellie tried to calm her.

'No, you don't! How can you? You had your nice, safe life with our aunt and uncle. You could have persuaded Father to let us come home, Ellie. And if you had, then Father would never have let someone like Maggie...'

'Connie, please.' Ellie looked white and strained. 'Please calm down and listen to me, getting yourself in this state isn't good for you or the baby. Please sit down and let me try to explain. Please.'

'Very well then,' Connie agreed miserably.

'I did go and see Father as I promised,' Ellie told her quietly. 'Mother protected us, Connie, and I suppose I was very young for my age. And... And immature. I wasn't prepared... I couldn't...'

Connie started to frown. 'I don't understand what you are trying to say.'

Ellie took a deep breath. 'When I went to see Father, Connie, it was already too late. You see, when I got to the house, Maggie was already there.'

'Maggie. What? I don't understand!'

Ellie's face had turned pink.

'I ... I went upstairs, never thinking ... not realising... When I went into the bedroom I found... I saw... Father was in bed with Maggie and they were... It was already too late. Had I been older, or more worldly, perhaps I could have challenged Maggie ... spoken with Father, but I was shocked and distressed... I...'

Connie could feel her heart thudding painfully.

'You mean that Father. That Maggie ... you mean that so soon after Mother?'

'Father is a man, Connie. He was lonely.' Ellie gave a sad sigh. 'I was upset and angry with him then, just as you were with me, but Father didn't know how much we all wanted to be with him. John and I have spoken at length about everything since then.

'Our aunts deliberately kept back the letters we wrote to one another and they kept them, too, from Father. Had they not done so, I suspect he would have lost no time in reclaiming us...

'Connie, you don't know how I have regretted not being stronger. And wiser. Not being older... Not knowing as I know now that I should have demanded immediately that Maggie leave. If I had done that...'

Instantly Connie got up and went to her side, taking hold of her arm, 'No, Ellie... You mustn't blame yourself – I had no idea. I thought...'

They looked at one another, both with tears in their eyes, and then suddenly they were in one another's arms, crying and laughing at the same time as they hugged each other as tightly as Connie's pregnancy would allow.

'I wanted so much to take Mother's place, for all that you thought I was the lucky one in our aunt and uncle's house.' Ellie bit her lip. 'I don't like to talk about it, Connie, but that household was not... Everything was not as it seemed, and our uncle...' She stopped, plainly unable to continue.

Tentatively Connie put her hand on her sister's

arm, the quiet calm she had learned as a nurse entering her voice as she told her. 'Please don't stop there, Ellie. I can sense from your voice that whatever happened must have been very painful for you. We are sisters, after all.'

Ellie started to shake her head. 'Connie, our poor Aunt Parkes had much to bear. I feel guilty that I do not go and visit her more often, but just to enter that house...'

Connie started to frown. There was no mistaking Ellie's distress.

'I thought you were so happy there. Our Aunt and Uncle Parkes treated you as though you had been their daughter, especially Uncle Parkes! I remember that ball he gave and how envious I felt when I saw your beautiful room, and how Uncle Parkes...'

'Don't!' Ellie begged her in a tortured voice, springing up to pace the floor in open agitation.

'Please do not speak of our Uncle, Connie, I can hardly bear it. Just to hear his name, and on your lips, when I know the fate he intended for you. For both of us, if I had not escaped into marriage to Henry.'

'Ellie, what on earth are you talking about?' Connie demanded, as she studied her sister's tear-stained face with concern.

Wretchedly Ellie shook her head. 'I cannot tell you!'

'You must,' Connie insisted, going to her side and taking hold of her hand again.

'You must, Ellie, for your own sake as much as mine.'

Ellie gave a deep shudder but allowed Connie

to lead her over to a chair, and then kneel down at her feet.

'Now tell me,' Connie instructed her firmly, still holding Ellie's hand in her own.

Ellie swallowed and struggled to control herself.

'Like you, at first when I went to live with them, I thought that our Uncle Parkes was kind. But then he started paying me particular attention, Connie, complimenting me,' she stressed, 'treating me, he claimed, as a daughter, as you said. But innocent though I was, I could sense that...'

Connie felt Ellie's fingers tighten within her own, and her heart missed a beat.

'I was in a most uncomfortable situation. Our aunt was often unwell, and I was left alone with our uncle, no matter how much I tried to avoid it. There is no easy way to tell you this, Connie... There was the most dreadful incident in Uncle Parkes' study when I feared not just for my virtue, but for my life as well. Indeed, had it not been for the quick thinking and bravery of my maid, I dread to think what would have happened.'

'Mr Parkes tried to rape you?' Connie asked her numbly.

Unable to speak, Ellie nodded her head.

Tears started to roll down Connie's face. Why had fate done this to them? Was it because they had been left motherless? Unprotected. Unloved.

Silently they hugged one another tightly, as though they were once again motherless children fearing being torn apart from one another. This was not the time to tell Ellie of her own burden of shamed grief, Connie decided, protectively.

369

Right now her sister had enough to bear, and Connie wanted to help her to bear it, and to show her how much she loved her. As gently as a mother, she wiped the tears from Ellie's face and kissed her.

When they were able to talk again, she said shakily, 'Oh, Ellie, I have accused you so often and so mistakenly inside my heart, and now it turns out that you were not to blame after all.'

Regret for the closeness they had lost shadowed Connie's eyes.

'Gideon tried so hard to find you after he and I were married, Connie. I wanted so badly to make things up to you; to have you here with me and to give you the life I knew you wanted: parties, pretty clothes...'

'I am sure Aunt Gibson would have had something to say to that! In her eyes such treats would have been the last thing I deserved, after the disgrace I had brought on myself by running away with Kieron.'

'Despite all the happiness Gideon and our children have brought me, losing you, believing you dead, has shadowed that happiness, Connie.'

Now the shy, loving, confidences poured from both of them.

Tenderly Ellie touched Connie's face, pushing a stray curl out of the way.

'But now my happiness is complete, for I have found you again and have all my family safe – you, John, Philip... I am indeed blessed, and will soon be blessed again by the birth of this child you carry.'

Pain pierced Connie's heart, and she was overwhelmed by a need to confess everything to her sister, and to remove the final barrier between them.

'Ellie, this child. I...'

The door to the parlour burst open to reveal a white-faced John standing there.

'Ellie! Connie! A message has just come from Friargate.'

'Father!' Connie guessed.

John nodded his head.

'Connie, what are you doing?' Ellie demanded, as Connie pulled away from her.

'I must go to him,' Connie told Ellie simply. 'I must Ellie; please don't try to stop me!'

The familiar bedroom Connie remembered from her childhood, had been scrubbed until it was spotless under her direction, and the whole room smelled of carbolic and clean linen. Maggie had stubbornly refused to allow her husband to be moved to the comfort of Ellie's home, but that was the only argument Connie had allowed her to win.

Maggie and her children were banned from Robert Pride's sick room unless allowed there by Connie herself. Ellie and Gideon had insisted that Connie must not, as she had wished, move into the house so that she could watch over their father night and day; but Gideon had willingly agreed to pay the wages of the excellent nurse Iris had found, to take over from Connie at night and who maintained Connie's own strict routine.

It had been fortunate indeed that Iris should have happened to visit Preston, and to call in at

Winckley Square to see how they all did, within hours of their father's collapse, Connie acknowledged. Their Uncle Gibson, although a doctor, had been reluctant to visit the Friargate house and administer to his wife's brother-in-law.

'It is cancer, isn't it?' Connie had asked Iris quietly, after the other woman had offered her services and skilfully examined her new patient.

'Yes,' Iris had confirmed, equally quietly.

Connie had exhaled her pent-up breath and turned her tear-streaked face to the fading light coming in through the window.

'He cannot have very long, I think.'

'It is hard to say, but I don't think so,' Iris had agreed gently.

'You will leave me something to give him for the pain?' Connie had asked her.

'I shall write a prescription for morphine for you, Connie, which I think you will have to have filled by the hospital dispensary. You know how.'

Numbly Connie had nodded.

'Fair upset 'im, that's what you've done,' Maggie had announced in a surly voice after Iris had left. 'What with 'im not being able to get 'is normal bottle of tonic from the chemist, and then you lot coming round.'

Remembering this conversation now, Connie closed her eyes. The Government had only recently brought in a law banning the sale of cocaine, and it was no doubt this that had been in the 'tonic' her father was no longer able to obtain, and which had probably held some of the pain of his condition at bay.

She looked toward the door as she heard soft

footsteps on the stairs. 'Ellie!'

'How is he?' her sister whispered as she entered the room.

'Sleeping,' Connie told her tiredly.

'Nurse has arrived, and I have come to take you home, Connie.'

When Connie looked reluctantly at the painfully thin figure in the bed, Ellie reminded her, 'Gideon will not have you staying here overnight, Connie. It is for your sake as much as anything else. It will not aid our father if your own health begins to suffer.'

'Yes, I know,' Connie agreed wearily.

It was the end of May and her pregnancy was well advanced now, with her baby due at the end of July.

As she and Ellie walked back in the warm evening air, tiny rivulets of perspiration began to form on her skin under the suffocating weight of her blacks, adding to Connie's discomfort. She would be almost as glad to be rid of her widow's weeds as she would the unwanted life inside her. Her future was something she did not dare allow herself to think about, even though Ellie had stressed to her more than once that she and her child would be wanted, and welcome, to live permanently under her roof.

'You are a widow after all, dearest, and what could be more natural than that you and your child should live with us?'

TWENTY-TWO

Harry stared at the letter. Slightly crumpled and grubby, it had obviously been opened at some stage in its journey from New Brighton.

Absently he rubbed his thumb over the envelope; his mother's best writing paper. A slight smile crooked his mouth. He turned the letter round in his hands, deliberately holding off from opening it, wanting to savour every pleasure of its arrival, even the smallest: the texture of the paper, the shape of the envelope, seeing his name written in his mother's familiar neat handwriting. He was like a man facing a meal after starvation.

The letter opener – loaned to him by the Baron, along with the privacy of this sun-soaked corner of the courtyard garden – trembled slightly in his good hand as he carefully slit the envelope.

The letter inside was satisfyingly bulky and his heart started to beat faster.

It couldn't be much longer, they all knew that. Even Maggie's surly outbursts had been tempered, whilst her two younger sons watched the comings and goings to the house in unfamiliar silence.

For Connie, there was some small comfort to be found in the familiarity of routine, and in making her father's sick room as close an approximation as she could of her Infirmary ward. But it was only a small comfort.

Witnessing her father's body being destroyed by what was growing inside him was very hard to bear, her emotions as a daughter constantly threatening to break through her professionalism.

One thing she was learning though was just how much she missed her work.

'You have a true vocation for this, Connie,' Iris commented gently, watching her as she tended to her patient.

'Matron put us all through a very rigorous training,' Connie answered her.

Iris shook her head. 'I don't doubt that, but I have seen many nurses employing their skills since this War began, and I am not flattering you when I say that you are one of those special few who have a natural instinct for their patient's needs.'

Connie didn't answer her for the simple reason that she couldn't. She was standing beside her father's bed, monitoring his pulse. It told her what the instinct Iris had just praised her for already knew.

'I've brought you a prescription for more morphine. If you are in any doubt as to how much to administer, then you must send for me, Connie. No matter what time of day or night.'

Silently they looked at one another in mutual understanding.

Too much morphine would send her father into a deep sleep and from there into death, without the need for him ever to have to wake again to the pain he had been suffering. The prescribed dosage would allow death to claim him at its own pace, whilst giving him only brief periods of respite from his agony.

'I won't do what I shouldn't,' Connie assured Iris woodenly.

Half an hour after Iris had gone, her father started to wake from his drugged sleep, his thin fingers plucking at the bedclothes and scratching at his own flesh as the morphine wore off.

Connie fed him the nourishing chicken broth Ellie's cook had made for him, and then gently washed his hands and face.

'Connie?' There was fear in his eyes as well as pain, as his gaze moved anxiously around the room.

The late afternoon sunshine spilled in through the window, emphasising the stark reality of his wasted body.

'I want to get up. I should be in the shop.'

He made the same fretful protest every day, and, just as she had done every day, Connie soothed him calmly, telling him, 'In a little while, Father, only wait until Ellie has been to visit you.'

'Ellie is coming?' He said it as eagerly as a child anticipating a long-awaited treat, and yet Ellie had visited him every single day.

There was a nagging ache low down in Connie's back and she massaged her flesh tiredly, determined to ignore it. From the window she could see her sister hurrying toward the house. The moment she was close enough, Ellie looked up at the window, her expression reflecting her anxiety.

Ten minutes later Ellie came into the room.

'I brought some more chicken soup with me,

and some food for the children. They look so much better now that you have given them both a bath, Connie, and supplied them with handkerchiefs. You have a real way with them!'

'I didn't want them spreading any germs around Father,' Connie answered her briskly, as though excusing her own behaviour.

Ellie shook her head tenderly. 'You are already behaving like a mother, Connie.'

'No!' Her denial was sharp and immediate, causing Ellie to frown, and Connie herself to stiffen. There was no point in trying to explain her feelings to Ellie. She would never understand. 'I ... I cannot think of such things whilst there is Father to care for,' she excused her reaction lamely.

'How is he?' Ellie whispered, looking toward the bed.

'Much the same,' Connie fibbed.

'Connie, I want you to promise me that... I want to be here,' Ellie told her steadily.

'One cannot always know these things,' Connie hedged.

'Promise me,' Ellie insisted.

'I shall do my best.'

Sighing slightly, Ellie sat down at the small table by the window. 'I have brought sewing with me.'

'More clothing for the men at the Front?' Connie asked ruefully, knowing that her sister, like so many other women of her class, was part of a group of women who met every week to sew for charity.

'See for yourself,' Ellie smiled serenely, holding

up a small bed gown. 'I have been making clothes for your baby, Connie.'

'You shouldn't have bothered!'

'It was no bother, I have enjoyed it. Do you have any names chosen for the babe? His father's, I imagine, if you have a boy,' Ellie answered her own question, before giving a small sigh. 'I had always intended that if I had a daughter I would give her our mother's name.'

Connie closed her eyes against the pain that felt like a knife twisting inside her heart. On the bed, their father cried out sharply and she turned to him, glad of the distraction.

'Can you not give him something to ease his pain?' Ellie asked in distress, as his moans grew louder and his movements more frantic.

Unable to speak, Connie shook her head.

The sun's dying rays bathed the letter in gold light as it lay on the stone seat beside him. Harry reached out toward it and then stopped. He didn't need to read it again. He had read it and re-read it so many times he knew every word by heart.

His mother's outpouring of joy that he was alive when they had all feared him dead, the passing away of his great-aunt, and the unexpected discovery that she had not, as she had always threatened, left everything to charity but had instead willed both the house and her capital to his mother. Harry thanked God for that, for his mother more than deserved it.

The letter also told of Frank's safe return from the War and the injury he had suffered, as well as his mother's delight that he and Mavis had made their home with her; Sophie's continued determination to follow in Mavis's footsteps and train as a nurse; and the fact that Rosa had given birth to a son, and he was now a father. He had a child. A son, and yet all he could feel was nothing. No joy, no pride, no gratitude at such a gift of promise for the future. Nothing...

She had hoped to return home in time for the birth, but the little one came early whilst she was staying with her mother's family in Ireland, and they are still there. She has named him Christopher, which she writes is a family name on her mother's side, and which she said would be less painful for her than naming him for you. We have despatched both a telegram to give her the happy news that you are safe, and written her a letter – although, my dearest Harry, I do grieve for the poor mother who must learn now that her son is gone from her.

A child. He and Rosa had a child. A deep shudder ran through him and he hated himself for the bitterness of his own inner denial.

Rosa was his wife, this child his own flesh and blood. He could not deny either of them their place in his life, and if he was to think himself an honourable man, he could not deny them a place in his heart either.

Unable to stop himself Harry reached for the letter, searching as hungrily as he had already done a dozen and more times for some mention of Connie, and knowing that he would find none.

So went the lover's heart, hoping when there was no hope. Longing when there could be no surcease. Loving when there could be no return of that love.

Connie gritted her teeth as she tried not to listen to the agonised sound of her father's breathing.

She had heard of – and seen – patients' deaths dragged out over many weary days by this dread disease, but she had still hoped that fate might be kind to her father.

Now as she witnessed his distress, she knew her hope was not going to be answered. Deliberately she tried not to look to where she had placed the morphine. There was enough and to spare if she could but bring herself to administer it. But to do so would be to murder her father!

Murder? An already dying man? And when she knew it would spare him further pain? Helplessly Connie paced the floor, torn between different duties, and oblivious to the commotion of an arrival downstairs, until the bedroom door opened.

'Iris!'

Relief shadowed surprise in her eyes, followed by her tensing at the unexpectedness of the arrival. But before she could say anything, Ellie edged round the door behind Iris causing Connie's eyes to widen even further.

'Doctors have instincts, too, you know,' Iris told Connie gently, as she removed her coat.

Tears welled in Connie's eyes. 'I'm glad you came,' was all she could manage to say. 'Both of you.'

'Oh, Connie.' As Ellie hugged her and they clung together, Iris asked matter-of-factly, 'I take it you haven't given him any morphine this evening?'

Numbly Connie shook her head, prising herself out of Ellie's arms as Iris pulled on a clean white gown, to demand agitatedly, 'Iris, you won't give him too much, will you? He's so weak now and...'

'Connie, I'm the doctor here,' Iris reminded her gently. 'But, no, I won't.'

Connie held her breath though as she watched Iris prepare the drug.

'Ellie, I think you had better go downstairs and ask your stepmother if she wants to be here,' Iris announced calmly.

Automatically Connie turned her head to watch Ellie leave. When she turned it back again Iris was saying calmly, 'I have mixed a full dose.'

'That will be too strong,' Connie protested.

'I only intend to use as much as we need, Connie. We can use the rest later...'

Reassured, Connie helped her to administer the drug, her eyes blistering with hot tears, as she did so.

From downstairs the noisy sound of Maggie's grief fractured the quiet calm of the bedroom, making Connie flinch. Her father took a deep gulping breath of air and trembled violently, before trying to throw off the bedcovers.

Connie had seen the signs of addiction many times before, but she still winced, and well understood the shocked look on Ellie's face as she came back into the room – without Maggie who had chosen to stay away, for now – and stood by the bed.

381

If one didn't know the true nature of that addiction, to watch the relief and release from pain soothe their father, could almost have been to witness a form of benevolent magic, Connie admitted.

His eyes were still open, and she could see recognition in them as he looked from her to Ellie and back again. 'My daughters. My lovely girls.'

Ellie was reaching for her hand and Connie held it tightly whilst they each, without needing to say anything, took hold of one of their father's.

His flesh felt cold, and his eyes were starting to close. Ellie bent her head to brush her lips against his forehead. When she raised it again, one of her tears lay against his skin.

His breathing had slowed.

'He looks so peaceful,' Ellie whispered shakily.

Connie felt for his pulse, her fingers tightening anxiously on his frail wrist. It had slowed, and was slowing still further. She looked toward Iris who, unlike her, seemed oblivious to the signs of death taking him from them.

'I shall put the rest of the dose over here, Connie,' she announced. 'How is he doing?'

'He is sleeping,' Ellie told her.

No, he is dying, Connie wanted to say, but the words refused to be said.

An hour passed, dragging second by leaden second, and yet at the same time flying by on the fleetest of wings.

Some urge that had to be obeyed, sent Connie toward the window to tug it open, and as she did so Iris gave her a long, wise look. And then said gently, 'Perhaps your stepmother should be here, now?' and then went to the door to summon her.

Connie had seen death many times and in many forms, but this was different, this was her father, the father who had given her life; the mortal flesh that had created her and Ellie as sisters.

At the bedside Maggie was sobbing noisily and uncontrollably. The frail chest lifted and stilled and then slowly fell. Maggie screamed and would have flung herself across the bed, if Iris had not had the presence of mind to take hold of her and say firmly, 'Let him breathe, Maggie.'

'Breathe! He is dead. Anyone can see that!' Maggie screamed back at her, but she still allowed Iris to hold her back.

Ellie had caught her bottom lip between her teeth, and Connie went to her and took hold of her hand in her own.

'Goodbye, Father.'

Connie heard herself saying the words, saw the familiar, last gasping breath being taken; heard the unmistakeable death rattle; felt the long, agonising, impossible wait before it was exhaled, as though somehow she was not a part of it, nor a part of her own pain.

Iris had gone, taking Maggie with her, and it was left to Connie and Ellie together to do those final things for him: washing and then laying out his body. It was a shared task, but with their roles reversed, so that it was Connie who was the more senior, and not her older sister.

When all was finally done, Connie started to tidy up, tensing as she picked up the remainder

of his drug dose. The fluid stood still and clear –
no powder in it; no crystals; no morphine? Her
heart started to thump heavily.

Ellie had gone downstairs and Iris had come
back into the room. Connie looked toward her.
'You gave him the full dose!'

'I gave him the medication I deemed necessary
as a doctor,' Iris corrected her firmly, and then
added softly, 'I did what I would want someone
to have done for me, Connie. I did what I could
do as a doctor, and you could not as a loving
daughter.'

Connie's tears came then, spilling down her
cheeks. Tears of relief and release – and acceptance.

There was one thing for sure, Connie decided
emotionally, she would never cease to be grateful
to Gideon for his insistence, against their Aunt
Gibson's ice cold wishes and Maggie's noisily
wept protests, that their father was buried with
their mother.

Connie looked out of the window of the Winckley Square house to where the funeral cortège had
stood only a fortnight earlier. She had a nagging
stitch in her side which had been there all morning
and Ellie, coming into the room and seeing her
rubbing it, hurried over to her immediately. 'It
cannot be much longer now, Connie. You must tell
me the minute you feel anything.'

'I am a nurse,' she had reminded her sister
drily.

The minute she felt anything? A bitter bubble
of pain rose up inside her. She felt everything:

anger, loathing, hatred, resentment...

'Oh, I can't wait to have another baby in the house. I am so excited, Connie. A wonderful new life ... and you know that Gideon and I want you to consider this house to be your home from now on. After all, where else should you go? You are my sister, and this baby will be as close to me as any of my own children.'

Restlessly Connie pulled away from her. 'Iris promised me that she would take me and show me round the hospital.'

Ellie frowned. 'Why on earth would you want to do a thing like that, and in your condition?'

'Ellie, I am a nurse,' she repeated, although in a different tone. 'Of course, I want to!'

'You were a nurse, Connie, now you are to be a mother!' Ellie reminded her.

Connie closed her eyes, in frustration and bitterness. Ellie didn't understand. How could she? Why should she?

But it was more than her wards that she missed, Connie admitted miserably. What she missed was her independence; her pride in managing for herself. When he had taken her body, the Captain had taken those from her as well, and in their place he had left her this ... this burden in her from which she felt she could never be free.

'I do not want to be a mother,' she told her sister emphatically. 'I do not want this child... I hate this child!'

Ellie stared at her. 'Connie, you don't know what you are saying.'

'Yes I do,' Connie assured her bleakly.

'But the baby's father. The man you loved...'

385

Connie started to laugh savagely. 'Love him? No, I loathe and hate the very thought of him; and I loathe and hate even more the seed he forced into my body.'

'Forced?'

Connie looked at her sister.

'I wanted to tell you when, when you had told me about Mr Parkes, but John arrived with the news of our father. Oh, Ellie, why are there such men? Wicked, wicked men. I knew that I had angered him by interfering in his seduction of one of the junior nurses, but I never imagined that he would take such revenge. If I had–'

'Forced, Connie?' Ellie stopped her. 'You mean you were raped, that this child you are carrying is the result of that attack? Oh, Connie, why have you not said? Why?'

'I did not think you would believe me.'

They looked at one another in mutual pain.

'And the accident, when Iris's car...' Ellie began hollowly, 'Connie, you were not trying... You did not deliberately?'

'No!' Connie stopped her. 'Although I did wish many times that I might be brave enough to take my own life. No, I was so filled with despair and misery that I simply did not see the car until it was almost upon me!'

'It was almost a miracle,' Ellie whispered. 'God recognised your need and your innocence, Connie, and gave you back to us!'

A solitary tear rolled down Connie's pale face followed by another.

'You believe me then, Ellie?' she asked painfully.

'Of course I do! How could you doubt it! I know you, Connie. I know that were this a child of love, you would be proud to acknowledge that love, with or without any marriage ties!'

Connie gave a small gasp.

'What is it? Connie what's wrong?' Ellie asked anxiously.

'My waters have broken,' Connie told her calmly.

Now she knew why they called it labour. It went on and on relentlessly, this hard physical business of giving birth, pain upon pain engulfing her, possessing her, and refusing to let her go.

The sky darkened whilst she toiled.

Ellie dampened her forehead and smiled, her hair as wet with sweat as Connie's own, as though she had laboured with her. 'Not much longer now, Connie.'

It was Iris who was attending her and not some mere midwife, her hands were bloody and slick with mucus as she urged Connie to push.

Did Iris think she wasn't already doing so? There was nothing Connie wanted more than to rid her body of its loathed burden, to be free of its possession of her! Gritting her teeth she tried to push harder, whilst the night drew on.

'And again, Connie.'

'I can't,' she sobbed. 'I can't bloody push any more.'

'Yes you can, Connie.' That was Ellie, her voice firm and big sisterish, and automatically Connie responded to it.

'That's it, Connie. Push. Nearly there...'

The warmth of the early August night filled the room, and all of them were sticky with it and with the travail of the birth, but no one more so than Connie as she yelled her resentment and loathing into the thick, stifling air, her body surging into a savage desire to be rid of its burden.

'Connie, yes! Oh, good girl... Good girl.'

She could hear Iris sobbing and laughing, in a totally un-Iris-like explosion of emotion, whilst she lay panting for breath, exhausted. And then she heard it, a thin, sharp sound that pierced her insides.

Ellie was beaming down at her, tears running down her face, as she told her, 'Connie, you have a little girl, a beautiful, beautiful daughter. Oh, Connie, look!'

Deliberately Connie turned her face away, refusing to look at the swaddled bundle Ellie was holding out to her. She looked instead to where dawn was paling the sky beyond the bedroom window.

She had given the wretched thing life, hadn't she? It had no right to expect anything more of her.

'Connie,' Ellie was protesting.

'Take it away!' she told her fiercely. 'I don't want it.'

It was lunchtime and the sun was well up, and the thing Ellie had insisted on placing in a crib beside her bed – after they had made her comfortable after its birth in the early hours of the morning – was making a high-pitched wailing

388

sound that was piercing her whole body.

Angrily Connie got out of the bed, ignoring the ache of pain seizing her. Without looking into the crib she gathered up its tightly-wrapped contents, stiffening when immediately she felt its unwanted warmth. With surprising strength it tried to squirm closer to her body seeking nourishment, but Connie held it at arm's length as she walked across the bedroom and opened the door.

'Connie!'

Grimly she looked at Ellie who had suddenly appeared from her own bedroom.

'What are you doing?'

'Putting this somewhere I can't hear it,' she told Ellie flatly.

'Give her to me!' Ellie demanded, her face softening as Connie handed her the small bundle.

'Oh, Connie, look at her. She is so gorgeous. Connie!' she protested as Connie turned round and started to walk back to her room.

'I don't want it, Ellie. If you want it, then you keep it.'

TWENTY-THREE

'What are you going to call her, Connie? She can't be "Baby" for ever!'

Connie stiffened, refusing to look at Ellie who was seated, lovingly cradling the baby in her arms. It was November and three months since she had given birth.

'Call her whatever you wish, Ellie,' she answered her curtly. 'I don't care.'

Between them Ellie and Iris might have been able to virtually force her to feed the wretched child, but she had no interest whatsoever in naming it. She loathed everything about it, especially that feeling that pierced her when she felt it tugging avidly on her nipple.

'Well, if you refuse to suckle her then I shall find a wet nurse who will,' Ellie had told her determinedly, when Connie had said the baby could starve to death for all she cared.

'Find one then,' she had answered her sister sharply.

But, in the end, nature itself had conspired against her, giving her an abundance of milk that flowed from her breasts every time the wretched child cried. Since it was hungry constantly, Connie had been forced to give in, if only to ensure that she had some peace.

'Connie, believe me I can understand how you feel,' Ellie told her gently. 'But it is not this poor baby's fault that you, that her father... She is not to blame, Connie!'

'No? It is her existence that has condemned me to a life of fabrication and dependency on others, Ellie. It is because of her that I am no longer Sister Pride. It is because of her that I have had to lay claim to a husband who never existed. John Smith!' She pulled a face. 'Couldn't Gideon have been a little more imaginative?'

'He chose the name because there were so many John Smiths amongst those who have fallen, Connie,' Ellie chided her quietly. 'With such a name, Baby will easily pass anonymously.'

Baby!

'If she must be named, then name her as Lydia Harriet!'

Connie didn't know which of them was the more astonished by her sudden outburst, Ellie or herself.

'Lydia Harriet! Oh, Connie, how pretty. And Lydia for Mama!' she approved.

Connie could feel her face beginning to burn, as she waited for her sister to ask her what had made her choose Harriet as the baby's second name, but Ellie seemed to be unaware of her self-conscious discomfort, prattling excitedly instead about christening bonnets and gowns.

Later, when she was alone with the wretched thing suckling eagerly and unwantedly at her breast, Connie asked herself what on earth had made her name her for Harry. She was not his child after all! His child! Had she, his wife – his widow – named her child for him as well?

The baby wailed as Connie pushed her away from her breast and put her down, to get up and pace the room in anguished pain. How different things would have been were this child Harry's. Angrily, she went over to the baby and looked down at her.

A pair of intensely blue eyes focused on her, their gaze open and innocent – trusting – untouched by the darkness of Connie's emotions. A pain, a feeling, a sense of her heart turning over slowly inside her chest gripped her.

Shakily, Connie crouched down and looked,

really looked, at her child for the first time.

'She has the Barclay looks, Connie,' Ellie had told her happily. 'More so than any of the other babies of our generation. Aunt Gibson might claim that Cecily's Charlotte is going to be the beauty of the family, but our little one here will outmatch her!'

Connie had ignored Ellie's prediction, but now she could see what her sister had meant. The dark cap of hair had already begun to curl; the delphinium blue eyes were beautifully shaped and set between thick, dark lashes. The little nose already showed signs of elegance.

Wonderingly Connie reached out and touched the soft skin. Immediately she got a smiling dimpled response and a happy gurgle.

'She is such a happy loving baby,' Ellie had told her.

Her small hand reached out and grasped Connie's finger. A feeling swelled inside Connie bursting past her own carefully built indifference. Unable to stop herself, Connie picked her up and held her tightly, whilst grief and pain flooded her.

This was her child. Hers! Emotionally she looked into the dark blue eyes gripped by a fiercely powerful surge of protective love.

'Well, I don't know why you claim she has the Barclay looks, Ellie, because I can see nothing of them in her myself.' Amelia Gibson sniffed as she looked disparagingly at the pretty face framed by the lacy christening bonnet.

It had been Ellie who had insisted on having a lavish family party to celebrate Lydia's christening, and now as she listened angrily to their aunt, Connie was beginning to wish she had not given way and agreed.

Ellie though, as proud godmother, was thoroughly enjoying showing off the new addition to the family to their assembled relatives.

'And besides,' Amelia Gibson was continuing, 'for all we know she may very well take after her father's family! There are none of them here today, I notice.'

Connie could feel herself beginning to stiffen, but she was spared the necessity of saying anything by Gideon who immediately stepped in and responded smoothly, 'Sadly Connie's husband was not in the fortunate position of having a large family around him.'

'But he must have had parents,' Amelia was insisting.

'Of course,' Gideon agreed. 'But both are dead.'

'I see. So your child has no father and no paternal family whatsoever, Connie. And what of her father? We hear nothing of him from you, and one might almost suppose...'

'I do not think we should be reminding Connie of such sadness on what is meant, after all, to be a happy occasion,' Gideon interceded firmly.

'I hope you realise what a very fortunate and privileged young woman you are, Connie, especially after the trouble you caused and the disgrace you brought on yourself!'

Her Aunt Gibson was determined to have her say and to make her disapproval felt, Connie recognised, trapped in a corner of the room whilst the older woman lectured and hectored her.

'Don't think though that I am deceived!'

Connie frowned and looked sharply at her. 'As to that, Aunt. I hope that you mean that you were deceived as to the wisdom of you, and my mother's other sisters stealing us from our father!'

'How dare you say such a thing! Although of course, it's typical of you that you do! You should think yourself lucky that you are still accepted as a member of this family, Constance, especially when...' Her lips pursed, and she looked deliberately from the rings Connie was wearing to where Ellie was holding Lydia Harriet.

'A leopard does not change its spots!' she pronounced darkly.

'Meaning what, exactly?' Connie demanded.

'You know perfectly well to what I refer! The disgrace you brought on yourself when you were in my sister's charitable care!'

Connie had had enough. 'Nothing will satisfy you, will it, Aunt, other than having your suspicions confirmed! What is it you want me to say? That I am not, and never have been, married? That my child is a bastard born out of wedlock. That...'

'Connie.'

She looked blindly at Ellie as she felt the gentle pressure of her sister's hand on her arm.

'Please excuse us, Aunt...'

As she swept Connie away, Ellie gave her arm a little shake and told her, 'You must try not to mind Aunt Gibson, Connie. I am afraid that much of the reason she is so unpleasant is my fault. She has never forgiven me for the fact that Gideon is so wealthy and well thought of! It would suit her much better if she were able to patronise us all. And despite what she says, our lovely little Lydia is the most beautiful baby in the whole family!'

'Ellie, I don't think she will ever believe that I was married, and what is more I feel she is determined to force me into admitting as much. She hates me!'

Ellie gave her a sympathetic look.

With Lydia Harriet over three months old, it had been agreed that Connie should be officially out of mourning, and for the christening she was wearing one of the new outfits Ellie had generously insisted on her having.

The cut and style of her dress with its matching coat was far more expensive than anything Connie herself could have afforded, and in some ways she felt almost a fraud wearing it. As she did in pretending to have a husband and the respectability to which she had no real right?

Despite her now genuine love for her baby, sometimes Connie felt as though she was suffocating in her new life. She longed to be back at the Infirmary. Working ... being amongst people with whom she felt she had things in common, and by whom she was accepted and valued.

'Connie, you have not been yourself these last few weeks. Is it because of what Aunt Gibson said at the christening?'

'Only sort of...' Connie answered her, and then

burst out, 'Ellie, I miss my work so much. Just listening to Iris talking about the hospital makes me feel so wretched, and since she mentioned the other week how all the hospitals are so desperately short of nurses, I've been thinking how wrong it is that I should be here doing nothing.'

'But Connie I thought you were happy here with us!'

Guiltily Connie bit her lip. 'I am Ellie. You've done so much for me; helped me so much. But I feel I should be doing something, Ellie. I miss the Infirmary, and my ward, my friends. I miss being useful.'

Ellie sat down, as she heard the emotion in Connie's voice. 'You're serious about this, aren't you?'

Eagerly Connie nodded her head. 'I've spoken with Iris, and she's agreed to have a word with Matron for me the next time she visits the Infirmary. She feels sure that Matron would allow me to return to work.'

'You mean you'd go back to Liverpool?' Now Ellie really did look shocked. 'I thought you were talking about finding work here in Preston! Oh, Connie, you can't do that! What about baby Lyddy? You can't return to nursing and be a mother!'

Connie had to turn away from her.

'No, I know,' she agreed quietly.

She had already known, of course, how impossible it would be for her sister, to whom her family was of paramount importance, to understand just how she felt; just how miserable and frustrated it made her to read almost daily in the

396

papers, of hospitals being unable to cope with the sheer number of injured soldiers returning from the Front, in part at least, because of the lack of trained nurses.

She ought to be doing her bit for the war effort; she needed to be doing her bit, Connie recognised, even if Ellie could not understand that.

'Lyddy is as close to you as she is to me, Ellie, if not closer. Sometimes I wonder if she actually knows which of us is her mother. I had thought...' she paused, and then went over to her sister, dropping down on her knees in front of her and taking hold of her hands.

'I know you won't understand this, Ellie, and I don't expect you to, but when nurses are needed so desperately, I feel that it's my duty to go. Lyddy will hardly notice that I am gone. Not when she has you to love her.'

'You will leave her here with me? Oh, Connie, you don't know how happy that makes me. I shall love her as though she were my own. In fact, I already do!'

There were tears in Ellie's eyes as they clasped one another's hands.

'You will see her often, Connie. On your days off, and whenever you choose. And I shall make sure that she doesn't forget you. But are you sure this is what you want? To return to nursing?'

'Yes,' Connie told her quietly.

A month later, Connie received the news from Iris that Matron was happy to have her back, although as a married woman, Connie would have to live out rather than have a room in the nurses' home.

'She has supplied me with a list of respectable lodging houses for you, Connie, as you are not the only married nurse returning to work.'

It had been decided that Connie would spend Christmas in Winckley Square and then return to Liverpool after the New Year.

Baby Lyddy was cutting her teeth, and making good use of the teething ring John had brought for her. He had returned home unexpectedly on leave, just in time to celebrate Christmas with them.

Connie doubted that there could be any family throughout the country for whom the Christmas festivities were not overshadowed, in one way or another, by the War. In every home there would be empty places and missing loved ones, and on Christmas morning the Vicar gave an extra sermon and read prayers for those far from home.

Even the boys were preoccupied by the War, and Connie saw the looks Gideon and Ellie exchanged when Philip asked if the War would be over before he was old enough to enlist.

'I am going into the Royal Flying Corps like John,' the elder of Ellie's sons announced.

'Pooh, that is nothing. I intend to join the Navy and command a battleship,' the younger one insisted.

'I pray that this War will be over soon,' Ellie told Connie as they went up to the nursery together, accompanied by Henrietta, to tuck Lydia in her crib.

'She is such a pretty baby, Aunt Connie,' Henrietta piped up admiringly as she stroked Lydia's soft curls.

'And sweet-tempered, too,' Ellie said tenderly.

'Well, in that at least, she is more like you than me,' Connie laughed.

But later, having gone into the nursery to check on Lydia before she went to bed, Connie studied the minute features slowly and intently – something she had grown into the habit of doing – and then exhaled on a jerky sigh of relief, having reassured herself once again that there was nothing of her father in her.

Her boxes were packed, and she had said her formal goodbyes to everyone – even Aunt Gibson – all she had to do now was go to bed and wait for the morning and her journey to Liverpool.

It had been a long and busy day and she should have been tired. Instead... Connie glanced toward the door. Opening it, she hurried quickly up the stairs to the nursery.

She knew she should not be doing this. She had already said her goodbyes to Lydia, but somehow she couldn't stop herself from opening the door and tiptoeing toward her baby daughter's crib.

There was more than enough light from the full moon shining outside the window to illuminate the room, and she could see Lydia's face quite clearly. Instead of being asleep, as Connie had expected, the baby was wide awake, the dark blue eyes looking solemnly into her own as she bent over her.

Ellie often declared that Lyddy wasn't just the prettiest baby she had ever seen, she was also the happiest, and it was true that she was a child who smiled much more than she cried.

She was smiling now as she kicked and gurgled, plainly pleased to have her mother's company. The new teeth she had been cutting were revealed by her gummy smile, the small hand closing determinedly on Connie's finger as she reached out to stroke her soft skin.

'I'm sorry for not loving you right from the very start,' Connie whispered softly to her. 'But I do love you now, little Lyddy.' Connie could feel the tears she was fighting not to cry, thickening her voice. 'I love you so very much!'

Lyddy seemed to be reaching out her arms to her. Unable to stop herself, Connie leaned into her crib and lifted her out. The baby scent of her turned Connie's heart over inside her chest with emotion. And she kissed one small, open, little starfish hand. How could she ever not have wanted this perfect little creation? Love for her filled her every single pore.

Lost in absorbing each minute detail of her, Connie didn't hear the door open.

'Connie.'

Clutching Lydia to her she whirled round, 'Ellie.'

'You know how much I love her, don't you, Connie!'

Numbly Connie nodded, but she was holding Lydia even tighter.

'And that she'll have everything she needs.'

Again Connie nodded, but the pain inside her was growing.

As Ellie walked toward her, Connie clutched Lydia as tightly as she could, as though half-afraid that Ellie might wrench her from her arms.

'I can't leave her,' she told Ellie fiercely. 'I can't! I know you love her, Ellie, but I love her, too, and I can't bear the thought of being without her! I'm going to take her with me!'

She couldn't bring herself to look at her sister, knowing what her reaction would be.

'Connie!'

There was a note in Ellie's voice she had never heard before, a sad sweetness that made her ache inside.

'I knew you wouldn't go without her. I've told Jenny to pack her things. But if things don't work out... If you should change your mind, I want you to know that you will both be welcome back here, Connie.'

'You knew I'd take her with me?'

Connie's voice wobbled as she ignored the last part of her sister's quiet statement.

'How could you? I didn't even know myself until just now. I swear to you I hadn't intended...'

'I've seen the way you look at her. Watched you with her... I've seen the mother love in your eyes, Connie, and known that it was in your heart.'

'I know you love her, Ellie.'

'Yes I do. And I love you, too. Do you really think I could be happy with your child, if you weren't happy? I'm not going to pretend that I wish, more than anything, that you weren't leaving, but we all have to be true to our own self, Connie.'

'Ellie!'

Tearfully they hugged one another, Lydia snuggled safely between them.

'This is from Gideon,' Ellie told her, once she had released her.

As Connie took the envelope Ellie was handing her, she frowned slightly. 'What is it?'

'A draft on his bank for a bank account in your name. It was Gideon's idea, Connie, and not mine. He wants to be sure that you have your own money should you need it.'

'He, both of you, have already been generous enough. I shan't touch it. I shall keep it safe for Lydia instead. For when she grows up!'

Ellie burst out laughing. 'I hope we may see each other before then Connie!'

'We shall see one another as often as we can. I shall bring Lyddy to see you on my days off, Ellie.'

'And I shall make frequent visits to Liverpool to make sure you have not disappeared, even if I have to beard your dragon of a Matron in the hospital itself, in order to do so!'

TWENTY-FOUR

'Yer want a room, yer say?'

Tiredly, Connie hitched Lyddy a little higher onto her hip. Disconcertingly she had discovered that it was not going to be as easy to find lodgings as she had assumed.

It was now nearly evening, and she had been trudging from lodging house to lodging house for what seemed like hours, only to be turned away by landladies who had made it plain that they were not prepared to let rooms to a woman with a child, even if the Queen herself was prepared to speak for her, never mind a mere Matron.

'Sorry, but I 'aven't any vacancies. Where's yer man?' she demanded suspiciously.

Connie had had enough. Holding Lydia tightly, she told her fiercely, 'I'm a widow. A nurse looking for accommodation so that I can go back to work! There are soldiers dying because there isn't anyone to nurse them. Do you want to have that on your conscience?'

'Conscience, is it!' The other woman sniffed tossing her head. 'Well, I've never heard of no nurses needing to find a room – lives at the 'orspital they do. And, any road, I only take single, respectable lodgers, and they don't want their sleep disturbed by crying babies.' She folded her arms over her chest and added sharply, 'And if you was a nurse, what would you be expectin' to do with 'er whilst you was workin'?'

'The same as other working mothers,' Connie told her equally sharply. 'There must be someone round here who minds children?'

'Mebbe there is, and mebbe there isn't, but yer ain't bringing 'er 'ere!'

Connie's arm ached from holding Lyddy, and she thought longingly of the comfort of Ellie's home.

'There must be someone who will rent me lodgings,' she pressed.

'Oh, aye, plenty,' the other woman agreed. 'There's a woman on the next street who'd like as not take yer – glad of anyone she is, wi' that mad brother o' hers to look after. Should be in Bedlam by rights, he should.'

The next street, she'd said, but as Connie checked the list she'd been given before turning wearily toward it, she could not find any lodgings listed for it.

Remembering the horror of some of the lodgings she had shared with Kieron, she hesitated, but then Lydia, tired and hungry, started to wail.

Comforting her as best she could, she started to walk down the street until she came to a window with a 'Vacancies' sign in it.

The house looked clean enough, she acknowledged, as she studied the polished windows and immaculate doorstep.

Hesitantly she knocked on the door and waited.

The woman who answered it, looked at her a little apprehensively.

'I'm looking for rooms,' Connie told her. 'There's just me and the baby, and I'll be wanting someone to keep an eye on her for me whilst I'm at work. I'm a nurse, up at the Infirmary...'

Lydia gave a hungry wail, and Connie's heart sank as she waited for the woman to turn her away, but instead her thin face lit up and she exclaimed, 'Oh, poor little thing! You'd better come in and I'll show you the rooms. They're on the second floor, a bedroom and a parlour. If you want meals then it will be extra.'

When Connie followed her up a flight of immaculately clean stairs her heart started to lift. To her relief the two small rooms were pin neat and clean, the furniture simple but adequate.

'I'm Nora Barstow, by the way.'

'Connie Pr ... Smith,' Connie introduced herself.

'I'll take the rooms, Mrs Barstow, and I'll pay you the rent now,' she added quickly, worried that the landlady might change her mind. But the woman looked as relieved as Connie felt.

'I'm not married. It's just me and my brother living here, and I'd prefer it if you was to call me Nora, if that's all right with you.'

She sounded almost shyly hesitant, and Connie found herself warming to her. She was certainly very different from any of the other prospective landladies she had encountered during the day.

'I've left my boxes at the station,' Connie told her. 'I'll have to find a carter to bring them here for me.'

'Well, my brother will probably do that for you. He's out at the moment.' She gave Connie a hesitant look, and told her awkwardly, 'I should perhaps warn you that he isn't quite... That is to say... Well, no matter what other folks round here think, he was as right in the head as anyone else before he went off to the War, but now...'

'It's all right, Nora,' Connie reassured her gently. 'I'm a nurse, and I've seen what the War can do to even the bravest of men.'

But inside, Connie admitted to feeling a little wary, and questioning the wisdom of her decision to lodge with the Barstows. Not on her own account, so much as on Lydia's.

'I've got a couple of days before I start work at the hospital but you needn't worry that I shall be under your feet. I need to find someone I can leave Lydia with whilst I'm out at work.'

405

'Well there's Cassie Halkowes over on Neville Terrace. She takes in bairns for women whilst they're working. There's a lot of women round here working at the munitions factory. But I would be quite happy to mind her for you,' she offered eagerly. 'I've got a bit of time on me hands and I don't mind admitting I'd welcome the company.

'Aye, and I could teach her her letters and that once she gets old enough. Taught at Sunday school, I did,' she informed Connie proudly, before adding with a small sigh, 'of course things were different in them days. Me mam and da were alive for one thing, and this was a respectable area then, with most folks owning their own houses. It's all changed now. Most of the houses round here have been bought up and are landlord-owned, and it's never the same once that happens. Tenants don't have the same pride in a place if it's not their own.'

Nora was lonely Connie guessed, and probably part of her loneliness stemmed from the fact that her neighbours shunned her on account of her brother. She would have to reserve judgement on whether or not the house was going to be a suitable place for Lydia until after she had met him, she acknowledged, as she gratefully accepted Nora's offer of a cup of tea and a bite to eat.

'You can come down and have it with me if you want. It's warmer downstairs in the kitchen.'

'I'll be right down,' Connie thanked her. 'Just as soon as I've got Lyddy sorted out.'

It had been a long day, and half an hour later,

comfortably ensconced in the rocking chair Nora had insisted on her having, Lydia already asleep in her arms, Connie could feel her own eyes closing.

Her stomach felt pleasantly full of the homemade chicken soup Nora had given her, and the kitchen was wonderfully warm, its floor clean enough to eat off. Lydia had devoured the bowl of porridge Connie had fed her. She was coming up for six months now and Connie had been weaning her in preparation for her return to work. Connie still breastfed her at night though, as much for her own sake as the baby's, since she cherished the opportunity to nurture her.

If it weren't for her concern about Nora's brother she would have thought she had really fallen on her feet, Connie admitted.

Reluctantly rousing herself, she told Nora, 'I'd better take Lyddy up and put her to bed, then I'll come down and give you a hand with those dishes.'

'You'll do no such thing! You look worn out yourself,' Nora told her firmly. She gave a small frown. 'I was expecting Davie to have been back before now, and you wanting your boxes.'

'They can wait until morning,' Connie assured her calmly. 'I've got enough with me for tonight.'

Her bed was as comfortable and clean as the rest of the house, its sheets smelling of fresh lavender, and as she snuggled into its warmth, Connie breathed a sleepy sigh of relief.

Tomorrow she would telephone Ellie and reassure her that all was well, and that she had found somewhere comfortable to live. She had written to Josie to say that she planned to return to the Infirmary, having received letters from her and from some of the other nurses as well, which Iris had brought with her to Winckley Square after one of her regular visits to Liverpool.

There had been a letter amongst them from Mavis too, a stilted wish for Connie's future happiness and for her safe delivery – the kind of note one might receive from an acquaintance rather than a close friend, and Connie had agonised over how she should reply to it.

She might be reconciled with her sister, but the loving relationship she now had with Ellie, rather than taking away the ache of pain the break in her friendship with Mavis had caused her, had somehow underlined it. The truth was that she missed Mavis for herself, and not just because she was Harry's sister. But she was reluctant to do anything to try to re-establish their old friendship.

For one thing, Mavis was bound to want to ask her questions about Lyddy's father, and why she had said nothing to her about meeting him and marrying him, and for another... For another, much as she yearned to be with her friend, Connie dreaded hearing about Rosa and Rosa's child – Harry's child!

So she had written back to Mavis in an equally stilted fashion thanking her for her concern, and informing her of her plans.

Her feet ached a little, and her last drowsy thought as she snuggled into her comfortable bed was the wry one that if they ached now, that was nothing to how they were going to feel after her first week back on the wards.

It was the sound of men fighting outside in the street that woke her. The room was in darkness and for a moment she couldn't understand where she was. The sounds of men brawling took her back in time. But then Lydia gave a small wail, and she realised with relief that she was not back with Kieron in some filthy tenement building, but tucked up snugly in a room still warm from the now dying fire Nora had insisted on lighting for her.

Exhaling in relief, she pulled Lydia closer to her, and then checked, as she heard the front door being opened followed by the sound of Nora's frightened voice as she pleaded, above the noise of punches and sobs of terrified pain, 'No. Please don't hurt him. Please let him go!'

Ignoring the small inner voice warning her not to get involved, Connie threw back the bed-clothes and pulled on the thick dressing gown Ellie had given her for Christmas, to run to the window.

Down below in the street she could see a small group of men bending over another man who was lying at their feet. He had curled into a ball as he tried to protect himself from their fists and feet, whilst Nora tried impotently to push them away.

Guessing that the man being attacked must be her brother, Connie reacted more out of instinct than anything else. She pushed open her window and threw the contents of the ewer of water she had used to wash her hands and face in before going to bed, over the nearest of the men.

The water hit him full in the face, and as he looked up at the window, Connie called out sharply, 'It'll be the chamber pot next, and if you lot wake my man up you'll soon know about it. Just back from the Front he is, where every decent man ought to be, not fighting in the street.'

Whilst they stood and stared up warily at her, Connie could see Nora helping her brother to his feet and dragging him inside. If the men chose to follow her and force their way into the house... Fiercely, Connie closed her mind to that thought.

To her relief, another couple of windows in the street were being opened, and irate voices demanded to know what was going on.

Hastily she closed her own window, and having checked to make sure that Lydia was asleep, hurried through their bedroom door to the top of the stairs. She could see Nora in the hallway bent over her brother, who was groaning.

'Nora, have you locked the door?' she called out.

'Yes! Oh, Connie. Thank you. I'd never have got Davie away from them if you hadn't been so quick-thinking. They've half killed him as it is.'

'I'll come down and have a look at him,' Connie told her, hurrying down the stairs. 'Do you think we can get him into the kitchen, so that we can clean him up a bit?'

'I'll try, but he's so afraid of them, I don't think he realises that he's safe yet. Davie, it's all right. You're safe now with Nora. Let's get you into the kitchen, love, and get you cleaned up a bit.'

The man crouching on the floor, his hands over

his head, started to shake and moan, 'No... No...', and then suddenly he made a sound like a burst of machine-gun fire.

'Oh, Davie. Love, no, not that. Don't pay any attention, Connie...' Nora was saying, but Connie ignored her to cross the hall and kneel down.

'Jinx?' she questioned gently.

Slowly he removed one hand from his head and then the other, and then turned his face toward her.

Angry pity clutched at Connie's heart as she saw how badly he had been beaten. Even in the dim light from the hallway it was possible to see the deep cuts steel-toed boots had made in the flesh just above his eye and his cheek, right across the telltale scar. One eye was already discolouring, and blood was trickling from the corner of his mouth.

'It's Sister Pride, Nora,' he suddenly started babbling thickly, pulling on Nora's arm rather as a child might have done.

'You know my brother?' Nora asked Connie warily.

'He was on my ward for a while when I was at the Infirmary,' Connie informed her.

'Kind,' Jinx, or Davie, as she now realised he was called, whispered and touched Connie's arm, 'kind.'

'He told me about the nurse who was kind to him,' Nora told her emotionally. 'Not that it's always easy to understand properly just what he is trying to say. But he doesn't mean any harm, Connie... I know they say round here that he's

411

mad and should be locked up in Bedlam, but there was nothing wrong with him before he went off to war,' Nora told her angrily, repeating what she had said earlier. 'Changed him it did, and no mistake. But I can't just have him put away. I promised me mother I wouldn't for one thing, and for another... Like as not he'd be dead within a fortnight if he didn't have me to look after him.'

'Let's get him into the kitchen and clean those cuts,' Connie suggested, waiting until she had cleaned them properly and was dressing them, before asking Nora, 'if this isn't the first time he's been attacked, why hasn't something been done about it? Have you reported it to the police?'

'It isn't as simple as that, Connie. You see all the houses around here bar mine are landlord-owned and the landlord he wants this one, too, but he doesn't want to buy it for a fair price. He wants to frighten me out of it like he's done others around here. And if you were to ask me, I'd say that's part of the reason those thugs of his keep attacking poor Davie. It's the same men he sends in if'n someone doesn't pay their special rent money.'

'Special rent money?' Connie queried.

Nora gave a heavy sigh.

'Aye, that's the extra he charges his tenants for making sure that they don't get no bother from anyone like. Thing is though, that the only ones they're likely to get bother from are his own men,' she told Connie bitterly. 'There's no need for you to worry though. They don't bother any of the lodgers. They bring in money, and he likes

412

to keep this street respectable so that he can show it off, if anyone comes round checking up like.

'I have heard as how he's got dozens of filthy tenements as is let out to poor souls who can't afford anything better, whole families living in one room, and all sorts rooming in the same building with them, if you know what I mean. Women as is looking to tempt the soldiers when they come home on leave, and keep them from their families,' she added darkly, obviously not willing to utter the word 'prostitute'. 'I warned Davie not to go out at night, but he never listens. Like a child he is...'

'Well, they've knocked him about pretty badly and he's got some nasty cuts, but nothing seems to be broken.'

'Connie? Connie Pride?'

'Josie!' Connie exclaimed in pleased surprise, as she paused halfway down the stairs leading to the hospital dispensary.

Enthusiastically the two friends hugged one another.

'When did you start working here again?' Josie demanded.

'About a month ago,' Connie answered her. 'When did you come back?'

'Oh, six months back now. The house seemed empty without Ted to look after. Vera suggested I got a job with her in the munitions factory but I didn't fancy it somehow, and then I heard as how the hospital was needing nurses, so I got meself up here and asked if I could come back like, even though I was married. Well, widowed now of course, and they was more than pleased to have me!

'And you?'

Connie hesitated, unwilling to lie, but all too aware of the fact that Matron had taken her back on as Connie Smith, even if everyone who remembered her, including Mr Clegg for whom she was now working as a surgical nurse, still referred to her as Sister Pride.

'The same,' she answered Josie as casually as she could. She gave a small shrug. 'I could have stayed in Preston with my sister and her husband, but I missed the work.'

'You means you was married? Well I never! I hadn't heard. And widowed, you say?' Josie added sympathetically.

'There are a lot of women lost their men to this War,' Connie responded truthfully. 'And at least I've got my little Lyddy...'

'You've got a babby! Fancy that! I saw Vera the other day, she's carryin'.'

'How's her Bert?' Connie asked drily. 'The last I heard he had claimed to be a conscientious objector so as to avoid being called up!'

'Well, there's bin a bit of trouble there. Fell out good and proper, they did. The next thing was that Vera moved out, and moved in with this soldier she'd gone and tekken up with. Aye, and this babby she's carryin' is his an' all, and him gone back to the War and left her with nowt but a swollen belly and a heap o' trouble on 'er hands.

'Bert won't have her back, and her family have turned their back on her. She's still working at the munitions factory and she's moved in with one of the girls she works with there. Seems like the pair of them was off having a good time when they should have been at home cooking their husbands' suppers, and that's how Vera met up with this soldier in the first place. Now he's gorn and left her and, like I said, she's in a right old mess.

'Still, if you ask me, it serves her right. Ted allus did say she was one as would come to a bad end, and to tell the truth, it isn't as though she hasn't got what she deserved, messing around like that. I mean what respectable woman ends up in her state, carryin' and no husband!' Josie demanded indignantly. 'I don't have anything to do with her any more,' she added virtuously. 'After all, I don't want to get tarred with the same brush as her, I'm a respectable widow!'

Connie's heart sank a little further with every word Josie said.

'Anyway, what about you, Connie?' Josie pressed sympathetically. 'You're a widow too. Was your husband...?'

'I don't want to talk about it, if you don't mind, Josie,' Connie stopped her quickly.

'Aye, I know how you feel. Hated talking about my Ted I did, at first.'

'I hardly knew John, really,' Connie told her in a low voice. 'He was a soldier ... and ... and not from round here.'

'There, Connie, don't you go upsetting yourself,' Josie sympathised, making Connie feel even more guilty. But she had Lyddy to think of, she reminded herself, as she acknowledged how right Gideon and Ellie had been to want to protect her, even if something in her balked at having to lie.

'Do you ever hear anything of anyone else?' Connie asked her.

'Anyone else. Like who?'

'Well ... Mavis, for instance.'

Josie's face broke into an immediate smile.

'Oh yes. She writes to me, regular like. It was through her that I 'eard that you'd left the hospital because she wrote and asked me if I knew where you were. Said as how she'd had some of her letters sent back to her.'

Connie bit her lip.

'I should have written, but what with ... everything.'

'Aye, well, Mavis 'ull understand. Allus was an understanding one was Mavis. So you won't have 'eard their good news then, I suppose?'

'I knew that Rosa was to have a baby,' Connie admitted cautiously.

'Oh that, yes, a fine boy she's had, but Mavis and them haven't so much as seen 'im, on account of how Rosa has gone living with some cousin or other. But that'll change once this ruddy War is over and their 'Arry comes back.'

The stairs moved sickeningly beneath her feet, and for a moment Connie thought she might actually faint.

'Harry? But he's dead?' she protested shakily.

'Aye well, they thought 'e was, but seemingly it were all a mistake and he's a prisoner of war! Harry wrote to the War Office about the mix up and they checked up on everything, and Mavis and them were allowed to send a letter to 'Arry...

416

Mavis says that she'd rather he was imprisoned than still having to fight, and I can't say as I blame her!

'And then, as if that weren't enough good luck, that old aunt of theirs went and died, and they found out that she'd left them the house and a fair bit o' money as well! 'Ere is that the time? Sister will have me guts for garters, if I don't get a move on,' Josie announced. 'How about the two of us meeting up for a proper chat over a cup o' tea next time we're both off. You can bring your little 'un, if you like.' Her face softened. 'Right fond of kiddies, I am. Pity that me and Ted never had any.' She gave a small sigh.

Connie was incapable of making any kind of rational response. Her heart was thumping and she felt sick with shock and pain.

Harry was alive. Harry wasn't dead. Harry was alive and once this War was over he would be coming home to his wife and his son, and the three of them would live happily ever after, whilst she...

Tears burned the backs of her eyes like raw acid. Thank God. Thank God, Harry would never know the extent of her shame! She couldn't bear to think of him knowing that she was not married and the mother of a child, because she knew what he would think...

Harry was alive. Pain and joy filled her in equal measure. Harry was alive, but a part of her wished that she were dead.

TWENTY-FIVE

'Connie, it is so lovely having you here with us, and little Lyddy too.'

Ellie smiled fondly at where Lydia was sitting happily in the late August sunshine, whilst the adults enjoyed the picnic they had brought to the lakeside with them.

'When Gideon first bought the house here I thought it was an extravagance, but I admit I do love the Lake District,' Ellie told Connie happily, before adding, 'but what I love even more is having us all together. I am so pleased that both you and John were able to be here at the same time.'

'Well I've only got two days off,' Connie reminded her tiredly.

Ellie frowned a little as she looked at her. 'I know how much you wanted to go back to nursing, Connie, but I have to say that it doesn't seem to be doing you much good. You look so thin and you've barely smiled or laughed the whole time you've been here. Is everything all right?'

'Yes, of course,' Connie answered her, but she knew that she was lying.

Something had happened to her with the birth of Lydia, something she had not bargained for – a combination of a deep need to be with her child, and an equally deep weariness of damaged

418

young bodies and death. Sometimes it seemed no matter how hard they worked, there was so little they could do.

And then of course there were her agonising, aching dreams of Harry and the unending pain of loving him.

'Tell me more about your landlady and her brother,' Ellie demanded.

Connie had given Ellie a brief description of Nora and Jinx, telling her about how much they both adored and spoiled Lyddy but omitting to mention the fact that Jinx, or rather Davie, had been beaten up twice whilst she had been living with them, and that Nora was in constant fear for her brother.

'Perhaps I should just give in and sell this house to Derek Walton,' she had told Connie wearily one evening, when they were sitting together drinking tea, whilst Lyddy slept peacefully in Nora's arms. In Nora, Connie had found the perfect person to care for Lyddy whilst she was at work, and Nora had refused to take so much as a penny for watching over the baby, saying that she ought to be the one paying Connie for the pleasure it gave her to have Lydia's company.

'He's an evil man. Him and that partner of his, they both are.'

'Perhaps you *should* sell and move somewhere else,' Connie had suggested more than once.

'I've got Davie to think of. And I'm afraid that no one would sell to me once they knew about him. He doesn't mean any harm Connie, you know that, but folks just don't understand.'

Now though it seemed Nora was being forced

to change her mind.

'Connie, I've been thinking,' Ellie broke into her thoughts. 'I know it will be hard for you, but why don't you leave Lyddy with us instead of taking her back to Liverpool with you? Gideon has decided that I'm to stay up here with the boys, instead of going back to Preston at the end of the month as we'd intended, because of the way this influenza is spreading. There are thousands dead of it already abroad, apparently,' she told Connie anxiously.

'We have been warned to take every precaution against it that we can,' Connie admitted soberly. 'As yet we haven't had any patients affected by it.'

'Oh, this wretched War! I wish so that it would be over! Gideon says that even in the Government now there are those who are insisting that something be done to bring it to a close, and that too many lives have already been lost. And now what with more food rationing on top of everything else.'

'Connie you're back. I have missed you so much. But where is Lydia?'

'I left her up in the Lakes with my sister,' Connie answered Nora as the other woman welcomed her in. 'Ellie is worried about this influenza and begged me not to risk Lyddy's health by bringing her back to Liverpool, especially with me working at the hospital.'

'Oh I shall miss her so much!'

'So shall I.' Connie gave her a rueful look. 'I miss her already and it hasn't been a full day yet

420

since I left her.'

It had almost broken her heart to say goodbye to her baby. But this time, unlike when she first came back to Liverpool, she knew she had to leave her behind, for Lyddy's own good. Gideon had alarmed her with his grim certainty that the influenza deaths being inflicted on other countries would also be inflicted on their own. He had already put in place stringent measures to prevent it infecting his own household.

If he should be proved right, Connie knew that Lydia would be far safer with Ellie in the fresh air of the countryside than in the close confines of Liverpool. Even so, she thought constantly of her little girl who had celebrated her first birthday earlier in the month with Ellie throwing a very grand party for her. She remembered how Lyddy had sat to have her photograph taken by her Uncle John wearing the beautiful silk and lace dress her Aunt Ellie had sewn for her.

'Oh, Connie she is such a beauty,' Ellie had whispered emotionally. 'Every time I see her she is even prettier. She is so like our mother.' Silently they had looked at one another, and then Ellie had squeezed Connie's hand reassuringly, 'She's all Barclay, with just the right amount of Pride common sense, Connie, and nothing else!'

By the end of September, Gideon's prediction had proved alarmingly correct, and the so-called 'Spanish' flu was sweeping the country.

'Have you heard the latest?' one of the nurses an exhausted Connie bumped into in the dining room on her way for her breakfast before she went on duty, asked her, continuing without waiting for Connie to reply, 'a friend of mine works at the Walton and they've had twenty-five nurses go down with the flu already.'

Connie said nothing. She had already heard privately from one of the other Sisters, the even more shocking news that seven nurses and one Sister had died from the pneumonia that was accompanying the influenza. The Liverpool hospital authorities were afraid that such news would panic people and affect the morale of the whole of the city's nursing staff.

She ate her breakfast as quickly as she could, and hurried onto her own ward, 'Sister Pride, Matron wants to have a word with you.'

No matter how many years she spent nursing, she would always feel this little quiver of anxiety whenever she was sent for by Matron, Connie acknowledged ruefully, as she hurried in obedience to her summons. It was a reflection, perhaps, on the number of times she had been summoned before her for misdemeanours during her early training. She was commanded to enter Matron's office the moment she knocked on the door, 'Ah, Sister Smith good!'

Although officially she was now Sister Smith, virtually everyone still referred to her as Sister Pride, much to Connie's relief, and it took her aback slightly to hear her unfamiliar surname.

'You may have heard about the sad deaths of our colleagues at Walton Hospital,' Matron began, waiting whilst Connie inclined her head in acknowledgement. 'Walton's Matron has sent me a message asking if I have any senior nurses, or even better a trained Sister, I can spare to take over two of their maternity wards. I am loath to part with any of my nurses, especially those most senior, but Walton's Matron, Mrs Roberts, tells me that they have had more admissions than they can possibly hope to cope with, and having already lost a Sister... Mrs Roberts herself has had the influenza but thankfully is now recovering. The choice must be your own of course...'

Wryly Connie listened, knowing that the reality was that the choice had already been made for her.

'When am I to report to the Maternity Hospital, ma'am?' she asked calmly.

'You may go immediately, Nurse. Or should I say, Sister,' Matron smiled approvingly.

There was no time for Connie to tell anyone where she was going, and when she reached the Maternity Hospital she was despatched immediately to make herself known to Mrs Roberts, the Matron, who greeted her with evident relief.

'One thing I am insisting on all my nurses doing, Sister, and that is making sure they take care of their own health – that means eating regular meals, whether one wants them or not! I have given our cooks instructions that soups, broths, fruit juices and whole fruit are to be made available to my nurses at all times! A nurse who does not take proper care of her own health is doing our patients as great a disservice as she is herself. I understand from the Matron at the Infirmary that you have an excellent nursing record.'

'I've worked most frequently on surgical

wards,' Connie felt bound to explain.

Matron's mouth compressed.

'As you will discover, I am afraid that our maternity wards have been turned into a form of surgical ward by this dreadful influenza.' She gave a faint sigh. 'We have mothers coming in who simply do not have the strength to fight this affliction, and dying virtually as they give birth. Naturally we are making every effort to save their child, even when that means...' She broke off and gave Connie a bleak look. 'I understand you are a mother yourself, Sister?'

Silently Connie nodded her head.

'Then I am sure you will understand how much it means to a mother, even in the throes of death, to know that her child is saved.'

Connie's stomach had started to knot, but she still nodded in agreement.

'The maternity wards?' a nurse commented to Connie, when she had asked Connie where she was to be working. 'Gawd, I pity yer. It's Bedlam up there, babies howling and screeching as the surgeons tek 'em from their dying mas. Poor motherless little sods, and who's to look after 'em heaven alone knows, 'cos mostly their das are at the Front.'

Connie had thought that nothing could be worse than what she had seen already, even if the rows and rows of tightly-packed beds filled with dying patients brought in by their families bleakened the heart and the soul; but she had been wrong, she admitted, several hours after she had first walked into the maternity ward.

Here indeed was a form of hell on earth that affected her emotions; tore at her heart as nothing else ever had or could.

Women, their bellies huge with their unborn children, lay dying – or dead – whilst surgeons worked to remove the living children from their bodies.

One young woman in the corner of the ward screamed to Connie to help her, but when Connie would have gone over to her, the surgeon shook his head and told Connie tersely, 'Leave her,' explaining grimly. 'She was brought in three days ago – she's nowhere near full term. We can't save her or her child.'

The newborn babies were taken screaming to the nursery for fear of them being infected, and none of the nurses from the maternity ward were allowed to accompany them. They had to pass the babies over to a masked nurse who bathed them and then passed them into the nursery itself.

Connie had come on duty at ten in the morning. At midnight she was still working, having stopped only to drink some broth as ordered by Matron and eat some fresh fruit.

As fast as one woman was delivered and her body removed to the makeshift morgue that had been set up to try to accommodate the growing number of bodies, another one arrived to take her place. Some poor souls were literally abandoned by their families at the door of the hospital itself, including women whose pregnancies had barely even begun.

Connie couldn't help but pity these poor souls;

already infected they had been brought here in reality to die, and their child with them.

'You will tell them to have me babby christened, won't yer?' one terrified woman begged Connie, her eyes bright with fear in her sunken face. 'Don't let the poor little bugger be buried unshriven.'

'She can't be any more than four months,' the doctor Connie had summoned to look at her, told Connie. 'She's hardly showing at all.'

'The mother swears she's gone seven, she's been starving herself thinking it would stop her getting the flu.'

The doctor shook his head. 'I've got forty women here close to term. I can't afford to waste time operating on one who it's obvious I can't deliver a living child from.'

'How would you feel if she was your wife, and that your child?' Connie demanded furiously.

He was only a young man although he looked grey and old.

'My wife died last week,' he told her emotionlessly. 'And our son died with her. He was just over a year old.'

Virtually the same age as Lyddy!

Thank God she had agreed to leave her daughter with Ellie! Gideon had banned anyone from visiting the lakeside house, and Connie had at his request given him over the telephone, instructions on how to keep everywhere disinfected.

In between doing what she could for her patients, she prayed that her family wouldn't contract the virus, and most of all that her precious Lyddy would be safe!

The child she had not wanted had become more precious to her than she could ever have imagined.

It was just over a week since Connie had first started working at the Maternity Hospital. Carpenters had had to be hired in order to cope with the demand for coffins, and Connie knew that the sound of newborn babies crying for their dead mothers would haunt her for the rest of her life.

Part of the problem was that terrified families were bringing their sick into the hospital at the height of their infection, when movement or disturbance of any kind was very bad for them, and Walton hospital itself contained row after row of beds of dying patients.

'We can't take in any new patients,' one of the maternity ward doctors told Connie as she came on duty. 'The wards and the corridors are already full of dying women, and we had another five brought in last night. Four of them will die before they can deliver,' he added bleakly.

'And the fifth?' Connie pressed.

'Dead already,' he told her curtly.

Adjusting her mask, Connie started to move down the ward, pity and anger wrenching at her heart. These women were so weak that even if they could survive the illness, they simply did not have the strength to endure labour.

'Connie... Connie... Is that you?'

Quickly she turned to look toward the woman calling her name, 'Vera!'

She could barely recognise her friend in the

woman lying in the bed. Her belly was huge with advanced pregnancy, but her face was sunken and waxen, death already staring from her eyes, as rigours shook her body.

'Vera it's all right,' Connie tried to soothe her.

'There's no need to lie to me, Connie. I'm dying, and I know it. That's why I came here. It's the baby... I knew if I could get mesel' here it 'ud have some chance. I'm full term, and from the way 'e's been kicking at me he's a healthy little varmint. Even if I don't go into labour before ... well, I know what it's all about, Connie. I've heard as how they're tekkin' the little 'uns from their dead mothers to save 'em like...'

She flinched as a convulsion suddenly seized her, her belly going rigid.

'See. He knows himself.' She gasped as a birth pang gripped her. 'Not that the poor little sod is going to 'ave much of a life. A bloody orphan that's what 'e's going to be!'

'What about Bert and your family?' Connie protested, as she monitored Vera's pains.

'Cast me off they 'av. Anyway, this 'un ain't Bert's.'

She was growing weaker in front of Connie's eyes.

Very few of the mothers lived long enough to see their child born, most of the babies being taken, as Vera herself had just said, from their bodies.

'Connie,' Vera was gripping her hand so tightly that Connie's fingers had gone white.

'I want yer to promise me that you'll look after the little 'un for me. I heard as how you've got

428

one of your own... Promise me, Connie. We was good friends once.'

'Vera. You should be saving your strength,' Connie urged her, but Vera was refusing to be placated or sidetracked.

'Promise me!'

'Very well,' Connie gave in helplessly. 'I promise.'

TWENTY-SIX

Numbly Connie looked at the sleeping baby in her arms. It was just over a week now since he had been born; just over a week since his mother had died; just over a week since she had promised Vera that she would look after him for her.

Unlike her own Lydia, he was the ugliest baby Connie had ever seen, thin as a skinned rabbit, blue-white, with a sheen of carrot-coloured hair.

He was also angry, noisy, and constantly hungry. The only reason he was asleep now was because the one way to get him to sleep was to walk up and down carrying him, and Connie had walked virtually all the way from the hospital to Nora's with him.

'Bloody 'ell, we'll be glad to be rid of 'im!' one of the nurses in the nursery had told Connie bluntly, 'a right little bugger he is. Upsets all the other babies with 'is crying an' sets them off as well!'

'What will happen to them all?' Connie had

asked her tentatively, as she had looked round the rows and rows of cribs, each containing a motherless child.

To know the full horror of the influenza epidemic one only had to walk into this room, and learn that not a single one of the mothers of these babies had survived the epidemic.

The nurse had given an exhausted dismissive shrug.

'Well they've all got families of one sort or another, and I suppose they will be taken in and brung up by them. We've had a fair few wimen in who 'aven't got husbands – it 'appens all the time, but we've had more of them recently on account of the War. Mind you, even if they 'ave got a dad, like as not he'll have to farm 'em out to someone who can look after them, if he can afford to. Them as can't will probably end up in the poorhouse orphanage. I could make mesel a fortune tekkin 'em in, if I was of a mind to do it.'

Listening to her had banished Connie's hope of trying to find a respectable woman who could take charge of Vera's son, which was why she had had to take him home with her, having already warned Nora of the addition to their household.

Fortunately Nora had been delighted by the news that there was going to be another child in the house. 'I miss your Lyddy so much...'

Connie was missing her desperately herself, but whilst the influenza was raging through the city she was not going to risk her daughter's health by going to visit her.

As she had known she would, she found Nora in the kitchen, 'Well, here he is Nora,' she announced wryly. 'Little Georgie, and a real little... Nora, what is it? What's wrong?' she demanded with concern as she saw Nora's tear-swollen eyes. 'Is it Davie? Have those men...?'

Blowing her nose, Nora nodded her head. 'They came round late last night, Connie, after you'd gone to work. Banged so hard on the door, they did, I thought they were going to put it through, never mind waking up half the street.'

She gave a deep shudder. 'Davie was that scared.'

'What did they want?' Connie asked her.

'Same thing as always! This house! Only this time...' Fresh tears filled her eyes. 'Oh, Connie, I've never said anything about this to you, and perhaps I should have done, but I was that pleased to have you lodging here, and I thought that if you knew you'd want to leave.

'You know how Davie is ... he doesn't mean any harm. But folks will torment him like, and he's a big strong lad.'

Connie's heart was beginning to sink. 'What are you trying to say?'

'There was this man ... posh chap ... been in the Army. I don't know the ins and outs of it, but someone did tell me as how they had seen him speaking to Davie, and having a bit of a go at him, like. Davie never said anything to me ... but seemingly...' Nora was crying so hard she could hardly speak, and Connie put a comforting hand on her arm.

'Nora, whatever Davie's done I know it wouldn't have been done out of malice. If someone's been tormenting him.'

'Well, that's what I've been thinking. But I was that shocked when they told me, Connie. I'd no idea ... I'd heard about this Captain being found dead, like, but it was a while back now, and I never imagined that Davie could have had anything to do with it.'

Connie clutched the baby more tightly, as her heart started to beat too heavily.

'Whether or not it's true... Last night... Well, when I said I wouldn't sell them this house no matter what, they said as how they knew about what Davie had done. How he'd started yelling something about murdering the Captain to them. Connie, I don't know if what they're saying is true or not, but what I do know is that they could get my poor Davie into a lot of trouble. "Mr Connolly said to tell you that iffen you don't sell him this house, he'll see to it that your Davie hangs for the Captain's murder," those were their very words to me!'

Two things hit Connie one after the other; both equally shocking in their different ways. The first was the realisation that Davie could well have been bullied by the Captain to the point where he had attacked him, and the second was the acid fear that the Mr Connolly Nora was referring to, might be Kieron's Uncle Bill.

'Mr Connolly?' she repeated through stiff lips. 'You've never mentioned him before. Who is he, Nora?'

'Bill Connolly! Everyone around here is afraid of him, Connie, even the menfolk. A real nasty piece of work he is... There's tales of all sorts of goings on to do wi' folks who've crossed him disappearing and never being found. No one will say so, but it's since he took up with the landlord that these bully boys have started coming round making decent folk pay money over, so as they won't have their shops and property attacked. Our Davie is terrified of him.'

Connie had to sit down.

Bill Connolly... A chill of icy horror shot down Connie's spine.

She did her best to reassure and calm Nora, but the truth was that she herself felt almost as sick with fear as she could see her landlady was.

She knew that it was illogical for her to fear that somehow Bill Connolly could harm her now; after all she wasn't the vulnerable, abandoned girl she had been when he had hurt and threatened her. But still she was afraid.

'It's no good, Connie. I'm going to have to let him have the house. I'll get no peace until I do, and I've got Davie to think of. Oh, Connie, if Davie did kill that man...'

'You mustn't think about that,' Connie told her sharply. 'Try not to worry, Nora.'

But inwardly Connie was equally as worried herself. Worried and afraid.

Bill Connolly! Anger and fear gripped her. Why hadn't she ended his life when she had had the opportunity? She paced the floor with Georgie, trying to stop him crying, whilst she worried exhaustedly at the problems confronting her.

She would never find another landlady as accommodating as Nora, nor one whom she liked so much. And she wasn't just responsible

433

for finding a home for herself now, she had Lydia and Georgie to think about. And then there was Nora herself, where would she go and what would she do? And Davie, what about him...?

Her head was aching with the effort of trying to think. What would happen if she couldn't look after Georgie? She had promised Vera after all, that he would not end up in an orphanage with no one to care for him.

Connie frowned as an idea suddenly occurred to her. Thoughts and the plans formed swiftly inside her head.

By morning, after a virtually sleepless night, she felt both exhausted and yet, at the same time, dizzily elated.

'You mean you'd look after other people's babies whilst they was working, and they'd pay you for it, like?' Nora demanded in disbelief when Connie told her what she was planning over breakfast.

'Yes,' Connie agreed eagerly. 'I thought I'd never want to do anything but nursing, Nora, but somehow having Lydia changed that. I still want to work, that's the way I am, but seeing all those motherless babies at the hospital...' She paused and shook her head. 'I sort of thought then that it was a shame that the poor little souls couldn't have someone like you to look after them.'

'Like me?'

'Yes... If I was to do this, Nora, I'd need you to be part of it with me. You see what I was thinking was that, if we could get hold of a decent-sized house with plenty of room and a decent-sized garden, then we could take in a fair number of little 'uns. We wouldn't need to charge their families very much, and if we had enough paying then we could take in a few whose families couldn't afford to pay. Give them a bit of proper mothering, and feed them up a bit. You'd be good at that,' she added coaxingly.

Nora's jaw had dropped and she was staring at Connie as though she had never seen her before.

'Well, I never did,' she exclaimed breathlessly. 'What on earth made you think of a thing like that!'

Desperation, Connie wanted to reply, that and the feeling the sight of all those small cribs had given her.

'Well, it's all very well to talk of it, Connie, but if I have to give up this place, I can't see how we could ever afford to find somewhere else.'

'You can leave that to me,' Connie assured her briskly. 'I just want you to promise me that you and Davie will help me.'

'Davie?'

'We'll need someone strong to help out, especially if we get somewhere with a garden,' Connie told her briskly, deliberately pretending not to notice the tears springing up in Nora's eyes.

'Well, I don't know, Connie. Of course me and Davie will help, but I have to say that I can't see folks paying someone else to mind their little 'uns.'

'Yes, they will,' Connie assured her firmly. 'This War has changed things, Nora. Women go out to work now just like men, and they'll be glad to pay someone a few pennies a week to take care of their babies. We can charge the better off ones a little bit more, and that way we'll have enough to take in some of those whose families can't afford to pay.'

'Well I can see the sense in what you're saying, but we'll never be able to afford to rent the kind of place you're talking about.'

'*We* may not, but I know someone who can and will,' Connie informed her confidently.

She would talk to Iris first, and then, once she had her support, she would take her plan to Ellie and ask her sister to approach her husband for her.

In the meantime she had work to do! Josie was as nutty about children as Nora and might be tempted to join them; Gideon owned property himself and would be able to put them in the right direction to find the right place...

'Oh, Connie what a wonderful idea! Isn't it Gideon?' Ellie appealed to her husband excitedly.

They, Connie, Iris, Ellie and Gideon were all sitting in Gideon's study, Connie having asked her brother-in-law if she might discuss a business proposition with him.

'It could be,' he agreed cautiously.

Ellie and Gideon with their family and, of course, baby Lyddy, had now returned to Preston. However, they were still taking every precaution against being infected by the influenza – as instructed by Connie. Connie and Iris too had taken steps to ensure they were not carrying infection with them on their visit.

'I think it's an excellent idea,' Iris said now.

'And it will certainly have my support in as many ways as I can give it. You are a budding philanthropist I think, Connie!'

'She'd better not be too much of one if this is going to be a business venture I'm investing my money in,' Gideon mock-growled.

'Oh, your money will be safe enough, Gideon,' Iris assured him firmly. 'There's a real need for what Connie wants to provide. And as for her plan to take in some babies at no cost, that is most generous of you, Connie,' she added warmly. 'I shall certainly want to sponsor some of those places myself!'

'Well what I was hoping Iris is that when you are in Liverpool, if you have time, you could call at the nursery and look at the little ones, just to be sure that none of them have anything contagious. I know the symptoms for some things of course, but I am not a doctor, and after what I saw at the Maternity Hospital...'

'Wait, Connie, you're trying to run before you can walk,' Gideon protested. 'You're going to need somewhere to house this business before you go taking on a doctor.'

'Well of course she does, Gideon, and that is where you come in, isn't it, Connie?' Ellie put in. 'After all, you already own a good deal of property, Gideon, so you will know what to look for and what to avoid. And once you have found one for Connie, your men can do whatever work needs to be done on it for her.'

'Can they now!' Gideon said drily, but Connie could see that there was a definite twinkle in his eye.

'It is a wonderful idea, Connie,' Ellie told Connie when Iris had left, 'and for all that he pretends to be so stern, I know that Gideon feels the same way. After all,' she said quietly, 'all three of us know what it is like not to have a mother. And anything you can do to give those poor little motherless mites some love will always have mine and Gideon's support, isn't that true, Gideon?'

Gideon looked at them both.

'Yes,' he agreed. 'But,' he warned them both, 'this is a business venture and must be treated as such!'

'I wouldn't want it any other way, Gideon,' Connie assured him – and meant it.

'Right then, we'd better start looking round for a suitable property for you, hadn't we!' Gideon responded calmly.

'By Connie, when you first told me what you was thinking I never thought it 'ud be like this,' Nora confessed admiringly.

They had opened just over a week ago, and already they had enough fee-paying babies for Connie to have been able to take in six babies for free, much to the relief of their desperate families.

It had helped of course that Gideon had generously bought the house outright for them, as well as agreeing to sponsor at least two of the babies whose families could not afford to pay anything for their first year. But Connie still felt justifiably proud of herself as she surveyed the sparkling clean room filled with cribs of clean and fed babies.

Ellie had protested at first when Connie had

told her where she planned to open her nursery, asking her if it wouldn't be better and healthier to find a house that wasn't in the heart of the city; but Connie had shaken her head pointing out firmly that people going out to work would want to leave their babies somewhere within easy reach of their workplace, and to her relief Gideon had immediately backed her up.

Connie had her own rooms on the second floor of the large house, whilst Davie and Nora shared the large attic floor.

Josie, who Connie had persuaded to come and work for them, had kept her own house and Connie was already thinking about looking for another trained nurse to help out on a part-time basis.

'Eeh, I still can't believe that the War is really over,' Nora continued.

Connie looked at her. The War had officially ended on the 11th of November, the week after they had opened the nursery.

'For some people it will never truly be over,' Connie told her quietly.

The War was over and he was back in England. He and the Baron had parted more as friends than enemies, and Harry had left the older man looking forward to the return of his son.

The grim faces of the other men around him told him that they, like him, whilst thankful to be home, were thinking of their fallen comrades. He had been lucky, Harry told himself determinedly, even if England's damp weather was already making him aware of the dull ache in his injured arm.

439

Liverpool looked dirty and shabby after the green freshness of the mountains, but he still took an appreciative and deep gulp of its salty, sooty air, already searching the busy crowds just in case he might somehow see Connie. It was ridiculous, of course, but ridiculous or not he could not help himself.

He had thought of her constantly on his way home, wishing beyond anything else, that he might be going home to her. If he had been, what a homecoming that would have been! But he had no right to have such thoughts, he reminded himself sharply. No right, at all! He had a wife and a child. The thought of having to spend the rest of his life with Rosa filled him with despair, and with guilt.

His natural inclination was to go first to New Brighton to see his family, but of course he must see Rosa first. He had heard nothing from Rosa himself, but Mavis had written to him to tell him that his wife and child were living with Rosa's cousins in Manchester.

There was no point in putting off the inevitable; Rosa was his wife no matter how much he might wish that she were not! Picking up his kitbag he climbed onto the waiting train which, like the one he had travelled up from the coast on, was packed with homecoming soldiers like himself.

For all those who had come home though, there were many thousands more who would not. All around him Harry could see that relief at the end of the War was tinged by disillusionment, and also bitterness as people counted the cost in the lost lives of their loved ones.

Harry wasn't particularly familiar with Manchester, but a fellow soldier gave him directions as to which bus he needed to take to get to the address he wanted. The mid-December day was fading into grey dusk when he finally walked up the steps of the terraced house facing onto the small park.

For some reason he had expected his knock to be answered by a maid, and so it came as a shock to see Rosa's shadowy face in the darkness of the hall as the door was pulled open. But it was not as much of a shock as his arrival obviously was to her.

'Harry!'

It quite definitely wasn't pleasure or happiness he could hear in her voice, Harry recognised grimly. She turned back into the hallway and looked frantically toward the half-open door behind her.

'Who is it, Rosa?'

Harry recognised her cousin Gerald's voice immediately, and he could see the sick panic in her eyes as she looked from him back into the house, and called out in a falsely bright voice, 'Gerald, it's Harry!'

Harry could hear her cousin cursing, and then the sound of a child crying, followed by the noise of a blow and a savage, 'Shut it you,' before Gerald himself emerged into the hallway.

Rosa's face was already crumpling, and she pushed impatiently at the howling child who had come into the hall and was trying to cling to her.

'I said shut it,' Gerald warned, aiming a kick at

441

the child's bottom that sent him tumbling forward onto the floor.

Instinctively Harry went to pick him up, unable
to stand by and see the boy so ill-used.

'Aye, might well pick him up, after all he is
yours!'

Harry stiffened. This was his son?

As he looked at the grubby, unkempt child with
his shock of black hair, and his features in which
Harry could see nothing of himself or his family,
he acknowledged that he felt nothing other than
a surge of pity, such as he might have felt for any
child who looked so uncared for.

His lack of fatherly feelings dismayed him. He
had been trying to tell himself that, once he saw
the boy, he would feel differently about him, but
there was just nothing within him that urged him
toward the child.

Nothing! He might have been anybody's rather
than his own.

'Saw yer front door was open, Missus, so I
thought I'd pop me head in and see if yer old
man was up for goin' out for a pint tonight, to
celebrate the victory, like!'

At any other time, Harry might have been
amused by the way both Rosa and Gerald froze,
as though part of a stone tableau, exchanging one
brief glance before looking away from one
another.

'Not tonight, mate,' Harry heard Gerald
answering his friend over-heartily.

'Aye, all right then. See yer, Missus. He's a
lucky chap your old man to have such a pretty
wife,' he flattered Rosa, before disappearing into

the street, whistling as he did so.

'Harry, I can explain,' Rosa started to say quickly, rushing to close the front door. 'It wasn't my fault ... I thought you were dead.' Tears filled her eyes. 'You have no idea how distressed I was. My father feared for my very reason ... and your family didn't help, going on at me to go and live with them, and that dreadful old aunt of yours. I was just so grateful when Phyllis and Gerald invited me to stay with them.'

Silently Harry waited.

'Look there's no call for us to stand around here in the hallway,' Gerald butted in. 'Come on in and sit down, Harry. And let me get you a drink. What 'ull you have. You soldiers are drinking men I know, and I bet that's not all you enjoyed whilst you've been in them foreign parts.' He gave Harry a knowing wink. 'All them pretty French women...'

Harry ignored him and turned to look at Rosa who was now sobbing noisily.

'Why did that chap refer to you as Gerald's wife?' he asked curtly.

'Don't look at me like that,' she demanded angrily. 'It's not my fault, I told you. I thought you were dead. And Gerald always has been sweet on me.'

'Sweet on you! I thought you had a wife of your own?' Harry challenged Gerald coldly.

'She died,' Rosa answered for him. 'And it seemed only natural that we should comfort one another. We are cousins, after all.'

'Cousins!' Harry exploded savagely. 'It's not as cousins that the two of you are living here together

443

though, is it?'

'Oh for Gawd's sake, Rosa, stop that bawling,' Gerald yelled. 'Look here, Harry. Let's talk about this man to man! You were dead, so we were told, and Rosa here, well, like she said, we have always had a fondness for one another. You know how it is. One thing led to another and, well, it seemed best that the two of us should make everything legal and respectable. So we decided we might as well get married. Of course then we found out that you weren't dead after all, but by then it was too late, we'd tied the knot.'

'That's bigamy,' Harry told him flatly, and then wished he hadn't as Rosa burst out into hysterical weeping. 'Why didn't you say something to my family?' he demanded. 'Why didn't you?'

'How could I?' Rosa yelled at him, 'and anyway I thought that maybe...' she broke off and gave him a sullen look.

'You thought what?' Harry challenged her. 'You thought that with any luck I might end up dead anyway. Well I'm sorry to disappoint you, Rosa, but I'm very much alive.'

He could hardly take it all in. Rosa was married to someone else. Rosa had committed bigamy.

'What are you going to do? If you make me live with you...'

Live with him! Harry was tempted to tell her that that was the last thing he wanted! 'There's only one thing I can do,' he told her grimly instead. 'I'll have to divorce you.'

'Divorce me! No, Harry! You can't do that. I shall be disgraced. Everyone will know what I've done.'

'It 'ud be much better if you were to allow Rosa to divorce you, old chap,' Gerald told him. 'And it could all be done quietly, so that no one's the wiser. Rosa and I are thinking about emigrating anyway ... having a fresh start, aren't we, Rosa love? You can have the brat. We don't want him anyway, do we, Rosa, and seeing as he's yours anyway.'

Harry could scarcely believe what he was hearing. 'Is that true?' he asked Rosa coldly. 'You don't want your own child?'

Rosa pouted and looked sullen. 'It's all right for you to say that, Harry, but you don't know what he's like! He's been nothing but trouble, always sickly and ailing, and besides, like Gerald says, we want a fresh start.'

A fresh start! Well, she wasn't the only one who wanted that. No, by golly, she wasn't. As the realisation of what her bigamous marriage to Gerald meant started to sink in, Harry could feel his spirits starting to lift. His own freedom, his own future beckoned, and it seemed a small price to pay to take on the responsibility of the child who was after all his, in order to have that freedom.

'Very well then,' he agreed, scooping up the child who was sitting on the floor. 'You'd better pack up his things.'

TWENTY-SEVEN

'But, Harry, what I don't understand is why you've chosen to teach at a school in the middle of Liverpool when you could have gone back to Hutton, or even taught here in New Brighton. Schools are crying out for teachers.'

'I know that, Mavis.'

'Come on, love,' Frank smiled gently. 'Harry has talked of nothing but hoping he would get this Assistant Headmastership at the City Merchant's School, ever since he applied for it weeks ago. I know that it would have been nice to have him here living close to us, but Liverpool is hardly the other side of the world,' Frank teased her fondly.

'No, I know that.'

Mavis gave a groan as she heaved her pregnant bulk out of the chair. She had only three weeks to go before she was due to give birth, and the midwife had already warned her that she should expect to deliver twins. Not that Mavis minded, after having waited so long, and almost given up hope of ever having a child, she was only too thrilled at the thought of having two!

'And what about Christopher?' she asked Harry uncertainly.

Harry suppressed a small sigh. He knew without intercepting it, that his sister and brother-in-law would be exchanging an anxious look, and he could well understand why.

Despite all Harry's attempts to love his son he still felt no closer to him; and as though the boy himself sensed it, he constantly threw tantrums and behaved so badly that even Harry's mother was beginning to make excuses to avoid spending time with him.

'I shall take him with me, of course,' Harry answered her.

'You won't be able to look after him yourself,' Mavis warned him.

'No,' Harry agreed drily.

Mavis paused and looked at Frank. 'I had news from a nurse at the Infirmary last week, and I heard that Connie Pride, Connie Smith as she is now, has taken on a house and is looking after other people's children. She's got a child of her own now, of course. I know she and I lost touch with one another what with one thing and another, but from what I've been hearing this nursery she runs might be just what you need for Christopher. I'll go and see her for you myself if you like. I'd like to see her again. I've missed her,' she admitted.

Harry was glad that he had turned to look out of the window before Mavis had told him about Connie, that way there was no risk of his sister seeing what he was afraid might be in his eyes.

'Connie's married?' He had to force his voice to sound natural, whilst his heart thumped in anguished pain, and the old longings he had thought he had successfully vanquished, came rushing back over him.

'Widowed,' Mavis corrected him absently. 'I

447

did hear about it at the time, but it all happened so quickly. I was here, and what with thinking you were dead... I wrote to her of course, and she wrote back. Living with her sister in Preston, she was.

'She's got Vera's little lad living with her as well, now. Connie was working at the Maternity Hospital when all the mothers were dying from influenza, and she promised Vera that she'd look after her baby for her. At least that's what I heard from Josie, says that that's when Connie got this idea of starting up her business.

'So much a week she charges for taking kiddies in whilst their mothers are at work, and those that can afford she charges a bit more, and then takes in some as can't afford to pay, for free,' Mavis finished.

'It's certainly worth considering,' Harry agreed as casually as he could. 'I'll perhaps go and see her!'

'Well, if you do go and see her, make sure you remember me to her,' Mavis told him, adding quickly, 'and you can tell her that I miss her, too, Harry, and that I'm sorry we lost touch.'

It was March already and almost Spring. She didn't know where the weeks and months had gone, Connie admitted, as she smiled down adoringly at Lydia.

'And just look at this pretty little dress your Aunt Ellie has sent for you,' Connie told her. She broke off from admiring her daughter, to smile in welcome, as her sitting-room door opened and Iris came in.

'I would have knocked, but you said to come straight in when I had finished. Connie, these children really are a credit to you,' Iris marvelled.

She sat down and gratefully accepted the cup of tea Connie poured for her.

'Their families must bless you for what you're doing.'

'Well I don't suppose they bless me when they're having to dig into their wages to pay me,' Connie answered her wryly. 'But we do like to think that we give value for money. Every child who comes here goes home clean and well fed. Not that it's all down to me,' she felt bound to add. 'It's Nora who cooks for them and feeds them, and Josie who's forever wiping their hands and faces.'

'And you who has given orders that every one of them has to have their hair checked every day for lice,' Iris pointed out, 'and sends so many of them home in far better clothes than they came in.'

'Oh well, as to that, Ellie keeps me supplied with good quality second-hand stuff she's begged from her well-to-do friends.'

'It's a wonderful thing that you're doing here, Connie,' Iris told her quietly. 'How many have you got here now who get free places?'

'Well we're up to ten now, mainly thanks to Gideon and Ellie sponsoring another two. I'm thinking of asking Gideon if he thinks we should look into buying the house next door to give us some more space. But I want to wait a bit and see what happens, now that the War's over and the men are coming home. There's a lot of talk about how the women won't be needed to work in the factories now, and if that's the case then I dare say there won't be as many women wanting to leave their babies here.'

'And you don't regret taking this on? You wouldn't rather be nursing?'

'Sometimes,' Connie admitted laughing. 'But only occasionally when I'm sick of crying babies. It's different when you have one of your own, Iris. You feel different yourself.'

After Iris had gone, Connie went out into the garden where Davie was busy digging over the vegetable beds. The first touch of the spring warmth to come was already in the air. As soon as it was warm enough they could bring the babies outside for an hour.

Humming to herself she went back inside.

'There's a chap waiting to see you,' Nora told her as she walked into the kitchen. 'Wants to know if you'd take his young 'un. He's waiting in the front parlour.'

If Nora had put their visitor in the front parlour that meant she thought she felt he could afford to pay a decent fee. And if that was the case, they might be able to take in the baby whose grandmother had pleaded with Connie, explaining that the child's mother had disappeared with her sailor lover.

Pausing only to pat her hair and straighten her dress, Connie hurried down the hall and opened the parlour door.

Harry had told himself that he was ready to see her and that he had his feelings properly under control, but when the door opened and Connie walked in, he knew that he had underestimated the effect seeing her was going to have on him.

When he got awkwardly to his feet, he could feel his head spinning and his heart thumping as heavily as though he had run a mile uphill.

'Harry!'

Connie felt the blood leave her face and then race back into it, turning it a burning hot red.

'Harry!' she repeated in agonised disbelief whilst emotional tears blurred her eyes.

'Mavis said to give you her best. It was her idea that I call. She heard from Josie about how you were minding other folks' little 'uns.'

He was gabbling away like an idiot, Harry told himself, but somehow he dared not stop talking, because he was so afraid if he did that he wouldn't be able to stop himself from taking hold of her and kissing her.

He had known how much he loved her and how much he longed for her, but the reality of seeing her brought home to him, with shocking intensity, the hot fierceness of his actual physical desire.

'Mavis! I haven't heard from her in such a long time... How is she?'

Did her voice sound as wooden and stilted as she felt? Had he taken one look at her and guessed how much she longed to throw herself into his arms?

'Very large and very tired,' Harry answered humorously, explaining, 'she's due to give birth any time and the midwife has told her to expect twins. I understand that you have a daughter.'

'Yes,' Connie answered automatically. 'Lydia Harriet.'

Immediately her face crimsoned. What on earth

451

had she told him Lyddy's full name for, as though ... as though she wanted him to know that she had named her in part for him?

'Mavis says that Josie has told her that she is very pretty. She must take after you, Connie.'

Was he really complimenting her, or was he just being polite?

'Ellie, my sister, says she's a true Barclay – my mother's family,' Connie explained dizzily.

She could hardly take her eyes off him, and it bemused her to see how tanned and well he looked, his skin several shades darker than she remembered, emphasising the colour of his eyes. His shoulders were surely broader too, his jaw leaner, harder. A man's jaw now.

'And this must be your son?' she said quietly, trying not to look at the squirming child Harry was holding in his arms. She did not want to give away how agonisingly jealous she was that another woman had given him his child.

Harry hesitated. The truth was that he was pretty sure that Christopher was not his son.

'Yes. This is Christopher,' Harry agreed, 'he hasn't really got used to being with me yet I don't think,' he apologised, as the little boy suddenly started to scream and contorted his body into a rigid arc.

'That's all right,' Connie tried to comfort him. 'We've got a lot of little ones here who haven't got used to their dads yet. How is... How is your wife?'

She could hardly bring herself to say the words, but good manners dictated that they had to be said.

Harry looked away from her. 'Rosa and I are to be divorced.'

'Divorced!'

Connie couldn't conceal her shock. It was virtually unheard of for anyone, other than the titled and wealthy, to divorce.

'But Mavis said. I thought...'

'Our marriage was a mistake from the outset,' Harry told her quietly. 'Rosa is to marry her cousin just as soon as she is free to do so, and they intend to emigrate to America. Christopher, of course, will stay with me.'

'Oh, Harry...'

'It's all right,' he told her hardily, hearing the shocked compassion in her voice. 'To be honest, Connie, I'm as glad to be free of the marriage as Rosa is. If not more so,' he admitted. 'I suppose you think it ungentlemanly of me to say that, but I can't see the point in lying.'

Before he could continue, Christopher kicked him in the stomach, driving the breath out of his lungs.

'Oh dear. Give him to me, Harry, and you sit down and get your breath back,' Connie urged him, quickly taking the angrily resistant little body from him and holding the boy deftly.

'How old is he now?' she asked, gently but firmly binding Christopher's hands into his body, and holding him in such a way that his struggles to hit out at her were defeated.

'He was two in January,' Harry told her, ruefully admiring the calm way she was dealing with Christopher's aggression.

'Two? He's a good size for his age then, I've got

453

boys here nearly six months older than him and nothing like his size,' Connie told him.

Harry made no response. Mavis had also commented on Christopher's size, but for him to have fathered the boy, Christopher would have had to have been conceived on the one solitary occasion he and Rosa had been intimate in the six months before he left for the Front.

And if he wasn't Christopher's father, as he was beginning to suspect, he thought he had a very good idea who might be, which made Rosa and Gerald's callous decision to leave the child behind when they emigrated, even more shocking.

Harry had seen for himself how Gerald had treated the little boy, and he had decided that whether or not he had physically fathered Christopher, he meant to be the best parent to him that he could.

'I was sorry to hear about your sad loss, Connie.'

The stilted, formal words hung in the air between them, and it pierced his heart to see how the colour left her skin.

'You must have loved him a very great deal?'

He had meant the emotional words more for himself than for her, but Connie gasped as though he had struck her.

'I can't take your son, Harry. We're already full.' She was speaking too fast, and too betrayingly, Connie knew, but she just couldn't stop herself. She wanted him to go before she betrayed herself any further. She wanted him to go so that she could give way to the tears she could feel burning behind her eyes. She wanted him to go before she flung herself into his arms and begged him to stay.

There was a loud knock on the parlour door, and before she could say anything, the door itself opened and two men came in. They pushed past the little tweeny Connie had hired more out of pity than anything else.

The moment she saw them, Connie knew who they were, and the blood ran cold in her veins with helpless fear.

'Out you!' one of the men ordered Harry, holding open the door, whilst the other walked over to Connie.

'What's going on?' Harry demanded immediately, recognising Connie's shocked terror.

'This is none of your business, and if you know what's good for you, you'll do as you're told,' the man by the door responded, spitting a plug of tobacco onto Connie's immaculate floor.

'Please go, Harry,' Connie begged him white-faced, handing Christopher to him.

He could hardly stay if Connie didn't want him to, but Harry had no intention of going very far. Not when he could see how afraid she was.

Quietly he walked into the hall, and then instead of leaving went into the garden. He had no idea what or who it was that had brought that look of tension and fear to Connie's face, but he intended to find out.

Like a lot of men returning from the War, Harry had discovered that he was now in many ways a different Harry to the one who had left England to fight for his country.

For one thing, since his return home he had

discovered within himself an unfamiliar strength, allied to a sense of purposefulness, and determination to live his life as he wished to live it, and not as others dictated.

Connie, he had sensed immediately, shared those feelings. They were, he felt, a part of a new generation who having gone through the War shared a special awareness of the frailty of life. And a special need to preserve it and nurture it, where and whenever they could.

Everything he had heard about her since his return, had not only strengthened his love for her, but had added admiration and respect. All this meant that, in his estimation, if she felt afraid then there was a very good reason for that fear.

He could see a man digging fiercely at the bottom of the garden as though his life depended on it, and Harry began to make his way toward him. Connie could send him away as many times as she wished, but whilst he felt she might need his help, he intended to return, and to go on returning.

Alone in the parlour with her visitors, Connie lifted her chin and faced them as calmly as she could.

'We've come from Mr Connolly,' one of the men told her.

She had guessed as much, of course, having recognised them as the thugs who had beaten up poor Davie. Bill Connolly must be getting very sure of himself and his power if he felt able to have his name spoken publicly by his men, Connie acknowledged.

Although she was struggling not to let them see it, she was seized with ice-cold dread. She could feel the frantic thud of her heartbeat, and the sick panic caused by her own fear.

So far as she knew, she was well outside the area Bill Connolly had marked out as his territory. Were his men here because he was planning on extending that territory, or for an even more sinister purpose? Had Kieron's uncle somehow realised who she was?

If her relationship with Kieron ever became public knowledge, she would be ruined, Connie acknowledged. And not just financially.

'Mr Connolly thought as how you would like to know about this business service he runs, protecting people from having their property damaged by some of these rogues that are about,' the man continued, watching her slyly.

Connie waited in silence, already knowing what was coming next.

'Mr Connolly reckons as how you must be making a tidy bit o' money here, and because you're a woman, he's prepared to be generous. Twenty per cent is normally what he charges for protecting his customers. He told us to say as how he will just take the ten from you. First Friday in the month we calls for it. In cash if you please... And seeing as we are halfway through March already, he's said as how he'll only charge you for half of this month, and he won't collect until the end of next month. Thirty pounds that u'll be, when we comes for it!'

Thirty pounds! Connie stared at them, anger swamping her fear.

'I can't pay you that much! It's impossible. I don't...'

'Don't give us any of that. Mr Connolly knows what you charge, and how many brats you've got here. Thirty pounds the last Friday next month, otherwise you'll be getting a taste of what happens to people's property if they don't appreciate Mr Connolly's generosity to them. Nice house you've got here. It 'ud be a shame if anything was to happen to it...'

When Connie made no response the second man, who so far had remained silent, demanded grimly, 'You do know who Mr Connolly is, don't you?'

Yes, Connie wanted to respond, he's a murderer and a thief, but of course she couldn't, instead she answered quietly, 'I hadn't realised he had extended his interests to this part of the city.'

The first man laughed. 'Aye, well, Mr Connolly knows how to spot a good business opportunity when he sees one, and he's already got a couple of properties hereabouts. It's thirty pounds, don't you go forgetting – Mr Connolly doesn't like customers who forget what's owing to him.'

From his vantage point in the garden where he had been talking with Davie, and more informatively with Nora, who had come down to see who was with her brother, Harry watched Connie's visitors leave.

Then, re-claiming Christopher who had struck up an immediate friendship with Davie, he headed purposefully for the house. Thanks to Nora's good offices, he was not only able to leave

458

Christopher safely in her hands, but also to make his way to the parlour via her kitchen.

Connie could not make up her mind what to do.

Ordinarily with any kind of problem, she would have turned immediately to her brother-in-law Gideon, and without the potential added complication of Bill Connolly recognising her, she would have done so.

But, although Gideon and Ellie knew about Kieron, they did not know all the facts, and the truth was that she felt so ashamed of, and so shamed by, them that she did not want them to know.

The book she had been reading the previous evening lay on a small table beside her chair, and more for something to keep her occupied than anything else, she picked it up and pulled out a set of library steps, intending to restore the volume to its correct place on the top shelf of the elegant mahogany cupboard.

She had opened the glass door and was just perching on the top of the library steps, when she heard someone knock on the parlour door. Her immediate fear was that Bill Connolly's men had returned.

At the same moment as Harry entered the parlour, Connie turned anxiously toward the door, forgetting that she was on the steps. The book fell to the floor first, and would have been followed by Connie herself had not Harry raced across the room to catch her.

She felt as light as thistledown in his arms, Harry thought achingly, and her eyes were the most magical colour he had ever seen. Even her tears could not disguise their beauty. He wanted to gaze into their deep green depths for ever.

When had Harry become so powerfully muscular? He was holding her as easily as she might have held a child. The warm, male scent of him surrounded her and there was a look in his eyes as his hot gaze held hers that turned her heart over.

'Connie!'

Her name seemed to be wrenched from his throat as though it hurt him to say it, and then shockingly, but oh so sweetly, he was kissing her. Not a hesitant, uncertain, youthful kiss this, but a man's kiss. Immediately Connie responded to it and to him, letting her love speak for itself.

'Connie, Connie... I have wanted you so. Loved you so...' The words thick with longing and need tumbled from his lips between the passionate kisses he pressed on hers – the sweetest of balms to her aching heart.

She wanted to stay held safe like this within his arms listening to his words of love for ever.

Upstairs one of the children fell over and cried out, bringing then both sharply back to reality; but even though Connie drew back from him, Harry continued to hold one of her hands.

'Throughout my darkest hours, it has been you and your sweetness, and my unending love for you, that I have thought of most often, Connie. It was my memories of you, and my longing to live to see you again, that sustained me when I would have given up hope.'

The simple words caught at her heart, reminding her of all the things she would rather have forgotten.

'If that is true, then you had no right to do so,' she answered him immediately. 'You had a wife to think of and to love.'

Harry shook his head. 'No. I can say this now without guilt – I never loved Rosa.'

'But you married her!'

Connie froze as she heard the betraying pain in her own voice.

'I had no choice,' Harry told her quietly, adding when he saw the white-faced look of shock Connie couldn't quite conceal, 'Rosa had made public announcements to the effect that we were to be married even though there was no intimacy of any kind between us, other than inside her head.'

'I thought that perhaps you had fallen in love with her because I had ... after you had realised that you did not, after all, care for me,' Connie told him painfully.

'If you are referring to the fact that you, very properly, chided me for my forwardness, then I have to tell you, Connie, that all that did was make me all the more determined to woo you,' Harry told her drily. 'But I know I should not be speaking to you like this. You may be the only woman I have ever loved; the only woman I shall ever love...'

'No, you should not,' Connie agreed, fiercely pulling her hand free of his, and turning her back on him.

She didn't know how she was to bear this! Harry loved her. He had always loved her! But

461

how could she allow him to give her that love?

'Connie, what is it? What's wrong? Those men?'

'Nothing's wrong,' Connie lied fiercely. 'And those men were just ... just enquiring about whether or not I could take another child!'

Harry wasn't going to be fobbed off. Not after what Nora had already told him, and even more importantly, not after the sweet passionate way Connie had just returned his kiss. She could say what she liked, he knew now that she shared his feelings!

'You and I both know that that's not true,' he told her quietly. 'Those men had been sent round to threaten you into paying them protection money!'

Connie's face paled.

'I don't want to talk about it. You had no right to come back in here.'

Her obvious distress tore at Harry's heart.

'I have the right of a man who loves you, Connie,' he stopped her fiercely. 'I have the right of wanting to protect you. Why won't you let me do that? You're treating me as though I'm your enemy, and yet five minutes ago in my arms, you returned my kisses as though... Is it because of your husband?' he asked her simply.

'There was no husband!'

Connie couldn't believe what she had said.

As he saw the way her eyes widened in shocked guilt, Harry went over to her and captured her hands in his own. 'Connie, please don't look like that! Please don't. I can't bear it. If you loved him, and he...'

'No!'

Despairingly Connie tried to drag her hands from his so that she could cover her face and hide her anger and shame from him.

'Harry, I can't let you love me,' she told him brokenly. 'I wish that I could. I wish that more than I have ever wished anything. But if I were to accept your love, ultimately you would end up hating and despising me. If the truth about me ever got out in the eyes of the world, I would be a creature to be treated with contempt and loathing. I would be dragged down, Harry, and you would be dragged down with me. You saw... You know yourself what I was ... what I am. If your family knew of that...' Connie bit her lip to prevent herself from crying.

'It was Bill Connolly who was responsible for the debased condition in which you saw me in Back Court. As a young woman I behaved very shockingly, Harry. I ran away from home with Kieron Connolly, Bill's nephew. Foolishly I believed I loved him, and we had planned to start a new life in America, only Bill paid Kieron to desert me.

'On the occasion on which you saw me, Bill had taken out on me his rage at finding that I had survived whilst Kieron had gone down with the *Titanic*. He had threatened to put me to work in one of his brothels. Fortunately I managed to escape.'

'Connie, Connie. I care nought for any of that. To me you have the only purity which really matters, and that is purity of heart! You are pure and good in ways that few other people can match.'

Now Connie couldn't control her tears. They welled in her eyes and rolled down her cheeks, causing Harry to groan and draw her into his embrace.

'My love, my precious, precious love. Do you really think what others might have to say would alter by so much as a breath how much I love you? And besides, as a divorced man,' he began more humorously, 'I am scarcely...'

'That is different,' Connie stopped him firmly, before adding more emotionally, 'Harry, I am so afraid that Bill Connolly might see me and recognise me, and if he does, he will blackmail me. If I don't pay him I shall be totally disgraced.'

Harry hugged her as tightly as he could, knowing that what she had said was the truth.

'I can't allow you to be disgraced and brought down with me, Harry. And I won't.'

'There is only one thing that will make me walk away from you, Connie,' Harry told her quietly.

Helplessly she looked up at him. 'What's that?'

'If you were to tell me that you care nothing for me.'

Connie took a deep breath. She ought to do it; she had to do it for his sake. But no matter how much she tried, she just could not say the words.

'Harry, you cannot do this,' Connie wept. 'And besides, you do not even know the whole yet.'

'Then tell me,' he encouraged her tenderly.

'I am not a widow. I do not have a husband, but I do have a child. And that child... I was attacked, Harry, r ... raped.'

'Connie! No! You do not have to say any more!'

'No please, please let me finish,' she begged him when he made to comfort her. 'I must tell you the whole, and if I stop now... It was an act of hatred and violence against me, Harry, a punishment rather than an act of lust.'

'Whoever he is, I shall–'

'Harry, he is dead,' she told him. 'And although I should not do so, I thank God for it! As I thank Him, too, that Lyddy has none of him in her. When I first discovered I was to have her, I couldn't bear it; I even thought of taking my own life. But then, by some chance, I stepped into the street in front of our friend Iris's car. She recognised me and took me home to Preston and Ellie.

'It was Ellie who counselled me to pretend that I had been married and widowed. You must despise me for such a lie!'

'No,' Harry told her vehemently. 'Never ... never, Connie. I could never ever feel anything for you other than love!' he assured her.

'No, Harry, you must not love me,' she protested. 'I cannot let you love me, Harry. Knowing my past, who would believe–'

Putting his fingertip against her mouth he corrected her lovingly, 'Knowing you, who would believe? You do yourself and those who love you the gravest injustice, Connie, if you think we cannot see you for what you are.'

'But you must see...'

'What I see is a beautiful, courageous woman from whom love and compassion shine out to others like a beacon. I can't wait to meet Lydia Harriet... We must be married before she learns to talk, Connie, so that she will learn to call me Daddy and not Harry.'

'There is Georgie as well,' Connie reminded him.

'And I have Christopher,' Harry agreed calmly, before adding softly. 'And I hope most sincerely that there will be others...'

Connie turned away from him. The temptation he was offering her was almost more than she could endure.

'Harry, I should not be allowing you to speak to me like this. You are a schoolmaster. You hold a position of great respect, my past...'

'I care nothing for any of that. If necessary you and I can create a whole new life for ourselves. There are other countries in which to live besides this one, Connie.'

'You are thinking of America?'

Harry shook his head. 'I was thinking more of Australia or New Zealand. But in all honesty, Connie, I do not care where we live, just so long as we live there together.'

'No, Harry. I...'

She gazed up at him as he took her back into his arms.

'Harry!' she began to protest, and then stopped as he cupped her face and kissed her. Just as she had so longed for him to do, for such a very, very long time.

'I can't believe the difference in Christopher, and it's all down to you!'

Harry shook his head in bemused disbelief as he watched his son playing happily with the other children under Connie's lovingly firm gaze.

'I didn't have to do very much,' Connie told him drily. 'All the poor little scrap needed was a bit of love, and to know that he wasn't going to be kicked or smacked every time he came near an adult. He must have had such a hard life with Rosa and Gerald. I get little ones coming here who haven't a piece of clothing to call their own, and who are so hungry it breaks your heart, but they are still loved, and well-loved, too. But Christopher... Are you really sure he isn't yours?' Connie asked him quietly.

They had no secrets from one another now, other than the most intimate special secret of one another's bodies.

'As sure as I can be!' he answered Connie grimly.

'He must never know that, Harry. Don't let him grow up feeling that he doesn't have anybody of his own. Ellie, John, and I, all know what that feels like and I would never wish it on another child! Lyddy and Georgie have me, even if Georgie isn't mine. After all, he's never known anyone else but me.'

'It's just as well the Headmaster's house at school is a good size,' Harry commented, grinning as Connie pretended to look severe and then blushed delightfully.

'Oh, so you're after Mr Dodd's job now, are you?' Connie teased him. 'Does the Headmaster know that you aim to take his place?'

'As a matter of fact, he does! And what's more it was his idea,' Harry told her, enjoying watching her expression change. 'And,' he told her, getting up out of his own chair and coming over to her to take hold of her hands and pull her to her feet, 'I've got some even better news for you.'

'What?'

'Mr Dodd thinks that the school governors will allow you to use the empty house adjoining the Headmaster's for the nursery.'

'What! Oh, Harry, are you sure? Is he serious?'

'Don't get too excited, it's nothing like as grand as this place,' he warned her. 'It will need a fair bit of work doing on it. There is a garden, although it's very overgrown. Still, I reckon that Frank will probably be prepared to give Davie a hand getting it straight.' When Connie stiffened he demanded quietly, 'What is it? What's wrong?'

'You haven't said anything to your family about us, yet, have you? Only you did promise that you wouldn't. Not, not until I've got everything sorted out here.'

'No, I haven't said anything,' Harry told her tersely, a frown replacing his normal smile. 'But you know how I feel about that, Connie. And it isn't just my family. What about your own? Your sister didn't seem too pleased to see me here the last time she called. I'll bet a guinea to a penny she thinks I'm not good enough for you.'

'No, Harry, Ellie doesn't think that at all,' Connie assured him truthfully.

'No? Then why did Gideon come over on that trumped-up excuse of wanting to check the roof timbers?' Harry asked her grimly.

Connie's face flushed guiltily. The truth was that Ellie and Gideon were concerned, as Ellie had worriedly put it, that Harry might have dishonourable intentions toward Connie!

'I've learned my lesson in that department, thank you, Ellie,' Connie had told her sister quietly.

'But he is forever calling here and it is plain that he is on very intimate terms with you, Connie. Only last week when Iris and I called, I could have sworn that prior to us entering the parlour, he had been embracing you,' Ellie had announced primly.

And since that had in fact been the case, Connie had not been able to come up with a very satisfactory denial. However she knew if she told Harry the truth, he would insist on making his intentions toward her very plain. And she was not prepared to allow him to do that until she felt confident that Bill Connolly had no idea who she really was.

Physically he may not recognise her – he hadn't known her that well – but if he were to hear her name...

Just thinking about him was enough to have her heart thumping anxiously. In two days' time his men would be coming for his money. Harry was adamant that she was not to pay it, but Connie was terrified of the consequences if she didn't.

'I wish you would let me tell Frank about this,' he had told her during one of their more heated discussions, 'he may not still be in the police but he has friends there.'

'Harry, you don't understand. Bill Connolly is not afraid of the police. He's a horribly cruel and violent man who enjoys frightening and hurting others.'

'I can't compel you to report him to the police, Connie,' Harry had acknowledged.

'No, you cannot,' Connie had agreed. 'Perhaps he will change his mind and not send his men round?' she had offered hopefully.

And there, for now, the matter had been left, neither of them willing to change their stance, but neither of them either wanting to deepen their quarrel over it.

'Mavis keeps asking me if you have said yet when you might have time to visit her and the twins,' Harry said now.

'I should like to see them Harry but...'

But she was afraid that somehow Mavis would guess how things stood between Connie and her brother.

'I don't like deceiving people like this, Connie. I love you and I want the whole world to know it, never mind those closest to us. Mr Dodd is all set to retire at the end of this term, and then the Board of Governors have already told me that they wish me to take over from him.

'I very much want us to be married before school re-starts at the end of the summer holiday. That way we can move straight into the Headmaster's house with our children, and you can run the nursery in the house next door.'

'You think I can be your wife, a mother to our children, a Headmaster's wife with all that that involves, and still run the nursery?' Connie demanded mock-indignantly.

'I think you can do anything you wish to do, Connie. You have such strength my love, such courage.'

'Courage? Me?'

'Yes, Connie,' Harry told her gently.

She didn't feel very courageous on Thursday,

already dreading Friday and the visit she knew it would bring.

They were up in the nursery, the children having gone home, leaving just Christopher, Georgie and, of course, her own precious Lyddy. And Connie couldn't help smiling indulgently when Harry picked Lyddy up.

'Did you really name her Harriet because of me?' he asked Connie softly.

'Yes.'

Still holding Lydia, he leaned across and kissed Connie lightly on the tip of her pretty nose.

'It's time these three were tucked up in bed,' Connie began, and then frowned as there was a sudden commotion on the stairs and the door to the nursery burst open. The open door revealed three men, one of whom, Connie realised with a sickening surge of shocked fear, was Bill Connolly himself.

'It's insurance money day,' one of the men told Connie, giving her an ugly leer.

'But I don't have it yet. You told me tomorrow evening,' Connie stammered shakily. 'I was going to go to the bank in the morning.'

'Oh, yer was, was yer... Don't give us that,' he derided her.

'Stop wastin' our time, unless you're wantin' us to look for it ourselves.'

'No! I am telling the truth. I haven't got any money here,' Connie protested. And it was the truth. On Gideon's insistence, she banked her takings as soon as her customers paid her, and never kept more than a few guineas in the house.

It had been her intention to withdraw the

471

money she had to pay over to the men in the morning, never imagining that they would arrive a day earlier than they had said.

She could feel Bill Connolly looking at her, and she wanted to turn and run.

'Get the money, and get it now,' he told her curtly.

Just the sound of his voice made her shudder with loathing and dread. But it seemed that he had not recognised her! She supposed that she must look very different now, dressed as befitted a widow and a respectable businesswoman, to the girl he had last seen, with her hair hanging down and her face swollen with the tears she had cried.

She remembered that, whenever she had seen him when she had been with Kieron, he had always ignored her as a mark of his dislike and disapproval of her.

His menacing attitude though, was making her feel too anxious to be relieved that he had not recognised her. Christopher had come to stand next to her and Georgie, never the easiest of children, suddenly started to wail loudly.

'Shut that brat up,' Bill Connolly snarled.

Automatically, Connie bent down to pick Georgie up, keeping Christopher close to her as she did so.

'Look Mrs Smith has just told you that she doesn't have the money. Why don't you come back tomorrow?'

'Because we're here today, and we're here today because a little bird has told us as how you're planning to do the dirty on us,' Bill Connolly announced savagely. 'Is that true?' he demanded, crossing the floor and grabbing hold of Connie's arm in a painful grip.

Immediately she cried out in fear.

'Let go of her!' she heard Harry demanding sharply, behind her.

In her spare arm, Georgie began to scream frantically, whilst Christopher kicked out at Bill Connolly's leg.

Giving a savage oath, he released her and made a grab for Christopher shaking him violently. 'Why you little varmint.'

'Put him down. You're hurting him,' Connie demanded, her own fear forgotten as she tried to go to Christopher's aid.

'The money now... Otherwise I'm going to give this brat something to really cry about.'

Connie went completely still, and she knew that Harry, who was standing next to her holding Lyddy, had done the same.

'No, please. You mustn't hurt him,' Connie heard herself begging frantically. 'I've got a few guineas, and I promise you if you come back tomorrow I'll have the money. Just, please, put him down!'

'The money,' Bill Connolly repeated, as he deliberately bent Christopher's arm.

Christopher had started to scream; a thin, piercing, shocking sound.

There was a sound from the open doorway. A low, dangerous roar of almost inhuman fury, as suddenly out of nowhere, Davie appeared and flung himself against Bill Connolly's back. He wrapped his arms around Bill Connolly's neck, and wrenched at it, ignoring the attempts of

473

Connolly's men to drag him off.

'Connie, hold Lyddy.'

Quickly Connie grabbed hold of her daughter as Harry handed her over, somehow managing to hold both her and Georgie.

With Harry standing between her and the men she couldn't see what was happening, but she could hear it!

'Get him off me!' she could hear Bill Connolly choking as he tried to break free from Davie.

She heard too the small thud as he dropped Christopher onto the floor before Harry quickly snatched him up.

Then she heard the grotesque, tearing, snapping sound of Bill Connolly's neck being broken, as Davie refused to release his powerful hold, even though Bill Connolly's thugs were thumping Davie and trying to tear his fingers from Bill's flesh and drag him away.

'Christopher, Davie's friend,' Davie was sobbing angrily, as he choked the last breath of life from Bill's lungs. 'You not hurt my friend...'

Connie could see the glint of light on the raised knife held in the hand of one of Davie's assailants.

Frantically she pushed past Harry, just in time to see Davie fall to the floor, the knife hilt deep in his back.

For a second there was total silence and then one of the thugs burst out to the other, 'It's too late for that, Bill's dead, and now you've killed him, an all. I'm gettin' out of here.'

The two men turned and fled through the still open door.

'Oh Davie!' Quickly putting the children down, Connie ran over to him and sat down beside him, cradling his head in her arms.

'Harry, go and get Nora,' she begged, adding, 'he's still alive, but there isn't much time ... and ... and take the little ones.'

Harry, who had been about to telephone the police, looked from her white, set face to the telephone, and then stepped away from it, heading for the stairs instead.

Left alone with Davie, Connie stroked his hair and whispered to him as though he were one of her charges, which in many ways she felt as though he was.

'Oh Davie, Davie, you were so brave ... and he's hurt you so badly ... but you saved poor little Christopher.'

The pain-filled eyes gazed up into her own, and he tried to say something, but it was blood and not words that bubbled from his mouth.

Biting her lip, Connie wiped it away with the hem of her skirt.

In the few minutes it had taken Harry to bring Nora, Davie's life had started to ebb away.

Sobbing noisily, Nora sat down beside him as Connie was doing.

'Hold his hand, Nora. And talk to him,' Connie whispered to her. 'He can hear you.'

'Oh Davie, Davie,' Nora sobbed. 'Oh, my poor little brother.'

Davie opened his eyes and Connie could see a look of exultation in them.

'Mam,' he whispered joyfully.

'Nora, he's gone,' Connie told her gently.

'Oh, I can't believe it. What on earth happened? I'd gone up to have a nap, and he'd said he was coming up to see Christopher; something about showing him some stones he'd found in the garden. He just doted on that boy.'

'He saved Christopher's life, Nora,' Connie told her emotionally, as Harry helped Nora to her feet, and then told Connie, 'I've just telephoned Frank. The police will be here soon, but Frank is having a word with someone he knows first. Why don't you and Nora go and get the children sorted out, Connie, and leave me down here to deal with Davie and all of this.'

Half in shock, she looked at him, 'But I'm the one who is the nurse.'

'And I'm the one who is the man,' he pointed out. 'Besides, Davie's won't be the first body I've sat a while with, and it will be best if I'm the one who speaks to the police.'

A look passed between them. Of strength and love on Harry's part, and gratitude and love on Connie's.

Unsteadily she got up, and then helped Nora to her feet.

'Harry, I'm so afraid of what might happen,' Connie whispered.

'Don't be, there's no need. Not now. Not any more!'

476

EPILOGUE

'Eeh, Connie but you make a bonnie bride.'

Connie smiled lovingly at Nora. It was just three hours since she and Harry had been married and the wedding breakfast was almost over. Soon she and Harry would be leaving for their honeymoon – children and all!

Gideon had loaned them the Lake District house, and Ellie had offered to have the children, but Connie had firmly refused. 'We're a family now and where Harry and I go, so do our sons and daughter.'

'Connie, I know it's wrong of me to say this, him being me brother an' all. But part of me can't help feeling glad that Davie has gone – not for me own sake, but for his,' Nora amended quickly.

'Nora, you don't have to explain that to me,' Connie assured her. 'And besides, whilst we live, a part of Davie will always live on. We will never forget what he did for Christopher.'

As she spoke, Connie looked across to where Christopher was sitting with Georgie and Lyddy, all of them vying excitedly and happily for Harry's attention, whilst Mavis looked on affectionately, her twins beside her. Thanks to Frank and his friends, the whole affair of Bill Connolly's and Davie's deaths had been dealt with quietly and discreetly.

477

The special, extra time Connie had convinced Harry to give to Christopher, had resulted in a much closer bond between the two of them, and had helped Christopher to recover from the terrible scenes he had endured.

She, too, had given him a special role to play, explaining to him that he was her eldest son, which meant that he had a very important part to play in their family life.

'Connie, I have never seen you so happy.'

She turned to smile at her sister.

'I never thought I would be so happy,' she admitted, as Nora went to join Harry and the children.

'Sometimes I have to pinch myself to make sure all this is real, Ellie. Having loved him for so long ... sometimes ... I know I don't deserve to have so much!'

'Connie, that is nonsense, and don't let me ever hear you say it again,' Ellie insisted firmly, taking hold of her and giving her a small, loving shake.

'What are you two talking about?' Harry demanded, coming over to join them.

'Connie's courage,' Ellie told him with a smile. 'And how much she deserves to be happy and loved.'

'Indeed she does. And I intend to make it my business to make sure that she always is.'

The publishers hope that this book has given you enjoyable reading. Large Print Books are especially designed to be as easy to see and hold as possible. If you wish a complete list of our books please ask at your local library or write directly to:

Magna Large Print Books
Magna House, Long Preston,
Skipton, North Yorkshire.
BD23 4ND

THIS BOOK
BELONGS TO:

BEATRIX
POTTER'S
GARDENING LIFE

BEATRIX POTTER'S
GARDENING LIFE

*The plants and places
that inspired the classic
children's tales*

MARTA McDOWELL

TIMBER PRESS
Portland, Oregon

Published in 2013 by Timber Press, Inc.

The Haseltine Building
133 S.W. Second Avenue, Suite 450
Portland, Oregon 97204-3527
timberpress.com

Printed in China
Book design by Marla Sidrow
Sixth printing 2016

Library of Congress Cataloging-in-Publication Data

McDowell, Marta.
    Beatrix Potter's gardening life : the plants and places that inspired the classic children's tales / Marta McDowell.—1st ed.
        p. cm.
    Includes bibliographical references and index.
    ISBN 978-1-60469-363-8
    1. Potter, Beatrix, 1866-1943. 2. Potter, Beatrix, 1866-1943—Homes and haunts—England. 3. Gardens—England. I. Title.
    PR6031.O72Z74 2013
    823'.912—dc23
                            2013001143

A catalog record for this book is also available from the British Library.

FRONTISPIECE: Beatrix Potter on holiday at Holehird, Windermere, 1889

OPPOSITE: Guinea pigs gardening from *Cecily Parsley's Nursery Rhymes*

For Kirke

CONTENTS

THE FLOWERS LOVE the house, they try to come in. The golden flowered great St. Johns wort pushes up between the flags in the porch, it has peeped up between the skirting and the flags inside the porch place before now. And the old lilac bush that blew down had its roots under the parlour floor, when they lifted the boards. Houseleek grows on the window sills and ledges; wisteria climbs the wall; clematis chokes the spout's casings. Wall flowers and cabbage roses in season; rosemary and blue gentian, and earliest to flower the red pyrus Japanese quince—but nothing more sweet than the old pink cabbage rose that peeps in at the small paned windows.

—Beatrix Potter's description of
Hill Top, part of an unpublished
sequel to *The Fairy Caravan*

PREFACE

———»✦«———

IRST, A CONFESSION. I did not read Beatrix Potter as a child. In fact, I learned about Peter Rabbit from a knockoff of sorts. The spoiled youngest of four, I would steadily pester my mother for books on outings to Woolworths, and one day she bought me a shiny-covered Golden Book called *Little Peter Cottontail* by Thornton W. Burgess. Its naughty rabbit cavorted in wildflowers and visited a farm, but never found Mr. McGregor's garden. My introduction to Beatrix Potter came much later in life.

In 1981, at a shower celebrating my upcoming nuptials, someone gave me a large cookie jar in the shape of a bonneted, apron-bedecked "porcupine" holding an iron. Wedding showers are awkward at best, particularly for learning about famous characters from childhood literature that one has somehow, in two-plus decades of life, managed to miss. What did I say when opening this gift in front of a sizeable, entirely female audience of friends, family, and future relations? That memory is lost. I have also repressed the identity of the gift-giver. Neither the Mrs. Tiggy-winkle cookie jar (a hedgehog, if you please) nor the marriage lasted long.

Fast-forward to 1997, when I set off with my second (and last) husband and two aged parents for a tour of Scotland and the Lake District. William Wordsworth was on our agenda. His homes, Dove Cottage and Rydal Mount, are both near Grasmere and not far from Windermere, where we were staying. And what of Beatrix Potter, that children's author and artist?

Our visit to Hill Top Farm, Miss Potter's beloved home on the other side of Windermere, turned out to be a highlight. For one thing, the sun came out that afternoon after a week of Scotland in the rain. (My mother, who had brought only one pair of shoes—my father would blow-dry them for her every night in our B&B—was especially grateful.) The Hill Top garden was at its August peak; the tour was engaging.

I learned that day that Beatrix Potter was a gardener. I garden, though some days I feel that I do most of my gardening at the keyboard. I am intrigued by writers who garden and by gardeners who write. The pen and the trowel are not interchangeable, but seem often linked. Emily Dickinson, poet and gardener, has long been an obsession of mine. Edith Wharton interests me, and Jane Austen, both novelists with a gardening bent. I once read all of Nathaniel Hawthorne, winnowing his words for horticultural references. Gertrude Jekyll and Vita Sackville-West also oblige. And now there was Beatrix Potter.

A rabbit sets off to garden, later adapted for *Peter Rabbit's Almanac for 1929*

So Beatrix Potter and the idea of her garden simmered quietly at the back of my mind. Over the years I saw some of Potter's marvelous botanical watercolors at the Victoria and Albert Museum in London and the Morgan Library & Museum in New York. *Miss Potter*, a Hollywood film, came and went. An adroit article by Peter Parker appeared in the gardening journal *Hortus*. But one day at the New York Botanical Garden shop, two books lay side by side on a display table: a new edition of Potter's *The Complete Tales* and Linda Lear's biography, *Beatrix Potter: A Life in Nature*. The simmer turned to a boil.

A few explanatory notes. You may be relieved or perturbed, depending on your druthers, that I have avoided botanical names in most of the book. Beatrix was not impressed with gardener's Latin, so I have bowed to her feelings on the matter. For those of you who are looking for these particulars, you will find lists of the plants she grew, wrote about, and illustrated, including their proper nomenclature, at the end of the book. Her grammar, punctuation, and spelling were loose, particularly in her letters, but they are reproduced as she wrote them. I would encourage you to have copies of her *Tales* at hand. The stories with their illustrations are a joy to read. They will increase your understanding of both Beatrix Potter and her gardens.

Part One is a gardener's biography of Beatrix Potter. In terms of her own name, I must beg her pardon on two counts. First, for taking the liberty of referring to her by her Christian name, I plead twenty-first-century customs. Second, during her married years I have generally stuck to her maiden name rather than switching to her preferred "Mrs. Heelis." As she continued to use Potter professionally throughout her life, she would, I think, understand that it is by that name that we continue to know her best.

Part Two follows Beatrix Potter through a year in her gardens. When she lived with her husband at Castle Cottage, it is not always clear whether she and her correspondents are discussing the garden there or across the road at Hill Top Farm. So in describing the progress of her gardens through the seasons I hope I will be forgiven for smudging the lines a bit, as her efforts and enjoyment encompassed both.

Part Three is a traveler's guide, intended as a lure to discover or rediscover Beatrix Potter's Lake District and the other parts of Great Britain that influenced her. The gardens at Hill Top Farm alone would merit a visit, and there are many other gardens and landscapes that still have echoes of her.

Welcome to Beatrix Potter's gardens . . .

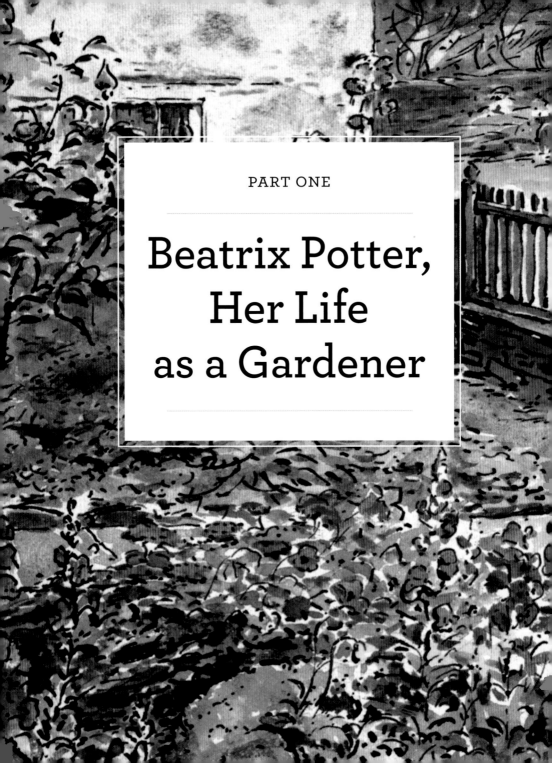

PART ONE

Beatrix Potter, Her Life as a Gardener

Beatrix Potter in the front porch at Hill Top Farm, 1913

EVERY GARDEN TELLS A STORY, if you know how to read it. The story of Beatrix Potter's garden begins on an October day in the village of Sawrey in the north of England.

A woman walks up a rise toward a farmhouse, tape measure in hand. She is small in stature, and some gray hairs are wound into her otherwise brown bun. Tiny lines around her mouth would fold into a smile, if there were one. It seems like happiness is not something she expects. She has just signed the contract for Hill Top Farm, her first property. Her blue eyes are wide, imagining the garden she will lay out, its walls and walks, and perhaps a long trellis like the one at her uncle's home in Wales.

Beatrix Potter can picture the garden built and full of flowers: snowdrops in the winter, a spring torrent of lilacs and azaleas and daffodils, summer covered with roses, chrysanthemums for autumn. Fruit trees are a must. A pear tree and some plums can go in with the old apples in the orchard, some currants and gooseberries with the flowers.

She should be happy, this Londoner, realizing the dream of a place of her own in the Lake District, yet an air of sadness clings to her, a hint of loss, like fog that refuses to burn off by midday. It is 1905. The garden beckons as a fresh beginning.

GERMINATION

B EATRIX POTTER was a late bloomer, gardening-wise. By the time she saw the first growing season progress through her garden at Hill Top she would be forty years old. In spite of a somewhat late start, the seeds of Potter's gardening interests were planted early on.

On a Saturday in the height of summer, July 28, 1866, Beatrix Potter was born at No. 2 Bolton Gardens in London. Her parents, Helen Leech Potter and Rupert Potter, were among the recently rich, due in large part to fathers who had made fortunes in Manchester's cotton industry. The Potters had just purchased this, their first home, newly built in the leafy neighborhood of South Kensington.

Behind the stylish four-story terrace house, the back garden where Beatrix played as a child was a low-key affair. It was walled to lend privacy and gated for access. A few small trees cast shade. A gravel path surrounded a central rectangular lawn. Between the path and the wall grew a simple bed

Beatrix Potter at a garden gate, about 1871

18

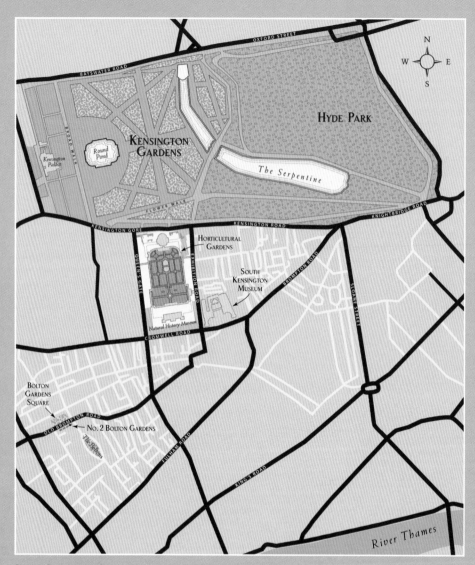

Beatrix Potter's London

of shrubs like laurel and aucuba along with a smattering of groundcovers. Hyacinths bloomed there in the spring, their fat, colorful spikes pumping out perfume. Brick set in a sawtooth pattern edged the bed. A rose was trained on the wall along with an assortment of climbing vines.

Across the street from No. 2 was a pocket park, a garden square exclusive to residents. To attract affluent buyers, London residential developers as early as the seventeenth century started offering a private park as an amenity. By the Potters' day such parks were must-have features for the fashionable. It was a bit of country in the city, *rus in urbe*. As was usual, the Potters paid for the privilege of the park. A garden tax covered their share of its upkeep. In exchange, they received a key to its iron gate. Young Beatrix, under the authority of Nurse MacKenzie, knew its shaded walks, winding through shrubberies, around lawns, and alongside flowerbeds.

Beatrix and her nurse continued their constitutionals to the Royal Horticultural Society's Horticultural Gardens, a pinnacle of Victorian prowess nestled next to the South Kensington Museum, now the Victoria and Albert Museum. At Beatrix's child's-eye view, the intricate flowerbeds (changed seasonally to maintain peak bloom) stretched out in fans and curves of color. The large glass conservatory was warm and tropical in winter, a jungle to a young, imaginative girl. On concert days, musicians played from cast iron

OVERLEAF: The square at Bolton Gardens, photographed by Rupert Potter, 1896

bandstands. A tiled arcade lent shade from the sun. The Potters' male heir, born when Beatrix was almost six, especially enjoyed the water features. "Once when Bertram was sailing his boat at the Horticultural Gardens," Beatrix remembered, "an elegant young man playing lawn tennis remarked to an elegant young lady, when the boat stuck in the reeds, that it reminded him of 'Moses in the Ark.'" The Gardens were an appropriate venue for chaperoned children, a place where fashionable society strolled.

The Horticultural Gardens were just across from Kensington Gardens, another regular destination for Nurse MacKenzie and the children. One of London's Royal Parks, it was laid out during the seventeenth and early eighteenth centuries in the then-popular Dutch style. Symmetry ruled. The great avenues of trees stretched radially from the formal Round Pond. A touch of English landscape style came into the garden with the natural-looking Serpentine, an artificial lake created by damming up Westbourne Stream. Young Beatrix and Bertram ambled among the gentry on the Broad Walk and explored the Flower Walk, playing under the watchful eye of Nurse MacKenzie.

MacKenzie was the first in a series of minders, the Potters adopting this common childrearing practice for their social class. Governesses taught Beatrix the basics—arithmetic and

The gardens of the Royal Horticultural Society, South Kensington, photographed by York and Son, about 1871

English, geography and map-drawing. A tutor came in for French. Her last governess, Miss Annie Carter, added German. Beatrix learned Latin. She enjoyed reading Virgil, so she had no problem with botanical names for plants later on, though in general she avoided them.

A shy child, Beatrix found quiet affection among a menagerie including, at various times, mice, frogs, snails, lizards, birds, a dog, a hedgehog, a bat, and of course, rabbits. Some were authorized, some smuggled. In addition to pets, her parents indulged her, and later Bertram, in their

Round Pond in Kensington Gardens, postcard, undated

OPPOSITE: Foxglove and periwinkle, pencil, 1876

artistic efforts. Beatrix Potter first gardened with her pencil and paintbrush.

With her father, Beatrix visited art galleries and the studio of his friend, successful society painter Sir John Everett Millais. Rupert Potter, an accomplished amateur photographer, shot sitters and landscape backgrounds for Millais, a great help to a painter who spent much of his time in the studio rather than *en plein air*. In later years Beatrix wrote, "When I was young it was still the fashion to admire Pre Raphaelites. Their meticulous copying of flowers & plants ...influenced me." By age ten, her drawings of plants showed promise. She learned from books in the Potter library—copybooks by James Andrews and Vere Foster. She learned from art lessons, both private and through the South Kensington Art School. She learned by looking, on family holidays as well as in London.

Helen Beatrix Potter. Feb 9. 1876.

Dalguise House,
undated

OPPOSITE: Beatrix and
her mother, about 1872

Scotland, a regular Potter holiday destination, provides
the first plant reference in family correspondence, appropriately referring to the first bloom of the year. Writing to his
seven-year-old daughter from a winter trip, Rupert noted,
"There are snowdrops on the lawn but the trees are all bare
and no bunnies are to be seen." The Potters spent eleven
long holidays in Dalguise (pronounced dahl-guys), a manor
house in the forested hills near Dunkeld on the western
side of the broad River Tay. From 1871 to 1881, the family
sojourned there for several months each year escaping the
dust, not to mention health risks, of London summers. In
contrast to Bolton Gardens, which Beatrix later described as
"my unloved birthplace," she remembered Dalguise as "beautiful, home sweet home."

Beatrix was a country girl at heart. Dalguise was as quiet as London was bustling. The air was clean, unlike the sludgy, sulfurous air of the Victorian city. Light slanted in through forests carpeted with the soft needles of conifers, delighting a fanciful little girl. "The woods were peopled by the mysterious good folk," she later wrote. "The Lords and Ladies of the last century walked with me along the overgrown paths." Beatrix flourished at Dalguise.

Childhood discipline loosened. There were flowers to pick along the lanes and in the garden's box-hedged beds. Beatrix remembered running to greet a favorite guest, William Gaskell, who was sitting comfortably on the front doorstep. "There are sounds of pounding footsteps," she recalled. "The blue-bottles whizz off the path. A little girl in a print dress and striped stockings bounds to his side and offers him a bunch of meadowsweet." Hardly behavior that would have been allowed in London.

While the Potters brought their retinue of staff with them on their long holidays, there must have been a Dalguise gardener who worked at the house year-round. He would have been occupied tending the roses, clipping the hedges and, in summer, answering the questions of an

Beatrix and Bertram at Dalguise, about 1876

Beatrix with governess Miss Madeline Davidson at Dalguise, 1878

inquisitive little girl. Her father photographed Beatrix and her governess in front of a carefully tended display of potted plants. While the gardener is invisible, his work is apparent—grooming, watering, and presenting the plants to their best advantage.

Beatrix made her own little gardens, fencing tiny enclosures and tending plants, pretend and real. They were important enough that her father took note of them when he wrote

to her from a solo visit to Dalguise. "I went up to look at your pretence garden under the fir trees above the orchard & I am sorry to say that the cows had been trampling about & had knocked over the little palings which you left."

When not in London or Scotland, the Potters often visited Camfield Place, her paternal grandparents' home. Jessy Crompton Potter and Edmund Potter bought the three hundred-acre estate in rural Hertfordshire north of London the

View from the terrace at Camfield Place, water-color, 1884

year Beatrix was born. To her, it had always been there. At Camfield "all is bound up together in fact and fancy, my dear grandmother, the place I love best in the world and the sweet balmy air where I have been so happy as a child."

She could run in the garden, only returning when the fire bell was rung as the summons home. Great banks of rhododendrons bloomed in the spring, concealing a faux medieval grotto. A hollow but living elm was perfect to climb and explore for birds' nests. A yellow rose grew up the brick wall of the kitchen garden, along with the more tender fruit trees. Edmund Potter employed fifteen gardeners to manage the park, walled garden, ornamental beds, and greenhouses.

The landscape of this childhood idyll acquainted the young Beatrix with the work of another artist, Capability Brown.

Lancelot "Call me Capability" Brown was England's supreme garden designer of the eighteenth century. Charming and affable, Brown was a landscape superstar who could exploit the "capabilities" of your country place. If England were a face, Capability Brown would have been its plastic surgeon. His nips and tucks involved extravagant earth moving: building hills, excavating vales, damming streams to create water features. He banished formal features, scraping allées and parterres alike. (All done in the pre-industrial era of manual labor and the original kind of horsepower.)

For his commissions, Brown would typically deliver an Arcadian lawn rolling out from the manor house as far as the eye could see. He painted with trees, planting them in wide belts, elegant clumps, and individual specimens. By the time Beatrix Potter played at Camfield, the trees had grown into mature plantings. The cedar of Lebanon was a particular favorite, "its branches resting on the ground, mixed up with summer growth of wild parsley and coarse grass." It must have made a wonderful childhood fort.

Taste in garden styles changes, but Beatrix later remembered Camfield Place, its trees and views, with fondness. She

Camfield's cedar, pen and ink, undated but later used in *The Fairy Caravan*

pronounced, "I believe it is the fashion to make game of Capability Brown, but, if this place is a fair example of his skill, I do not agree." Beatrix Potter was never a slave to fashion.

Beatrix developed her inner gardener on the three-legged stool of South Kensington, Dalguise, and Camfield Place. But in 1882, the year she turned sixteen, her father broke the news that he was unable to renew the lease for Dalguise. Swimming in the midst of adolescence Beatrix cried, "the memory of that home is the only bit of childhood I have left." With the loss of Dalguise, she would look for a new balance.

OFFSHOOTS

———✦———

I**T WASN'T EASY** being Beatrix Potter. She had the normal adolescent woes, compounded by chronic shyness. She was clumsy in company, once moaning, "I feel like a cow in a drawing room." While other girls her age, including her cousins, were charming in society, Beatrix was awkward. Bertram went off to boarding school. Beatrix was kept at home. She was prone to fainting spells and headaches. She complained of colds and bouts of influenza. Her health problems were capped by a serious case of rheumatic fever. Her mother was difficult, her father distracted. She was, in short, discontented.

She fought back with her paintbrush and her pen. "I cannot rest, I must draw, however poor the result, and when I have a bad time come over me it is a stronger desire than ever, and settles on the queerest things, worse than queer sometimes." She confessed, "I caught myself in the back yard making a careful and admiring copy of the swill bucket, and

A study of a garden scene with cold frames, watercolor with pencil, undated

the laugh it gave me brought me round." She wrote these observations in her journal in a code she invented when she was fifteen years old.

In her journal, she recorded a life of arrivals and departures. After more than ten years of long summers at Dalguise—holidays stretching for three to five months—over the next two decades the Potter family seemed almost to drift among a selection of summer homes. They sampled five different places in the Lake District. Some years they took houses in Hertfordshire, near her aging grandparents at Camfield Place. Nor did Rupert abandon Scotland—he rented other properties in and around Dunkeld. Add to this at least one seaside trip for several weeks each spring to allow a top-to-bottom cleaning of London's soot and grime from No. 2 Bolton Gardens, and one is left with a sense of Beatrix's rootlessness.

Rupert Potter chose the Lake District the first year Dalguise was unavailable. It had some obvious appeals. There were similarities to Scotland: weather (wet) and upland scenery (sublime), not to mention excellent fishing. It was a

Beatrix, hair shorn during a bout of rheumatic fever, with her pet dormouse, Xarifa, 1885

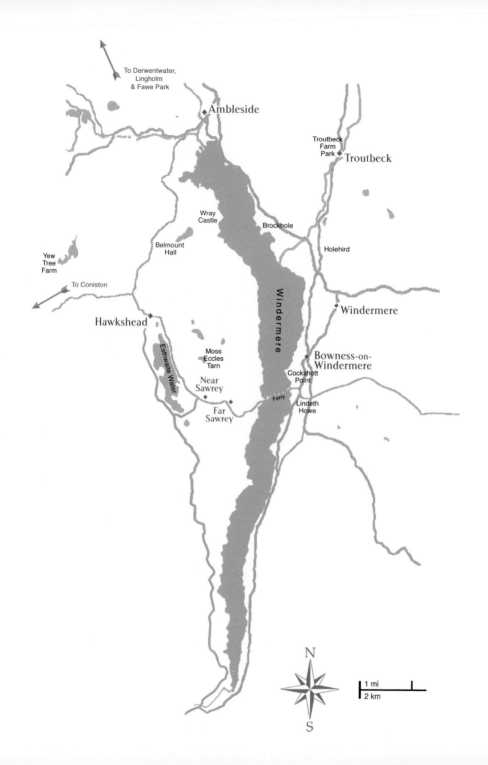

The Potters including spaniel, Spot, at Wray Castle, 1882

OPPOSITE: Beatrix Potter's Lakes

popular destination. Other London and Manchester families summered there, giving it the social imprimatur. A great-grandfather on the Crompton side had once owned property in the Southern Lakes near Coniston Water.

When Beatrix and her parents, her brother, assorted pets, and staff emerged from the train station at Windermere, they proceeded to Wray Castle on the far shore of the lake. Unlike the staid classical façades of Bolton Gardens and Dalguise, Wray Castle was a neo-Gothic concoction built in the 1840s, complete with crenelated towers and picturesque garden.

Rupert and Beatrix Potter (far left and far right) with Edith Rawnsley, Reverend Hardwicke Rawnsley, and their son Noel, 1887

The summer at Wray was Beatrix's initiation into country life in the Lakes. One Saturday in August, she headed out on a solo walk to Hawkshead, the closest market town about two miles away. In her journal she recorded, "Had a series of adventures. Inquired the way three times, lost continually, alarmed by collies at every farm, stuck in stiles, chased once by cows." Her misadventures introduced her to the land and its smallholdings with their patchwork of enclosed pastures, hayfields, and gray farmhouses. The lanes were bounded with stacked slate walls and hedgerows, where public paths, those ancient rights-of-way, often required a stile, a purpose-built ladder, to cross over a wall. Sometimes the footpaths cut across unmarked pastures, and it was a toss-up whether the walker or the ruminants were more surprised by the encounters.

The Reverend Mr. Rawnsley, the Potters' neighbor at
Wray and canon of the local church, would have encouraged
her walks. Public footpaths were among his many advoca-
cies. Hardwicke Rawnsley was a man of words and action.
He erupted with enthusiasm, and to shy, teenaged Beatrix
he must have been pure pleasure. He and his wife, Edith,
became friends with the Potters on that visit and remained
so for the rest of their lives. One of his passions was large
scale: the preservation of the landscape of Lakes. As President of the Lake District Defence Society and later a co-
founder of the National Trust, he was tenacious. He once
wrote in a visitor book: "He came and pleaded till he bust;
The sacred cause of National Trust." His sacred cause would
eventually become hers.

In the course of the familial peregrinations, Beatrix Potter began to appreciate gardens in a new way. Her father taught her the basics of photography and gave her a camera. Among her exposures and his are many landscapes and designed outdoor spaces. In Salisbury she admired the Cathedral Close, "with its fine elms, green meadows and old red-brick houses in gardens where the *Ribes* and *Pyrus japonica* are coming into flower." Years later she would plant gooseberries and currants, both *Ribes*, and japonica in her own garden. Beatrix admired the wrought iron gates and a sundial inscribed "life's but a walking shadow." She also made note of their lunch at the White Hart where "the cooking is not so handsome as the bill."

She began to focus a critical eye on the gardens she visited. Describing a valley garden on the Cornish coast, she wrote, "It is the most successful and striking piece of landscape-gardening I ever met with, but struck me as being almost too picturesque." She was intrigued by the tropical plants, tree ferns and the like, but felt they were "rather out of place in an old English garden. There is nothing like a box-border and the scent of wall-flower and polyanthus over a snug brick wall."

Her travels also brought on a more serious study of plants. She referred to Sowerby's *British Wild Flowers*, a gift

Black currants, water-color with pen and ink, about 1905

A flower garden, water-color with pen and ink and pencil, undated

from Grandmother Potter. She recorded encounters with plants. On one trip she itemized sea pinks, a dwarf creeping willow, and a spotted-leaved orchid. She noted their locations. She compared different sites. "With regard to ferns, further inland it is equal to Devonshire in profusion of all the commoner sorts." She found a rare plant blooming late for its season, recording, "The boggy ground was literally dry, and I waded through the sweet bog myrtle to look for the long-leaved sundew, which I remembered covering the black peat like a crimson carpet."

Botanizing was part of her wider interest in natural history that gathered speed in her twenties. She bagged insects, dug for fossils, drew Roman archaeological findings and, of

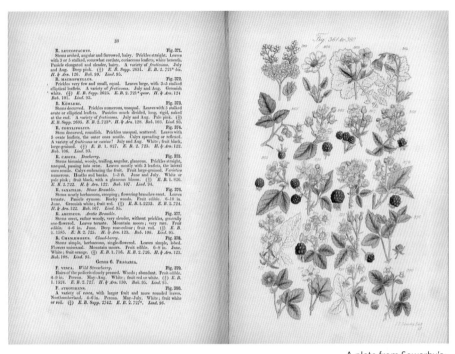

A plate from Sowerby's *British Wild Flowers* showing various bramble fruits and strawberries, 1882

course, studied animals. Intensely. She and Bertram were known to prepare skeletons of departed pets. (When her journal was first published, *The Times of London* ran the story with the headline "Beatrix Potter Boiled Squirrels.") In her day the sciences—geology, botany, biology, chemistry—were just splitting into their separate and academically regulated disciplines. Darwin had studied orchids, barnacles, birds, earthworms, and climbing plants as well as primates to develop his theories of natural selection. Even Gilbert and Sullivan's modern major general had "information vegetable, animal, and mineral."

For Beatrix, it was fungi that commanded her focus. Between 1883 and 1897, she spent much of her time studying

A study of natural history subjects, lithograph, 1896

and painting mushrooms, lichens, and the like. They were plentiful in the moist, green holiday locales chosen by Rupert Potter.

She got encouragement from some unlikely quarters, including their Scottish postman. In Dunkeld, postman Charlie McIntosh was well known as the "Perthshire Naturalist." He was an improbable scientist with his mumbling speech, humble clothes, and uncertain posture yet, as Beatrix noted, "He is a perfect dragon of erudition, and not of gardener's Latin either." He used the miles of his postal delivery route as a great outdoor laboratory. "His successor has a tricycle," Beatrix observed. "It will save his legs, but modern habits and machines are not calculated to bring out individuality or the study of Natural History." When Beatrix was introduced to Charlie, he warmed to her burgeoning portfolio of mushroom portraits, "and his judgement speaking to their accuracy in minute botanical points gave me infinitely more pleasure than that of critics who assume more, and know less." A fruitful correspondence followed. Letters, drawings, and specimens were exchanged through the twice-daily mail. In one letter she notes, "*Agaricus variabilis* is almost like a pansy and *A. velutipes* also very handsome . . . It is a real pleasure to copy them, they are such lovely colours."

In her letters to McIntosh, she regularly uses the botanical names for the specimens under discussion and shows an understanding of their relationships to one another. After all, botanical classification is a hierarchy not unlike the class distinctions among the people in her day-to-day life. She began to concentrate on the fungi, to the exclusion of other lines of Natural History study. "I do not often consider the stars," she wrote in her journal, "they give me a tissick. It is more than enough that there should be forty thousand named and classified funguses." She intended to master them.

Beatrix explored the growth habits of fungi. Her schoolroom was transformed into a botanical laboratory. She devoted time to sprouting spores (forty or fifty different

OVERLEAF LEFT: Mr. Charles (Charlie) McIntosh, naturalist and postman, undated. (His left hand was injured in a sawmill accident in his teens.)

OVERLEAF RIGHT: Mushrooms, watercolor with pencil, undated

Agaricus sylvaticus.

species), to studying slides under her microscope, and always, to drawing. She consulted the collections at the Natural History Museum. Her explorations piqued the interest of her uncle, Sir Henry Roscoe, knighted for his contributions to chemistry and married to Rupert Potter's sister Lucy. Roscoe accompanied her to the Royal Botanic Gardens, Kew, to meet the experts there. Is it any surprise that their reception was cool? Beatrix Potter was an amateur, without credentials and, to make matters worse, an almost-thirty-year-old unmarried woman.

She returned to Kew repeatedly. On one visit she saw a botanist growing spores in his laboratory in the herbarium. "I opine that he has passed several stages of development into a fungus himself," she wrote. "I am occasionally conscious of a very similar transformation." On another visit, she confronted the Director and his Principal Assistant: "There is no harm in giving an opinion, so long as it is made clear whether it is only an opinion, or the result of observation, we find some people make theories out of dried specimens without the least experience of the way things grow." In addition to growing mushrooms, Beatrix Potter was growing up.

Uncle Harry, now fully convinced, worked with her to document her findings in an essay—she refers to it over several months in her journal as "my Paper"—refining it into an acceptable academic piece. As women were not generally admitted to the Linnean Society, London's premier botanical group, it was Roscoe who brought her paper there and one of the gentlemen from Kew who read it. The paper was deemed unpublishable without more work. Beatrix Potter withdrew it without further comment in her journal. It has

The herbarium at Kew, about 1890

since been lost. The Society's minutes are silent. We are left only with her title, "On the Germination of the Spores of *Agaricineae*." Beatrix Potter's scientific investigations into botany largely end. Her journal ends too.

It is easy to envision a different path for Beatrix Potter. With more encouragement at Kew or the Linnean Society she might have become an illustrator of botanical books, in the legion of Victorian women who painted plants. Even she could see it. To her cousin Edith Gaddum's ten-year-old son Walter, she wrote "I have been drawing funguses very hard, I think some day they will be put in a book but it will be a dull one to read."

Mushrooms in the woods, watercolor with pencil, undated

Still, she treasured her fungus paintings, getting them out over the years to show select visitors. She made folios in which to store them, calico-covered, lined with cambric, and fastened carefully with neat ties. Before she died she ensured that the paintings would go to a museum that would appreciate them. Decades after her death, a mycologist, W. P. K. Findlay, used her paintings to illustrate his book, *Wayside and Woodland Fungi*, which is dull only if you are interested neither in mushrooms nor Beatrix Potter.

FLOWERING

→»✦«←

SOMETIMES A HEAVILY pruned shrub comes suddenly into flower. In her thirties, unmarried but clever, opinionated and quietly ambitious, Beatrix Potter wanted to *do* something. She yearned for something other than assuming the rounds of calling cards, menu planning, and household management as her parents aged. She had always invented stories. Even during the most scientific days of her fungus phase, she imagined a group of mushrooms in a Lake District landscape looking like tiny "people singing and bobbing and dancing in the grass and under the leaves all down below, like the whistling that some people cannot hear of stray mice and bats, and I sitting above and knowing something about them."

She had written these words during her first stay in the village of Sawrey, where her family lighted for their summer sojourn of 1896. Unlike Wray Castle, isolated in its estate acreage, the Potters' summer lease in Sawrey, Lakefield, was part of the village, merely set back from the main road with a large lawn. She painted watercolors of the garden at the house there, with its views over the small, exquisite Esthwaite Water.

She found a beautiful quality of light in these gentle Southern Lakes, mellowed by the water and broken by the heights. The weather, often wet, was changeable, with clouds that moved and refracted. Morning mist on the surface of the water turned pale pink as the sun rose. The smells of the moorland with its gorse and heather mingled with agricultural smells, fresh mown hay and equally fresh manure.

She drove her pony cart. She went on walks with Bertram, "not without a sense of trespass, but the air and wild herbage very pleasant." She collected seeds of wild plants like balsam. She drove down to the ferry and up to Wray, catching the light reflecting off Windermere. She went to the Hawkshead agricultural show where, "The only prize *we* took was for *common turnips*, which little Mr. James Rogerson [the gardener] seemed to think almost an insult."

Strolling among the slate-roofed houses of Sawrey, she made the acquaintance of the locals and admired their small flowery gardens. "It is nearly as perfect a little place as I ever lived in, and such nice old-fashioned people in the village,"

The garden at Lakefield, watercolor with pen and ink, about 1900

Windermere.

Beatrix driving her pony
cart, photographed by
Rupert Potter, 1889

OPPOSITE: Windermere,
watercolor with pencil,
undated

she exclaimed. It would take another ten years before Beatrix
Potter would have a flowery little garden of her own in this
perfect place in the Lakes.

Like many creative people, Beatrix Potter had peaks of
inspiration and output, and the 1890s was one of hers. While
musing about the reproductive processes of mushrooms she,
with the help of Bertram and Uncle Harry, got a few of her
drawings published as holiday cards and illustrations. She
also started writing down stories for children, very specific
children, stories with flora as well as fauna.

Beatrix, Bertram, and
Rupert Potter, 1892

Her last governess, Annie Carter, just three years older
than Beatrix, was now married to Edwin Moore and living in
Wandsworth, a suburban neighborhood in southwest London. Beatrix had taken a special interest in the Moore children, visiting them when in London, sending them letters
when away. The letters were picture letters, stories and traveler's tales illustrated with quick pen and ink sketches. Having
real children as an audience stoked her active imagination.

In the first of these letters, written to four-year-old Noel
Moore from Falmouth in April 1892, she tells him, "I have
come a very long way in a puff-puff to a place in Cornwall,
where it is very hot, and there are palm trees in the gardens
& camellias & rhod[od]endrons in flower which are very

pretty." The next spring she writes him again from Falmouth, mentioning, "I saw a man & a little boy getting sea-weed, they had a nice donkey with panniers to carry to their garden, for manure, it makes the cabbages grow." In her most famous letter, written that September from Eastwood in Scotland, she introduced the rabbit quartet of Flopsy, Mopsy, Cotton-tail, and Peter, living with their mother under the roots of a fir tree. It was Annie Moore, friend and confidante, who suggested that Beatrix might adapt this story letter to her son into a publishable book. Beatrix borrowed the letter back, recopied it, and designed: "The Tale of Peter Rabbit and Mr. McGregor's Garden."

Hardwicke Rawnsley, her preservationist friend from Wray Castle days, helped her submit the manuscript through the appropriate channels. Publisher after publisher sent rejections. Beatrix finally gave up and turned to self-publishing her little book with an abbreviated title, *The Tale of Peter Rabbit*. The first printing, 250 black-and-white copies dated December 16, 1901, sold out, so she printed another 200 the following February. In the midst of this, Frederick Warne & Co. reconsidered and took on the book, subject to the illustrations being redone in color. Warne published *The Tale of Peter Rabbit* in 1902.

OVERLEAF: Part of a letter to Noel Moore, 1892

This is a pussy
I saw looking for
fish —

These are two little
dogs that live in
the hotel, + two tame

Sea gulls
+ a great many

cocks + hens in
the garden.

I am going today to a place called the Lizard
so I have no time to draw any more pictures,
+ I remain yours affectionately

Beatrix Potter.

Felmouth Hotel
Falmouth
March 11th 92

My dear Noel,

Thank you for your very interesting letter, which you sent me a long time ago.

I have come a very long way in a puff-puff to a place in Cornwall, where it is very hot, and there are palm trees in the gardens & camellias & rhodendrons in flower which are very pretty.

The story opens in a woodland setting, with a mother rabbit sending her children out foraging for blackberries. The three obedient if somewhat dull daughters take their baskets and crooked sticks and get to work picking the thicket clean. The plot's main action centers on their blue-jacketed brother in Mr. McGregor's now famous garden.

The garden is more likely that of McGregor's employer. Look at McGregor, kneeling in the dirt with unkempt beard, dibbler, and hobnailed boots. Compare him to his work place with its high walls, grand box-edged beds, and goldfish pond. While he was no doubt the general of the potting shed, it was a property that was beyond his means. He and his rabbit pie–preparing Missus would have lived in an estate cottage as caretakers, not owners. Beatrix Potter was economical in the clues that she laid out in her words and pictures.

In *The Tale of Peter Rabbit*, written in Potter's matter-of-fact voice, the garden is not sentimentalized. From page one, she takes off the white gloves, noting that Peter's unwise father had ignored his wife's good advice and ended up in a pie on the McGregor table. Rabbits in most gardens were not pets like her Peter Piper, Benjamin Bouncer, and all the rest. While Beatrix had been known to free a wild rabbit from a trap, she stated unequivocally, "They are regular vermin, but one cannot stand by to see a thing mauled about from one's

Peter Rabbit meets
Mr. McGregor

friendship for the race. Papa in his indignation pulled up the snare. I fancy our actions were . . . illegal."

The country houses that the Potters occupied over the years had gardeners who would not have appreciated their animal rights activities. Scottish gardeners were the norm, both north and south of the borders. Scotland was a known exporter of gardeners and botanists. In *Adam Bede*, novelist George Eliot wrote, "But a gardener is Scotch, as a French teacher is Parisian."

Mr. McGregor was a type, and Beatrix knew the type up close. Her grandparents employed gardeners, as did the country house owners from whom her father let. In 1894, staying in Lennel, yet another property in Scotland, she wrote about the ripening cherries on the tree in the garden, reporting "the rooks are so tame they will scarcely leave it for stone throwing, and the thrushes sit and stare. I have been tying up some bunches in little muslin bags, also weeding, to the amusement of the old gardener."

Beatrix wrote for the record that she never knew a gardener named McGregor though "several bearded horticulturists have resented the nick-name." He and Peter seemed to have emerged fully clothed as it were—"their names especially seemed to be inevitable." Beatrix Potter took memories of gardeners over decades of country estate summers and came up with a composite character. "Mr. McGregor was no special person unless in the rheumatic method of planting cabbages," she wrote, "I remember seeing a gardener in Berwickshire extended full-length on his stomach weeding a carriage drive with a knife."

As well as characters, Beatrix Potter drew garden settings for *Peter Rabbit* from various holiday homes. One was particularly influential. "If . . . [Mr. McGregor's] vegetable garden and wicket gate were anywhere it was at Lingholm near Keswick," Beatrix wrote, "but it would be vain to look for it there, as a firm of landscape gardeners did away with it, and laid it out anew with paved walks." Beatrix knew Lingholm well, having spent ten summers there with her family. Lingholm's walled kitchen garden was a standard feature for nineteenth-century estates. The wall segregated the more mundane members of the plant family from the ornamental flowerbeds.

In her *Tale*, Peter Rabbit wriggles under a gate into a kitchen garden with a realistic mix of fruits and vegetables. His illegal actions begin with trespass but quickly descend into poaching. Peter's binge eating takes place in an early summer garden where rows of French beans provide shade to the maturing lettuce, carrots, and radishes. Cabbages are being transplanted for a fall crop. Ripening gooseberries are netted against the birds—which later act as a cheering section for the struggling bunny.

When Beatrix Potter signed on with Warne to publish the commercial edition of her book, she worried about "the rather uninteresting colour of a good many of the subjects which are most of them rabbit-brown and green." She solved this problem by adding flowers. Nasturtiums bloom orange and yellow outside the potting shed. Peter knocks a shower of potted red geraniums from a windowsill. And what geraniums! These specimens are not only floriferous, but sport variegated leaves.

Proper procedures of horticulture are evident. When "feeling rather sick, he went to look for some parsley," Beatrix poses the bilious-looking Peter in front of a pot filled with cuttings. They look like stem cuttings of geraniums, setting roots in wet sand. They are tidy and carefully labeled. Peter stands next to a cucumber frame. Inside the frame, a deep pit would have been filled with a thick layer of manure, then a layer of soil. As the manure decomposes, it heats the soil and, along with the sun concentrated by the glass, creates its own self-powered greenhouse for long-season vegetables like cucumbers. Clearly Beatrix Potter, who at this point did not have a garden of her own, had absorbed lessons from the gardeners she had met over the years.

Peter Rabbit takes a leap

Mr. McGregor's fictional garden shed is well stocked: a broom for sweeping, a spade for heavy digging, a trowel for transplanting. He has different sizes of flowerpots: small "thimbles" for starting seeds and "long toms" for growing on deep-rooted seedlings. Some pots are rimmed; some are not. The tools of horticulture—soil sieve and watering can, rakes and spades—set the stage in Potter's unique style. Peter hides in a watering can, unfortunately for him filled with water. Mr. McGregor just misses trapping him with a soil sieve, normally used for filtering out large bits out of the compost rather than trapping young rabbits.

In the garden we see Mr. McGregor using a dibber to set out the young cabbages in his rheumatic way. He picks up a hoe to cultivate the onions. To get a better view, Peter climbs

There must be a rabbit
in here somewhere

up into a traditional wooden wheelbarrow. McGregor grabs a rake when he chases Peter. And with Peter's abandoned clothes, he makes up a little scarecrow, ineffective with the birds but effective for setting up the sequel.

The Tale of Peter Rabbit was a surprise success. As a result, Beatrix went on to publish one or two books with Warne every year, arriving, as one reviewer put it "as much a manifestation of autumn as falling leaves." *The Tale of Squirrel Nutkin* has its own falling leaves that the squirrels use as little boats to make their way to an island in Derwentwater. Nutkin's rhymes highlight the trees: beech, oak, cherry, hazel, and crab, but it is a story of the woodland, not of the garden. Nor does *The Tailor of Gloucester*, set in a city shop, have anything to do with gardening, though the embroidery, deftly managed by mice, includes some exquisite flowers. It wasn't until the next bunny book, *The Tale of Benjamin Bunny*, published in 1904, that the garden came once again into play.

Fawe Park, the neighbor to Lingholm on Derwentwater, was the Potter family rental for the summer of 1903. Beatrix, enthusiastic about her illustrations, set to work with verve drawing and painting in the garden. The Fawe Park sketchbook matches the *Benjamin Bunny* illustrations in lockstep. A pear tree espaliered on the walls of the Fawe Park kitchen garden provides the entry point for two fictional rabbit burglars. Striped carnations that bloomed at Fawe Park that summer appear as lanky specimens in McGregor's garden and in costume as Benjamin's boutonnière. The little rabbits walk on wooden planks laid through the garden, used to avoid compacting the soil. Onions, drying in the Fawe Park vegetable beds, become the booty for two marauding bunnies. When Mr. Rabbit, who is Benjamin's father and Peter's uncle, enters, he sports his pipe of rabbit tobacco, or, as Beatrix tells us, "what *we* call lavender." Beatrix told her editor that rather than ending the book with the "rather . . . trite" happily ever after, she preferred to end with "old Mrs Rabbit strung up the onions and hung them from the kitchen ceiling, with the bunches of herbs and the rabbit tobacco" as she thought "rabbit tobacco" was a rather fine phrase.

Drawing at Derwent-
water, 1903

Her little books brought Beatrix Potter out of her shell,
her letters from the period indicating stronger relationships
with friends and cousins. With her publisher, F. Warne &
Co., she was assertive. About a possible new project she
wrote, "I cannot design pattern borders, but I like drawing
flowers. I will go on with it on approval if you are undecided,
or for myself if you decline it." Warne's was a family business,
and the large, sociable Warne clan opened its arms to her.
Norman was her project manager; she interacted with his
older brothers, Fruing and Harold. Norman and his sister
Millie welcomed her to their Bedford Square home where

Peter and Benjamin on alert among flower pots, frames, and tubs

OPPOSITE: Flower pots, frames, and tubs, water-color, 1903

they lived with their widowed mother. They were a delight to know—Millie and Mrs. Warne who gardened, Norman who believed.

As time progressed, Beatrix's letters to Norman softened with playful and affectionate undertones. She gave Norman a nickname, Johnny Crow, and delighted in the little glass-sided box that he made for Hunca Munca, the star of *The Tale of Two Bad Mice*. In Lyme Regis with her family she wrote Norman about primrose-covered banks along the Pinney footpath. "I don't know whether I shall get as far as the big land slip by myself," she confessed, "I have not any-one to walk with." She enjoyed his company as well as his

Peter letting go of the red handkerchief

OPPOSITE: Carnations at Fawe Park, watercolor with pen and ink, 1903

professional advice, and of their latest project, *The Tale of Mrs. Tiggy-Winkle*, she wrote, "I do *hate* finishing books, I would like to go on with them for years." It appears it wasn't only the book she had in mind.

Beatrix compared herself to Anne Elliot in Jane Austen's *Persuasion* when, on July 25, 1905, she received a letter from Norman asking for her hand. Her position changed from spinster daughter one day, to cherished fiancée the next. Alas, her parents objected. Norman was not in the right set. He was, after all, in the trades, and the Potters were a generation removed from the sullying influence of cotton manufacturing.

The Warne siblings, with Norman and Millie on the left, undated

To keep the peace, Beatrix and Norman agreed to a quiet engagement. She wore his ring, but for the time being nothing was announced beyond the immediate families.

Beatrix Potter's happy ending was short lived. The garden that they might have planted together was not to be. Just a month after their betrothal, Norman Warne died after the sudden onset of leukemia. He was buried in Highgate Cemetery. Beatrix visited with Millie and wrote his brother's wife, fussing as one does about the details when, in the face of death, there is the enormity of grief. "The stone is put back quite neatly again; . . . I don't believe the grass will ever grow

Mr. Jeremy Fisher
swimming

well under the fir tree, I was wondering whether white Japanese anemonies would grow where it is rather shaded, Millie says you have them in your garden & know their habits." For her dear Norman all that was left to consider were flowers for his grave. She wore his ring always.

In the days after Norman's death, Beatrix fled to Gwaynynog in North Wales, the home of her widowed Uncle Burton. While there, work was her comfort, as well as letters from Norman's siblings. She worked on the proofs of *Tiggy-Winkle*. She laid out a book about a frog named Mr. Jeremy Fisher, with drawings of forget-me-nots and water

Mr. Jeremy Fisher and friends in his garden

OPPOSITE: The garden at Gwaynynog, watercolor with pencil, 1911

lilies. She wrote Harold Warne, "I know some people don't like frogs! But I think I had convinced Norman that I could make it a really pretty book with a good many flowers & water plants." And sketching, particularly in the garden, was good therapy.

Gwaynynog had a large garden that she had described years earlier as "two-thirds surrounded by a red-brick wall with many apricots, and an inner circle of old grey apple trees on wooden espaliers. It is very productive but not tidy, the prettiest kind of garden, where bright, old fashioned flowers grow amongst the currant bushes." The gardens at Gwaynynog later became the setting for *The Tale of the Flopsy Bunnies*, published in 1909, but first would influence, at a reduced scale, the design of her garden at Hill Top Farm.

ROOTS

T HE YEAR they were engaged, Norman and Beatrix had been working on *The Tale of the Pie and the Patty-Pan*, a complicated story with beautiful drawings of those flowery little gardens around the village of Sawrey. By that time, Beatrix was already on the hunt for property there, no doubt with the thought that Mr. and Mrs. Norman Warne, publisher and writer, would maintain an address in London but have a permanent country home in the Lake District. Now, less than two months after his death, she bought thirty-four-acre Hill Top Farm. Purchased with royalties from her books supplemented by a legacy from an aunt, it was a declaration of independence. She had the pride of a new owner, though locals grumbled that she had paid too much for the place.

Hill Top Farm sits on a rise with its back to Near Sawrey, its lane bending at an acute angle up Tower Bank. Sawrey is a two-part village made up of the hamlets prefaced Near and

The invitation from
*The Tale of the Pie and
the Patty-Pan*

Far. They are connected like Siamese twins by the main road and a stream named Wilfin Beck. In one of those contradictions of history, Near Sawrey, the location of Hill Top, is farther from the ferry where most visitors arrived in Beatrix Potter's time. The "Near" in Sawrey refers to its proximity to the market town of Hawkshead, more important in the years when the village was named.

The main road bends through Near Sawrey as if it couldn't decide whether to stay or go. The farmsteads strung

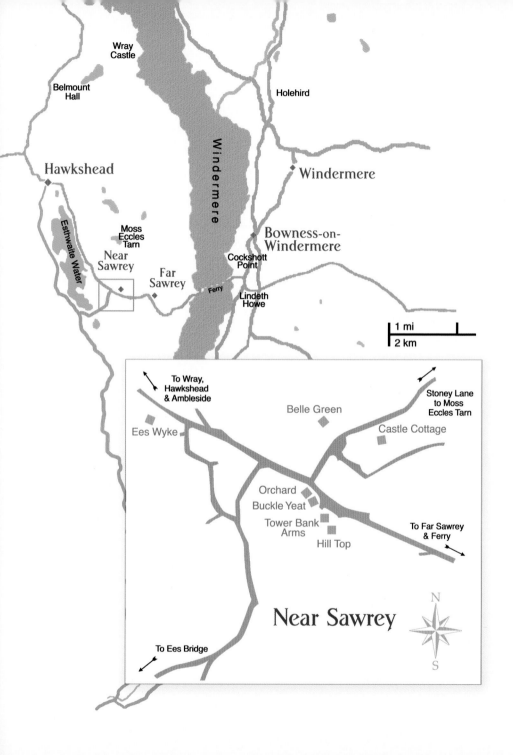

The garden in front of Buckle Yeat Cottage in Near Sawrey, water-color with pen and ink, undated

OPPOSITE: Near Sawrey and environs

along the road include cottages like Buckle Yeat (its lovely dooryard garden was featured in *The Tale of the Pie and the Patty-Pan*) and Tower Bank Arms, the public house with its drape of roses. A long lane perpendicular to the main road stretches up Oatmeal Crag toward the tarns, small upland lakes. When Beatrix settled in, the lane was lined with the post office, the local market (later to be featured in *The Tale of Ginger and Pickles*), and various cottages including the blacksmith's home, Belle Green. Another road turned down the hill toward Esthwaite Water, eventually making its way over Ees Bridge along the shore and back to Hawkshead. "I have often been laughed at for thinking Esthwaite Water the most beautiful of the Lakes," said Beatrix.

Having spent family holidays in the area, Beatrix found that Hill Top Farm had the modest comforts of familiarity. She knew the tenants, John Cannon and his family, as they had boarded the Potters' coachman. Impressed with Cannon's honesty, she decided to keep him on to run the farm.

Her first thoughts were for redoing the garden and adding on to the house. The cottage pleased her with its old cabinets and fireplaces, in spite of an infestation of rats to battle. A new wing for the Cannons would reserve the charms of the old house for her.

Gardening eases grief. Beatrix launched herself into the pleasant distractions of making her first garden. She engaged a local mason to move the entry drive away from the front door, giving her more space for beds at the front of the house. Millie Warne, Norman's sister, became her garden confidante and first guest. To her, Beatrix wrote, "The garden is very overgrown & untidy, I hope next time you come it will be straighter, I have got the quarryman making walks & beds, it would not have been work for a visitor! But it will be a great pleasure to show you the result some day."

Snapdragons, water-
color with pen and ink,
about 1903

A sketch of Hill Top's addition, pencil, undated

She laid out the main garden with a long axial path paved with stones. Deep beds stretched out on either side. The cottage was the focal point, its pointed porch of great slabs of slate drawing the visitor up. She commissioned a long wall to separate her garden from Tower Bank Arms on the right. On the left, the bed seemed too large and open to the orchard. Beatrix solved the problem by adding a long trellis, reminiscent of Gwaynynog. She made a garden that felt protected, a safe harbor from the high winds that she had weathered. Even the word *garden* comes from an etymological root that means *enclosed*.

The small scale of Hill Top Farm is surprising given Beatrix Potter's four decades of experience with country houses and their gardens. Rather than choosing an estate house, with a sublime view of lakeshore or upland "fells" and a grand, terraced landscape, she chose a working farm with a modest cottage and garden. Contrast this with her cousins Edith and William Gaddum who settled in 1899 at Brockhole, an estate on the other side of Windermere, and called

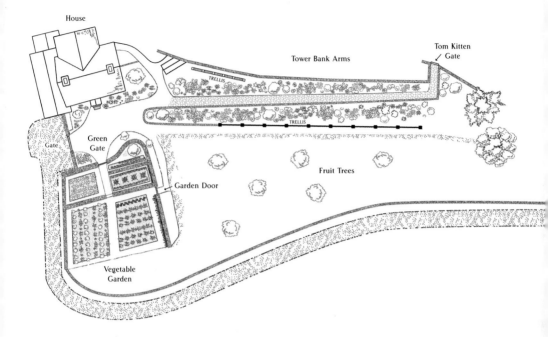

The gardens at
Hill Top Farm

in designer Thomas Mawson to lay out the acres of terraces and plantings. Beatrix chose her own path.

In creating her garden, Beatrix used stone from a quarry on her own land and local craftsmen, in sync with the Arts & Crafts style. The style celebrated the handmade in a world of increasing mechanization. While she had a separate walled vegetable garden and a linear garden divided with a symmetrical wooden trellis, her garden was not formal. She mixed loose drifts of hardy flowers with bulbs, flowering and fruiting shrubs, even some vegetables. Her cottage garden is in a distinct genre that emerged in the late nineteenth and early twentieth centuries. Designers such as William Robinson and Gertrude Jekyll popularized this vernacular gardening style combining traditional materials, informal dense

A garden path and trellis at Gwaynynog, pencil, undated

plantings, and a mixture of ornamental and edible plants. An Arts & Crafts garden encompasses the house; Hill Top's garden and house are fused into a complete whole.

In her first years as owner of Hill Top Farm, Beatrix did not live there; she only visited. As unmarried daughter she dutifully resided in London with her parents, though they seemed willing to part with her periodically. So she left many projects in the hands of contractors. Her first spring, 1906, she arrived to find that one of them had created a huge flat expanse for a lawn. Oh no! She moaned to Millie, "I believe the word 'tennis' was mentioned but I have never played it, so it conveyed nothing particular to my mind. I could not think why he was taking such a time & now I discover a thing big enough for playing football!" As she was disinclined to pay more money to have it fixed, she had the farmer plant out

The cottage garden
and trellis at Hill Top,
watercolor with pencil,
undated

potatoes there. Why are so many gardening lessons learned the hard way? She consoled herself that the fruit trees that she had planted were showing their first blooms.

While the addition was underway at Hill Top, Beatrix lodged with the blacksmith and his wife, Fred and Harriet Satterthwaite, at their home, Belle Green, in Near Sawrey. Mrs. Satterthwaite had an opinion about all things gardening, including the weather. She introduced Beatrix to the tradition of the rain and Saint Swithin's day, July 15: "St. Swithin's day if thou dost rain / For forty days it will remain / St. Swithin's day if thou be fair / For forty days 'twill rain nae mair." Beatrix, ever-practical, worried about the hay and countered, "I should hope that tonight's downpour may be the end of it, in spite of St. S." In later years Beatrix took up the St. Swithin method of forecasting herself.

The Hill Top garden in early spring with enthusiastic pansies, undated

Beatrix wisely spent most of her first year with the Hill Top garden watching what came up and how things bloomed. An old rose clambering up the farmhouse had a neglected look but was pushing out new growth. She gathered up a swarm of bees in a borrowed skep. Mr. Satterthwaite fixed a box hive for them. When the Ees Bridge below her farm was pulled down, she gathered some wall-rue fern to install in her garden wall. "I like old walls," she avowed.

She had come to the right part of the world. Stacked, dry-laid stone walls lined the roads and pastures around Sawrey, dividing its dales and vales into small holdings framed in gray. The wall stone was laid horizontally until the top, with

Sawrey landscape with stone wall and hogg hole, watercolor with pencil, 1910

the capstones set at an angle like a long row of teeth. Occasionally the walls were pierced with low "hogg holes," which allowed yearling sheep (hoggs) to pass from one pasture to another while keeping in the cows.

That August she was called from Hill Top to Lingholm to stay with her parents at their summer rental on Derwentwater. Only twenty miles from Sawrey, it still paled in any comparison with her new home. Lingholm was windy; Hill Top was protected. Lingholm's air was stuffy; Hill Top's was crisp. "I miss the sheltered open air & the gardening," she wrote Millie, "I think I might start weeding here! but it might be an uncivil reflection on the gardener, the weeds are awful!"

Phlox, watercolor with
pencil, undated

Back at Hill Top in September, she started adding plants of her own to the garden. They were mostly pass-along plants, taken from other gardeners. Divisions of London pride, a type of saxifrage that Millie had given her, looked as if "they quite enjoyed the change of climate," as did their new owner. A quarryman with a garden near the ferry offered some glorious phlox that she decided to intersperse with laurel bushes. Lilies from Millie would combine nicely with the azaleas. Her cousin Edith gave her "some bits" of another tiny saxifrage. Her gardening mentor, the indomitable Mrs. S., offered cuttings of crimson- and purple-flowered "white rock," also known as aubrieta. Beatrix wondered if she would ever get it to grow as well as Mrs. Satterthwaite's.

Neighbors started arriving unbidden with contributions. Mrs. Taylor was first, bringing "a very well meant but slightly ill-timed present of saxifrage . . . she brought out a large newspaper full!" from the corner cottage. Beatrix, the new gardener on the block, was impressed with their generosity. "I am being inundated with offers of plants! It is very kind of people; and as it really is the right time to thin & replant, I don't feel such a robber of the village gardens."

Speaking of thievery, like many a guilty gardener before and since, Beatrix added to her plant palette with occasional pilfering. After all, "Mrs. Satterthwaite says stolen plants always grow." To Millie she confessed that she was becoming light-fingered as well as green-fingered. "I stole some 'honesty' yesterday," she wrote, "it was put to be burnt in a heap of garden refuse!" (The honesty she pinched was *Lunaria annua*, a freely self-sowing biennial with pink flowers in spring and profuse translucent seedheads in the fall.)

One September day, Beatrix announced to Millie, "I have got a large bed in the garden prepared by digging. I am going to the nursery at Windermere this week to choose some bushes." Traveling along the long hill that wound down below Far Sawrey, she paid the toll for her horse and cart on the open ferry. (The ferry still offers a fare for horses.) The short boat ride across the waist of the lake took her to

Bowness, next to the town of Windermere where she went to a nursery gaining fame: Lakeland Nursery, sometimes called Mawson Brothers', the firm of Isaac and Robert Mawson. Their brother Thomas, the landscape architect, started it with them in the early 1890s. She was delighted with her purchases: lilac, mock orange, rhododendrons, and more. And even Beatrix Potter couldn't resist a new plant, snapping up a red fuchsia. "They say it will grow out of doors here all winter." She never mentions the fuchsia again; perhaps the nursery's marketing was superior to the fuchsia's hardiness.

Flowering shrubs were the workhorses of the garden, adding a middle layer to her design. Trees, trellis, and cottage created the largest partitions in her garden, the walls of her outdoor rooms. Smaller flowering plants—perennials, annuals, and bulbs—added drifts of color, like the watercolor paint seeping into the paper in her paintings.

The garden seemed to be working its cure. She felt better, and was eating so well that she told Millie she was nearly ashamed of her appetite. "There's nothing like open air for soothing present anxiety and memories of past sadness," she later wrote.

The old apple trees in the Hill Top orchard turned out to bear good cooking apples. She ate them for dinner, though she didn't specify whether she prepared them herself. "Moreover I am absorbed in gardening," she announced to Millie. "I am in course of putting liquid manure on the apple trees!! It is a most interesting performance with a long scoop." Beatrix was no hothouse flower, waiting for a gardener to do her bidding.

An old advertisement for the Mawson Brothers' nursery, undated

ROSE ARCH AND SILVER BIRCH IN

MAWSON BROS.' NURSERIES,

WINDERMERE.

One of the most important industries in the Lake District is the growing of Trees, Shrubs and Hardy Plants, many of which are used by Mawson Bros. in furnishing the gardens laid out by them in various parts of the country, whilst others are purchased by a large clientele who find that Hardy Trees and Shrubs from the Lake District succeed admirably.

These Nurseries are delightfully situated, and are always open to visitors, who may inspect the many rare and beautiful flowers at their leisure. Catalogues free.

She got her hands dirty, taking an interest in her property from the ground up. "I think I shall attack the county council about manure," she wrote in an assertive tone to Millie, "I am entitled to all the road sweepings along my piece, & their old man is using it to fill up holes, which is both illegal & nasty." She never reported whether or not she resolved this particular business. For her lily bulbs, she mixed old mortar and peat, balancing the light, acidic soil. She had a new pump put in at the same time the plaster ceiling was repaired. (She had fallen through the old ceiling of the back kitchen, much to her amusement and the alarm of the workmen.)

She was abuzz with her garden, declaring, "My news is all gardening at present. I went to see an old lady at Windermere, & impudently took a large basket & trowel with me." Now able to put her horticultural knowledge to work, she reported, "I got nice things in handfuls without any shame, among others a bundle of lavender slips, if they "strike" will be enough for a lavender hedge; and another bundle of violet suckers, I am going to set some of them in the orchard." She had obviously learned propagation techniques.

Beatrix started learning the techniques of farming too. She observed John Cannon cutting the tall bracken fern, starting to dry after a September frost, to use for bedding the livestock stalls in winter. His children, Ralph and Betsy,

Beatrix in a Sawrey
garden, 1913

At the front door

The puddle-ducks
go past

Mrs. Tabitha Twitchit
and the kittens go up
the garden path

were enlisted to help. "He has cut it about a mile off up the
lane behind Belle Green, it is a rough road to bring it down. I
think I will go up next time with the cart & help the children
to rake it, it is such nice dry crackly fern."

Not all children were welcome in the Hill Top garden,
at least not unsupervised. *The Tale of Tom Kitten* (1907) is
dedicated to "All Pickles—especially to those that get upon
my garden wall." As a new gardener, she wanted to protect
her plants and dry-laid walls from their thoughtless steps. In
Tom Kitten, Beatrix shares much of the front garden at Hill
Top with her readers. Tom's mother, Mrs. Tabitha Twitchit,
turns her three little kittens out into the garden in their best

The little boy finds
Jemima's eggs among
the rhubarb

and most uncomfortable party attire. Her injunctions are
specific as, toast fork in hand, she sternly escorts them out
the door into the splendor of climbing roses and snapdragons. Tom, Moppet, and Mittens don't even make it down the
path before their clothes are stained green. They climb the
Hill Top rockery among the rhododendrons and tall ferns.
Stoney Lane winds up through the fells in the background.
A double picket gate, the gate to Hill Top's garden path, is a
key feature. When Tabitha finds the miscreants minus their
clothes (you must read the story if you want to know to
whom the clothes have been transferred, in Shakespearean

Jemima Puddle-duck meets the "gentleman with the sandy whiskers"

comedy–fashion), she inflicts corporal punishment to a floriferous backdrop of irises and peonies. The illustration is true to a gardener's eye, as these plants bloom through the glorious peak of an English summer.

On mornings in June when the sun rose early, Beatrix Potter looked out her bedroom window at Hill Top. The old glass in the farmhouse windows contorted the view, making the sheep and the trees and the hill and the garden ripple like reflections on the tarn. She liked to watch the calves, Norah and Rose and Blossom. Everything was delightful. Even watching the cow being milked was an adventure.

The following year, *The Tale of Jemima Puddle-Duck* was written as "A Farmyard Tale for Ralph and Betsy." This story of a simpleton duck has a beautiful drawing of the walled vegetable garden at Hill Top, including the rhubarb patch where Jemima tries unsuccessfully to hide her eggs. The

Jemima collecting herbs

beehive is in its special niche in the stone wall. The wrought iron gate sets off the vegetable garden from the dooryard garden. Plants are part of the joke in *Jemima*, as foxgloves appear with the sandy-whiskered gentleman, in front of his house and behind his log seat. Silly Jemima doesn't get the clues, though the reader knows he is a fox. When asked to bring an assortment of herbs to cook her own goose, so to speak, Jemima collects "sage and thyme, and mint and two onions, and some parsley" from the Hill Top garden. Beatrix's favorite sheepdog, Kep, is the hero of the story.

In one of her letters to children, Beatrix told of another of her dogs with a particular talent for entrances. "I had a dog, old Fleet, ... who used to open a ... similar latch in the iron

A detail of the green wrought iron gate at Hill Top

garden gate, and what's more she (standing on her hind legs) holding the latch used to step backwards pulling the gate open towards herself. I could never teach her to close it." The green iron gate at Hill Top is of particular note, with its bold form and perfect color. Its bright green color blended with the garden and offset the dark stone wall. She installed a matching gate in the side yard of the new extension of the house.

Beatrix loved to walk the paths and lanes of her new home. In *The Tale of Samuel Whiskers* (originally called *The Roly-Poly Pudding*), published the same year as *Jemima*, she incorporates an illustration of the countryside—her orchard in bloom and the rolling meadows and copses beyond. It is literally a bird's-eye view. Two sparrows and a small dark

A view with Hill Top's chimney and roses

bird perch on Hill Top's chimney, and the roses reach up, up, to the top of the gable. In the stillness of a favorite trek uphill to Moss Eccles Tarn between Oatmeal Crag and Cuckoo Brow Woods, the silence was broken by the chatty course of Wilfin Beck, the munching of sheep and cows, and the occasional caw of a crow that must have brought Norman, her "Johnny Crow," to mind.

RIPENING

———⟫⟪———

BEATRIX POTTER did not cultivate celebrity. Instead, she spent her spare time in a quiet country life on her farm and behind her garden wall. Still, word leaked to the locals that she was the Peter Rabbit lady. Working in her garden, she overheard a driver tell a group of sightseers, "That's 'er 'ouse." The passengers responded "Hah? 'oo's?" requiring a lengthy explanation of her life and works. Beatrix smiled, feeling this demonstrated "refreshing ignorance of [Peter Rabbit] . . . on part of cargo who have obviously never read that book. Such is fame."

Beatrix continued writing books and designing spin-off merchandise—toys, china, wallpaper, and the like—in part to fund her garden efforts. Money, her own money, meant emancipation from constraints, parental and otherwise, and the garden always called for more. Gardening can be described as a hole one digs in the ground into which to shovel funds. There is always a new project, a new plant,

The Flopsy Bunnies
follow Mr. McGregor

or a new tool. Buying Hill Top and making the first altera-
tions to garden and cottage had exhausted her savings. She
wrote at intervals to Harold Warne, asking about how much
she might expect. "The place is not at all expensive to keep
going," she observed, "but there is still ample opportunity to
lay out the garden and surroundings."

With these opportunities in mind, her new book
returned to a location that was popular with her readers:
Mr. McGregor's garden. In *The Tale of the Flopsy Bunnies*

Gardens neatly razed

(1909) we learn that Peter has grown up and is in the nursery business with his mother. They advertise special services: "Gardens Neatly Razed, Borders Devastated by the Night or Year." Benjamin has married Peter's sister Flopsy, and their offspring are the book's title characters. The bunnies appear in Mr. McGregor's garden with its box borders and elegant trellising. The geraniums have been restored to the McGregors' windowsill and marigolds bloom along their cottage wall.

Many gardeners remember *The Tale of the Flopsy Bunnies* best. It is not for the plot, which is slender. Nor is it for the charming garden illustrations based on the Burtons' garden at Gwaynynog. Instead the opening line sticks in the mind: "It is said that the effect of eating too much lettuce is 'soporific.'" Soporific stands out. Paired with an illustration of the six little rabbits in Mr. McGregor's lettuce patch, this wonderful word is a beacon to the botanically inclined. Beatrix had her sources for this pharmaceutical plant fact including the sixteenth-century *Herball* by John Gerard, a book she added to her own collection. She might have read the report by Scottish doctor Andrew Duncan on "Observations on the preparation of soporific medicines from garden lettuce," published in 1811. Whatever the original reference, Beatrix Potter transplanted it permanently into children's literature.

Her garden did not sleep. Her perennials filled in to the point that she offered divisions to friends. She ordered hand-glasses, miniature greenhouses made of iron and glass, that looked like lanterns without bases. During cold snaps she set them over precious plants, and they seemed to speed up her propagation efforts, especially in spring. She thought of her garden even when she was back in London, so much so that she was driven outside to putter behind the house there. "I have been rolling the lawn in our back garden today . . . I am

Soporific means sleepy

very impatient to go up north and plant a few more shrubs before things begin to bud."

Not every shrub worked out. Beatrix discovered that gardening is an ongoing experiment, and sometimes a trial to one's patience. She waited and waited for one of the bushes she planted to bloom, then reported to a friend, "my specimen of that rubbishy bush flowered! And after waiting 4 years it was a sort of dirty maroon coloured flower, like a single holyhock, only not so handsome. Some samples flowered

Beatrix looking over the wall in Sawrey, undated

at Mawson's nursery garden at Windermere also; Mr Mawson & I agreed that we would go without the flower in future rather than put up with such another summer for gardens!" She doesn't reveal the type of plant, though from her description it sounds like a member of the hibiscus family.

Near Sawrey was her adopted home, if only part time, and the Hill Top garden sang its siren song. She wrote to Millie in 1910, "I am now taking a few days rest i.e. gardening violently when I ought to be sketching pigs." The people of the village were dear to her. She featured many of them along with the village's wisteria-bedecked shop in *The Tale of*

Ginger and Pickles (1909). An aged wisteria vine also grew up Hill Top's façade, blooming exuberantly each spring.

Beatrix was infected with the gardener's imperialistic tendency. There is never enough space for all of the plants that one lusts after or the design ideas that come to mind. She was on the lookout for space to expand. When a farm across the road from Hill Top came on the market, she bought it. Castle Farm included a farmhouse, a cottage, and a pasture called Post Office Meadow. This time she was not going to overpay. She avoided that embarrassment by working with a local solicitor, Mr. William Heelis from Hawkshead.

Beatrix was pleased with Mr. Heelis, and with more than his legal counsel. In her journal decades earlier, she wrote of her cousin's intended, saying, "Love in a cottage is sentimental, but the parties must be very pleasing to each other to make it tolerable." Willie was more than tolerable. In the winter of 1912, he proposed. He was tall, where Beatrix was short. Willie was athletic. He hunted, fished, bowled, and played golf. He was from a large family. He was a part of the country that Beatrix loved. Beatrix was forty-seven; her Willie was forty-one.

Is it surprising or predictable that her parents objected? He was beneath her, they argued. She should root him out of her life. Who were his people? While Heelis and Rupert Potter were in the same profession, a solicitor was hardly a

Beatrix Potter and William Heelis at No. 2 Bolton Gardens, on the eve of their marriage, 1913

barrister. And what of London society? Thankfully, brother Bertram intervened. Arriving in London from his country home in Scotland, he made the stunning announcement that he had been secretly married for ten years to Mary Welsh Scott, a farm girl he had met there. And they thought he had been occupied painting landscapes! Not long after, Beatrix and William are posing for a pre-wedding photograph in front of the flower border at Bolton Gardens. A fig tree is trained onto the wall behind them. They were married at St Mary Abbot's in Kensington on October 15, 1913. Beatrix remembered her Shakespeare, "What are the words in the 'Tempest'? 'Spring came to you at the farthest, in the latter end of the harvest.'" Having missed out on much happiness in the first half of her life, she was making up for it.

Castle Cottage, after the renovations, about 1925

With Willie, she was planted permanently in Sawrey. Rather than moving into Hill Top with its antique (read non-existent) indoor plumbing and close proximity to her tenants, the Heelises chose to expand Castle Cottage for their marital home, doubling its modest size. It would be their bastion, their keep. They hired a builder to open up the old front rooms, taking out partitions and breaking new doors into walls. They added a bathroom. Their upstairs bedroom, while not palatial, afforded a fine view of Hill Top across the road, where Beatrix still enjoyed gardening and drawing, writing and arranging her growing collection of antique furniture. Hill Top became a sort of still life into which she inserted bouquets from the garden as well as overnight guests. She continued to treat it as her special place, "a

Pansies, watercolor with
pencil, undated

house of one's own" that she had created as her first declaration of independence.

A wise gardener once said that if husband and wife garden together they should have separate beds. In the case of the Heelises, Beatrix did most of the gardening, though Willie sometimes helped plant the vegetable seeds. She set box hedges around her garden beds at Castle Cottage, filling them with flowers: pansies and roses, bellflowers and phlox. As at Hill Top, she mixed in soft fruit, like currants and strawberries, and herbs like sage. It was "a regular old fashioned farm garden," in keeping with the house. To Beatrix, calling a garden old fashioned was high praise.

The year of their marriage saw the publication of *The Tale of Pigling Bland* (1913), a charming romance with a small pig who sighs, "I wish I could have a little garden and grow potatoes." Instead his overburdened mother sends Pigling and his brother Alexander to market—without a shopping list. Alexander, through a plot twist, is escorted home to Hill Top by a policeman, illustrated with a perfect view of the garden and the flagged walk to the house. Pigling's many adventures and close calls end with his finding a mate, Pig-wig. The two appear in landscapes around Sawrey: at a signpost near Esthwaite and looking over a rolling view of hills and farms. Lest we read too much into the story, Beatrix wrote to a friend, "The portrait of two pigs arm in arm—looking at the sun-rise—is *not* a portrait of me & Mr Heelis, though it is a view of where we used to walk on Sunday afternoons! When I want to put William in a book—it will have to be as some very tall thin animal." After *Pigling Bland*, Beatrix took a hiatus from writing. She enjoyed married life and her increasing commitments to farm and garden, raising sheep and cows, chickens and turkeys, as well as flowers, fruits, and vegetables, on her 120 acres.

While Willie continued his law practice, Beatrix was in charge of the farm as well as the household. The farm manager checked with her every morning about the work planned for the day. Beatrix also made sure that meals were served promptly for her ever-appreciative husband. They enjoyed afternoon walks up to the tarns where Willie would fish—truth be told, poach—and Beatrix would row or paint. For the village, they must have been a baffling sort of gentry, living in a cottage but having retainers: a chauffeur and car for Beatrix, a housekeeper and a girl to help with the cooking, men to farm the land and help with the gardening.

Beatrix continued to be responsible for the endless logistics of aging parents. Her father declined quickly, dying the May after her marriage. With the start of the Great War in August 1914, Beatrix moved her mother close by, first in rented accommodations in Sawrey then, wisely, to the other side of Windermere. Her parents had taken Lindeth Howe as a summer's lease in the past, and now Mrs. Potter was installed there permanently with her London furniture, coach, horses, and servants. Mrs. Potter had a proper gardener, Benjamin Dawson, at Lindeth Howe. Her gardens included a peach house and greenhouse, lawns and bedding flowers, and the newly stylish herbaceous border.

Weekly, Mrs. Potter would arrive, driven by her liveried coachman like some imperious copy of Queen Victoria, and expect Beatrix to drop everything. Interrupted during the harvest Beatrix, on one occasion, jumped into the carriage with armfuls of corn. One can only imagine what her mother said to that.

In March 1916, short-handed from the war, Beatrix wrote a letter to *The Times* on employment opportunities for women in farm labor. She was unimpressed with the

Alexander follows the policeman up the garden walk to Hill Top from *The Tale of Pigling Bland*

formation of the Women's National Land Service, an organization that trained and supervised women in agricultural jobs, and what she termed their "ridiculous and vulgar" uniforms. But she added, "I am perfectly ready to employ the right sort of woman." The letter was signed "A Woman Farmer."

She received a response from an applicant. Her name was Eleanor Louise Choyce, known as Louie. Beatrix, intrigued, enquired by return post about Miss Choyce's age and experience and detailed the work. "I have poultry, orchard, flower garden, vegetables (help with heavy digging, no glass), cooking here with the girl's assistance; Mrs C. I & this girl all help with hay, & I single turnips when I can find

time, & look after some . . . land on the fell." By April, Louie had arrived, accepting the offer of wages and lodgings at Hill Top. Louie wrote her mother at the end of May about the lilacs and azaleas. "I have never seen so many & so fine, it is perfectly beautiful." She described working with Mrs. Heelis, propagating Scotch broom collected on the fells and lavender cuttings from the garden. On their walks they collected foxglove leaves from wild plants, used during World War I to distill digitalin, a heart medication. She added, "I get up early but Mrs Heelis isn't a bit of a driver. She finds me odd jobs if it is too hot or wet to garden & never fusses. I simply do like her exceedingly."

Louie became a regular, coming back many summers to help. Gardening is a solitary occupation, often soothing for that reason. For a change it was a joy for Beatrix to have a kindred spirit working next to her in the garden. Louie brightened up the Heelis home as well, singing and playing Beatrix's piano. Beatrix and Willie called her their "singing bird." Just ten years younger than Beatrix, she started as an employee and ended a friend. She and Beatrix wrote to each other about their gardens and their families for the rest of their lives. While Beatrix always opened her letters with the formal salutation "Dear Miss Choyce," they are full of affection and flowers.

Louie Choyce in later years, undated

In 1917, the year after Louie Choyce first came to Sawrey, Beatrix's publisher, Frederick Warne & Co., declared bankruptcy. Shocking. Harold Warne had borrowed from the coffers with the perhaps understandable intent of propping up another of the family businesses. He went to prison. Beatrix, with her deep-rooted attachment to the rest of the Warne family, agreed to some new work for the reorganized company. She spent time in 1918 on *The Tale of Johnny Town-Mouse*. She was really too busy to write and paint, but this she did—on top of the happiness of her married life, the demands of the farm, and the worries of the escalating war in Europe. There was a pall of family grief as well. She worked in the shadow of her brother's sudden death on his farm in Scotland.

She and Bertram had both chosen country life over city, just as Timmy Willie did in *Johnny Town-Mouse*, an adaptation of a fable dedicated to "Aesop in the shadows." Timmy Willie, a mouse born in a garden, is drawn among heartsease, small yellow-, purple-, and white-petaled pansies. Timmy finds a hamper of vegetables, particularly the peas, irresistible. In the illustration the hamper sits beside Hill Top's green metal gate. Hijacked to town, Timmy is befriended by Johnny Town-Mouse, but yearns for home, "And when the sun comes out again," he tells Johnny, "you should see my

Timmy Willie's garden
with pinks and pansies

garden and the flowers—roses and pinks and pansies—no
noise except the birds and bees, and the lambs in the meadows." Timmy goes back to his garden. Johnny later visits, but
finds Timmy's life and lodgings too quiet. Beatrix closes the
story with the statement, "For my part, I prefer to live in the
country like Timmy Willie."

SETTING SEED

A COUNTRY MOUSE, Beatrix went native. As Mrs. Heelis she took on the customs and picked up, if not the accent, then at least the jargon of her new home. By living beyond the pale of London society, she jettisoned its obligations and conventions. Her costume changed to a straw hat for the garden, simple woolen jacket and skirt, and clogs or boots to lift her feet out of the mud. A cloudburst? There was sacking to throw over her shoulders. Sudden sunshine? She could tie a rhubarb leaf on top of her head. If villagers raised eyebrows at her wayward wardrobe, what did it matter? She was comfortable with herself, even if a glance in the mirror reminded her of one of the pigs.

In the garden Beatrix planted more roses, including a pink 'Queen of Bourbons.' Roses smothered the walls of Castle Cottage, their fragrance wafting into the open windows like an exhalation of summer. As at Hill Top, she planted a Japanese quince beloved for its early bloom. She

Beatrix Potter's "self-portrait," sepia ink and pencil, 1924

tended ferns and alpine plants in her rockery. But as she got older, her garden sometimes got out of hand. To her cousin Caroline Clark, she confessed a Darwinian approach to gardening, calling it a case of the survival of the fittest. It was "always very full of flowers and weeds, presently it will be a sheet of self sown snow drops, and later on daffodils. It always seems too wet or too busy at the right time for digging over—consequently I just let the plants alone until they have to be divided, and small things like gentians have got crowded out." Yet she couldn't resist adding just a nugget of advice. "I think they [the gentians] will stand wet if you mix pebbles or old lime with the soil, for drainage."

Beatrix enjoyed the fruits of her labor. By the 1920s she owned not only Hill Top and Castle Farm in Near Sawrey, but also Courier Farm. Courier Farm had a great expanse of fruit trees, dubbed by Beatrix "the orchard opposite the Castle." She had room to try different varieties of apples. Some were best eaten directly from the trees—Worcester Pearmains, Quarrendens from Devonshire—others, like the sour crabapples, were best preserved with plenty of sugar. She was a great preserver of fruit, making quantities of jams, jellies, and marmalades. To visitors, she served bread and preserves with tea, a simple country fare.

Margaret "Daisy" Hammond, the niece of one of her childhood governesses, moved to Sawrey in 1922 with her friend Cecily Mills. The two women rented the front half of the old Castle farmhouse and an adjoining cottage from Beatrix and became fast friends with their landlady. They were avid gardeners. One June when Daisy and Cecily were away, Beatrix was looking after their garden and temptation proved too great. She penned her confession in a letter to Daisy. "I have also thieved a few lettuces and some truly magnificent aquilegias," she admitted, "—never saw finer ones and more variety." She reported on their roses and described the honeysuckle, "hanging into the porch as though the house was uninhabited—or only tenanted by Sleeping Beauty!"

Beatrix proffered invitations to Willie's large family, and his siblings and their offspring arrived regularly to call on the couple. Ann Lorraine, a grandniece, remembered wildflower walks with Aunt Beatrix, accompanied by the two Pekingese dogs that came into the household in 1936 and

Beatrix with her sheepdog Kep next to Hill Top's rockery, 1913

Honeysuckle, water-
color with pen and ink,
about 1895

1937, Tzusee and Chuleh. When asked the name of a plant,
Beatrix quipped, "It's called Enchanter's Nightshade. It isn't a
nightshade and it isn't at all enchanting, but apart from that
I suppose it's quite a good name." (Enchanter's nightshade,
Circaea lutetiana, is a prolific weed, related not to poison
nightshade nor to the tomatoes, potatoes and eggplants that
share its family, but to evening primroses and willowherb.)
Beatrix passed on plant lore freely, in the same way she delivered flower posies from her garden to friends in the village.

Beatrix the hostess was sometimes a contradiction. Usually publicity-averse, she enjoyed select appreciative callers,
especially those from abroad. The first of these appeared in

Apples and quince,
watercolor, 1880

1921. Anne Carroll Moore, a children's librarian from New York City, was assertive. Planning a trip to Grasmere, she contacted Warne and asked if Beatrix Potter would like to see photographs of French children and their grandmothers reading *Pierre Lapin* and *Jeannot Lapin*, the bunny books in translation. A rare invitation from Mrs. Heelis came by return post. Miss Moore arrived on a morning in June and walked up the long hill from the ferry. She remembered the wild roses in hedgerows and the fresh smell of mown grass. Beatrix came out of the hayfield, "looking for all the world as Beatrix Potter should look." By the time they walked up the lane, Moore felt as if she had always known her. Many years later, she recalled standing in the Castle Cottage garden, "The familiar flower garden of her picture books tempted us to linger there, for the foxgloves were in their glory."

Visitors enjoyed potted geraniums lining the windowsills outdoors in warm weather. These colorful slips of summer spent the off-season sunning themselves on the broad interior sills of Castle Cottage and Hill Top. Cacti joined them, not the spiny denizens of the desert, but the jungle varieties. Orchid cactus was a particular favorite, and Beatrix exchanged different types and colors with Louie Choyce, sometimes sending cuttings through the mail. The plants, hybrid epiphyllums, are easy to propagate. With patience, small pieces of the green leathery leaves will root and eventually bloom in a range of ruddy colors—magenta, fuchsia, salmon—like red paint mixed with different amounts of blue and yellow. One summer, Beatrix wrote, "Thank you for the cutting I hope it may be lucky. I am very fond of cacti, and with half doz pots there are always two or more that flower—though the largest scarlet is only every 4th year."

A small but steady stream of visitors found their way to her garden over the coming years, looking for Peter Rabbit and his creator. Marian Perry came from Philadelphia and became a friend for life. The Coolidge family arrived from Massachusetts with well-behaved children in tow. Beatrix

Foxgloves, watercolor with pen and ink, about 1903

Beatrix Potter in the garden at Hill Top, 1913

recognized like-minded individuals in these friends from across the sea. She showed them her flowers and furniture, her artwork and animals. "They appreciated the memories of old times, the simple country pleasures—the homely beauty of the old farm house, the sublime beauty of the silent lonely hills," Beatrix wrote.

Her American friends sent her books. From Marian Perry, she particularly enjoyed Sarah Orne Jewett's *The Country of the Pointed Firs* with its piecework narrative set in the woods and village gardens of Maine. One visitor, Alexander McKay, was a Philadelphia publisher. He sent

Orchid cactus,
watercolor, 1886

her the poems of Joyce Kilmer. She thanked him for the
beautiful book, and added, "There are other verses as good
as "Trees"—almost." (The poem to which she refers begins,
"I think that I shall never see / A poem as lovely as a tree.")
Henry P., one of the Coolidge children, convinced Beatrix to
share a new set of stories with an American audience.

Beatrix Potter had stories in reserve. As she put it,
"Through many changing seasons, these tales have walked
and talked with me." *The Fairy Caravan*, published in 1929,
was a set of interconnecting tales, threaded together by a
magic circus. The book is a dog and pony show, literally, run

Xarifa's birthplace among the primroses in *The Fairy Caravan*

by Sandy, a West Highland terrier, and Pony Billy. *Caravan* is full of plants, almost a catalog of wild flowers of the North Country. It describes her sheep and her sheepdogs, the smithy and his forge, the weavers and their rhymes, the farms and orchards of her home place. A very personal book, she wove in the birds and blooms of memory, writing of the old gardens and woodland of her grandparents' home at Camfield Place.

Just as Beatrix did not rest on her writing laurels, she was also not finished with land and garden acquisitions. In

Tom Storey with Herd-wick sheep, undated

1923 Troutbeck Park Farm, encompassing over two thousand acres on the opposite shore of Windermere, had come on the market. Beatrix knew the place, had known it for thirty years, with its river valley and becks, its tableland and bulwark of high fells. She had, in the 1890s, looked for fossils there. Now she bought it, and paid farm managers and a sheep expert, Tom Storey, to rebuild it and its herd. Beatrix built her own expertise in Herdwick sheep, an ancient hardy stock that was well suited to the lean life on the mountain fells. She became a regular at agricultural shows, showing the best of her rams

Cow, pen and ink with
pencil, undated

and ewes. In 1943 she was elected president of the Herdwick
Sheep Breeders' Association.

While Beatrix liked the traditional ways, she considered
herself forward thinking, a scientific farmer. She was entering an era of farming with the magic of modern chemicals.
She used a new drug to combat liver fluke in her sheep flock.
In one letter she informed Louie Choyce, "I used a weed
killer for the first time at Hill Top in the stone paving, it was
said to be non-arsenical and probably *was* harmless—it did
not kill deep rooted weeds!" She tried ammonium sulphate,
a fertilizer, to green up the pastures earlier. She corresponded
with other farmers on methods for improving her cattle
herd. When bracken spread to the point of invasiveness, she

acquired a set of mechanical bracken crushers to share with her tenant farms. Though nostalgic for the draft horses, she bought a tractor and a motorized mower.

Beatrix's life bridged from the age of steam and railroads to the age of the internal combustion engine. Not all of this change was to her liking. She sold drawings to her American friends to raise funds to prevent the development of a strip of lakeshore on Windermere. She wrote to *The Times*, decrying an airplane factory and its noisy test flights. She supported those who protested against widening the road that passed through Wordsworth's daffodil fields. "This little corner of the country should be kept unchanged for people who appreciate its beauty," wrote Beatrix to Marian Perry in 1928.

In 1930, she acquired another huge estate, Monk Coniston, with proceeds from *The Fairy Caravan*. Now interested in genealogy, her own roots, Beatrix was particularly attracted to Monk Coniston because it included a parcel once owned by her great-grandfather. While it might seem that she was working her way to becoming a land baron, or baroness if you will, Beatrix Potter had a higher purpose in mind. She had stayed involved with her old friend Hardwicke Rawnsley's efforts to conserve the Lake District and, more broadly, sites of history and natural beauty around England. After he founded the National Trust in 1895, Beatrix was a supporter in word and deed. This was, in a sense, landscaping on a regional scale. "I'm sure I am doing good in trying to save anything I can of our Lake country from being vulgarized," she wrote, "For, as true education advances, the beauty of unspoilt nature will be appreciated; and it would be a pity if the appreciation came too late." From her childhood romps through Camfield and Dalguise to her wanderings around the misty hills and valleys of her adopted Lakes, she treasured her home ground. With Willie, she arranged that all of their real estate would go to the National Trust after they both died.

Between now and then, there was more hands-on gardening to do. She was still "the busy Bee" as her uncle Hutton called her in her twenties. Through Willie, she had gotten to know an expatriate American, Rebecca Owen, who lived at Belmount Hall, a stately Georgian house between Hawkshead and Ambleside. Miss Owen, a unique individual in all respects, eventually decamped to Rome and sold Belmount to Beatrix in 1938. It seems that Beatrix had been itching to get her hands on the garden. She wrote to cousin Caroline the next year reporting, "My eccentric old friend Miss Owen has died in Rome . . . so I have a free hand in an old walled garden of over an acre." It was like having a new sketchbook, or perhaps more like being presented with one of her Peter

"This little corner of the country," watercolor with pencil, 1912

Rabbit painting books, as the outlines were there. Along the garden walls at Belmount azaleas bloomed. Spring bulbs were a carpet, a dream. But the old fan-trained fruit trees were verging on decrepit, and Beatrix trained clematis into them to hide their flaws. She put in new flowering shrubs to eventually take their place.

Shrub planting seems to increase proportionally with a gardener's age. Flowering shrubs are more self-reliant than perennials, requiring fewer horticultural interventions. Beatrix, now seventy-three, remembered Caroline saying she was "going in for shrubs—and for the same reason." She asked Caroline about *Chimonanthus fragrans*, wintersweet. Did Caroline think it would grow at Belmount? (Interesting that in this case, Beatrix made an exception to her usual avoidance of botanical nomenclature.) She had already planted

Ceanothus—California lilac. She stated, as if for the record, "I should like to plant some bushes that might grow on at Belmount Hall without much attention." Woody plants tend to live longer, especially untended, than herbaceous perennials, an attribute devoutly to be wished for an older gardener.

Beatrix was feeling her "anno domini." In 1938, she had some gynecological procedures in the Women's Hospital in Liverpool. She came home but soon landed back in hospital. With the doctors recommending a difficult hysterectomy, she left detailed instructions in the event she did not recover. She made up lists for Willie, and to her friends she wrote, "I have failed in strength more than people know this last 2 years. Most times it has been an effort to walk to Hill Top. I am so glad I was feeling particularly well last week; and I have seen the snowdrops again." But recover she did. It was hard to keep her down. She observed, "I am always better on fine days when I can work in the garden." She was joined in the garden by her two little dogs, playing hide and seek around the boxwood hedges.

Not long after her return home, World War II descended even on distant Sawrey. Men and boys joined up. The Ministry of Agriculture asked for more plowing and more potatoes. The Heelises blacked out their windows at dusk.

Clematis, watercolor, undated

Relatives of Beatrix, the Hyde Parkers, turned over their manor house to the army and moved into Hill Top. Bombs fell, though much less in the country than the cities. There was worry of invasion. Willie signed up as a local warden as he had during the last war, though Beatrix felt he was better suited to the Agricultural Committee than patrolling nights wearing a tin hat. "And the rest of us 'carry on', and grow sheep and cabbages and rabbits," Beatrix wrote to an American friend. She was undaunted. "What a pretty country it is at the Lakes is it not? Hitler cannot spoil the fells; the rocks and fern and lakes and waterfalls will outlast us all."

She did not outlast the war. On December 22, 1943, weakened from influenza and fighting bronchitis, her heart gave out. She was seventy-seven years old. Beatrix Potter Heelis died in her bed with Willie at her side. Just three weeks before, she had written to Louie of one of her last forays into the garden, "I am still under the weather. We had some really fine dry frosts, but I was disappointed to find I was not ready to stand the cold—it was really severe frost—so I got a cough again, but it did not last long. Today has been pleasant sunshine. I have been pruning creepers against the wall in the sun here."

Her friend, Tom Storey, spread her ashes in an undisclosed location on her land in Sawrey. Tradition has it that

Beatrix in the doorway at Castle Cottage, undated

Beatrix with one of her Pekingese dogs in the garden at Castle Cottage, 1930

it was on the little hill overlooking the farmhouse at Hill Top. She would merge with the soil, down-to-earth to the last. The best of stewards for the land, in her will she left over four thousand acres to the National Trust, retaining some life interest in the properties for her spouse. William Heelis died in August 1945, only eighteen months after his wife's passing. Our access to the views, the lakes and hills, the cottages and pastures of Cumbria, are thanks in great part to Beatrix Potter and her *Tales*. The lakesides are not strewn with holiday cottages. The jagged vertebrae of the fells are free of vacation homes perched on unlikely heights. She left a legacy of land as well as words and pictures.

She also left a garden. It frames Hill Top, it ushers visitors in, and while no garden can remain frozen in time, it is a living link to a remarkable woman and her interest in plants and gardening.

PART TWO

The Year in Beatrix Potter's Gardens

Violets, watercolor with pencil, undated

IF BEATRIX POTTER kept a garden journal, it did not survive. Perhaps it was destroyed after her death according to her wishes, along with the many letters she received from friends, fans, and relations. Perhaps it, along with nursery catalogs, garden magazines, and books, went to a waste-paper collection during World War II. "I have been sorting papers and books this afternoon— a perplexing task as regards books," Beatrix wrote to Anne Carroll Moore in the winter of 1942. "'Salvage drives' are a craze; at the present moment being overdone. Things are being destroyed that ought not to be." Many of her gardening books were dispersed after her death, so perhaps more information will surface to the delight of some future garden historian. Meanwhile let us garden with Beatrix Potter through the seasons, informed by her writing, artwork, and photographs past and present.

WINTER

———◆——◆———

*"There has been some lovely
weather—to look at."*

WINTER PERCHES on Sawrey like a large black bird. The nights draw out into the darkness of the north, cut by glow of lamplight and the smell of fireplaces burning wood and coal in the village cottages. It is the selvage of the year.

The weather can be wild with gales, closing down the ferry and stranding passengers and freight for days. Chimneys moan with wind. Pipes freeze and burst. The roads are treacherous. One hopes for a dry, crisp frost, but more often it is, to use Beatrix's term, "sloshy," with cold fog hanging in the dark valleys. Like an annoying guest that keeps postponing departure, the short days of winter hang on, and on.

At least the frost serves a purpose for farm and garden. On her bookshelf is H. Rider Haggard's *A Farmer's Year*, in which a winter entry reads, "frost in moderation is a good thing for the land, as it pulverizes the earth and destroys noxious insects by the thousands." And it is pretty to see the

Hill Top on a wintry
night, watercolor, about
1910

148

March 5.07

Hill Top's orchard in the snow

OPPOSITE: Footprints in the snow, watercolor with pencil, 1909

villagers skating on Esthwaite Water. As one of the shallower lakes, it freezes quickly.

While one can always hope for a "green winter," if the weather pulls up cold and wet from the "low east," there is heavy, drifting snow. Up in the peaks and crags and fells, blizzards can trap sheep, sending the shepherds and their dogs to the uplands to dig them out. The more dependent livestock, cows and horses under cover for the winter, need feeding, and Beatrix the farmer keeps an eye on the supply of hay. Walking back from the barn, her eyes absorb the silent snowy landscape reflecting blue light.

In her garden, structure dominates. The garden's skeleton is laid bare. Beatrix's investment in its bones is repaid in winter. At Hill Top, the long trellis acts as a spine. Snow clings to it. The stacked stone walls of the vegetable garden

The green gate at Hill Top

OPPOSITE TOP: Castle Cottage

OPPOSITE BOTTOM: Hill Top's vegetable garden in winter

are gray; the green wrought iron gate is a shot of color. The walls and stone paving maintain the spatial set of the garden, just as in Beatrix Potter's illustrations the backgrounds, natural and architectural, frame the characters. At Castle Cottage the beds are outlined in trimmed evergreen boxwood hedges; at Hill Top they are edged in slate. The houses, Hill Top's gray pebble-dash with green trim and Castle Cottage's

Hill Top's garden trellis

RIGHT: The handle of a
spade at Hill Top

buff with pink, take on a significance in the winter garden
in proportion to their importance for comfort and survival.
Structures stand up to the season, design-wise.

Garden tools take on a quality of still life. A wooden
spade handle stands out in relief. A wheelbarrow is sculptural.

The garden's woody plants—its trees and shrubs—are
unveiled. The deciduous tribe drops its leaves. Looking at
the bare outlines of her garden shrubs in winter, Beatrix
observes the way they grow: the honeysuckle opposite-
branched, with side shoots developing off the main stem
in pairs; the azaleas alternate-branched, with shoots offset.
Nature, ever thrifty, repeats the pattern at a larger scale in the
trees around Sawrey: ash–opposite; oak–alternate; maple–
opposite; beech–alternate. Beatrix writes, in 1937, to an artist
protégé, Delmar Banner: "We can tell every tree in winter

without reference to foliage by its mode of growth. So study them in some spare moments, . . . they will repay—they are in the right place as beautiful as rocks. They have a nobility of growth which is usually entirely overlooked."

The evergreens take a lead role. Across the rest of the year, you might call them retiring, their green needles fading into the background with the distractions of flowers, fruit, or foliage. In winter, especially with a dusting of snow, their dark color and strong contours stand out. Close to the road at Hill Top, a Scotch pine with red bark and bluish needles defines the garden in winter. Large enough to be seen from Castle Cottage, the tree is a visual connection between the two halves of Beatrix Potter's horticultural whole.

Other details too subtle to notice in the growing season move forward. The roots of the older apple trees at Hill Top

A robin in the
winter garden

The morning frost
lights the remains of
last year's plants

OPPOSITE: Dried
seedpods

and in the orchard across from the Castle look like arteries, penetrating the ground. Their bark stands out like the plates on a turtle shell. In the garden the lilac's bark is smooth and gray. Dried seeds and stalks on plants like meadow rue and goatsbeard stand up to a good bit of weather, though by leaving them the gardener contends with a bigger spread of seedlings the following year. The robins, sedentary birds, add a spot of color and movement in the winter garden.

Leaves of the roses,
edged in frost

On the rose canes, frost outlines the remnant leaves.
Shriveled red hips and recurving thorns add interest. To be
botanically correct, the sharp bits on roses are called prickles.
Beatrix Potter would have enjoyed the term, as she particularly liked the sound of its rhyme, pickle.

Little bulbs that would be overlooked in the peak season
have their day. The snowdrops are improbable if not prepos-
terous. Their leaves brush off the descent of winter, Beatrix
reporting their "noses" emerging as early as October. As the
season progresses, they slice through soil frozen solid, making
the gardener question their motivation. The small, bell-shaped

Rose hips, watercolor,
about 1878

flowers opening on wiry stems seem to ring in the New Year. Each flower has three white outer petals that hang down like three drops of cream, appropriately enough as the botanical name, *Galanthus*, is from the Greek for "milk" and "flower."

Varieties differ in small ways. Are there green markings on the outer petals? Are the petals narrow? Do they have a yellowish or greenish hue? These minutiae are of great interest to snowdrop enthusiasts, though practical-minded Beatrix sticks to the common species, *Galanthus nivalis*. Still, as she collects other things, oak furniture in particular, she would have sympathized with these galanthophiles.

Snowdrops, watercolor, undated

From *Peter Rabbit's Almanac for 1929*

One might wonder what all the fuss is about, as snow-drops seem like the runts of the bulb world litter. The largest tops out at about twenty-six centimeters or ten inches tall. Their appeal is in their shape, their pristine color, and their sense of timing. Snowdrops bloom when there is little floral competition. This is the flower that Beatrix most often mentions in her letters, though snowdrops do not appear in any of her books save *Peter Rabbit's Almanac for 1929*, assembled

Snowdrops at Hill Top

from spare drawings. With the exception of the wintery *Tailor of Gloucester* and one chapter (out of twenty-three) in *The Fairy Caravan*, she set her stories in a perpetually sunny garden balanced at its late-spring to early-summer peak.

Looking out onto her own garden one February, Beatrix admires the snowdrops. "There are thousands in front of the windows and in the orchard and in the lane. That is why I have an untidy garden. I won't have the dear things dug up in summer, they are so much prettier growing in natural clumps, instead of being dried off and planted singly." Snowdrops have the bonus of being prolific self-sowers. Where they are happy, given undisturbed soil and some patience, you too can have your thousands.

Beatrix's thousands of snowdrops harmonize with the outdoor palette in their green-and-white color scheme. But

Cloth-of-gold crocus

for a vivid touch in the bleak midwinter, Beatrix adds yellow aconite and crocus. Their brightness seems to vibrate. Their splashy hue signals the earliest pollinators. For gardeners, yellow is the starting pistol for the race to the growing season.

The early-blooming yellow crocus at Castle Cottage push up on pallid tubes in February from corms, solid little parcels that store food over their long dormancy. While she doesn't say, perhaps Beatrix planted them in the small lawn, as these early crocus are amenable to naturalizing in the grass. Their foliage matures well before the lawn needs to be mowed. They were probably the cloth-of-gold crocus, so-called because they reminded the namer of fabric woven with a gold-wrapped weft.

Winter aconites grow from unlikely little tubers that look strangely reminiscent of droppings from Beatrix's

Witch-hazel

ever-present pet rabbits. She no doubt planted her aconites in a visible spot, along a path or in a direct view from
a window or door of Castle Cottage where they would lie
undisturbed during their dormancy the rest of the year. Their
buttercup flowers—they are in the same family as summer
buttercups—deign to open only on sunny winter days. They
are worth the wait. As someone who did embroidery and
made moveable paper toys for children, Beatrix would have
appreciated the finely cut collars of strappy green leaves that
encircle the yellow petals.

The aconites in her garden have a matching neighbor,
the first shrub to bloom in the annual cycle at Castle Cottage.

With its low arching branches, winter jasmine—Beatrix calls it "jessamine"—is perfect for growing over a low slate wall. Its yellow buds open on bare wood. Leaves come later. It is a spreader, setting roots wherever it touches the ground. Beatrix may have gotten it from a gardening friend, as it is so easy to share. Its only fault is a tendency to catch leaves, the way Mr. Jeremy Fisher accidentally snagged a stickleback. Winter jasmine catches so much detritus that it needs to be cleaned out in late winter to look its best.

The unruly petals of a Chinese witch-hazel bush add to the yellow festivities in her late winter garden. As a bonus, Beatrix could step out her door on a sunny February morning

The darling buds of winter

to enjoy the fragrance of the witch-hazel. Spicy and sharp, it is understandable that someone thought to distill its cousin, the American witch-hazel, into an astringent.

Winter wipes the gardener's slate clean. In Beatrix Potter's sometimes-messy garden everything herbaceous dies back, including the weeds. The beds that do not get dug will still be there next year.

Among Beatrix Potter's possessions left at Hill Top is a 1911 catalog from Fox Hill Hardy Plant Nursery in Kent. How could any gardener resist the title "Novelties of New and Rare Plants Supplement to the Catalogue of 1911"? It boasted selections of "the best narcissi, late and early flowering tulips and forcing bulbs." Beatrix kept it through all the years, treasuring its litany of flowers—just the thing to page through on a dreary cold day.

Winter is a time of watching. "I have stopped indoors since the snow, except just feeding birds in the garden." The progress of buds is monitored. For a taste of summer, at least the jam cupboard is well stocked. When the sun finally rises earlier than Beatrix does, she knows that spring can't be far off. "March has come in—like a polar bear! So it may go out as a lamb. The snow is not much but the wind is bitter. The week before was really fine, quite warm in the sun. I was doing a bit of gardening at Hill Top and it was almost hot under the wall." Bliss.

SPRING

———→←———

*"You are as welcome as the
flowers of spring!"*

IF THERE IS NO SETBACK, spring can elbow its way in
by the first week of April. Compared to the gardens of her
friends in warmer parts of England, Beatrix's garden is often
"more backward." Branches remain bare, the leaves and flowers seem stubborn in their refusal to open. A late snow is
not unknown, a reminder that this is north, Beatrix Potter's
true north. "Today is mild and 'growy' quite a spring smell"
she writes to a friend, "let's hope it has not come a fortnight
too soon!" As the ground begins to thaw and the sun moves
higher in its arc, the new season exhales.

On the roadsides and in the open woodlands around
Sawrey, the English primroses push up in the grass with
their pale yellow petals and bright yellow centers. This is the
first wildflower in abundance, and must have been for the
Romans as well, the word "primrose" coming from the Latin
for first, *prima*, and rose, *rosa*. They are well settled in around
this valley with its moist, acidic soil. In *The Tale of Little Pig*

English primroses,
watercolor with pencil,
undated

168

Hawthorn in bloom,
watercolor with pen and
ink, undated

Robinson, the last official tale published by F. Warne & Co.
in 1930, the soon-to-be-shanghaied pig picked a bunch of
primroses to sell in the market at Stymouth.

Primroses and other wildflowers—violets and lady's
smock—bloom under the hedgerows, living fences planted
by generations of fell farmers. Their utilitarian function
aside, hedgerows have created a unique habitat for plants
and animals. They come alive in spring. Pointed beech buds
unfurl into fresh leaves. Hawthorn, black thorn, and sloe
thorn open in succession with their frothy flowers. Beatrix
waits for "black thorn winter," a cold snap that seems to coin-
cide with the bloom.

Post Office Meadow, on the slope between Castle Cottage and Hill Top, is full of tiny lawn daisies. Beatrix listens for the first cuckoo call, another sure mark of the season. Above Far Sawrey one of the woodlands is called Cuckoo Brow Woods. Walking there, she can hear the bright chattering sound of Wilfin Beck, running fast and clear from the snowmelt in the uplands. March is the month of mud. The dirt roads and lanes are slick. "It has been so dirty in the fields it nearly pulls my big boots off."

It is a good time for pruning the evergreens in her garden—the laurels and the like—and the roses. The woody plants are just about to break dormancy, rousing up like some heroine from the Brothers Grimm. A haircut will energize them for the growing season, though for a while they look like newly shorn sheep. For the flowering shrubs she will wait until after they bloom to avoid cutting off this year's buds. In fact, the honeysuckle bush is open by now. Its little flowers would not be worth having if not for the sweet smell that they exude on sunny, cool March mornings.

Up on the fells, the Scotch broom is just starting its yellow sweep across the landscape. It blooms on erect green stems with vertical brushstrokes. The plant's yellow flowers are like butterflies: five petals divided into an upright banner, two outfacing wings, and two in the center forming a keel. Beatrix has invited Scotch broom into her garden. All of its pea family relations that are already there—wisteria, sweet peas, beans—share the same flower shape. The plants are starting to get a bit out of hand in her richer garden soil, but she decides to leave them in for at least one more year.

To another friend planning a visit, Beatrix suggests holding off until later into April "for the wild daffies do not like the winds of *March* in the north." William Wordsworth made Windermere's wild daffodils famous a century before Beatrix moved there. In 1804 he enshrined that host of golden daffodils along its eastern shore in his poetry: "Beside the lake, beneath the trees, / Fluttering and dancing in the breeze." They bloom in Sawrey courtesy of Beatrix Potter.

Wild daffodils grace her uncle's garden in Wales, and Beatrix transplants some from there in 1906, writing to Millie, "I am going to get some of the wild daffodil bulbs which grow in thousands here. They grow about Windermere but there are none in my orchard, though plenty of wild snowdrops." Beatrix remembers them from Easters past. On family vacations to the sea, she saw children selling cheerful bunches of "Lent lilies." She adapts this years later when she has Pig Robinson pick a bunch for market and call out, "Who'll come and buy my eggs and daffodillies?"

These wild daffodils are a so-called straight species, *Narcissus pseudonarcissus* to those not befuddled by Latin binomials. *Homo sapiens* have not meddled with them by selecting or hybridizing. While not native to the Lakes, botanists and garden historians speculate that the Romans introduced the wild daffodils to Great Britain, as their nativity

Daffodils in front of Castle Cottage

is Mediterranean. The daffodils have certainly made themselves at home in the Lake District.

While Beatrix sang the charms of the wild daffodil, she grows many cultivated varieties in her flowerbeds. Plant people have been always been a restless lot, seeking unusual traits that will show and sell well, rather like breeders of dogs or Herdwick sheep. The daffodil has been the target of centuries of unnatural selection. They come tall and short, early and late. The central cup, or corona, can be long, as in trumpet daffodils, or short as in flat-cupped. Some have a windblown look, with the outer petals swept back. The inner corona and outer perianth can be the same color or contrasting, in combinations of yellow, white, orange and red, even

Post Office Meadow,
ready for grazing

pink and green. In *The Fairy Caravan*, Beatrix pointed out daffodils that were "the big bunchy tame ones that we call 'Butter-and-eggs.'" With enough different kinds, Beatrix has them blooming in the garden for at least two months in spring. Some, like the tazettas, are so fragrant that with just a few cut stems, the entire house will smell sweet.

Even though Beatrix herself never traveled beyond Great Britain, she assembled a garden of plants that was geographically diverse. Just as Pig Robinson sailed to the land of the Bong Tree, Sir Joseph Banks introduced Japanese quince, or japonica, to England in 1796. She remembers it from her trip to Salisbury, so many years ago, with her parents. The quince flowers early against Hill Top's front wall, its sweet coral buds opening before the leaves emerge.

Spring rains and warmer temperatures bring on a rush of new grass. For a farmer like Beatrix Potter, the growth is more than welcome. From the fells where the Herdwick sheep overwinter, ewes are brought down to "intakes," walled pastures where the new lambs are born in April. The ewes rely on fresh grass to ensure ample milk. The hay for the cows and horses in the barn has almost run out, and the livestock are let out into the pastures once again. The wild cherries in the woods are a haze of white blossoms. The hazel bushes in the coppices and hedgerows sway with drooping catkins. Birds nest in her garden.

Beatrix Potter could be called a locavore, though she might have found the term pretentious, eating out of her own larder and locally sourcing from the village shops and farmers. In order to have vegetables for the table, Beatrix starts as early as the garden soil can be worked. It is a time to plant, quoting Ecclesiastes in her King James Bible. In her garden Beatrix picks up a handful of soil. Compress in fist; disperse through fingers. Friability is the question. Too wet and the seeds will rot. The walls around the Hill Top vegetable beds reflect the spring sun and dry the soil out earlier than the rest of the garden.

Rabbit holding a cauliflower from *Peter Rabbit's Almanac for 1929*

The cool-weather crops are ready to go in. Cabbages like the cold, along with their cousins, broccoli and cauliflower, and Beatrix plants all three. Turnip seed can be planted. After they germinate and grow on for a few weeks, when she has time Beatrix "single[s] the turnips," pulling out the extras to give each seedling its own space, room for their roots to fill out. And it is time for lettuces and other greens.

Every spring Beatrix fulfills Pigling Bland's wish for a little garden to grow potatoes. Her potatoes are ready to be planted, preferring the cool spring days. The seed potatoes that go in the ground now were saved in the cellar from last year's crop. Only a few eyes, the growth buds, are necessary to get each new plant started. Beatrix can "chit" them in late

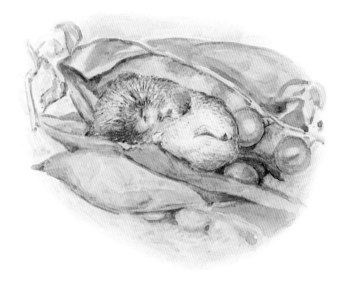

Timmy Willie asleep
among peas from
*The Tale of Johnny Town-
Mouse*

winter to give them a head start. Exposing the blunt ends
of the seed potatoes to light encourages them to sprout. In
the garden she might mix a handful of old mortar into the
soil, not for the lime—potatoes prefer acidic soil, and lime
"sweetens" it, raising the soil pH—but for the calcium. She
lays them in the trenched soil carefully, shoots up, and covers them over. If any potatoes have softened or are too small
to plant, the Hill Top pigs will be glad to oblige. On a farm
nothing goes to waste.

The sooner the peas are planted, the better. When they
aren't in by mid-April, Beatrix describes herself as "behindhand." The taste of spring peas, fresh picked, is a phenom-
enon. If the weather cooperates and she has time to put in
a second sowing, she can sometimes get a second crop of
peas. Succession planting is a great idea in principle, though
the mice seem to eat them as fast as she puts them into the
ground. She noted mice eating peas in more than one of her

tales. Still, some of the peas take hold and spiral up the pea stakes, branchy twigs saved from pruning that she has stuck in the ground beside the plants.

Beatrix's feelings about animals shifted somewhat over time in proportion to the upswing in her gardening enthusiasms. She did not entirely switch allegiance from Peter to Mr. McGregor, but on occasion she came to view animals as pests instead of pets.

The birds that strip the flowers from her fruit trees incur her wrath. "Plum blossom was destroyed last spring by the bullfinches," she complains. "They have become a perfect nuisance, they stripped the buds from the currant & gooseberry bushes too." As an experienced gardener, Beatrix knows that no buds equals no fruit for the coming season. She is left with that violated feeling. Of the birds responsible, she writes, "They are very pretty, but they really want shooting, whether protected or not." The deer usually keep to the woods, but occasionally do "a lot of mischief" in the potato or turnip fields. One night sheep get into the walled garden at Hill Top and eat the middle out of every cabbage. Even the chickens get into the act. When the seed goes in she has to move the Hill Top flock, in particular a hen named Fenella, over to Castle Cottage so they won't scratch up the newly planted beds. And then there are the rabbits.

Beatrix Potter in Bolton Gardens holding her pet rabbit, Benjamin Bouncer, 1890. Note the wire mesh protecting the plants.

Rabbits were her special pets growing up and into adulthood. She always had a few hutch rabbits for young visitors who expected "Miss Potter" to have bunnies on hand. But she did not appreciate wild rabbits in the garden. She shared a poem, doggerel really, with her friend, Marian Perry. Perry later wrote it out from memory. It is entitled, "How to Lose Furry Friends:"

When I was still in my infant glory
And delighted in many a bed-time story,
No fairy-princess could quite compare
With the furry friends from a leafy lair.
Flopsy, Mopsy, Cotton-tail, Peter.
The last of whom was my special hero,
Who dared to defy the rustic Nero,
That wicked Monster, the mean old beggar
That horrible ogre—Mr McGregor.

But now that I'm a bit too hoary
To lose myself in a bed-time story,
I've slightly altered my firm conviction
Regarding my furry friends from fiction;
And might not weep at a grim autopsy
Oh Peter, Cotton-tail, Mopsy, Flopsy.
All of whom plus countless dozens
Of nameless ravenous rabbit cousins,
Pay frequent calls on my straggling garden–
Mr McGregor, I beg your pardon.

Rhubarb emerging in
the Hill Top garden

At least the pests leave the rhubarb alone, no doubt deterred by the oxalic acid in its leaves. The rhubarb crop is coming on, its crowns uncurling into large sturdy leaves. She picks some young, discarding everything except the thick central stems to use for cooking. When the rhubarb is more mature, the stems will be less stringy if peeled. In her well-used copy of *Mrs. Beeton's Cookery Book* Beatrix reads, "This is one of the most useful of all garden productions that are put into pies and puddings . . . . Rhubarb comes in season when apples are going out." The apple supply at Castle Cottage is dwindling by this time of year, but the last few apples are especially good cooked with the rhubarb, their sweetness balancing the tart flavor of the stems. Jemima, or

Hill Top's lilacs

some later puddle-duck, could have easily nested in the big patch, though she might have gotten huffy when it was time to harvest for the evening's pudding. Rhubarb likes fertile soil, so the addition of manure, duck or otherwise, keeps the patch going year after year.

The seeds of the annual flowers that Beatrix collected last fall can go into the ground. While she works, she is supervised by a robin, like the one she drew with Peter Rabbit's shoe in the potato patch. It watches her with "bright little beady eyes, and a very red cap—no, not a cap, a red waistcoat," waiting for her to turn the soil and expose fresh worms. It flutters away into a tree and keeps a lookout, warbling its song, twittering in alarm at the silent appearance of one of the cats.

By mid to late May, the black buds of the lilacs open with their lush panicles of bloom and heady aroma. Their heart-shaped leaves precede the blooms, adding a green underpinning. Lilacs are long-lived plants, and one antique shrub works its roots under the parlor floor at Hill Top, lifting up the floorboards. To keep the lilacs a manageable height, where the blooms can be enjoyed by those smaller in stature than Mr. Heelis, Beatrix prunes them as soon as the bloom is over, taking out the oldest branch or two every year to encourage new, shorter growth. Some she leaves tall, draping luxuriously over the wall of the kitchen garden in the front of Hill Top.

Azaleas, the deciduous variety, bloom in the shade of her lilacs, in pinks and yellows and—heavens!—even orange. They are showier than the smaller evergreen hybrids that are typical in gardens today, as the blooms are larger and open on bare branches ahead of the leaves. And they are wonderfully fragrant. Happy in Hill Top's acidic soil, azaleas, and their evergreen cousins, the rhododendrons, are among the first shrubs that Beatrix mentions planting in her garden.

The ferns near the rockery unfurl their croziers. The little alpine plants have a better chance in the protected crevices she has created in the corner near the farm gate.

Hill Top's spring façade

Sea thrift, with flowers small, round, and pink, nods in the breeze agreeably. The gentians and tiny saxifrages, the rock plants and succulents can send their roots down undisturbed. In the larger garden beds, the hardy perennials would crowd out the alpines. Sometimes she grows little plants in an old stone horse trough; now that they have fewer horses and more motors, the troughs might as well be put to an alternate good use.

The garden primroses are starting to bloom. A gaggle of candelabra primroses cluster at the feet of the azalea, their tall flower spikes sturdy over rosettes of green leaves. They have expanded year by year, and as they are easy to divide she shares some with Millie. They self-sow when they are happy, as they seem to be at Hill Top. Beatrix also grows polyanthus

A period photograph of the Hill Top garden in spring, undated

primroses; with the white around their petals they look like they are trimmed in lace. She likes to gather little bunches for arrangements to adorn favorite pieces of furniture.

Among the fading bulbs, the summer perennials are jostling their way through the soil, breaking dormancy and bulking up in anticipation of a later display. The gaps are filled with self-sowing biennials. A haze of forget-me-nots, each flower blue and yellow—complementary colors from nature's palette—settles in every year. Taller honesty blooms in pink, or sometimes in white. Their flowers have four petals apiece spread into a cross, typical of its brethren in the cabbage family. Nearly every garden in the village has at least a few of these flowers, as it is so easy to share (or steal) the seeds.

On either side of the porch at Hill Top, she coaxes some small bits of cousin Edith's mossy saxifrage into large masses. She doesn't know the variety name, but she sketched the plant for Millie Warne when she first began to grow them. Through the spring, their mossy leaves are covered with wiry stems and dainty white flowers. The name saxifrage means "stone breaker," as its native habitat is in rocky crevices. The namers of plants thought that saxifrages caused the cracks, but really they just like to send their roots down to find pockets of moisture in difficult settings.

Along the slate edging in the Hill Top beds, columbine gathers in clusters, bobbing in the breezes as if exchanging village gossip. Columbine cultivars often hybridize with one another, so it is more than gossip that they are trading. Despite this whiff of impropriety, columbine does set seed though it tends not to "come true." This has nothing to do with fairy tales, but rather with a tendency for ornamental traits and colors to revert back to their simple blue-purple ancestor.

Beatrix lets the seed that the columbine drops each year germinate in the concentrated heat of the slates. It always seems like they should be further back in the border, but with long tap roots they are hard to transplant. She likes a loose cottage style and the self-sowers settle in wherever they are happy. It adds an element of surprise to the garden each spring, as the composition changes.

Spring exuberance at Hill Top in Beatrix Potter's day, undated

Columbine and foxglove

The pensive faces of pansies bloom in between them. Some of them are the larger hybrids that she sowed from fresh seed. Others, like the wild pansies, drop seed here and there, popping up all over the garden. The name "pansy," as Shakespeare put it, "is for thought," coming from the French word *pensée*, meaning "thought." She had mice embroider pansies on the cherry-colored corded silk coat in *The Tailor of Gloucester* and surrounded Timmy Willie with them in *The Tale of Johnny Town-Mouse*.

Timmy Willie eats
strawberries from
*The Tale of Johnny Town-
Mouse*

Pansies are related to the common violet that grows
in the hedgerows around Sawrey, and that Beatrix planted
around the base of the fruit trees in the Hill Top orchard.
With the longer days, the strawberries are setting and the
apple blossoms are opening. As her experience in the garden grows, Beatrix is able to assess the quality of the fall crop
from its spring bloom. She writes one May, "The fruit damson seem set, plums doubtful, apples not out, & not much
budding. The daffodils have been most lovely, the garden is
very pretty, tulips coming on."

Spring is that wonderful if somewhat delusional time
for a gardener when the sap rises and everything seems possible. The changes to the garden that Beatrix envisioned last
year, but ran out of time or energy for, surely can be achieved
in the coming months. The weeding is manageable, spring

Violets, watercolor with
pencil, undated

weeds like bittercress and chickweed being easy to pull and,
in a pinch, edible.

Bluebells carpet the May woods around Sawrey and
Beatrix describes them "like a bit of sky come down." Her
words verge on the sentimental, but anyone seeing them
en masse will bubble with similes. A blue crowd in a city
of trees? An inland sea? Perhaps as in *The Fairy Caravan*
the bluebells need to jingle for themselves. The bluebell-
bedecked wood up the lane behind Castle Cottage makes
an appearance in *The Tale of Mr. Tod*, in which Benjamin
Bunny notes the difference between their sweet smell and
the musky scent emanating from Mr. Tod's stick house. The

Hill Top's border in
early spring

scene reappears in *Cecily Parsley's Nursery Rhymes*. As their
name implies, English bluebells are native to this green and
pleasant island. They differ from the larger and arguably
coarser Spanish bluebell, another species entirely. Like the
local red squirrel, the English bluebell is a national treasure.
Beatrix Potter would have appreciated the efforts that wildflower enthusiasts around the British Isles are undertaking
to preserve them.

Beatrix treasures wildflowers as a part of nature and an
extension of her own garden. To a visitor planning a trip
in late May, she is encouraging. "It will be a lovely time to
see the Lake district. If the bluebells are over, the foxgloves

Jemima Puddle-duck and the fox among foxgloves

OPPOSITE: Bluebells

OVERLEAF: Wisteria in full bloom at Hill Top

will be in flower—and I will show you the real woods and lanes." Foxglove flowers are tall spires of pink pendulous bells, beloved of bees, adding height and color to a border. The individual blooms look the perfect size for small fingers. The botanist who gave it the scientific name *Digitalis* must have agreed, as "digit" means finger. In old Anglo-Saxon, the name became "foxglove."

Foxgloves are biennials, growing in the woods and fells around Sawrey, as well as in the borders at Hill Top and Castle Cottage. Their first season they grow into great clusters of fuzzy green basal leaves. The next year they bloom, seeds mature and drop, and the cycle begins again. "I have just been

Clematis on Hill Top's façade

weeding a quantity of seedling foxgloves," Beatrix writes to Millie, "I think they would make better rooted plants than out of the wood. I shall save some for next spring."

The façade of Hill Top is a canvas for climbing plants. A vigorous clematis winds itself around the great canes of the climbing roses and into the downspouts, but spring makes its messy habits worthwhile. The front of the house is festooned with bloom from the foundation to the slate roof. The wisteria soon follows, its craggy trunk shooting out spurs of buds that open into flowers that look like hanging bunches of grapes.

The ancients had it right, thinking that goat-footed Pan, impish god of fertility and spring, could pipe the season in with an instrument of reeds. In the shallows of Esthwaite Water the green reeds are just pushing up through last year's hollow stems. Frogs wake up. Birds come back. The season ferments like a crock of cowslip wine, fizzing with smells and giddiness. Beatrix proclaims, "Spring is the most beautiful time of the year," though she seems to say that about every season in the Lakes.

SUMMER

"Excuse a scribble I have just come out of the hay—It is uncommonly warm!"

THE PENDULUM SWINGS. The calendar turns. By June, flowers seem in a hurry to open. The gardens at Hill Top and Castle Cottage are buoyant with bloom.

The German iris with their glaucous, dagger-pointed leaves cut through the fluff of lesser plants. Beatrix monitors them for years, waiting for them to bloom. One year her neighbor, Cecily Mills, yanks hers out in disgust, pitching them onto the rubbish heap on top of some old mortar. Wouldn't you know they flowered there? Now both Beatrix and Cecily have marvelous irises in the garden, grown in soil mixed with pulverized mortar rubble. No doubt the plants appreciate the drainage, the lean soil, and the addition of lime from the mortar. Their fleur-de-lys flowers are a joy. The fuzzy beards on their lower petals are like her father's mutton chop sideburns.

The peonies are like her; once settled, they resist moving. They are undemanding plants, blooming without fuss.

Iris and tulip, pencil and watercolor, undated

198

A close up of peonies in the Hill Top garden, undated

Energetic ants seem to be doing a country dance on the fat round buds. (Willie is the one for traditional dancing—he practices and enters competitions with friends from the village. Beatrix enjoys the dances too—from the sidelines.) The ants are delirious with collecting the sweet fluid exuded by the plant.

The insects in Beatrix's garden are endlessly interesting. Sometimes watching them takes all her attention. She invited many into *The Tale of Mrs. Tittlemouse* (1910): beetles and bees, spiders and butterflies. Butterflies and moths

Mrs. Tabitha Twitchit disciplines the kittens with peonies and irises in the foreground from *The Tale of Tom Kitten*

remind her of brother Bertram who hunted them like African game as a boy. Sometimes he let her draw their wings at the microscope before he pinned them like trophies with glee in a case. She has hung one of his display boxes in the "New Room" at Hill Top, along with some of his large, somber landscapes. The canvases surround her when she sits inside and works.

The spiders are comfortable at Hill Top both indoors and out. "I rather like spiders too," Beatrix writes to a young correspondent, "they are useful [for] catching flies." Unlike

A spinning spider leaves a web on Hill Top's fence

Mrs. Tittlemouse, Beatrix underlines, "I won't have them brushed away in summer, only when we do the spring white-washing we have to sweep down their webs." Back in the day when she painted at the microscope, she painted precise bio-logical renderings of furry arachnids.

The insect life in the garden is attracted by smell as well as sight, and summer is the season of the nose. The herbs are at their best. Great bushes of sage bloom on their square stems. Flavor accrues in their silvery leaves over the long days. Mrs. Beeton called sage a "sweet herb," along with thyme,

Moths, watercolor with pen and ink, undated

mint, marjoram, savory, and basil. You might roast a duck with them, but they also add flavor to the soups and stews and savory pies.

Rosemary blooms. It seems a miracle that this Mediterranean native is so at home in the soggy north. Perhaps it is sort of a reverse vacation, with so many British heading to points south for the winter. The Sawrey soil conditions are just right, quickly drying out after each rain.

Shakespeare wrote, "There's rosemary, that's for remembrance." In her twenties Beatrix could recite so many of Shakespeare's plays by heart. She remains a person of solitary pursuits: painting, reading, writing, gardening. Close up, the rosemary has tiny purple-blue flowers that look like orchids, needles green with a stripe of gray—contrast and complement for an artist to appreciate, lovely in design and even lovelier to smell. Brushing a hand against a branch releases the fragrance. Sharp. A cue, or perhaps a memento.

The bushes of gray lavender give her a glow of nearly maternal accomplishment. She rooted the plants from cuttings over the years, small pieces of stem stuck into a sandy mix. Every time a cutting takes root, it seems like a miracle. From the Latin lessons in the Bolton Gardens schoolroom she knows that *lavare* means "to wash." Lavender does make the linens fresh. The bees like it too.

Lavender, watercolor with pencil, undated

She is pleased with her pinks, small carnations with their zigzag edges and gray-green stems. They are perfect for her cottage garden, antique flowers beloved of the English since the sixteenth century. In fact, the color pink was named for the flower, not the other way round. The word "pink" originally meant to pierce or perforate, in the same way that pinking shears cut a decorative edge on fabric. She remembers a great bed of pinks growing at Fawe Park and drawing them there with thoughts of Benjamin Bunny. Their gray leaves form a tight mat at the edge of the stone path at Hill Top.

The sweet william, cousin to the pinks, are from her cousin Edith's garden at Windermere. The best thing about sharing plants is that they always bring the giver to mind.

Unlike spring when each flower can be appreciated on its own, in summer the garden is crowded with flowers. "The garden here is very gay," Beatrix beams, "white bell flowers everywhere amongst the weeds, and the house covered with roses. The pinks are very full."

More shrubs bloom. The spiraea flowers look like little posies. Currants and gooseberries have tiny inflorescence that soon progress into round fruit. Privet buds open in the hedges around Castle Cottage, luring the bees. The honey-bees fill tiny holders on the backs of their legs with pollen,

Carnations, watercolor with pen and ink, about 1904

Summer border at Hill Top

like the pannier baskets that the donkeys and horses used as far back as the Middle Ages to cart wool over the humped-back stone bridges around the Lakes.

Houseleeks have settled into the sills and slate of the house at Hill Top. They aren't leeks at all, but one of the handful of succulents native to the British Isles. Looking up houseleek in the index of her gilt-edged Sowerby's *British Wild Flowers*, Beatrix could find it listed as genus *Sempervivum*, literally "always alive," and species *tectorum*, meaning

Hill Top's summer garden, undated

"of roofs and houses." Its little rosette of leaves is spongy, and a flower stalk pops up in July with pink flowers. In past times, it was thought to protect the house from lightning; today it has been rediscovered as a plant for twenty-first-century green roofs. The old becomes new again.

Some years there can be too much of a good thing. If the blooms on the apple trees were heavy in spring, the developing fruit will need to be thinned on the spurs. "And what a crop of apples!" Beatrix exclaims one summer. "I am

Apple tree at Hill Top

thinning ours with a pair of scissors, so high as I can reach." Otherwise the apples will be stunted, their energy dissipated over so many fruits.

The first rose opens before the end of June, beginning a show of color and fragrance that arcs across the high days of summer. They must be pruned and tied, fed and deadheaded. If untended, they start to look like ragamuffins. Roses by any other name would still be an effort, but she wouldn't be without them. As she notes there is "nothing more sweet than the old pink cabbage rose that peeps in at the small paned

Bud and bloom at
Hill Top

windows." Some modern rosarians describe cabbage roses
as "dumpy." Beatrix, happily describing her own physique as
"stout and active," embraces their chubby blooms.

With the roses at the windows, Beatrix coordinates the
front rooms at Hill Top with the garden, connecting indoors
and out. She chooses colors to blend, floral paper for the
front hall and kitchen, green paint for the stairway. Upstairs
the sitting room is a peach tone, and the many landscapes on
the walls echo her landscape out the window. The bedroom
is the prize, with its glorious William Morris wallpaper,

Hill Top with roses

its bold Daisy pattern above the chair rail. In the Treasure Room at Hill Top, her own cabinet of curiosities, she hangs two original botanicals, one of a rose and another of a primrose, by the artist Valentine Bartholomew.

At Castle Cottage the moss roses she planted are in bloom. The flower stalks and buds are covered with little hairs that look like moss, or a hedgehog. The flowers are fragrant, as are many of the flowers in Beatrix's garden. She surrounds herself with color and perfume, a luxury for the senses.

What Beatrix calls syringa, and we call mock orange, is another olfactory delight. The scent is so sweet it turns her

From the front door at
Hill Top, undated

visitors' heads, a visceral response. Is there a word for that?
With eyes it would be called staring, but they are using their
noses. The white flowers are unassuming, and its growth
habit is unkempt. Only the fragrance maintains its place in
her pantheon.

St. John's wort is knocking on the door at Hill Top. Beatrix notes that it, "pushes up between the flags in the porch,
it has peeped up between the skirting and the flags inside the
porch place." At Hill Top, St. John's wort blooms in time for
its eponymous saint's day, June 24. ("Wort" is the Old English word for plant.) Really it is most satisfactory, blooming

bright and yellow for months and growing to the size of a shrub without much encouragement at all. When she looks at the leaves with the sun shining through them, she sees small round dots like little windows. Small wonder that from ancient Britain forward, the plant has been celebrated for its power to drive away witches and depression. Since Beatrix's time, chemists have endorsed its depression-alleviating ability. The jury is still out about the witches.

The lilies are a spectacle with their great trumpeting flowers. From her first year in her garden, she declares to Millie Warne, "I shall plant the lilies between the azaleas." She puts them in "most carefully, in a mixture of sand, old mortar & peat. I ought to do well with lilies, having a supply of black peat soil." It almost seems a shame to plant them, the bulbs so big and beautiful with imbricated scales. But above ground, their flowers open against the wall each year, proclaiming summer.

The white bellflowers are a favorite. They spread around the garden, dropping seed with some abandon. They seem like the summer equivalent of snowdrops, green and white and popping up wherever they like.

Beatrix's spring seed planting pays profits in summer. The sweet peas have sent their tendrils spiraling up tripod poles, making wigwam houses for fairies who are so inclined.

Tiger lily, watercolor with sepia ink, about 1900

A poppy in bud

OPPOSITE: White bellflowers

She cuts the pastel flowers and makes arrangements for the house and bouquets to share—the more she cuts, the more they bloom. Poppies unfurl from their buds like butterflies from cocoons. Mignonette and stocks add perfume and petals. Zinnias and hollyhocks bloom in a festival of color all the way until frost. She reminds herself to collect seeds when they are ripe.

The lanes are frothy with meadowsweet. In the spacious days of summer, Beatrix enjoys a stroll. The wildflowers and

Fungus in a Sawrey
pasture

birds, the animals both wild and domestic, are part of her
home, her domestic ecology. Late in the season she starts
spotting her old favorites, the funguses, around the pastures
and woods. While she is done painting botanicals, she has
inserted a few of them into her books over the years: gilled
mushrooms stand by Squirrel Nutkin's tree stump, a shelf
fungus acts as Timmy Willie's table, toadstools are a plot
device in *The Fairy Caravan*. Walking around Sawrey is an
indulgence, when she can tear herself away from the clamor-
ing demands of plants and animals domestic.

Squirrel Nutkin playing marbles on a mushroom-encrusted stump

Warm sunny stretches of weather call for rowing. There were years when Beatrix would row on Esthwaite while Bertram or her father fished—not that she didn't occasionally throw in a line herself. Now Moss Eccles Tarn is the usual destination. She glances over fondly at Willie as he casts into the tarn from their flat-bottomed rowboat. The red and white water lilies that she and their niece Nancy planted in the tarn have established nicely.

Beatrix monitors the progress of a few alpine rhodo-dendrons that she put in up by the tarns, as if in exchange

Moss Eccles Tarn

for the wildflowers that she digs up and replants in her valley garden. She puts up wire netting to provide protection
from wandering sheep. Some Cornish heath, out of place in
the Lakes, starts growing near them, and she posts a sample
to Louie Choyce to confirm the identification. It probably
hitchhiked along with the rhododendrons in their nursery
pots, as heath was sometimes used for packing roots. The
name "heath," referring to both the plant and the barren
places where it is at home, is from the Anglo-Saxon *haeth*,
a wasteland. The word "heathen" comes from the same root.

Water lilies, watercolor
with pen and ink, 1906

Summer visitors descend like a heathen horde, outnumbering sheep in the Lake District. Beatrix notes traffic issues, writing to Louie in 1922: "I wonder what the roads will be like in a few years, the motor traffic last summer between Windermere & Ambleside was 120 per cent increased from the summer before." Yet she does appreciate the automobile. When Marian Perry arrives from afar, a drive in the country complete with a picnic makes it a red-letter day.

Visitors, both expected and unexpected, often find her in the hayfields. Summer is time to make hay. Her letters link

Beatrix and Marian Perry picnicking in 1930. Of the photograph, taken by Perry's niece Betty Harris, Beatrix wrote: "Your long-suffering aunty looks rather like an elderly sheep. But I am more like a good tempered witch than a cow."

hay and weather, weather and hay. "Four days of it were hot," she reports, "and we got in two fields of hay and the ley [lea] corn without a drop of rain . . . We were a fortnight in the post office meadow; except during the dry week we have had to cut little bits, and work it over & over." The grasses and grains must be cut and dried, then stored. If it rains during the process the hay must be raked over to dry. Enough rain and the hay rots and is ruined. Hay is fodder. It feeds the cows and horses over the winter. (Not the Herdwick sheep—they prefer their own lean mountain pastures.) If her hay crop is short, some cows will have to be sold. Beatrix is a practical farmer, and she expects the farm to make a profit, however small.

Sheaves in a Sawrey field, watercolor with pencil, undated

Phlox is the stalwart of Beatrix's late summer garden, blooming until August. Tall and fragrant, the phlox must be staked to prevent the big round flower heads from pulling the plants down in heavy rain. Beatrix supports her plants with small branches left over from pruning the shrubs and fruit trees. The natural color quickly blends in with the green leaves in the garden.

The yellow loosestrife is blooming. Her Gerard's *Herball* notes that tying flowers to the bridles of a team of oxen or plough horses would make them more congenial, lose their strife in short. She likes them for their upright golden touch in her summer garden beds. Though she must say that the

Phlox

RIGHT: Yellow loose-strife

loosestrife seems to be settling in somewhat too happily in her garden, growing like Topsy from underground runners.

Beatrix has help in the garden. Or does she? Unlike her mother who has an experienced gardener at Lindeth Howe, Beatrix makes do with young men from the village unless Louie Choyce is in residence. In a letter to Miss Choyce, Beatrix writes that her latest helper was hopeless. "He has not the recognizing to take up docks & dandelions but he has scraped the 'weathering' & moss off the outdoor stairs including a little saxifrage which I valued; no sense and does not listen either." She wants the garden and house to merge. The sweet greenery that planted itself on the steps was a cherished part of the effect.

Summer is the battleground for weeds. In spring they are small and inconsequential, easy to pull, easier to ignore. Turn your back until summer, and the garden becomes, as

Summer in the Hill Top garden

Beatrix puts it, "an overgrown tangle" or "an outfacing mess." Annuals weeds like groundsel, and perennials like dandelion and dock, can turn the garden into a reproach. Yet Beatrix can excuse the garden everything for the pleasures it brings.

By the end of August the damson plums are starting to come in, ripening into a taste of the antique and exotic. Roman history interests her, and it was the Romans who introduced the "plum of Damascus," or damson, to England. Plums in general appreciate high moisture, so the Lake District weather suits them perfectly. They are stone fruit, so-called because of their round pits. After she pits them, Beatrix adds plenty of sugar to her damson preserves. They are high in acid and too tart to be eaten straight off the tree. Just as well, or the neighborhood children would be into them.

The apples and pears are coming on strong. Many years the crop coincides with the arrival of the Boy Scouts. She

Gooseberries

PREVIOUS: The summer
border in Beatrix
Potter's day, undated

graciously agrees to host their campsite on her farm, but
often finds them in her apple trees. Even after negotiations
with their troop leader, and a truce that includes access to
some of the *smaller* apples, she still discovers "specimens of
scouts, distended with green fruit inside clothes." She sends
them off with instructions to cook the fruit, while they chant,
"Three cheers for the *old* lady!" So much for feeling young.

With the sun high and the days long, thoughts of winter
are banished—almost. They creep in when the potatoes are
ready to be dug and stored in the cellar. When the vegetable marrows proliferate or get too big, she makes vegetable

Blackberries

marrow jam. There is fruit to be preserved. From the orchard come crabapples, damsons, and plums. From the garden: strawberries and raspberries, gooseberries and currants. From the countryside: elderberries, rowanberries, and blackberries. She remembers a neighbor at Wray, coaching her that the blackberry "is a kindly berry, it ripens in the rain." The season of fruit is short and the winters are long. Every jar of jam or jelly will be a taste of summer in the dark days. But no use rushing things. There is still autumn to enjoy.

AUTUMN

———→✦←———

"Perfect autumn days—still, sunshiny
mists ... golden haze."

BEATRIX THE WEATHER-WATCHER observes autumn edge into the garden. The light changes, slicing with an angled brightness. When the sun makes it through the clouds, that is. Sometimes the climate seems inhospitable to humans, let alone plants. The skies are slate, and it seems to rain every day. Surely it will break soon. "The weather is rather rough & unsettled," she reports in a letter. "It is a little colder today, if it comes frosty it will probably be finer." She must remember to rescue the potted geraniums, bringing them indoors. Frost clears the skies, welcoming sharp clear days and nights when the Milky Way is so bright it looks like its own long, endless lake.

The leaves spark, then flame. Oaks turn to russet, beeches to copper, birches to gold. The larch needles yellow. During the war, the second war, she has to take down some of the great plantations of larch around her properties. They are needed as pit props for the mines, a part of the war

Pink thistles, watercolor
with pencil, undated

Mist over Esthwaite
Water

effort. But she thinks ahead, going around with pockets full of future oaks, dibbling in acorns for the next generation. At Troutbeck, she plants five acres of larch saplings thinking forward to when the fence posts around the great park will need replacing. "An estate should always have a stock of larch coming on, no matter what sentimentalists may say against the tree," she writes to her liaison at the National Trust. "I should like to plant Scotch firs on Hall's Hill, before the house, and some oaks on the south slope of the Tongue & the Colt Park, but it is useless to plant specimen trees or groups without heavy fencing" (because of the sheep). Beatrix remembers Capability Brown's tree-scaping at Camfield Place, and she now has a broad enough canvas to create an

Beech tree beginning
to color, watercolor with
pen and ink, undated

estate-sized composition of her own. "It would be both orna-mental & good shelter for stock," she adds, ever practical.

Nature makes its own composition above Castle Cot-tage. Up toward the tarns the long grasses turn shades of brown. A few wildflowers still bloom among the tussocks and little bogs—tiny harebells, red hawkweed, white yar-row. Leaves fall. The thistles go to seed, with soft down float-ing in the air like fairies. Light frost burnishes the bracken in great swathes. It tarnishes gently, like polished copper turning brown.

The bracken is ready to be gathered for the farm, and Beatrix walks up after dinner to help with the raking. She enjoys the climb. Sheep dot the lean meadows that rise above

Castle Cottage in
autumn

Sawrey. Their fuzzy coats have grown back since their June
shearing, ready for the cold. Busy with grazing, they barely
note her progress up the hill. She spots the Cannon children
already at work among the bracken, loading the cart for their
father. "I think it is the pleasantest 'harvest,'" Beatrix writes
to Millie, "It is not so hot as the haymaking, but it is a funny
place to take a cart, we always expect the wheels will be coming off, it is such an awful road up & down." While in the
garden it would be a weed, to Beatrix the farmer, bracken is a
marvel of economy. In exchange for labor and modest trans-
portation, it provides free bedding for her stabled livestock
all winter.

Forest scene with bracken, watercolor with pencil, about 1894

OVERLEAF: Trees and hills, Sawrey

The stubble in the fields reads like a code for the end of her farmer's year, but now that the harvest is in, there is time for the agricultural fairs. Beatrix is busy with them, their commerce and their competition. She dons her best woolen suit and, driven by her chauffeur, Mr. Stevens, enjoys the autumn colors en route. At the fair, she socializes with friends and farmers, honest country folk she has learned to love. Her surplus sheep are sold, with "Mistress Heelis" carefully monitoring the prices. While she does not depend on farming for her daily bread, she wants her agricultural efforts to make economic sense. Sometimes she is in the market for a new ram, called a "tup" by Beatrix and her sheep farmers,

Creepers with their
seasonal blush

to add to the bloodlines, being a "believer in 'breed'." She is
proud of her "little Baa's" that take ribbons in the judging.

Home from the fair, she walks through her garden.
Creepers on the walls are coloring. Michaelmas daisies
bloom like a galaxy of stars, backlit in the luminous afternoon. Beatrix's New England friends call them asters. This
North American wildflower was rechristened in England
for the saint's day of Michael the Archangel and his cohort,
September 29. In Old England, Michaelmas was a "quarter
day," signaling the beginning of one-fourth of the year. Rents
were due. Help was hired. Now the saint and his flower con-
note autumn.

Hill Top's roses with their last hurrah

LEFT: Japanese anemones in bud

Japanese anemones flower, as they do on Norman's grave. They are tall and sturdy; over the years they have made great clumps. Beatrix remembers the day that the hamper of plant donations arrived from cousin Edith's garden in Windermere. It was 1906, her first anniversary at Hill Top. She had marveled at the anemones' coarse roots, gnarled underpinnings for a graceful plant. Growing in her garden its six-petaled flowers are akin to the little white wood anemones that pop up wild in spring, but these bloom pink on long wiry stems, stretching over the back of the border. She likes them almost as much when they are finished flowering, the round seedheads pirouetting in the wind.

AUTUMN   239

Autumn view of Hill Top, watercolor and pencil, undated

The roses carry on, with intermittent, almost defiant blooms. Of all the flowers and plants in Beatrix's art and authorship, roses make the most frequent appearance. She loves them in her garden at any season, but at the bookends—the first of summer and the last of the year—they tug at her heart. The rose hips redden. They blush the way she did as a child, when her father's friends teased her.

The dahlias are footprints of summer, still glorious with flowers. Their round buds form and open, form and open. The more Beatrix cuts them for bouquets, the more they seem to bloom. Then one morning around the middle of October a heavy frost—the locals call it a white frost—leaves them black. She wishes hers were more protected. Her

neighbor Cecily's dahlias outlast hers. Gardening is undeniably a competitive sport, but it won't be many nights until Cecily's are down too. Is the twinge of satisfaction a sin? Ah well, if so, it is certainly venial.

Once the frost has killed the dahlia foliage to the ground, Beatrix sets to lifting the swollen dahlia tubers out of the ground. They can be stored in the root cellar for next year's garden. It is always a wonder to see how they've multiplied underground. Next year she'll have to give some of them away. Perhaps she can post a few to Louie.

Speaking of post, next spring's new bulbs have arrived. The tulips with their smooth brown tunics look good enough to eat. It is too easy to succumb to the temptation to order a few more varieties of daffodils. Then the bulbs arrive and want to go in, always a logistical puzzle while the garden is still growing. As long as she can keep the bulbs cool and dry, she can put off planting them. Sometimes waiting for frost to set the garden back is easier—where the dahlias come out, the new bulbs can go in. Beatrix would rather have them all planted by the middle of October to let them settle in before the ground freezes solid, but often she simply has too much to do.

The chrysanthemums are the last flowers to bloom in her garden. The last seems sometimes dearest. Beatrix has many associations with this plant, and over the years, she has woven associations—with people, with places—into the fabric of her garden. Her maternal grandparents grew chrysanthemums, many different varieties; her uncle Crompton Potter won ribbons for his in the Manchester flower shows. She remembers her teenaged self, sitting on the train with Uncle Henry Roscoe, carrying "a bunch of chrysanthemums as large as cauliflowers." They were coming back to London from Woodcote, his country home in Surrey, where he and Aunt Lucy took great pleasure in their garden. She now understands that pleasure completely.

Chrysanthemums aside, the rest of her garden is looking slightly forlorn. It takes some cajoling to cling to any vestige

Dahlia, watercolor with pen and ink, about 1903

of prettiness, but to her the garden is beautiful in any state. Perhaps, though, it is time for a big dig.

A garden always gives another chance, an opportunity for a makeover. It is a permanent impermanence. If a plant pouts she can relocate it. When a bed is overgrown, she can dig it up and replant it. Beatrix reports to Louie, "I got most of Hill Top dug with assistance, it was in a great mess." She gets rid of the clutter, dividing the phlox and sorting out the campanula seedlings that come up willy-nilly. She beats back the yellow loosestrife that should have come with a warning label. Every gardener has fantasies of jettisoning everything and starting over, but she is too practical-minded for that.

The plants appear appreciative of a fresh start. Odd, but the perennials seem to get stuck when they have been in the same place for too long. "It is anxious work to dig up a border," notes Beatrix, "but . . . it has done good to most of the plants; they get 'set', as we say in Lancashire about a pig or calf that has stuck in its growing. I think the plants do well in nursery gardens because they are lifted frequently, & start afresh." She lifts the plants and digs over the soil with her garden fork. This is her opportunity to rearrange. She can play with the composition, imagining the progression of flowers and hues, working with the scale and texture of the

Hill Top's garden in autumn

leaves. Even if she feels like her aging eyes aren't up to doing color work with her paints any more, she can still play with color in the garden.

Many of her perennials enjoy being divided, split into pieces. They seem to tell her when the time is right. The centers of the plants hollow out, with growth coming up in a donut shape around an empty middle. Once divided, they will reward Beatrix's work with a better show in years to come. It seems a shame to waste the leftovers, so she tries to place them in good homes. "I think I will post you a Japanese cowslip," she proposes to Millie Warne. "I don't know if they would grow in London, they like a damp corner." Beatrix likes her damp corner of the world too.

Japanese cowslips in Beatrix Potter's garden, eventually dug and divided

Other plants arrive by post from her network of gardening friends with similar surplus. One of them, Charlie Cooper, sends her a bit of his garden in Devon one September. She sends him a thank you along with a dash of soil science. "What a lovely present of irises—(and what curious red earth? I had nearly forgotten the Devonshire red). The soil is curiously different here; but I do not doubt that these liberal roots will *grow*—in fact I rather doubt if cow manure is necessary in this wet climate and loose soil; usually our plants grow *too freely*."

Seedheads of honesty

Beatrix promises him the roots of tway-blade, a little local orchid, in return. In her day, there was no feeling of trespass when digging up wild plants. The supply seemed endless. She goes out with her trowel to the edge of the woods where she knows they grow. Charlie would see how the tway-blades like his red Devon soil.

She is busy gathering closer to home as well as in the woods. Seed collecting is a gardener's act of optimism, not to mention frugality. Seeds are tiny bundles of next year's garden, there for the asking. They are magic, like the fern seeds

One of the cabbage tribe

that cloaked *The Fairy Caravan* with invisibility. (She knew that ferns, like funguses, have spores. For her little readers, perhaps she felt that the word "seed" sounded better, in spite of the bad natural history.) She is a seed saver, though she sometimes tries to do too many things at once. "I wrote your address on an envelope that I was collecting flower seeds in," she confesses, "then I put it away with the other seed packets here—and I could not remember." Seeds from the vegetable garden are targets too. "Carrots, onion, leeks are useful . . . . We have lots of the cabbage tribe which ripen seeds in profusion." She spreads her seeds out in the parlor on old sheets of paper by the front windows to dry before storing them. Her

The warm wall in the
kitchen garden at Hill Top

stash grows from year to year. One of these days she will need
to sort them out.

The flowering perennials in her garden are drawing in
for winter. When she has the time, she cuts back most of
them to the ground, leaving a few of the stalks with interesting seedheads standing. The goatsbeard gets covered with
white hoar frost, looking more like an old man's beard than a
goat's. The honesty drops its sheath and could easily be paper
money. What seeds the birds don't eat will provide some
punctuation for the beds in winter. She worries about the
birds, this lifelong animal lover. As the year recedes, Beatrix
feeds them in the garden, attracting fluttering crowds. They

Apples, photographed by Beatrix or her father, about 1907

OPPOSITE: Apple picking, from *Peter Rabbit's Almanac for 1929*

enliven the landscape, a hungry host, and provide entertainment for the price of some seeds, much as the Fairy Caravan did for its audience.

In the vegetable garden she considers cutting a few last stalks of rhubarb, but she abstains, leaving the plants to gain strength for next spring. The fruit trees trained on the hot brick wall are losing their leaves. Some of the late vegetables seem to perk up with the cold. The cabbages are great globes with ruffs like Elizabeth Tudor. Beatrix looks with pleasure

Autumn berries
including hawthorn,
watercolor with pen and
ink, about 1905

on her best row of celery ever. They are banked up with soil to blanch the bases, making them sweet and tender. Lettuce makes a comeback, opening in frilly rows. A light frost doesn't faze lettuce, but she needs to pick it before a hoar frost freezes the watery leaves.

The late apples are yet to be picked in the orchard. Perhaps this year she will dry some apple rings. She walks out into the tall orchard grass, but avoids the nettles, still sporadically blooming with their well-known sting. Her collection of wildflowers planted in the orchard has recovered from her nieces' misguided efforts to "weed." She was angry, really angry, when she spotted the girls pulling out her carefully placed transplants, even though they were trying to be helpful.

The blackberries on the edge of the meadows are still bearing. The fruit of the hawthorn are bright red in the hedgerows. It is appropriate that the hawthorns are growing there. Hawthorns are named not for their fruit, but for the Old Saxon word for hedge. They must have seemed the perfect plant to that tunic-clad Saxon yeoman. His hawthorn plants grew, vigorous and thorny, into a fence that even sheep couldn't penetrate.

The hollies around the property are heavy with berries. Some years Beatrix sells small conifers from the farm to Christmas tree dealers. She wonders if she should sell the holly branches for decorations too. It is a quandary. If sold, "the dealers are so greedy they cut back the poor holly trees to bare poles" if not the branches are stolen, ripped off the trees in gaping tears. She wishes they could be saved in place. "The trees are lovely in secluded places where they have been left alone, glowing red and shining green." She can save only so much of the countryside.

When the cold sets in, she swaddles the outdoor pumps with sacking. Daylight diminishes. Beatrix and her garden are left on the doorstep of winter. The trees are bare, but she can already see snowdrops peeking through the soil.

PART THREE

Visiting Beatrix Potter's Gardens

Beatrix Potter's world: England, Scotland, and Wales

Y<small>OU WON'T COME UPON</small> Beatrix Potter's gardens by accident. You will have to seek them out. A Beatrix Potter gardening pilgrimage might start in London. Her South Kensington neighborhood, fallen into seediness after World War II, has revived. Though many of the terrace homes have been divided into pricey flats and their mews turned into luxury residences, there remains a sense of Potter's place from the tree-lined streets and sedate architecture. Damaged in the Blitz, No. 2 Bolton Gardens was demolished, though many of its neighbors still stand. Fittingly, a primary school was built in its place so that the site of Beatrix Potter's London home is alive with children. If you walk in front of the school, you will find a commemorative wall plaque, complete with a few of her favorite characters.

Turn around, and you will see the garden she saw. Still proprietary behind its iron fence and locked gate, the Bolton Gardens square is busy with playing toddlers and watchful caregivers, those in love and those at leisure, strolling and sitting among the plantings. Residents continue to pay a garden levy to enjoy the privilege, just as the Potters did.

From there it is an easy walk past the South Kensington Underground station, very much in operation by Beatrix

Bolton Gardens now

Potter's day, then alongside the home and studio of Sir John Millais on Cromwell Place to the former location of the Horticultural Gardens. If you walk on Imperial College Road or Prince Consort Road you will be ambling over the gardens where Beatrix and Bertram once played. The roads and the buildings of the Science Museum and Imperial College swallowed up the available land over the years, starting in 1888 when the gardens closed. The Chelsea Flower Show started here. To be more precise, the Great Spring Show of the Royal Horticultural Society was held here from 1862 to 1888 until it

moved first to Temple Gardens and then, in 1912, to its present home on the grounds of the Royal Hospital.

Beatrix would easily recognize Kensington Gardens. The Broad Walk is still anchored by Round Pond. The Flower Walk blooms, and birds sing in the shade trees. The palace where Victoria lived as a child is easily visible again, thanks to a recent project undertaken by the Royal Parks. Dozens of trees were removed to open up the view for Queen Elizabeth II's Diamond Jubilee, part of a 2012 redesign of the gardens by Todd Longstaffe-Gowan. It is still full of children and "children-who-never-grow-up," as Beatrix once called herself, an allusion to another children's hero, Peter Pan, who resided in Kensington Gardens in a J. M. Barrie book.

And what of the two country houses that left the largest imprint on young Beatrix Potter's gardening biography? Camfield Place in Hertfordshire, the place she loved best in the world, is still intact as an estate and private residence, most recently the home of the late romance novelist, Barbara Cartland. While Camfield itself is not open to visitors, you can visit the extensive gardens of Hatfield House nearby, just as Beatrix Potter did. The estate includes the palace where the young Elizabeth Tudor lived. Beatrix wrote to Louie Warne, one of Norman's nieces, in 1907, "I was showing my cousin an old oak tree at Hatfield where Princess Elizabeth was sitting when they came to tell her that Queen Mary was dead and she was Queen Elizabeth [I]. She wore a ruff and had a big nose; she could not sit under the tree today because there is nothing left except the trunk with no branches!" Queen Elizabeth II planted a new oak in the original location in 1985, marked by a plaque that does not mention the nose.

In Scotland, Dalguise House still stands, but is converted into a lodge and activity center for school trips and holidays. Children and adults take nature walks, discovering, one hopes, the same wonder that Beatrix and Bertram did in

The Tudor garden at
Hatfield House

the woodlands that surround the house. Unlike the Potter
children, today's guests at Dalguise can also take advantage of
organized adventures that include trapeze and zip wire. The
gardens that remain are minimal, but the landscape resonates.

Around the nearby villages of Dunkeld and Birnam are
well-marked trails along the broad meanders of the River
Tay. Groves of mature trees include some the largest in the
United Kingdom. Eighteenth-century follies, the Hermit-
age and Ossian's Cave, invite imagination. These forests are a
likely habitat to spot red squirrels like Nutkin. Gray squirrels
à la Timmy Tiptoes were introduced to nineteenth-century
Britain—the acquisitiveness for exotics extended beyond

National Trust signpost to Hill Top Farm with Castle Cottage in the background

plants to the animal kingdom. The grays have outcompeted the reds in most areas further south in England, including the Lake District.

Birnam, which shares a train station with Dunkeld, boasts the Birnam Arts and Conference Centre. A unicorn-topped pillar, which stood in the Dalguise garden in the Potters' day, is installed there along with a permanent exhibit celebrating Beatrix Potter in Scotland. Outdoors, bronze statues of many of her most famous characters frolic in the Beatrix Potter Garden. When it was opened in 1992, the designers wrote, "Wild flowers, water plants, mosses and fungi will not be discouraged, nor will wildlife (of the more congenial sort)."

Thirteen miles south, you can take in the Perth Museum and Art Gallery. It houses a choice collection of Potter's

Near Sawrey

fungus paintings along with the story of the mycological friendship that developed between Charlie McIntosh, the Perthshire postman-naturalist, and a young artist-scientist named Beatrix Potter.

The largest concentration of Beatrix Potter's gardens is folded into a corner of Cumbria. Most of them are dotted around Windermere. The major draw, Hill Top Farm, sits in an area that locals called the "back o' t' lake." It still feels remote. You can approach it from the Bowness ferry, at least in summer, and hike the two miles up the long hill through Far Sawrey, or wait for the next 525 bus. With a car you might take the B-road from Hawkshead, curving around Esthwaite Water following the signposts for Sawrey. When the road takes a sharp zag through the village look quickly, or you may miss Hill Top Farm.

Tower Bank Arms today

PREVIOUS: The magic of Hill Top Farm

A National Trust parking lot is tucked unobtrusively off the road. Sadly, you are parking atop Beatrix's orchard across from the Castle, so you will have to summon up a vision of her fruit trees—apple and pear, damson and plum—and the meanders of spring bulbs and summer wildflowers that bloomed beneath them. Did she envision the number of visitors she would attract to her village in summer, like swarms of bees?

On the short walk from the parking lot to Hill Top, take time to explore the narrow lanes and enjoy the houses with their slate porches and little flowery gardens, much as Beatrix did in 1896 when she first stayed with her family in Sawrey. You will pass Buckle Yeat Cottage, painted in lush detail for

The Tale of the Pie and the Patty-Pan. It still sports a colorful,
flowery front garden. The farmhouse where Beatrix lodged
during Hill Top's renovations, Belle Green, remains a private
residence. If you peer over the wall, you can spy a back garden that would have made Mrs. Satterthwaite proud. The
village shop and smithy are long gone, though the buildings
remain. These days the business of the village is mostly seasonal, the customers mostly tourist.

The seventeenth-century Tower Bank Arms is still
bedecked with roses in summer, as it was in *The Tale of
Jemima Puddle-Duck*. This is a friendly inn, where dogs, children, and wellies are welcome. On chilly days, patrons enjoy

A still life of garden tools at Hill Top

their drinks and meals in front of the old-fashioned fireplace. Spend the night if time permits. The four upstairs guest rooms are numbered in the old dialect that Beatrix learned from her shepherds—Yan, Tan, Tethera, and Methera—and used in *The Fairy Caravan*. Night in the village is dark and, after the bar closes, completely quiet. You may wake in the morning to the lowing or baaing of Hill Top's livestock. The views from the deep-set upstairs windows make Beatrix's love affair with Sawrey perfectly understandable.

Next door to Tower Bank Arms and sharing a wall is Hill Top Farm, the magnet for Beatrix Potter's fans, garden and otherwise. One no longer enters the garden through the

A descendent in the Hill Top garden

Tom Kitten gate; it was closed when crowds got too large. A new gate at the far corner of the property channels visitors into the garden. The garden is laid out along her stone path much as she would have known it. It is cozy and welcoming: fruits and vegetables amid the flowers, loose sweeps of plants that are kept in a carefully careless style. Roses and clematis bloom. The walled vegetable garden has peas and potatoes, radishes and rhubarb. A wooden beehive, much like the one that Mr. Satterthwaite made, sits in the bee bole, a purpose-built shelf in the stone wall. An arrangement of tools—a watering pot, spade, and soil sieve—is set in homage to Mr. McGregor's garden.

Castle Cottage seen over the Hill Top garden gate

In season, Hill Top Farm is beset by sightseers—you need a timed ticket to tour the house—but the garden can be seen at any time during opening hours. Come early or stay late to see it in morning or evening light, and to catch a glimpse of the garden alone. Next to the garden a few apple trees are cordoned off into a small paddock. You will often see a rabbit or two moving lippity-lippity through the grass.

The National Trust has made some necessary concessions in the garden for the volume of visitors. The area in front of the house has been paved to withstand the shuffle of feet waiting for the next tour. A bench under the parlor windows is there to sit on, though Beatrix rarely took time to rest during the growing season. A second paved path has been added behind the long trellis to direct the stream of visitors downhill to the inevitable gift shop and exit.

As you look at the garden and its swath of flowers, realize that few of the actual plants that Beatrix tended are still growing in the garden. The trick to preservation gardening is to keep the garden looking more or less as it did in her day while dealing with the inexorable fact that plants grow, spread, and sooner or later die. The Hill Top garden has been dug and replanted several times in the scores of years since Beatrix last gardened there. Peter Tasker, the National Trust's gardener at Hill Top Farm, selects plants to mimic those that appear in period photographs, in her correspondence, and in her *Tales*. You may spot the occasional weed or shaggy shrub. The mild untidiness is a deliberate nod to the cottage garden style and Beatrix Potter's gardening habits. She never aimed for a show garden.

As you step from the garden into the house, turn around and look out the door for a Beatrix Potter–eye view. The deep doorway and front windows framed the garden for her. Flowers entered, rather than tourists. Inside the color green dominates, bringing the outside in. The floral touches— wallpaper, fabrics, botanical art—speak to the garden on the other side of the walls. Landscape paintings merge nature with home.

As you set out through the gate at Hill Top, look across Post Office Meadow. Beyond it you can see a modest pale house, angled to the road. Its picture window looks towards Hill Top. It hardly looks a castle, but it was for Mr. and Mrs. William Heelis. If you walk up the lane next to the meadow, you can look over the gate into the Castle Cottage garden. It has changed greatly since they gardened there.

That gardens don't last may be one of their perverse charms. They are ephemeral, the intersection of time, place, and plants plus the effort of one or the efforts of many. Castle Cottage is a perfect example. While the National Trust owns it, since William Heelis's death in 1945 it has primarily been a private residence. Beatrix's niece Joan Duke and her husband lived at Castle Cottage and terraced the garden, changing out plants, and adding features of their own including a topiary bird.

Take time to wander in Sawrey. Below the village is Esthwaite Water, where you can see Mr. Jeremy Fisher's reeds and the signposts that appear behind Pigling Bland and Alexander. Along the roads, depending on the season you will still find wild balsam and hawthorn and blackberries. There are patches of yellow loosestrife, escapees from a garden, perhaps hers.

Castle Cottage, 1946,
during the Dukes' tenure

Above the village is Moss Eccles Tarn, beloved of Beatrix
and Willie Heelis. If you walk up Stony Lane and keep walking directly up hill, you will find it. The footing is a bit rough
and you will get a good workout, but it is well worth it. You
may have to cross a stile, but never climb the walls. Beatrix
welcomed visitors on her land, but once remembered "the
exasperation of seeing a large party of young women steeple-
chasing over a succession of newly cammed walls in pursuit

Sheep safely grazing on
Heelis land

of mushrooms." She liked seeing them up on the fells, "if they
would shut the gates when they come down again."

From the fells, you can see Sawrey from above, and the
broader landscape of the Southern Lakes that Beatrix Potter
loved. The fields are dotted with sheep and cows, placidly
ovine and bovine, busy with grazing and unlikely to bother
the hapless tourist. Wildflowers bloom there. Moss Eccles
Tarn seems unlikely, a lake at this high elevation, like some
kind of inverse drainage. If you are lucky, the water lilies will
be blooming there, just as Beatrix hoped when she planted
them with her niece. If you have the time, you can follow the
footpath next to Wilfin Beck and descend into Far Sawrey.

If you want a sense of the opulent gardens that were
prevalent in Mr. and Mrs. Potter's Lakeland, you can visit
many of the grand houses that were their summer homes.

The house where Beatrix first stayed with her family in 1896 is still in Sawrey, though its name had changed from Lakefield to Ees Wyke by the time the Potters returned there in 1902. It is still available to let, though by the room, as it is now a country house hotel. If you can stay there or partake of a meal in its dining room, you will get a hint, a whisper, of the lifestyle that the Potters maintained and that Beatrix largely left behind in her day-to-day life as Mrs. William Heelis. The garden that Beatrix painted is gone, though the pristine views over Esthwaite Water to the Langdale Pikes are unchanged.

In Hawkshead itself, William Heelis's old law offices are now the Beatrix Potter Gallery, where the National Trust displays a rotating selection of its Potter watercolors, first editions, and other treasures. Look carefully. Almost any exhibit will include images of plants, flowers, and gardens.

On the road from Hawkshead to Ambleside, you will pass the entrance gate for Belmount Hall, the stately stone house that once belonged to Beatrix's friend, Rebecca Owen. Its walled garden, which Miss Owen was convinced was haunted by the ghost of a cloistered monk, is now a ghost itself. Only the walls remain, and the memory that Beatrix adopted the garden after she bought the property from her friend in 1938. Belmount, like so much of the land in the

Sawrey valley, was part of Beatrix Potter's gift to the National Trust. Of late, the house and the garden beds that skirt it have been lovingly restored into a venue for weekend parties, weddings, and conferences.

Wray Castle, the Potters' 1882 rental, still perches above Windermere like a picturesque transplant from Sir Walter Scott. A property of the National Trust, the house is open in season, but the grounds are open year-round from dawn to dusk. The remains of the kitchen garden are there, with a surprising serpentine wall. The fernery is empty, awaiting a gardener with a fascination for fronds. A princely collection of specimen trees graces the Wray property, including the great conifers that Beatrix admired and the mulberry that, tradition has it, Wordsworth planted on his first visit. You can walk the lanes between Wray and Hawkshead that Beatrix explored on foot and in her pony cart.

A visit to the Armitt in Ambleside is a must. The Armitt is a quirky small gem of a museum, founded by a group of intellectuals in 1912 to preserve the heritage of their beloved Lakes. Beatrix chose the Armitt as the ultimate destination for her collection of natural history paintings—hundreds of funguses, with a smattering of fish, fossils, and Roman archaeological finds. In the gallery today you will find a sampling of Potter's paintings on display. The library upstairs

Belmount Hall with its restored gardens near the house

includes books on topics of natural and local history from Beatrix's collection, including some of her father's and grandfather's books.

From Ambleside, you might go west toward Coniston and spend the night at Yew Tree Farm, part of the Monk Coniston Estate that Beatrix purchased in 1930. Yew Tree Farm was the stand-in for shots of Hill Top Farm in the Renée Zellweger movie, *Miss Potter*. The front garden reflects the set designer's intent. Produce of Yew Tree Farm furnishes the table at the B&B. The farm family that runs

Yew Tree actively manages their flocks of Herdwick sheep in accordance with Potter's wishes and the National Trust's management policies.

Turning south from Ambleside along Windermere's eastern shore, Beatrix Potter would be pleased to find that her Gaddum cousins' home, Brockhole, is now the Lake District National Park's Visitor Centre. Its thirty-acre gardens with terraces and rose beds were grand in comparison with Beatrix's cottage plantings. Still, cousin Edith was always so generous with cuttings.

Just south from Brockhole is a hairpin turn that takes you up out of the valley to Holehird. Beatrix and her family stayed there in 1889 with its greenhouses and kitchen garden, but she was so sick she could barely walk. When they returned in 1895, she and Bertram "found the pleasant old gardener dead and gone, and a bustling self-important personage in his place, who [gave] Bertram... permission to pick raspberries." Beatrix was amused by the new gardener's attitude; Bertram was exasperated. Today they would both be amazed by the changes to the gardens. After the Potters' holiday sojourns there, William Grimble Groves bought Holehird in 1897. Groves, like the Gaddums, hired Thomas Mawson to improve his garden. Mawson added on to the greenhouses to house Groves's substantial orchid collection and dammed a stream to create a series of descending water

gardens. With its spectacular prospect of the Langdale and Coniston Fells, Holehird is one of the few of the Potters' Lakeland holiday rentals without a water view, so perhaps Groves was rectifying that.

Holehird at present is the headquarters of the Lakeland Horticultural Society, founded in 1969. The walled garden that Beatrix would have known, where Bertram picked raspberries and where they passed the time with the pleasant old gardener, is now a spectacular display garden with colorful island beds and deep borders. Beatrix the painter would have appreciated the color combinations, the complements and harmonies, in the carefully tended gardens, shepherded through the seasons by a group of dedicated volunteers.

About a mile further up toward Kirkstone Pass is Troutbeck Park Farm, the 1,900-acre sheep farm of which she was so proud. A Potter landscape gardening pilgrimage would not be complete without seeing the panoramas of Windermere that unfold below it, and the mature stands of trees that she first recommended planting in the 1920s. Two streams, Trout Beck and Hagg Beck, run akimbo on either side of the fell. "They meet and unite below the southern crags, making the tableland almost an island, an island haunted by the sounds that creep in running water," Potter wrote in an essay called "The Lonely Hills." She saw the magic of the land; it was there she first spotted the little tracks of the Fairy Caravan.

South to Bowness, you can tread other Beatrix Potter paths. In 1925, Cockshott Point, lake frontage on the eastern shore of Windermere, was on the brink of development. To support the National Trust's efforts to save it, Beatrix sent fifty autographed Peter Rabbit drawings to a contact in America to sell on her behalf. "Peter Rabbit is not begging for himself," she wrote. "Alas! so many of our heirlooms—our pictures, our ancient books, even our old timbered houses—are crossing the Atlantic—would not American friends help to save a bit of our scenery?" The woodland and meadow trails that wind along the half-mile of shore are proof of her success.

Holehird Gardens, maintained by the Lakeland Horticultural Society

The scarecrow in rabbit's clothing from *The Tale of Peter Rabbit*

OPPOSITE: Peter Rabbit Garden at The World of Beatrix Potter Attraction

In the town center, The World of Beatrix Potter Attraction has made a substantial contribution to garden enthusiasts by reimagining her horticultural territory. It brings her illustrations and cottage garden style to life. True to her Arts & Crafts bent, the builders of the Peter Rabbit Garden used locally sourced brick and slate and installed a greenhouse built by the great-grandson of Beatrix's shepherd-friend, Tom Storey. Heirloom fruits, flowers, and vegetables are carefully tended. Chelsea Gold Medal–winning designer Richard Lucas meticulously researched the project, down to identifying the likely variety of radish ('Long Scarlet') that

Peter Rabbit eating radishes

Peter consumes in what is arguably Beatrix Potter's most iconic image.

Continuing south along Windermere, you can dine and reside in style at another country house, Lindeth Howe, occupied by the Potters as a summer home and purchased by Mrs. Potter in her widowhood. If the garden's former glories have somewhat waned, the views of the lake are still superb.

The best place to end this tour of Beatrix Potter's gardens is in your own. Plant a gooseberry or a foxglove, as she did. Steal ideas, if not plants, from other people's gardens. Be inspired by Beatrix Potter's books to grow a potato, a rose, or a radish. If you have only a windowsill, try a geranium. Observe your garden, its progress in every season, and be happy every year that you can see the snowdrops bloom again.

I have lots of flowers, I am very fond of my garden, it is a regular old fashioned farm garden, with a box hedge round the flower bed, and moss roses and pansies and black currants & strawberries and peas—and big sage bushes for Jemima, but onions always do badly. I have tall white bell flowers I am fond of, they are just going over, next there will be phlox; and last come the michaelmas daisies & chrysanthemums. Then soon after Christmas we have snowdrops, they grow wild and come up all over the garden & orchard, and in some of the woods.

THE END

—➤◄—

H.B.P. 1886.

BEATRIX POTTER'S PLANTS

This section consists of two tables: "Plants Beatrix Potter Grew in Her Gardens" and "Plants in Beatrix Potter's Books." The plant information in the tables is organized by common name, as was Beatrix Potter's preference. Because common names at times overlap—moss rose to some refers to a shrubby member of the genus *Rosa* and to others an annual *Portulaca*—I have deferred to usage in a book that Beatrix owned, David Thomson's *Handy Book of the Flower-Garden* (1868). Her copy is still at Hill Top Farm.

The plants that Beatrix Potter grew in her gardens are documented by mentions in her surviving letters, reminiscences of friends and neighbors, the jottings of visitors, and period photographs. The abbreviations in the primary sources are keyed to the list on pages 309–310. Where there are multiple sources for a plant, only one is included. While Beatrix Potter grew fruits and flowers mixed together, I have separated fruits as well as vegetables into distinct categories in this table.

We love our little garden from *Cecily Parsley's Nursery Rhymes*

The second table, showing the plants that she illustrated or wrote about in her books, expands the list for Beatrix Potter garden aficionados. Although there is less certainty that she grew all of these plants, she appreciated them enough to make them part of her durable creations. I have omitted spinoffs such as games and painting books. This table also serves as a chronological list of all books written by Beatrix Potter; the date refers to the year of the first commercial publication.

Plants Beatrix Potter Grew in Her Gardens

Common name	Botanical name	Type	Primary source
aconite, winter	*Eranthis hyemalis*	perennial	Letter to M. Perry, 20 Feb 1934; *BPA*, p. 56.
anemone, Japanese	*Anemone japonica*	perennial	Letter to M. Warne, 12 Oct 1906; *Letters*, p. 148.
apple	*Malus domestica*	fruit	Letter to M. Wight, 26 June 1942; *Letters*, p. 450.
azalea	*Rhododendron* spp.	shrub	Letter to L. Choyce, 13 May 1921; *TCL*, p. 19.
bean, broad	*Vicia faba*	vegetable	Letter to L. Choyce, 7 Apr 1934; *TCL*, p. 54.
beet	*Beta vulgaris*	vegetable	Letter to H. Fish, 13 Nov 1941; *BPA*, p. 158.
bellflower, white	*Campanula lactiflora* 'Alba'	perennial	Letter to Dulcie (no last name), 29 July 1924; *LTC*, p. 184.
blackberry	*Rubus fruticosus*	fruit	Letter to L. Choyce, 16 Aug 1943; *TCL*, p. 74.
bluebell	*Hyacinthoides non-scripta*	perennial	Letter to H. Coolidge, 28 June 1928; *BPA*, p. 16.
box(wood)	*Buxus sempervirens*	shrub	Letter to Dulcie, 29 July 1924; *LTC*, p. 184.
broccoli	*Brassica oleracea* var. *italica*	vegetable	Letter to L. Choyce, 26 May 1943; *TCL*, p. 70.
broom, Scotch	*Cytisus scoparius*	perennial	Letter to L. Choyce, 23 Aug 1924; *TCL*, p. 38.
Brussels sprout	*Brassica oleracea* var. *gemmifera*	vegetable	Letter to L. Choyce, 29 June 1943; *TCL*, p. 72.
cabbage	*Brassica oleracea* var. *capitata*	vegetable	Letter to J. Steel, 2 June 1931; *DIDJ*, p. 47.
cactus, orchid	*Epiphyllum* cv.	houseplant	Letter to L. Choyce, 19 July 1939; *TCL*, p. 64.
carrot	*Daucus carota*	vegetable	Letter to H. Fish, 13 Nov 1941; *BPA*, p. 158.
cauliflower	*Brassica oleracea* var. *botrytis*	vegetable	Letter to L. Choyce, 29 June 1943; *TCL*, p. 72.
celery	*Apium graveolens* var. *dulce*	vegetable	Letter to L. Choyce, 20 Oct 1934; *TCL*, p. 51.

Common name	Botanical name	Type	Primary source
chrysanthemum	*Chrysanthemum* hybrids	perennial	Letter to Dulcie, 29 July 1924; *LTC*, p. 184.
clematis	*Clematis* spp.	vine	Sequel to *Caravan*; *HWBP*, p. 312.
columbine	*Aquilegia vulgaris*	perennial	NT Archives Photo HIL R 169 3
corn	*Zea mays*	feed crop	Letter to C. Cooper, 10 Sep 1936; NT Archives.
crabapple	*Malus sylvestris*	fruit	Letter to L. Choyce, 16 Aug 1943; *Letters*, p. 74.
crocus, cloth-of-gold	*Crocus angustifolius*	perennial	Letter to M. Perry, 20 Feb 1934; *BPA*, p. 56.
crown imperial	*Fritillaria imperialis*	perennial	Letter to M. Warne, 6 Apr 1911; FLP Archive.
currant, black	*Ribes nigrum*	fruit	Letter to Dulcie, 29 July 1924; *LTC*, p. 184.
daffodil	*Narcissus* cv.	perennial	Letter to C. Clark, 8 Apr 1934; *Letters*, p. 362.
daffodil, double	*Narcissus*, Division 4	perennial	Letter to M. Warne, 12 Mar 1914; unpublished.
daffodil, wild	*Narcissus pseudonarcissus*	perennial	Letter to C. Clark, 8 April 1934; *Letters*, p. 362.
dahlia	*Dahlia* cv.	annual	Letter to L. Choyce, 16 Oct 1925; *TCL*, p. 44.
damson	*Prunus domestica* subsp. *insititia*	fruit	Letter to L. Choyce, 12 May 1924; *TCL*, p. 35.
fern, ostrich	*Matteuccia struthiopteris*	perennial	NT Archives Photo 145997_HD21
fern, wall-rue	*Polypodium vulgare*	perennial	Letter to M. Warne, 18 July 1906; *Letters*, p. 142.
forget-me-not	*Myosotis sylvatica*	biennial	Memories of Susan Ludbrook; *BPSN 72* April 1999, p. 6.
foxglove	*Digitalis purpurea*	biennial	Memories of Anne C. Moore; *SIT*, p. 16.
fuchsia, red	*Fuchsia* spp.	perennial	Letter to M. Warne, 30 Sep 1906; *Letters*, p. 146.
gentian, blue	*Gentiana* spp.	perennial	Sequel to *Caravan*; *HWBP*, p. 312.

Common name	Botanical name	Type	Primary source
geranium, zonal	*Pelargonium ×hortorum*	houseplant	Letter to D. Hammond, Apr 1939; *Letters*, p. 403.
goatsbeard	*Aruncus dioicus*	perennial	NT Archives Photo HIL R 169 17
gooseberry	*Ribes grossularia*	fruit	Letter to L. Choyce, 12 Apr 1934; *TCL* p. 49.
grape	*Vitis vinifera*	fruit	Letter to M. Warne, 22 Aug 1912; *BPL*, p. 199.
hay	mixed grasses, etc.	feed crop	Letter to L. Choyce; 19 Sep 1922; *TCL*, p. 20.
holly	*Ilex aquifolium*	shrub	Letter to M. Perry, 12 Dec 1935; *BPA*, p. 62.
hollyhock	*Alcea rosea*	annual	Elizabeth Stevens, *The Horn Book Magazine*, Apr 1958, pp. 131–136.
honesty	*Lunaria annua*	biennial	Letter to M. Warne, 12 Oct 1906; *Letters*, p. 148.
honeysuckle	*Lonicera* spp.	vine	Sequel to *Caravan*; *HWBP*, p. 312.
houseleek	*Sempervivum tectorum*	perennial	Sequel to *Caravan*; *HWBP*, p. 312.
hyacinth	*Hyacinthus orientalis*	perennial	Letter to N. Moore, 6 Apr 1896; *LTC*, pp. 38–39.
iris	*Iris germanica*	perennial	Letter to C. Cooper, 10 Sep 1936; NT Archives.
iris	*Iris unguicularis* (syn. *I. stylosa*)	perennial	Letter to C. Cooper, 10 Sep 1936; NT Archives.
jessamine, winter	*Jasminum nudiflorum*	shrub	Letter to M. Perry, 23 Jan 1943; *BPA*, p. 194.
larch	*Larix decidua*	tree	Letter to L. Choyce, 9 Dec 1939; *TCL*, p. 67.
laurel	*Prunus laurocerasus*	shrub	Letter to M. Warne, 30 Sep 1906; *Letters*, p. 146.
lavender	*Lavandula angustifolia*	perennial	Letter to M. Warne, 12 Oct 1906; *Letters*, p. 148.
leek	*Allium ampeloprasum* var. *porrum*	vegetable	Letter to H. Fish, 13 Nov 1941; *BPA*, p. 158.
lettuce	*Lactuca sativa*	vegetable	Letter to L. Choyce, 29 June 1943; *TCL*, p. 72.

Common name	Botanical name	Type	Primary source
lilac	*Syringa vulgaris*	shrub	Letter to L. Choyce, 13 May 1921; *TCL*, p. 19.
lilac, California	*Ceanothus americanus*	shrub	Letter to C. Clark, 18 Mar 1939; *BPL*, p. 396.
lily	*Lilium* spp.	perennial	Letter to M. Warne, 12 Oct 1906; *Letters*, p. 149.
London pride	*Saxifraga ×urbium*	perennial	Letter to M. Warne, 6 Sep 1906; *Letters*, p.143.
loosestrife, yellow	*Lysimachia punctata*	perennial	Letter to L. Choyce, 23 Aug 1924; *TCL*, p. 38.
magnolia	*Magnolia* spp.	tree	Letter to D. Hammond, 30 Sep 1936; unpublished.
mangold	*Beta vulgaris* subsp. *vulgaris*	feed crop	Letter to L. Choyce, 26 May 1943; *TCL*, p. 70.
marrow, vegetable	*Cucurbita pepo*	vegetable	Letter to L. Choyce, 16 Aug 1943; *TCL*, p. 74.
Michaelmas daisy	*Aster* spp.	perennial	Letter to Dulcie, 29 July 1924; *LTC*, p. 184.
mignonette	*Reseda odorata*	annual	Elizabeth Stevens, *The Horn Book Magazine*, Apr 1958, pp. 131–136.
oat	*Avena sativa*	feed crop	Letter to L. Choyce, 19 Sep 1922; *TCL*, p. 20.
onion	*Allium cepa*	vegetable	Letter to H. Fish, 13 Nov 1941; *BPA*, p. 158.
pansy	*Viola* spp. and hybrids	annual	Letter to Dulcie, 29 July 1924; *LTC*, p. 184.
pea	*Pisum sativum*	vegetable	Letter to Dulcie, 29 July 1924; *LTC*, p. 184.
pear	*Pyrus communis*	fruit	Letter to L. Warne, 12 Aug 1911; *LTC*, p. 128.
peony	*Paeonia lactiflora*	perennial	NT Archives Photo HIL 169 2
phlox	*Phlox paniculata*	perennial	Letter to Dulcie, 29 July 1924; *LTC*, p. 184.
pink	*Dianthus caryophyllus*	perennial	Letter to L. Choyce, 29 June 1943; *TCL*, p. 72.
plum	*Prunus domestica*	fruit	Letter to L. Choyce, 2 May 1923; *TCL*, p. 26.

Common name	Botanical name	Type	Primary source
poppy, opium	*Papaver somniferum*	annual	NT Archives Photo HIL R 169 32
potato	*Solanum tuberosum*	vegetable	Letter to L. Choyce, 29 June 1943; *TCL*, p. 72.
primrose, Japanese	*Primula japonica*	perennial	Letter to M. Warne, 16 Sep 1909; FWA.
primrose, polyanthus	*Primula ×polyantha*	perennial	Letter to M. Warne, 6 Apr 1911; FLP Archive.
privet	*Ligustrum vulgare*	shrub	Letter to A. C. Moore, 25 May 1940; *BPA*, p. 105.
quince, Japanese (japonica)	*Chaenomeles japonica* (syn. *Pyrus japonica*)	shrub	Sequel to *Caravan*; *HWBP*, p. 312.
raspberry	*Rubus idaeus*	fruit	Interview with Harry and Ethel Byers, 17 January 1991, (NT).
rhododendron	*Rhododendron* spp.	shrub	Letter to M. Warne, 30 Sep 1906; *Letters*, p. 146.
rhododendron, alpine	*Rhododendron ferrugineum*	shrub	Letter to L. Choyce, 16 Oct 1925; *TCL*, p. 44.
rhubarb	*Rheum rhabarbarum*	vegetable	Memories of C. Clark; *TBP*, p. 85.
rock, white	*Aubrieta deltoidea*	perennial	Letter to M. Warne, 30 Sep 1906; *Letters*, p. 146.
rose	*Rosa* spp.	shrub	Elizabeth Stevens, *The Horn Book Magazine*, Apr 1958, pp. 131–136.
rose, bourbon	*Rosa* 'Queen of Bourbons'	shrub	Memories of Joan Duke, 1987, Ambleside Oral History Project.
rose, moss	*Rosa communis*	shrub	Letter to Dulcie, 29 Jul 1924; *LTC*, p. 184.
rose, pink cabbage	*Rosa ×centifolia*	shrub	Sequel to *Caravan*; *HWBP*, p. 312.
rosemary	*Rosmarinus officinalis*	perennial	Sequel to *Caravan*; *HWBP*, p. 312.
sage	*Salvia officinalis*	perennial	Letter to Dulcie, 29 July 1924; *LTC*, p. 184.
saxifrage	*Saxifraga rosacea*	perennial	Letter to M. Warne, 6 Sep 1906; *Letters*, p. 143.
Scotch fir	*Pinus sylvestris*	tree	NT Archives Photo HIL 169 27d

Common name	Botanical name	Type	Primary source
sea pink	*Armeria maritima*	perennial	Letter to J. Shapland, 26 Sep 1913; *The Times*, 9 Mar 2006.
snapdragon	*Antirrhinum majus*	annual	Elizabeth Stevens, *The Horn Book Magazine*, Apr 1958, pp. 131–136.
snowdrop	*Galanthus nivalis*	perennial	Letter to M. Perry, 4 Feb 1935; *BPA*, p. 64
Solomon's seal	*Polygonatum giganteum*	perennial	NT Archives Photo HIL 169 2
spinach	*Spinacia oleracea*	vegetable	Letter to H. Fish, 13 Nov 1941; *BPA*, p. 158.
spiraea	*Spiraea* spp.	shrub	Letter to C. Clark, 18 Mar 1939; *Letters*, p. 396.
St. John's wort	*Hypericum perforatum*	perennial	Sequel to *Caravan*; *HWBP*, p. 312.
stock	*Matthiola* spp.	annual	Elizabeth Stevens, *The Horn Book Magazine*, Apr 1958, pp. 131–136.
strawberry	*Fragaria ×ananassa*	perennial	Letter to Dulcie, 29 July 1924; *LTC*, p. 184.
sweet pea	*Lathyrus odoratus*	annual	NT Archives Photo HIL R 169 28
sweet william	*Dianthus barbatus*	biennial	Letter to M. Warne, 12 Oct 1906; *Letters*, p. 148.
syringa	*Philadelphus coronarius*	shrub	Letter to M. Warne, 30 Sep 1906; *Letters*, p. 146.
tulip	*Tulipa* cv.	perennial	Letter to M. Perry, 12 Dec 1934; *BPA*, p. 61.
turnip	*Brassica rapa* var. *rapa*	feed crop	Letter to L. Choyce, 26 May 1943; *TCL*, p. 70.
violet	*Viola* spp.	perennial	Letter to M. Warne, 12 Oct 1906; *Letters*, p. 148.
wallflower	*Cheiranthus cheiri*	biennial	Sequel to *Caravan*; *HWBP*, p. 312.
wisteria	*Wisteria* spp.	vine	Sequel to *Caravan*; *HWBP*, p. 312.
witch-hazel	*Hamamelis mollis*	shrub	Letter to M. Perry, 4 Feb 1935; *BPA*, p. 64.
zinnia	*Zinnia elegans*	annual	NT Archives Photo HIL R 169 32

PLANTS IN BEATRIX POTTER'S BOOKS

Book	Date	Common name	Botanical name (shown with first instance)	Text	Art
The Tale of Peter Rabbit	1902	bean, French	*Phaseolus vulgaris*	◆	◆
		blackberry	*Rubus fruticosus*	◆	◆
		cabbage	*Brassica oleracea* var. *capitata*	◆	◆
		chamomile (tea)	*Matricaria recutita*	◆	
		cucumber	*Cucumis sativus*	◆	
		currant, black	*Ribes nigrum*	◆	
		fir	*Pseudotsuga menziesii*	◆	◆
		geranium, zonal	*Pelargonium* ×*hortorum*		◆
		gooseberry	*Ribes grossularia*	◆	◆
		lettuce	*Lactuca sativa*	◆	
		nasturtium	*Tropaeolum majus*		◆
		onion	*Allium cepa*		◆
		parsley	*Petroselinum hortense*	◆	
		pea	*Pisum sativum*	◆	
		potato	*Solanum tuberosum*		◆
		radish	*Raphanus sativus*	◆	◆
		turnip	*Brassica rapa* var. *rapa*		◆
The Tale of Squirrel Nutkin	1903	beech	*Fagus sylvatica*	◆	◆
		cherry	*Prunus avium*	◆	
		chestnut	*Castanea sativa*	◆	
		crabapple	*Malus sylvestris*	◆	◆
		dock	*Rumex obtusifolius*	◆	
		fir		◆	◆
		hazel	*Corylus avellana*	◆	
		oak	*Quercus* spp.	◆	◆

Book	Date	Common name	Botanical name (shown with first instance)	Text	Art
The Tale of Squirrel Nutkin (continued)		pine	*Pinus* spp.	◆	
		plum	*Prunus domestica*	◆	
		rose, dog	*Rosa canina*	◆	
		stinging nettle	*Urtica dioica*	◆	
		strawberry	*Fragaria ×ananassa*	◆	
The Tailor of Gloucester	1903	cornflower	*Centaurea cyanus*	◆	
(flowers in embroidery)		pansy	*Viola ×hybridus*	◆	
		poppy	*Papaver* spp.	◆	
		rose	*Rosa* spp.	◆	
The Tale of Benjamin Bunny	1904	bean, broad	*Vicia faba*		
		chamomile		◆	
		carnation	*Dianthus* spp.		◆
		cherry		◆	
		fir		◆	
		lavender	*Lavandula angustifolia*	◆	◆
		lettuce		◆	◆
		onion		◆	◆
		pear	*Pyrus communis*	◆	◆
		rosemary	*Rosmarinus officinalis*	◆	
The Tale of Two Bad Mice	1904	(no *live* plants)			
The Tale of Mrs. Tiggy-Winkle	1905	bracken fern	*Pteridium aquilinum*	◆	◆
		currant	*Ribes* spp.	◆	
		daisy, lawn	*Bellis perennis*		◆

Book	Date	Common name	Botanical name (shown with first instance)	Text	Art
The Tale of Mrs. Tiggy-Winkle (continued)		forget-me-not	Myosotis scorpoides		♦
		foxglove	Digitalis purpurea		♦
		onion		♦	
		rush	Juncus spp.	♦	
The Tale of the Pie and the Patty-Pan	1905	carnation			♦
		clematis	Clematis spp.		♦
		daisy, lawn			♦
		dandelion	Taraxacum officinale		♦
		geranium			♦
		Kenilworth ivy	Cymbalaria muralis		♦
		lily, tiger	Lilium lancifolium		♦
		mallow, musk	Malva moschata		♦
		phlox	Phlox paniculata		♦
		poppy, Welsh	Meconopsis cambrica		♦
		rose			♦
		snapdragon	Antirrhinum majus		♦
The Tale of Mr. Jeremy Fisher	1906	buttercup, marsh	Caltha palustris	♦	♦
		forget-me-not			♦
		ragged robin	Lychnis flos-cuculi		♦
		reed	Juncus spp.	♦	♦
		water lily	Nymphaea alba	♦	♦
		water plant	Sagittaria spp.	♦	♦

Book	Date	Common name	Botanical name (shown with first instance)	Text	Art
The Story of A Fierce Bad Rabbit	1906	carrot	*Daucus carota*	♦	♦
The Story of Miss Moppet	1906	(no plants)			
The Tale of Tom Kitten	1907	anemone, Japanese	*Anemone japonica*		♦
		carnation			♦
		clematis			♦
		daffodil	*Narcissus* cv.		♦
		fern	*Matteuccia struthiopteris*	♦	♦
		fern, wall-rue	*Polypodium vulgare*		♦
		forget-me-not			♦
		geranium			♦
		iris	*Iris germanica*		♦
		pansy			♦
		peony	*Paeonia lactiflora*		♦
		rhododendron	*Rhododendron* spp.		♦
		rose			♦
		rose, Scots yellow	*Rosa spinosissima*		♦
		snapdragon			♦
		wallflower	*Cheiranthus cheiri*		♦
		water lily			♦
		water plant			♦
The Tale of Jemima Puddle-Duck	1908	foxglove		♦	♦
		mint	*Mentha* spp.	♦	
		onion		♦	♦

Book	Date	Common name	Botanical name (shown with first instance)	Text	Art
The Tale of Jemima Puddle-Duck (continued)		rhubarb	*Rheum rhabarbarum*	◆	
		rose			◆
		sage	*Salvia officinalis*	◆	◆
		thyme	*Thymus vulgaris*	◆	
The Roly-Poly Pudding later renamed *The Tale of Samuel Whiskers*	1908	geranium			◆
		fern, wall-rue			◆
		horse-chestnut	*Aesculus hippocastanum*		◆
		lilac	*Syringa vulgaris*		◆
		rose			◆
The Tale of the Flopsy Bunnies	1909	boxwood	*Buxus sempervirens*		◆
		cabbage		◆	◆
		cyclamen	*Cyclamen europaeum*		◆
		fuchsia	*Fuchsia* hybrid		◆
		geranium			◆
		lettuce		◆	◆
		marigold, French	*Tagetes patula*		◆
		marrow, vegetable	*Cucurbita pepo*	◆	◆
		pansy			◆
		rose			◆
		turnip		◆	

Book	Date	Common name	Botanical name (shown with first instance)	Text	Art
The Tale of Ginger and Pickles	1909	wisteria	*Wisteria* spp.		◆
		wood sorrel	*Oxalis acetosella*		◆
The Tale of Mrs. Tittlemouse	1910	cherry		◆	
		clover, white	*Trifolium repens*		◆
		cowslip	*Primula veris*	◆	
		oak (acorn)		◆	
		pennywort	*Umbilicus rupestris*		◆
		thistle	*Cirsium* spp.	◆	◆
The Tale of Timmy Tiptoes	1911	maple	*Acer* spp.		◆
The Tale of Mr. Tod	1912	bluebell	*Hyacinthoides non-scripta*	◆	◆
		cabbage		◆	◆
		bracken fern			◆
		cowslip		◆	
		dandelion		◆	
		lavender		◆	
		oak		◆	
		pig nut	*Conopodium majus*	◆	
		willow	*Salix* spp.	◆	
		wood sorrel			
The Tale of Pigling Bland	1913	carrot		◆	◆
		larkspur	*Consolida ambigua*		◆
		potato		◆	

Book	Date	Common name	Botanical name (shown with first instance)	Text	Art
Appley Dapply's Nursery Rhymes	1917	ash	*Fraxinus excelsior*	♦	♦
		carrot			♦
		potato		♦	♦
The Tale of Johnny Town-Mouse	1918	cabbage		♦	♦
		carnation		♦	♦
		corn		♦	
		daisy, lawn			♦
		lords-and-ladies	*Arum maculatum*		♦
		pansy		♦	♦
		pea		♦	♦
		pink	*Dianthus caryophyllus*	♦	
		rose		♦	
		strawberry		♦	♦
		violet	*Viola* spp.	♦	♦
Cecily Parsley's Nursery Rhymes	1922	bluebell			♦
		carrot		♦	♦
		cowslip			♦
		gooseberry			♦
		potato			♦
		turnip			♦
Peter Rabbit's Almanac for 1929	1928	apple	*Malus domestica*		♦
		boxwood			♦
		cabbage			♦

Book	Date	Common name	Botanical name (shown with first instance)	Text	Art
Peter Rabbit's Almanac for 1929 (continued)		daffodil			◆
		daffodil, wild	*Narcissus pseudonarcissus*		◆
		fern, wall-rue			◆
		geranium			◆
		ivy	*Hedera helix*		◆
		laurel	*Prunus laurocerasus*		◆
		pansy			◆
		primrose, English	*Primula vulgaris*		◆
		snowdrop	*Galanthus nivalis*		◆
The Fairy Caravan	1929	alder	*Alnus* spp.	◆	
		apple		◆	
		balm	*Melissa officinalis*	◆	
		beech		◆	
		birch	*Betula* spp.	◆	
		bluebell		◆	
		bracken fern		◆	
		bramble	*Rubus* spp.	◆	
		broom, Scotch	*Cytisus scoparius*	◆	
		buttercup	*Ranunculus* spp.	◆	
		carrot		◆	
		cedar	*Cedrus libanotica*	◆	◆
		cherry		◆	
		chestnut		◆	
		clover		◆	

Book	Date	Common name	Botanical name (shown with first instance)	Text	Art
The Fairy Caravan (continued)		corn		◆	
		cowslip		◆	
		crabapple		◆	
		currant, red	*Ribes rubrum*	◆	
		daffodil, wild		◆	
		daisy, lawn		◆	
		daylily	*Hemerocallis flava*	◆	
		elderberry	*Sambucus nigra*	◆	
		elm	*Ulmus campestris*	◆	
		fair-maids-of-France	*Ranunculus aconitifolius*	◆	
		fern		◆	
		fir		◆	
		flax	*Linum usitatissimum*	◆	
		forget-me-not		◆	
		foxglove		◆	
		fungi/toadstool	*Amanita* spp.	◆	
		germander	*Teucrium chamaedrys*	◆	
		ginger, green	*Zingiber officinale*	◆	
		gooseberry		◆	
		grass, bent	*Agrostis capillaris*	◆	
		ivy, ground	*Glechoma hederacea*	◆	
		hawthorn	*Crataegus monogyna*	◆	
		hazel		◆	
		holly	*Ilex aquifolium*	◆	
		ivy		◆	
		kesh	*Pastinaca sativa*	◆	

Book	Date	Common name	Botanical name (shown with first instance)	Text	Art
The Fairy Caravan (continued)		lady's slipper	*Cypripedium calceolus*	♦	
		lady's smock	*Cardamine pratensis*	♦	
		lamb's toes	*Lotus corniculatus*	♦	
		larch	*Larix decidua*	♦	
		lords-and-ladies		♦	
		mary bud	*Calendula officinalis*	♦	
		meadowsweet	*Filipendula ulmaria*	♦	
		milkmaid	*Cardamine pratensis*	♦	
		milkwort	*Polygala vulgaris*	♦	
		oak		♦	
		onion		♦	
		orchid, spotted	*Dactylorhiza fuchsii*	♦	
		parsley, cow	*Anthriscus sylvestris*	♦	
		pear		♦	
		peony		♦	
		periwinkle	*Vinca minor*	♦	
		pine		♦	
		potato		♦	
		primrose, English		♦	
		ragged robin		♦	
		raspberry	*Rubus idaeus*	♦	
		rue (herb of grace)	*Ruta graveolens*	♦	
		rush		♦	
		rose		♦	
		rowan	*Sorbus aucuparia*	♦	
		savin	*Juniperus sabina*	♦	

Book	Date	Common name	Botanical name (shown with first instance)	Text	Art
The Fairy Caravan (continued)		sele	unidentified	◆	
		snowdrop		◆	
		speedwell	*Veronica* spp.	◆	
		spruce	*Picea* spp.	◆	
		stinging nettle		◆	
		strawberry, wild	*Fragaria vesca*	◆	
		sycamore		◆	
		violet		◆	
		wallflower		◆	
		yew	*Taxus baccata*	◆	
The Tale of Little Pig Robinson	1930	apple		◆	
		asparagus	*Asparagus officinalis*	◆	
		bong tree	*Araucaria heterophylla*	◆	◆
		breadfruit	*Artocarpus altilis*	◆	
		broccoli	*Brassica oleracea* var. *italica*	◆	
		buttercup		◆	
		cabbage		◆	
		cauliflower	*Brassica oleracea* var. *botrytis*	◆	◆
		corn		◆	
		daffodil		◆	
		daisy, lawn		◆	
		elm		◆	
		onion		◆	
		pea		◆	
		potato		◆	

Book	Date	Common name	Botanical name (shown with first instance)	Text	Art
The Tale of Little Pig Robinson (continued)		primrose, English		♦	
		pussy willow	*Salix discolor*	♦	
		rhubarb		♦	
		turnip		♦	
		water crowfoot	*Ranunculus aquatilis*	♦	
		wheat	*Triticum* spp.	♦	
		yam	*Dioscorea* spp.	♦	
Sister Anne	1932	bour tree	*Sambucus nigra*	♦	
Wag-by-Wall	1944	balm		♦	
		borage	*Borago officinalis*	♦	
		cabbage		♦	
		eyebright	*Euphrasia officinalis*	♦	
		hyssop	*Hyssopus officinalis*	♦	
		meadowsweet		♦	
		pansy		♦	
		rose		♦	
		sedge	*Cyperus* spp.	♦	
		sundew	*Drosera* spp.	♦	
		thyme		♦	
		wallflower		♦	

NOTES &
FURTHER READING

Any exploration of Beatrix Potter's life and works should include membership in The Beatrix Potter Society. Its members are interesting and good-humored, as was Potter herself. As a group, it is welcoming and sociable, yet it holds itself to high standards. Its meetings, newsletters, and publications are informative and serious, as well as quirky in the best sense of the word. At my first conference, the first lecture I heard was by Peter Hollindale, a lecturer on Elizabethan Drama and Children's Literature from the University of York in which he introduced himself with, "My wife sometimes calls me Squirrel Nutcase." I was hooked.

To learn about Beatrix Potter, read Beatrix Potter's books. Frederick Warne & Co., now part of Penguin Random House, continues to produce lovely editions. The core of the literature about Beatrix Potter is included in the collections and published works listed in this section. The new reader might start with the biographies by Linda Lear, Judy Taylor, and Margaret Lane; the engaging collections of letters edited by Judy Taylor; and one of letters to Americans, by Jane Crowell Morse. The abbreviations of books and archival sources were adapted from the list in *Beatrix Potter: A Life in Nature* with the kind permission of Linda Lear.

Regal pelargoniums,
painted at Camfield,
watercolor, 1886

ABBREVIATIONS USED IN NOTES AND CITATIONS

AML   Armitt Museum and Library

ASC   Judy Taylor, *Beatrix Potter: Artist, Storyteller and Countrywoman*. London: Frederick Warne, 1986; revised edition 2002.

BPA   Jane Crowell Morse, editor. *Beatrix Potter's Americans: Selected Letters*. Boston: Horn Book, 1982.

BP/AW   Judy Taylor, Joyce Irene Whalley, Anne Stevenson Hobbs, and Elizabeth Battrick, eds. *Beatrix Potter, 1866–1943: The Artist and Her World*. London: Frederick Warne, 1987; revised edition 1995.

BP/LC   Cotsen, Margit Sperling, *The Beatrix Potter Collection of Lloyd Cotsen*. Los Angeles: Cotsen Occasional Press, 2004.

BPLN   Linda Lear, *Beatrix Potter: A Life in Nature*. New York: St. Martin's Press, 2007.

BPS   The Beatrix Potter Society, London (Archives on loan to V&A)

BP/Scot   Lynne McGeachie, *Beatrix Potter's Scotland*. Edinburgh: Luath Press, 2010.

BPSN	*The Beatrix Potter Society Journal and Newsletter*
BPSS	*Beatrix Potter Studies*
BP/V&A	Anne Stevenson Hobbs and Joyce Irene Whalley, *Beatrix Potter: The Victoria and Albert Collection*. London: Frederick Warne, 1985.
CCP	Cotsen Children's Library, Princeton University
DIDJ	Beatrix Potter, *Dear Ivy, Dear June: Letters from Beatrix Potter*. Toronto: Friends of the Osborne and Lillian H. Smith Collections, 1977.
FF	Beatrix Potter, *Beatrix Potter's Farming Friendship: Lake District Letters to Joseph Moscrop, 1926–1943*, edited by Judy Taylor. London: The Beatrix Potter Society, 1998.
FLP	Free Library of Philadelphia
FWA	Frederick Warne Archives, London
HWBP	*A History of the Writings of Beatrix Potter*, edited by Leslie Linder. London: Frederick Warne, 1981; revised edition, 1987.
Journal	Beatrix Potter, *The Journal of Beatrix Potter, 1881–1897*. Transcribed from her code writings by Leslie Linder. London: Frederick Warne, 1966; revised edition, 1989.
Letters	Beatrix Potter, *Beatrix Potter's Letters*. Selected by Judy Taylor. London: Frederick Warne, 1989.
LPC	Beatrix Potter Collection, The Linda Lear Center for Special Collections and Archives, Connecticut College
LTC	Beatrix Potter, *Letters to Children from Beatrix Potter*. Edited by Judy Taylor. London: Frederick Warne, 1992.
MY	Margarget Lane, *The Magic Years of Beatrix Potter*. London: Frederick Warne, 1978.
NT	National Trust
SIT	Judy Taylor, editor. *'So Shall I Tell You a Story . . .': Encounters with Beatrix Potter*. London: Frederick Warne, 1993.
TBP	Margaret Lane, *The Tale of Beatrix Potter*. London: Frederick Warne, 1946; revised edition, 1958.
TCL	Judy Taylor, editor, *The Choyce Letters: Beatrix Potter to Louise Choyce 1916–1943*. London: The Beatrix Potter Society, 1994.
TMH	John Heelis, *The Tale of Mrs William Heelis–Beatrix Potter*. Stroud, UK: Sutton Publishing, 1999.
V&A	Victoria and Albert Museum, London
VN	Eileen Jay, Mary Noble and Anne Stevenson Hobbs, *A Victorian Naturalist: Beatrix Potter's Drawings from the Armitt Collection*. London: Frederick Warne, 1992.

Preface and Germination

Page

8. "The flowers love": *HWBP*, p. 312.
21. Hyacinths at No.2 are noted in a letter to Noel Moore, *LTC*, p. 38.
24. "Once when Bertram": *Journal*, p. 16.
24. In addition to visiting the Horticultural Gardens as a child, Beatrix attended international exhibitions held there: the Fisheries exhibition of 1883, the Health exhibition of 1884, and the Inventions exhibition of 1885. Of the 1884 visit she wrote, "Band nice, food and most things related to health, very dull": *Journal*, p. 90.
26. "When I was young": *Letters*, p. 455.
29. "There are snowdrops": *BP/Scot* p. 27.
29. "my unloved birthplace": *BPA*, p. 213.
29. "beautiful, home sweet home": *Journal*, p. 85.
30. "The Lords and Ladies": *Journal*, p. 85.
30. "There are sounds": *Journal*, pp. 93–94.
33. "I went up": Unpublished letter from Rupert to Beatrix Potter dated Dalguise 1874, V&A/LPC.
34. "all is bound up": *Journal*, p. 444.
35. "its branches resting": *Journal*, p. 445.
36. "I believe it is the fashion": *Journal*, p. 446.
36. "the memory of that home": *Journal*, p. 84.

LONDON: For more on London's squares and their place in the city's horticultural history, see *London's Pride* by Mireille Galinou (London: Anaya Books, 1990) and Todd Longstaffe-Gowan's *The London Square* (New Haven: Yale University Press, 2012). Victorian horticulture in general is captured in Penelope Hobhouse's "The Eclectic 19th Century," a chapter in *The Story of Gardening* (London: DK, 2002), and in Jenny Uglow's *A Little History of British Gardening* (London: Pimlico, 2005).

For more information on the Royal Horticultural Society's South Kensington Gardens, the Royal Institute of British Architects provides an illustrated article on its website, www.architecture.com.

Beatrix Potter's London can be navigated in map view in *The A to Z of Victorian London* (London Topographical Society, 1987), plates 13 and 21, and *London: A Life in Maps* by Peter Whitfield (London: The British Library, 2006). The history of South Kensington is available in the rich *Survey of London*, F. H. W. Sheppard, editor, 1975, volumes 38 (South Kensington Museums Area) and 41 (Brompton), available through British History Online.

For a study of Beatrix Potter's education, particularly the books she read and artbooks to which she referred, Linda Lear's *Beatrix Potter: A Life in Nature* (*BPLN*) is essential.

CAMFIELD PLACE: Beatrix Potter wrote an epistolary essay about Camfield Place around 1891. (Her grandmother, Jessy Crompton Potter, died in September of that year.) It is included in *Journal*, pp. 444–450. A chapter in *The Fairy Caravan*, "Springtime in Birds' Place," includes a detailed description of an old garden that Beatrix remembered from Camfield. Birds' Place was an old house, torn down in 1833, according to *A History of the County of Hertford*: volume 3 (1912), pp. 458–462, available through British History Online. The present owners have a map designating a field on the Camfield estate as "Birds' Place" though the vestiges of the garden described in *Caravan* are gone.

While Beatrix Potter attributed Camfield Place to Capability Brown in her journal, other corroborating documentation has not been found. Brown's biographers, from Dorothy Stroud in 1975 to Jane Brown in 2011, exclude Camfield from his list of commissions though many other properties in Hertfordshire are included. The characteristics of the landscape at Camfield—two artificial lakes, sweeping views, grotto, summerhouses, and large scale tree plantings—are typical Brownian touches. If he did not design the property himself, he certainly influenced it.

DALGUISE HOUSE: For more on Dalguise and its surroundings, see David C. Duncan's essay "The Significance of Dalguise for Beatrix Potter," *BPSS* XI, and Lynne McGeachie's book, *Beatrix Potter's Scotland* (*BP/Scot*).

Offshoots

37. "I feel like a cow": *Journal*, p. 83.
37. "I cannot rest": *Journal*, p. 109.
42. "Had a series": *Journal*, p. 21.
43. "He came and": *BPSS* VII "Canon Rawnsley and the National Trust" by Elizabeth Battrick, p. 35.
44. "with its fine elms" and "the cooking": *Journal*, p. 380.
44. "It is the most" and "rather out of place": *Journal*, p. 222.
46. "With regard to ferns": *Journal*, p. 239.
46. "The boggy ground": *Journal*, p. 397.
48. "He is a perfect dragon": *Journal*, p. 305.
48. "His successor has": *Journal*, p. 306.
49. "and his judgement": *Journal*, p. 305.
49. "*Agaricus variabilis* is": *VN*, p. 66.
49. "I do not often": *Journal*, p. 421.
52. "I opine that". *Journal*, p. 425.
52. "There is no harm": *VN*, p. 108.
53. "I have been drawing": *LTC*, p. 100.
54. Beatrix Potter's handmade art folios are now housed in the rare book collection at AML.

ADOLESCENCE AND EARLY ADULTHOOD: Beatrix Potter's journal is the primary source of information on her adolescence and early adulthood. It was deciphered after years of effort by independent scholar, Leslie Linder. Among her many interests, Beatrix Potter noted plants, gardens, farms, and landscapes in her journal entries, all written in the years before she had a garden of her own.

For a discussion of the Potter family's propensity for travel and long holidays, see Judy Taylor's essay "The Potters on Holiday", *BPSS* III, pp. 41–48. The list of dates and locations assembled by Anne Stevenson Hobbs and Joyce Irene Whalley (*BP/V&A*, pp. 222–229) is invaluable.

NATURAL HISTORY: The study of natural history was well established in the English marketplace of ideas by the time Beatrix started germinating fungi and searching out snails, sundews, and sea anemones. The seminal book of natural history in England is Gilbert White's *Natural History of Selborne* (London: B. White & Son, 1789). Ann B. Shteir's book, *Cultivating Women, Cultivating Science* (Baltimore: Johns Hopkins University Press, 1996) explores in detail women's role in botanical studies in the years from 1760 to 1860; the epilogue, "Flora Feministica" is devoted to Beatrix Potter. *The Heyday of Natural History: 1820–1870* by Lynn Barber (London: Jonathan Cape, 1980) is a detailed and entertaining study of this popular passion. See Anne Stevenson Hobbs's essay "Flora and Fauna, Fungi and Fossils" (*BP/AW*, pp. 71–94).

For Unitarianism's influence on Beatrix's meticulous observations of nature, see Linda Lear, *BPLN*, pp. 41–42; it was Lear's own meticulous research that highlighted the provenance of Sowerby's *British Wild Flowers*, (*BPLN*, p. 469), which is now in the collection of Daito Bunka University's Beatrix Potter Reference Library.

FUNGI: If you are unable to visit the Armitt in person, you can enjoy its extensive collection of Beatrix's drawings in the essays and reproductions published in *A Victorian Naturalist* (*VN*). Her curious connection with Charles McIntosh, the naturalist postman, is the subject of *A Fascinating Acquaintance*, a booklet published by the Perth & Kinross Council in 1989. Dr. W. P. K Findlay, a British mycologist, published *Wayside and Woodland Fungi* (London: Frederick Warne, 1967) using Beatrix Potter's paintings to illustrate the book. I'm sure she would have been pleased. The Linnean Society's website (www.linnean.org) includes a précis and link to Roy Watling's article "Helen Beatrix Potter: Her Interest in Fungi" (*The Linnean*, January 2000). More details on the interactions with Kew botanists and the Linnean Society may be found in Linda Lear's *BPLN*, chapter 5 "Discoveries."

Flowering

55. "people singing and bobbing": *Journal*, p. 435.
56. "not without a sense": *Journal*, p. 426.
56. "The only prize": *Journal*, p. 431.
56. "It is nearly as": *Journal*, p. 427.
60. "I have come": *LTC*, p. 21.
61. I saw a man": *BP/LC*, p. 114.
64. "They are regular vermin": *Journal*, p. 307.
65. "the rooks are": *Journal*, p. 327.
66. "several bearded horticulturists" and "their names especially": *Letters*, p. 422.
66. "Mr. McGregor was": *Journal*, p. 363.
66. "If . . . [Mr. McGregor's] vegetable garden": *BP/AW*, p. 104.
67. "the rather uninteresting colour": *Letters*, p. 55.
69. "as much a manifestation": *ASC*, p. 95.
70. "rather . . . trite" and "old Mrs Rabbit": *Letters*, p. 96.
71. "I cannot design": *Letters*, p. 66.
73. "I don't know": *Letters*, p. 91.
74. "I do *hate*": *Letters*, p. 121.
74. Beatrix compared herself to Jane Austen's Anne Elliot in a letter to Millie Warne, *Letters*, p. 139.
76. "The stone is": *Letters*, p. 132.
78. "I know some": *Letters*, p. 125.
78. "two-thirds surrounded": *Journal*, p. 387.

PICTURE LETTERS AND LITTLE BOOKS: Judy Taylor's book, *Letters to Children* (*LTC*) is a charming window into Beatrix Potter's life as it intersects with those of her young correspondents. Potter repurposed many of her picture letters into book form. Leslie Linder's detailed scholarship in *History of the Writings of Beatrix Potter* (*HWBP*) informs the discussions about the details of her books. Linda Lear and other scholars argue that Mr. McGregor was patterned after Charlie McIntosh; see Lear's discussion in *BPLN*, p. 86.

HOLIDAY GARDENS: Most of the gardens that the Potters would have known at their holiday addresses have been swept away but persist in period pictures. The Cotsen Collection (CCP) catalog (*BP/LC*) and its facsimile of the family's photograph album (Los Angeles: Cotsen Occasional Press, 1998) are works of art themselves as well as primary sources on the Potters and their summer gardens. The curators of the Victoria and Albert Museum (V&A) have paired Beatrix Potter's watercolors of gardens with her book illustrations, showing their background/foreground relationships on its website: www.vam.ac.uk.

Roots

84. "I have often": *MY*, p. 86.
84. "The garden is": *Letters*, p. 134.
88. "I believe the word": *Letters*, p. 140.
89. "I should hope": *Letters*, p. 141.
89. Beatrix invokes St. Swithin for weather prediction in *DIDJ*, p. 19 and *TCL*, p. 51.
90. Beatrix notes an old rose on the Hill Top farmhouse in a letter to Millie during the summer of 1906, unpublished.
90. "I like old": *Letters*, p. 142.
91. "I miss the sheltered": *Letters*, p. 142.
92. "they quite enjoyed": *Letters*, p. 143.
93. "a very well meant": *Letters*, p. 143.
93. "I am being inundated": *Letters*, p. 146.
93. "Mrs Satterthwaite says" and "I stole some": *Letters*, p. 149.
93. "I have got a large": *Letters*, p. 146.
94. "they say it will": *Letters*, p. 148.
94. "There's nothing like": *Letters*, p. 450.
94. "Moreover I am absorbed": *Letters*, p. 148.
96. "I think I shall attack": *Letters*, p. 146.
96. "My news is all": *Letters*, pp. 148–149.
99. "He has cut": *Letters*, p. 147.
101. Beatrix described looking out through Hill Top's wavy glass window in *LTC*, p. 124.
102. "I had a dog": *BPA*, p. 33.

BEATRIX POTTER'S GARDEN AT HILL TOP FARM: Peter Parker's article "The Gardens of Beatrix Potter" in *Hortus Revisited* (London: Frances Lincoln, 2010) is the perfect starting place. Susan Denyer's *At Home with Beatrix Potter* (London: Frances Lincoln, 2000) gives marvelous detail on Potter's projects in the garden at Hill Top Farm and later at Castle Cottage. In 2004, the Armitt Museum published a pamphlet entitled "Beatrix Potter Gardener" with text by Elizabeth Battrick.

For details about wall building and other lore of the Lakes, see William Rollinson's sumptuous *Life and Tradition in the Lake District* (Worthing, UK: Littlehampton Book Services, 1974).

THOMAS MAWSON AND THE MAWSON BROTHERS' NURSERY: Beatrix did not leave a description of her cousin Edith's garden, Brockhole, though she mentions receiving plants from those laid out by landscape designer, Thomas Mawson. The work of Thomas Mawson as well as Mawson Brothers' nursery in Windermere, frequented by Beatrix Potter, are well documented in Janet Waymark's *Thomas Mawson: Life, Gardens and*

Landscapes (London: Frances Lincoln, 2009). Waymark's work adds to an earlier biography by Elizabeth Kissack, *The Life of Thomas H. Mawson*, (UK: Published by the author, 2006) as well as Mawson's classic, *The Art and Craft of Garden Making* (London: B.T. Batsford, 1901).

GARDENING AND THE ARTS & CRAFTS MOVEMENT: To appreciate the Arts & Crafts Movement as it filtered into garden design and horticulture in Beatrix Potter's day, see *The English Flower Garden*, first published by William Robinson in 1883, and the baker's dozen books on gardening subjects written by Gertrude Jekyll between 1899 and 1918. A thorough analysis of Robinson, Jekyll, and their circle may be found in Judith Tankard's *Gardens of the Arts and Crafts Movement: Reality and Imagination* (New York: Harry N. Abrams, 2004).

Ripening

105. "That's 'er 'ouse": *Letters*, p. 258.

106. "The place is": *Letters*, p. 161.

108. "I have been rolling": *TBP*, p. 110.

109. "my specimen of that": Letter to Fanny Cooper, 11 December 1911, [NT], LPC.

111. "Love in a": *Journal*, p. 156.

112. "What are the": *BPA*, p. 209.

114. Elizabeth Stevens mentioned roses and other summer flowers growing inside the box hedges at Castle Cottage in her article "A Visit to Mrs. Tiggy-Winkle" (*The Horn Book Magazine*, April 1958, pp. 131–136).

114. That William sometimes directed the work in the vegetable garden is documented in the National Trust Sound Archives interview with Harry and Ethel Byers who worked for the Heelises, 17 January 1991, NT.

114. "a regular old fashioned": *LTC*, p. 184.

115. "The portrait of two pigs": *Letters*, p. 214.

116. Mrs. Potter's garden at Lindeth Howe is described tangentially in a recommendation for her gardener, written by Beatrix after her mother's death in *Letters*, p. 357.

116. Beatrix's niece, Nancy Nicholson, described the carriage-drawn arrivals of Mrs. Potter in Sawrey in *TMWH*, p. 119.

117. "ridiculous and vulgar" and "I am perfectly ready": *TCL*, p. 11.

117. "I have poultry": *TCL*, p. 11.

119. "I have never": *TCL*, p. 17.

119. Beatrix wrote of collecting wild foxglove during World War I in *BPA*, p. 109

119. "I get up": *TCL*, p. 17.

GARDENING WITH BEATRIX POTTER: *The Choyce Letters* (*TCL*), edited by Judy Taylor, is a gift to gardeners, as it is collects the correspondence from one plantophile to another. It puts one in mind of other collections such as the letters between Christopher Lloyd and Beth Chatto (*Dear Friend and Gardener*; London: Frances Lincoln, 1998) and between Nancy Goodwin and Allen Lacy (*A Year in Our Gardens*; Chapel Hill: University of North Carolina Press, 2000). Beatrix Potter was a careful letter writer, suiting her topics to the interests of the recipient. We learn much about Beatrix and Louie, their joint and separate horticultural efforts, and more. For example, through these letters one discovers that Louie wrote the verses for Beatrix Potter's gardening guinea pigs in *Cecily Parsley's Nursery Rhymes*. Sadly, Louie Choyce's replies were destroyed along with the most of the letters received at Castle Cottage, as was Beatrix Heelis's practice in her later years (see *Letters*, p. 449).

Setting Seed

123. "always very full" and "I think they": *Letters*, p. 336.
123. "the orchard opposite": *TCL*, p. 44.
124. Beatrix listed some of her apple varieties in *TCL*, p. 74.
124. "I have also thieved" and "hanging into the": Letter to Daisy Hammond, 22 June 1929, [V&A], LPC.
126. "It's called Enchanter's": *TMH*, p. 35.
127. "looking for all": *SIT*, p. 15.
128. "The familiar flower": *SIT*, p. 16.
128. "Thank you for": *TCL*, p. 65.
130. "They appreciated the": *BPA*, p. 11.
131. "There are other": *BPA*, p. 34.
131. "Through many changing": *BPA*, p. 25.
134. "I used a": *TCL*, p. 48.
134. Beatrix wrote of using chemical fertilizers, specifically ammonium sulphate in *FF*, p. 79.
135. "This little corner": *BPA*, p. 14.
136. "For, as true education": *BPA*, p. 14.
136. "the busy Bee": *Journal*, p. 319, footnote.
136. "My eccentric old": *Letters*, p. 396.
137. "going in for shrubs": *Letters*, p. 396.
138. "I should like": *Letters*, p. 396.
138. "anno domini": Letters, p. 228.
138. "I have failed": *Letters*, p. 398.
138. Delmar Banner underscored Beatrix's concern with her garden, describing her scramble out of her sickbed dishabille to pull up cabbages devastated by slugs in *SIT*, p. 49.
138. "I am always": *Letters*, p. 207.

138. The year before she died, Beatrix wrote to Joe Moscrop that weeding her garden was the best cure in *FF*, p. 80.

140. "And the rest": *BPA*, p. 123.

140. "What a pretty": *BPA*, p. 95.

140. "I am still": *TCL*, p. 76.

FARMING WITH BEATRIX POTTER: For a peek into Potter's world of sheep farming, peruse *Beatrix Potter's Farming Friendship* (*FF*), a small volume of letters from Beatrix Potter Heelis to her master shepherd, Joseph Moscrop, edited by Judy Taylor with an essay "The Fell Farmer's Year" by Christopher Hanson-Smith (London: BPS, 1998). *The Tale of Mrs. William Heelis* (*TMH*) by Willie Heelis's nephew John includes a chapter entitled "Mrs. Heelis, Farmer."

Part Two Preface and Winter

147. "I have been sorting papers": *BPA*, p. 166.

148. "There has been some": *BPA*, p. 151.

148. "sloshy": *TCL*, p. 39.

148. "frost in moderation": Haggard, H. Rider *A Farmer's Year*, (London: Longmans, Green & Co., 1899), p. 81.

151. Beatrix refered to skating on the Lakes in *LTC*, p. 188. For the freezing properties of Esthwaite, see *Tait's Edinburgh Magazine*, 1839, Volume 6:96, available on Google Books. For those interested in other literary connections, Wordsworth skated there as a schoolboy and described his memories poetically in "The Prelude."

151. "green winter": *BPA*, p. 64.

151. "low east": *BPA*, p. 18.

154. "We can tell every tree": *BPSS* IX, "Keeping the Pieces Together: the Beatrix Potter Jigsaw in the United Kingdom" by Judy Taylor, p. 26.

158. "pickle" used by Potter to refer to kittens: *LTC*, p. 131, and children, *BPLN*, p. 414.

162. "There are thousands": *BPA*, p. 56.

167. "I have stopped indoors": *BPA*, p. 83.

167. Beatrix described the lengthening days and the winter sunrise in *BPA*, p. 151.

167. "March has come in": *TCL*, p. 31.

Spring

168. "You are as": *FF*, p. 57.

168. "Today is mild": *FF*, p. 64.

170. "black thorn winter": *TCL*, p. 35.

171. Beatrix captured the first cuckoo call in *DIDJ*, p. 116

171. "It has been so dirty": *LTC*, p. 185.
172. "for the wild": *BPA*, p. 20.
172. "I am going to get some of the": *TBP*, p. 103.
175. Beatrix wrote of the many birds nesting in her garden in *DIDJ*, p. 58.
176. "single the turnips": *TCL*, p. 13.
177. "behindhand": *TCL*, p. 50.
178. "Plum blossom was": *TCL*, p. 51.
178. "They are very": TCL, p. 49.
178. "a lot of mischief": *LTC*, p. 201.
178. Beatrix described the sheep in the walled garden in *DIDJ*, p. 31.
178. Beatrix complained of chickens in the seed beds, including Fenella in *TCL*, p. 49.
178. Beatrix wrote of "horrid little Peter Rabbits" eating her vegetables in *DIDJ*, p. 48.
180. "When I was still": FLP Rare Book Department, letter from Marian Perry, undated.
182. "bright little beady": *LTC*, p. 176.
189. "The fruit damson": *TCL*, p. 26.
190. "like a bit of sky": *Letters*, p. 312.
191. "It will be a lovely": *BPA*, p. 35.
193. "I have just been": Letter to Millie Warne, 11 June 1910, FWA.
197. "Spring is the most beautiful": *BPA*, p. 20.

Summer

198. "Excuse a scribble": *BPA*, p. 4.
201. "I rather like spiders": *LTC*, p. 192.
206. Edith Gaddum's contribution to the garden is documented in Letters, p. 149.
206. "The garden here": *TCL*, pp. 71–72.
209. "And what a crop": *Letters*, p. 450.
210. "nothing more sweet": *HWBP*, p. 312.
211. "stout and active": *DIDJ*, p. 13.
213. "pushes up between": *HWBP*, p. 312.
214. "I shall plant the lilies" and "most carefully, in a": *Letters*, p. 146.
219. Beatrix's niece Nancy remembered planting water lilies with Aunt Beatrix on the tarn in *TMH*, p. 115.
219. Beatrix described planting alpine rhododendrons near the tarn, enclosing a specimen of Cornish heath in *TCL*, p. 44.
221. "I wonder what": *TCL*, p. 24.
222. "Your long-suffering aunty": *BPA*, p. 38.
222. Beatrix mentioned hay and hay making in many letters including *Letters*, p. 392.

222. "Four days of it": *TCL*, p. 20.
224. "Growing like Topsy" refers to *Uncle Tom's Cabin*, a book Beatrix knew from childhood and re-read in 1939: *Letters*, p. 400; DIDJ, p. 77.
224. "He has not": *TCL*, p. 62.
225. "an overgrown tangle": *TCL*, p. 61.
225. "an outfacing mess": *TCL*, p. 62.
225. Willow Taylor, who grew up next door to Hill Top Farm, described "scrumping" apples in the orchard in *Through the Pages of My Life* (London: BPS, 2000), p. 31.
228. "Specimens of scouts": *LTC*, p. 128.
229. "is a kindly berry, it ripens in the rain": *Journal*, p. 433.

Autumn

230. "Perfect autumn days": *BPA*, p. 38.
230. "The weather is": *Letters*, p. 149.
232. Beatrix noted planting acorns: *TCL*, p. 67.
232. "An estate should": *Letters*, 297.
234. "I think it is": *BPLN*, pp. 230, 500.
238. "believer in 'breed'": *BPA*, p. 207.
238. "little Baa's": *BPA*, p. 38.
242. "a bunch of chrysanthemums": *Journal*, 436. Uncle Harry's garden, Woodcote, is among all-things-Roscoe recorded in his autobiography *The Life & Experiences of Sir Henry Enfield Roscoe* (London: Macmillan, 1906).
244. "I got most of": *TCL*, p. 47.
244. "It is anxious work": Letter to Fanny Cooper, 5 January 1911, LPC.
245. "I think I will post": Letter to Millie Warne, 16 September 1909, FWA.
246. "What a lovely present": Letter to Charlie Cooper, 10 September 1936, NT.
248. "I wrote your address": *LTC*, p. 156.
248. Seed saving from her garden is mentioned in *LTC*, p. 156; *BPA*, p. 158; and in the memoir of Ulla Hyde Parker in *Cousin Beatie* (London: Frederick Warne, 1981), p. 13.
248. "carrots, onion, leeks are useful": *BPA*, p. 158.
252. The story of her nieces accidently weeding her wildflower garden in the orchard is related in *TMH*, p. 125.
253. "the dealers are so": *BPA*, p. 62.
253. Beatrix mentioned Christmas tree and holly sales: *DIDJ*, p. 53.
253. Beatrix described wrapping the pumps for winter: *LTC*, p. 189.

Visiting Beatrix Potter's Gardens

260. "I was showing": *LTC*, p. 125.
262. "Wild flowers, water plants": *BPSN* 47, p. 8.
273. "the exasperation of seeing": *BPSS* IV, p. 36, "Mrs. Heelis Settles In" by Elizabeth Battrick.
278. "found the pleasant": *Journal*, p. 391.
280. "They meet and": *BPA*, p. 171.
280. "Peter Rabbit is not": *Letters*, p. 304.
285. "I have lots": *Letters*, p. 290.

TRAVELS WITH BEATRIX POTTER, ARMCHAIR AND AFOOT: There are many delightful travel guides to the Lake District, but for finding your way through Beatrix Potter's home turf none better than *Walking With Beatrix Potter* by Norman and June Buckley (London: Frances Lincoln, 2007). The Beatrix Potter Society has a beautifully illustrated and annotated map of Near Sawrey (London: BPS, 1999), available through the Society's website: www.beatrixpottersociety.org.uk. The National Trust's souvenir book *Beatrix Potter and Hill Top* by Judy Taylor (1997) provides an excellent summary of her first Lake District property. *Beatrix Potter's Lake District* by Gilly Cameron Cooper (London: Frederick Warne, 2007) is sumptuous as well as informative. Sue Tasker's *A Year in a Lake District Garden* (Ammanford, UK: Sigma Leisure, 2001) outlines the pleasures and challenges of gardening today at the Gaddums' former estate, Brockhole. The Lakeland Horticultural Society has an excellent brochure, *Guide to Holehird Gardens*, edited by Fred Dunning. A favorite book of travel essays, *The Art of Travel* by Alain de Botton (London: Hamish Hamilton, 2002), includes a selection on the Lake District. For sweet and lively concoctions about Beatrix Potter's life, see Susan Wittig Albert's eight-book mystery series, *The Cottage Tales of Beatrix Potter* (New York: Berkeley Publishing Group, 2004–2011).

PHOTOGRAPHY
& ILLUSTRATION
SOURCES & CREDITS

Frederick Warne & Co. is the owner of all rights, copyrights, and trade-marks in the Beatrix Potter character names and illustrations. Unless otherwise noted, images used in this book are copyright © Frederick Warne & Co., reproduced by permission of Frederick Warne & Co.

Pages 2, 19, 31: courtesy of The Beatrix Potter Society.

Pages 11, 32, 39, 42, 60, 71, 97, 112, 141, 142, 179, 309: Cotsen Children's Library, Department of Rare Books and Special Collections, Princeton University Library.

Pages 20, 40, 82, 87, 256: © Yolanda Fundora.

Pages 22–23, 25: reproduced by permission of English Heritage, National Monuments Record.

Pages 26, 47, 53, 95: from the author's collection.

Pages 38, 46, 48, 58, 75, 123, 133, 134, 137, 203: used by permission of the Rare Book Department, Free Library of Philadelphia.

Pages 50, 51: © courtesy of Perth Museum & Art Gallery, Perth & Kinross Council.

Pages 54, 59, 86, 90, 110, 130, 185, 187, 200, 209, 213, 226–227, 246, 250, 323: © National Trust.

Pages 62–63: The Pierpont Morgan Library, New York. MA 2009.1. Gift of Colonel David McC. McKell, 1959.

Pages 76, 118, 222: courtesy of a private collector.

Pages 103, 151, 152, 153 (top and bottom), 154 (left and right), 155, 156, 157 (top and bottom), 158, 162, 165, 166, 173, 174, 181, 182, 184, 191, 192, 194–195, 210, 234, 236–237, 238, 245, 247, 249, 262, 264–265, 269, 270, 274: © Photography by Ward.

Mushrooms surrounded by woodland plants and dried leaves, watercolor, undated

Pages 131, 286–287: The Pierpont Morgan Library, New York. 2000.34. Gift of Charles Ryskamp in honor of Eugene V. and Clare E. Thaw on the occasion of the 75th anniversary of the Morgan Library and the 50th anniversary of the Association of Fellows.

Page 163: © Bogomaz / Shutterstock.

Pages 164, 188, 196, 202, 208, 211, 212, 216, 217, 218, 220, 224 (left and right), 225, 228, 232, 239 (left and right), 248, 258, 261, 263, 266, 268, 277, 281: © Marta McDowell.

Page 229: © Kawia Scharle / Shutterstock.

Page 259: © Victoria and Albert Museum, London.

Page 273: © George Rodger / Getty Images.

Page 279: © Kevin Eaves / iStock Photo.

Page 282: © courtesy of Richard Lucas.

Sept 1. 03

ACKNOWLEDGMENTS

Thanks seems a small word, but I offer it to Jenny Bent, niece and agent, and Tom Fischer, editor-in-chief at Timber Press, who believed in this book from the outset. Linda Lear and Judy Taylor Hough were its fairy godmothers; they shared their extensive research, read drafts, and offered facts, advice, encouragement, and friendship to a newcomer on the Beatrix Potter scene. Dear friends Susan Castellan, Jane Davenport, Cathy Messmer, Gail Reuben, Sandra Swan, and Pamela Zave spent time on the drafts, their suggestions were appreciated and incorporated. Mollie Firestone, editor, transformed a manuscript into a book.

Yolanda Fundora, friend and artist, created marvelous maps and, with Pamela Zave, helped to select modern day photographs. Speaking of which, Dayve Ward captured lovely images of Beatrix Potter's gardens for a client across the sea whom he had only met virtually. Richard Lucas, designer of the Peter Rabbit Garden at the World of Beatrix Potter Attraction, kindly provided images of his work. Professor Yoshide Kawano drove my husband and I from Tokyo to Daito Bunka University's Beatrix Potter Reference Library and spent the day with us to further our quest. Betsy

Broad beans in bud, watercolor with pen and ink, 1903

Bray, Kathy Cole, Rowena Godfrey, Libby Joy, Jacqueline Mock, and other members of The Beatrix Potter Society sent materials and answered questions. Ian McCorquodale put out the welcome mat at Camfield Place, his childhood home, and offered information about the Potters' tenure on the property.

The professionals who safeguard the Beatrix Potter collections deserve special kudos for their assistance: Andrea Immel and Aaron Pickett at Princeton University's Cotsen Library, Inge Dupont and Maria Isabel Molestina at the Morgan Library & Museum's Reading Room, Ben Panciera at Connecticut College's Linda Lear Center for Special Collections and Archives, Deborah Walsh at the Armitt Museum & Library, Jane Renouf at the Ambleside Library, and the National Trust's Liz Hunter-MacFarlane and Jacquelyn Crofts. Nicola Saunders and Jennifer Greenway at Frederick Warne helped negotiate proper permissions.

I am indebted to Catharine Pritchard, National Trust house manager at Hill Top Farm, for details on the books and catalogs that Beatrix owned, as well as her observations about the interior décor reflecting the garden outside. Peter Tasker, Hill Top's gardener, provided timely, thoughtful answers on the plants and the garden and welcomed me as a volunteer one drizzly October morning to help him cut back the perennials in the long border. The plant information specialists at the New York Botanical Garden identified a particularly puzzling saxifrage in one of Rupert Potter's photographs of his daughter's garden. Edie Loening, archivist at the Garden Club of America, and the librarians at the Library of the Chathams sought out an article by Marian Perry's niece.

Finally, love always to Kirke Bent who was there for every step in the making of this book, even when they led us "over the hills and far away."

INDEX

orchid cactus, 128, 131, 290
Owen, Rebecca, 136, 275
Oxalis acetosella, 301

Paeonia lactiflora, 293, 299
pansy, 49, 90, 114, 188–189, 285, 293
   in BP's books, 120–121, 297,
      299, 300, 302, 301, 303, 307
Papaver spp., 297
Papaver somniferum, 294
Parker, Peter, 12, 315
parsley, 67, 102, 296
parsley, cow, 35, 305
Pastinaca sativa, 304
pea, 120, 172, 177–178, 267, 285,
   293, 296, 302, 306
pear, 70, 264, 293, 297, 305
Pelargonium ×hortorum, 292, 296,
   308–309
pennywort, 301
peony, 101, 198, 200–201, 293, 299,
   305
perennials in BP's gardens,
   184–187, 198–209, 213–214,
   223–224, 242–247
periwinkle, 26–27, 305
Perry, Marian Frazer Harris,
   128, 130, 135, 180, 221–222,
   290–292, 295, 319
Perth Museum and Art Gallery,
   262
Peter Rabbit's Almanac for 1929,
   11, 161, 176, 250–251,
   302–303
Petroselinum hortense, 296
pets, 25, 39, 41, 47, 64, 102–103,
   124–126, 138, 142, 178–180
Phaseolus vulgaris, 296
Philadelphus coronarius, 295
phlox, 92, 114, 223–224, 244, 285,
   293, 298
Phlox paniculata, 293, 298
Picea spp., 306

picture letters, 60–63, 314
pig nut, 301
pink, 121, 206–207, 293, 302
Pinus spp., 297
Pinus sylvestris, 294
Pisum sativum, 293, 296
plants in BP's books, 296–307
plants in BP's gardens, 288–295.
    See also annuals; bulbs;
    fruits; perennials; shrubs;
    vegetables
plum, 178, 189, 225, 229, 264, 288,
   293, 297, 319
polyanthus primrose, 44, 184–185,
   294
Polygala vulgaris, 305
Polygonatum giganteum, 295
Polypodium vulgare, 291, 299
poppy, 217, 294, 297, 298
poppy, opium, 294
poppy, Welsh, 298
Post Office Meadow, 111, 171, 174,
   222, 272
potato, 89, 138, 176–178, 228, 267,
   285, 294, 296
   in BP's books, 115, 182, 301,
    302, 305, 306
Potter, Bertram, 24–25, 37, 41, 47,
   56, 59, 112, 120, 201, 219,
   278–279
   photographs of, 30–31, 60
Potter, Crompton, 242
Potter, Edmund, 33–34, 277
Potter, Helen Leech, 18, 29, 37, 116,
   224, 316
   photographs of, 28, 41
Potter, Jessy Crompton, 33–34,
   46, 312
Potter, Rupert, 18, 26, 29, 32–33, 38,
   41, 44, 65, 111, 116, 219
   photographs by, 21–23, 59, 250,
    259
   photographs of, 33, 42, 60

Warne, Fruing, 71
Warne, Harold, 71, 78, 106, 120
Warne, Norman, 71, 73–74,
    76–78, 80, 84, 104, 239, 260
water crowfoot, 307
water lily, 77–78, 219, 221, 274, 298,
    299, 319
water plant, 298–299
Wayside and Woodland Fungi,
    54, 313
weeds in BP's gardens, 91, 123, 134,
    189–190, 224–225, 252, 271
Wharton, Edith, 10
wheat, 307
white rock, 92, 294
wild daffodil, 172–173, 291,
    303–304
wildflowers in BP's gardens, 172,
    191–193, 247, 264
Wilfin Beck, 81, 104, 171, 174
willow, 46, 301
willowherb, 126
Windermere, 40–41, 58–59, 86,
    93–96, 135, 172, 263, 278, 280
winter aconite, 163–164, 290

winter jasmine. *See* jessamine
wisteria, 8, 110–111, 172, 193–195,
    197, 295, 301
Wisteria spp., 295, 301
witch-hazel, 165, 167, 295
Women's National Land Service,
    117
wood anemone, 239
wood sorrel, 301
Wordsworth, William, 10, 135, 172,
    276, 318
Wray Castle, 40–43, 55–56, 61, 82,
    229, 276

yam, 307
yellow loosestrife, 223–224, 244,
    272, 293
yew, 306
Yew Tree Farm, 40, 277–279

Zea mays, 291
Zellweger, Renée, 277
Zingiber officinale, 304
zinnia, 217, 295
Zinnia elegans, 295